"Not very often does an avid reader chance upon a book which is enjoyed in a single gulp the first time, then installed on over-crowded shelves to be savored again and again. I cannot count now the number of times I have read TOO MANY MAGICIANS—each time with the same pleasure.

"The puzzle of the locked room murder is, of course, a classic device, but Lord Darcy and Master Sean O Lochlainn, Sorcerer, are characters who have become as real to me as my neighbors, and of whom I never grow tired. I owe a deep debt to Mr. Garrett for bringing them into our own time world. I have not the least doubt they do exist and live very full lives in their own!"

—ANDRE NORTON

Other *Lord Darcy* titles by Randall Garrett:

Available from Ace Science Fiction:

 —Murder and Magic
 —Lord Darcy Investigates

# TooMany Magicians

## RANDALL GARRETT

SF

ace books

A Division of Charter Communications Inc.
A GROSSET & DUNLAP COMPANY

51 Madison Avenue
New York, New York 10010

TOO MANY MAGICIANS

Copyright © 1966 by The Condé Nast Publications, Inc.

All rights reserved. No part of this book may be reproduced in any form or by any means, except for the in-
clusion of brief quotations in a review, without permission in writing from the publisher.

All characters in this book are fictitious. Any re-
semblance to actual persons, living or dead, is purely
coincidental.

An ACE Book
by arrangement with
Doubleday and Company, Inc.

This Ace printing: September 1981

2 4 6 8 0 9 7 5 3 1
Manufactured in the United States of America
Published simultaneously in Canada

# PART ONE

THE LIBRARY OF
THE UNIVERSITY OF
CALIFORNIA

# 1

COMMANDER LORD ASHLEY, Special Agent for His Majesty's Imperial Naval Intelligence Corps, stood in the doorway of a cheap, rented room in a lower middle-class section of town near the Imperial Naval Docks in Cherbourg. The door was open, and a man lay on the floor with a large, heavy-handled knife in his chest.

His lordship lifted his eyes from the corpse and looked around the room. It was small; not more than eight by ten feet, he thought, and the low ceiling was only a bare six inches above his head. Along the right-hand wall was a low bed. It was made up, but the wrinkles in the cheap blue bedspread indicated that someone had been sitting on it—most likely, the dead man. A cheap, wooden table stood in the far left corner with a matching chair next to it. An ancient, lumpy-looking easy chair—probably bought second-hand—stood against the left wall, nearer the door. Another wooden chair, the twin of the one at the table, stood at the foot of the bed, completing the furniture. There were no pictures hung on the green-

3

painted walls; there were no extraneous decorations of any kind. The personality of the man who lived here had not been implanted forcibly upon the room itself, certainly.

Lord Ashley looked back down at the body. Then, cautiously, he closed the door behind him, stepped over to the supine figure, and took a good look. He lifted up one hand and felt for the pulse that should throb at the wrist of a living man. There was none. Georges Barbour was dead.

His lordship took a step back from the corpse and looked at it thoughtfully. In his lordship's belt pocket were one hundred golden sovereigns, money which had been drawn from the Special Fund to pay Goodman Georges Barbour for his services to Naval Intelligence. But Goodman Georges, My Lord Commander thought to himself, would no longer be any drain upon the Special Fund.

My lord the Commander stepped over the body and looked at the papers on the wooden table at the far corner of the room. Nothing there of importance. Nothing that would connect the man with the Imperial Naval Intelligence Corps. Nonetheless, he gathered them all together and slipped them into his coat pocket. There was always the chance that they might contain information in the form of coded writing or secret inks.

The small closet in the right-hand corner of the room, near the door, held only a change of clothing, another cheap suit like the one the dead man wore. Nothing in the pockets, nothing in the lining. The two drawers in the closet revealed nothing but suits of underwear, stockings and other miscellaneous personal property.

Again he looked at the corpse. This search would

have to be reported immediately to My Lord Admiral, of course, but there were certain things that it would be better for the local Armsmen not to find.

The room had revealed nothing. Since Barbour had moved into the room only the day before, it was highly unlikely that he could have constructed, in so short a time, some secret hiding place that would escape the penetrating search of my lord the Commander. He checked the room again and found nothing.

A search of the body was equally fruitless. Barbour had, then, already dispatched whatever information he had to Zed. Very well.

Lord Ashley looked around the room once more to make absolutely certain that he had missed nothing.

Then he went out of the room again and down the hall to the narrow, dim stairway that led to the floor below. He went down the stairway briskly, almost hurriedly.

* * *

The concierge, who sat in her office just to one side of the front door, was rather withered but still bright-eyed little woman who looked up at the tall, aristocratic Commander with a smile that was as bright as her eyes.

"Ey, sir? What may I do for ye?"

"I have some rather sad news for you, Goodwife," my lord said quietly. "One of your tenants is dead. We shall have to fetch an Armsman at once."

"Dead? Who? Ye don't mean Goodman Georges, good sir?"

"None other," said his lordship. He had told the concierge only a few minutes before that he was going up to see Barbour. "Has he had any visitors in the past half hour or so?" The body, my lord the

Commander reasoned to himself, was still warm, the blood still fluid. By no stretch of the imagination could Barbour have been dead more than half an hour.

"Visitors?" The old woman blinked, obviously trying to focus her thoughts. "Other than yourself, sir, I saw no visitors. But there! I mightn't have seen him at all. I was out for a few minutes, a few minutes only. I went to the shop of Goodman Fentner, the tobacconist, for a bit of snuff, as is the only form of tobacco I uses."

Commander Lord Ashley looked sharply at her. "Exactly when did you leave and when did you come back, Goodwife? It may be of the utmost importance that the time be known."

"Why . . . why . . . it was just afore you come, good sir," the old woman said rather nervously. "As I come in, I heard the bell of St. Denys strike the three-quarter hour."

Lord Ashley looked at his own watch. It was one minute after eleven. "The man must have waited until he saw you leave; then he came up and came down again before you returned. How long were you gone?"

"Only as long as it takes to walk to the corner and back, sir. I don't like to stay too long away in the daytime when the door is open." She paused and a vaguely puzzled frown came over her face. "Who was it must have come up and gone down, sir?"

"Whoever it was," said my lord the Commander, "stabbed your tenant Georges Barbour through the heart. He was murdered, Goodwife, and that is why we must call an Armsman without delay."

The poor woman was absolutely shaken now, and Lord Ashley realized that she would be of no use whatever in dealing with the Armsmen. He was glad that he had asked her about any possible visitors before he had mentioned that the death was murder; otherwise, her valuable testimony might have flown from her head completely.

"Sit down, Goodwife," he said in a kindly voice. "Compose yourself. There is nothing to fear. I shall take care of summoning the Armsmen." As the old woman practically collapsed into the shabby overstuffed chair she kept in her office, Lord Ashley stepped to the outer door and opened it. He had heard the noise of boys' high-pitched voices outside, shrill with excitement over the game they were playing.

Because of his years of Naval training, it was easy for my lord the Commander to spot the urchin who was the obvious leader of the little group.

"Here, my lad!" he called out. "You, lad, with the green cap! How should you like to earn yourself a sixth-bit?"

The boy looked up, and his slightly grimy face broke into a smile. "I would, my lord!" he said, snatching the rather faded green cap from his head. "Very much, my lord!" He had no notion whether the personage who had addressed him actually was a lord or not, but the personage in question was most certainly a gentleman, and such a person one always addressed as "my lord" whenever there was a job in the offing.

The other boys became suddenly silent, obviously hoping that they, too, might gain some small pecuniary advantage from this obviously affluent gentleman.

"Very well, then," said Lord Ashley briskly. "Here is a twelfth. If you return here with an

Armsman inside of five minutes, I shall give you another like it."

"An . . . an *Armsman,* my lord?" It was obvious that he could not conceive of any possible reason why any sane person would want an Armsman within a thousand yards of him.

"Yes, an Armsman," Lord Ashley said with a smile. "Tell him that Lord Ashley, a King's Officer, desires his immediate assistance and then lead him back here. Do you understand?"

"Yes, My Lord Ashley! A King's Officer, my lord! Yes!"

"Very good, my lad. And you others. Here is a twelfth-bit apiece. If you come back with an Armsman within five minutes, you, too, will get another twelfth. And the first one to come back gets a sixth-bit for a bonus. Now run! Off with you!"

They scattered to the winds.

* * *

At half past two that afternoon, three men met in a comfortable, clublike room in the Admiralty Headquarters Building of His Imperial Majesty's Naval Base at Cherbourg.

Commander Lord Ashley sat tall, straight, and at ease, his slightly wavy brown hair brushed smooth, his uniform immaculate. He had changed into uniform only twenty minutes before, having been informed by the Lord Admiral that, while this was not exactly a formal meeting, civilian dress would not be as impressive as the royal blue and gold uniform of a full Commander.

Lord Ashley might not have been called handsome; his squarish face was perhaps a little too ruggedly weatherbeaten for that. But women admired him and men respected the feeling of determination that his features seemed to give. His eyes were gray-green with flecks of brown, and they had that seaman's look about them—as though Lord Ashley were always gazing at some distant horizon, inspecting it for signs of squalls.

Lord Admiral Edwy Brencourt had the same look in his blue eyes, but he was some twenty-five years older than Lord Ashley, although even at fifty-two his hair showed touches of gray only at the temples. His uniform, of the same royal blue as that of the Commander, was somewhat more rumpled, because he had been wearing it since early morning, but this effect was partially offset by the gleaming grandness of the additional gold braid that encased his sleeves and shoulders.

In comparison with all this grandeur, the black-and-silver uniform of Chief Master-at-Arms Henri Vert, head of the Department of Armsmen of Cherbourg, seemed rather plain, although it was impressive enough on most occasions. Chief Henri was a heavy-set, tough-looking man in his early fifties who had the air and bearing of a stolid fighter.

Chief Henri was the first to speak. "My lords, there is more to this killing than meets the eye. At least, I should say, a great deal more than meets *my* eye."

He spoke Anglo-French with a punctilious precision which showed that it was not his natural way of speaking. He had practiced for many years to remove the accent of the local *patois*—an accent which betrayed his humble beginnings—but his effort to speak properly was still noticeable.

He looked at My Lord Admiral. "Who was this Georges Barbour, your lordship?"

My Lord Admiral picked up the brandy decanter

from the low table around which the three of them sat and carefully filled three glasses before answering the Chief's question. Then he said: "You understand, Chief Henri, that this case is complicated by the fact that it involves Naval Security. Nothing that is said in this room must go beyond it."

"Of course not, my lord," Chief Henri said. He was well aware that this area of the Admiralty offices had been carefully protected by potent and expensive guarding spells. His Majesty's Armed Forces had a special budget for obtaining the services of the most powerful experts in that field, magicians who stood high in the Sorcerer's Guild. These were far more powerful than the ordinary commercial spells which guaranteed privacy in public hotels and private homes.

Such tactics were necessary because of the international situation. For the past half century, the Kings of Poland had been showing an ambitious streak. In 1914, King Sigismund III had begun a series of annexations that took bite after bite out of the Russian states, bringing under his sway all the territory between Minsk and Kiev. As long as Poland was moving eastward, the policy of the Anglo-French Empire had been to allow her to go her way. The Imperial domain was expanding rapidly in the New World, and Asia had seemed remote.

But Sigismund's son, King Casimir IX, was having trouble with his quasi-empire. He dared not push any farther east; the Russian states had formed a loose coalition in the early 'thirties, and the King of Poland had stopped his advances. If the Russians ever really united, they would be a formidable enemy.

Now Casimir IX was looking westward, toward

the Germanic states that had for so long formed a buffer between Poland and the Anglo-French borders. The Germanies had kept their independence because of the tug-of-war diplomacy between Poland and the Empire. If the troops of Casimir IX tried to invade, say, Bavaria, Prince Reinhardt VI would call for Imperial aid and get it. On the other hand, if King John IV tried to collect a single sovereign in tax from Bavaria, and sent troops in to collect it, His Highness of Bavaria would scream just as loudly for Polish help.

So Casimir, his ambitious plans stalled for the moment, was doing his best to disrupt the Anglo-French Empire, to weaken it to the point of helplessness, before actually using armed invasion to take over the Germanies.

That would not be an easy job. The Empire had been a growing, functioning, dynamic force ever since the time of Henry II in the Twelfth Century. Henry's son, Richard the Lion Hearted, had neglected the Empire for the first ten years of his reign, but his narrow escape from death at the Siege of Chaluz had changed him. The long bout with infection and fever, caused by a wound from a crossbow bolt, had caused a personality change, and for the next twenty years Richard I had ruled wisely and well. His nephew, Arthur, had become king in 1219, three years after the death of the exiled Prince John, and had done an even better job of ruling than had Richard. He had gone down in history as "Good King Arthur," and was often confused in the popular mind with the earlier King Arthur of the Sixth Century.

Since then, the Plantagenet line had—by diplomacy when possible, by the sword when necessary—

forged an Empire which had already lasted nearly twice as long as the Roman Empire and still showed no signs of deterioration.

Casimir IX couldn't use his armies, and his Navy was bottled up in the Baltic. No Polish fleet could get through the North Sea without running into trouble with either the Imperial Navy or the Navy of the Empire's Scandinavian allies. The North Sea and the Western Baltic were Imperial-Scandinavian property. Polish merchant ships were allowed to pass only after they had been boarded and searched for armament. King Casimir had tried to smash the blockade back in 1939 and had had his fleet blown out of the water for his troubles. He'd not likely try that again.

Instead, King Casimir had tried another kind of warfare—sabotage, insidious forms of terrorism, economic crises brought about by devious and underhanded methods, and a thousand other subtle forms of subversion. Thus far, he had wrought no real damage; his thrusts had been pinpricks only. But it was the vigilance of the Empire and of the King's Officers that had thwarted the Polish attempts to date.

\* \* \*

Admiral Brencourt carefully replaced the glass stopple in the brandy decanter before he spoke again. "I'm afraid I must apologize to you, Chief Henri. Acting under my orders, Commander Lord Ashley has withheld information from the plainclothes Sergeant-at-Arms who questioned him about the Barbour murder this morning. That was, of course, for security reasons. But I have now authorized him to tell you the entire story. If you will, my lord . . ."

Lord Ashley tasted his brandy. Chief Henri waited respectfully for him to speak. He knew that certain things would still be omitted, that Lord Ashley had been briefed as to which details to reveal and which to conceal. Nevertheless, he knew that the story would be much richer in detail than it had been when he first heard it.

Lord Ashley lowered his glass and set it down. "Yesterday morning," he began, "Monday, October 24th, I received a special sealed packet from the Office of the Lord High Admiral in London. My orders were to deliver it to Admiral Brencourt this morning. I left London by train to Dover, thence across the Channel by special Naval courier boat to Cherbourg. By the time I arrived, it was nearly midnight." He paused and looked candidly at Chief Henri. "I should point out here that if my orders had been marked 'Most Urgent,' I should have immediately taken pains to deliver the packet to My Lord Admiral, no matter what the hour. As it was, my orders were to deliver it to him this morning. I give you my word that that packet never left my sight, nor was it opened, between the time I received it and the time it reached the Admiral's hands."

"I can verify that," said Admiral Brencourt. "As you are aware, Chief Henri, our Admiralty sorcerers cast spells upon the envelopes and seals of such packets—spells which, while they do not insure that the packets will not be opened by unauthorized persons, *do* insure that they cannot be opened without detection."

"I understand, my lord," said the Chief Master-at-Arms. "You had your sorcerer check the packet, then." It was a statement, not a question.

"Yes," said the Admiral. "Continue, Commander."

"Thank you, my lord," said Lord Ashley. Then, addressing Chief Henri, "I spent the night at the Ho-

tel Queen Jeanne. This morning at nine, I delivered
the packet to My Lord Admiral." He glanced at the
Admiral and waited.

"I opened the packet," Admiral Brencourt said
immediately. "Most of what it contained is irrelevant
to this case. There was, however, an enclosure which
I was directed to hand over to Commander Lord
Ashley. He was directed to take a certain sum of
money to one Georges Barbour. That was the first
that either of us had ever heard of Georges Barbour."
He looked back at Lord Ashley, inviting him to take
up the tale.

"According to my instructions within that sealed
envelope," Ashley said, "I was to take the money immediately to Barbour, who was, it seems, a double
agent, working ostensibly for His Slavonic Majesty
Casimir of Poland, but in actuality working for the
Naval Intelligence Service of the Imperial Navy. The
money was to be delivered to Barbour between fifteen minutes of eleven and fifteen minutes after. I
went to the appointed spot, spoke to the concierge,
went upstairs, and found the door partially open. I
rapped, and the door swung open farther. I saw
Georges Barbour lying on the floor with a knife in his
heart." He paused and spread his hands. "I was surprised by that development, naturally, but I had my
duty to do. I removed his private papers—those on
his desk—and I searched the room. The papers were
turned over to the Admiral."

"You must understand, Chief Henri," said Admiral Brencourt, "that there was a possibility that
some of those papers might have borne coded or secret messages. None of them did, however, and the
lot will be turned over to you. Lord Ashley will describe to you where each item lay in the room."

Chief Henri looked at the Commander. "Would you mind submitting a written report, with a sketch map indicating where the papers and so on were?" He was more than a little piqued at the Navy's high-handed treatment of evidence in a murder case, but he knew there was nothing he could do about it.

"I will be happy to prepare such a report," said Lord Ashley.

"Thank you, your lordship. A question: Were the papers disarrayed in any way—scattered?"

The Commander frowned slightly in thought. "Not *scattered*, no. That is to say, they did not appear to have been thrown around haphazardly. But they were not all in one pile. I should say that they were ... er ... neatly disarrayed, if you follow my meaning. As though Barbour had been going through them."

"Or someone *else* had gone through them," said the Chief thoughtfully.

"Yes. That's possible, of course," the Commander agreed. "But would the killer have had time to look through Barbour's papers?"

"Suppose," the Chief said slowly, "that there was one single paper—or maybe a single set of them—that the killer was after. And suppose he knew enough to be able to recognize those papers on sight. He wouldn't have needed more than a few seconds to find them, would he?"

The Commander and the Admiral glanced at each other.

"No," said the Commander after a moment. "No, he wouldn't."

"Do you have any idea what such paper or papers might pertain to?" Chief Henri asked with deceptive casualness.

"None," said My Lord Admiral firmly. "And I give you my word that I am concealing nothing. This office was not even aware of the very existence of Georges Barbour; we have no idea what he was doing or what sort of papers he may have been handling. This was our first knowledge of him, and we have received no further word from London. Thus far, London does not, of course, even know he is dead. One day, perhaps, some sorcerer may discover a way to get teleson lines across the Channel, but until then we must rely on dispatches sent by courier."

"I see." Chief Henri rubbed his hands together rather nervously. "I trust that your lordships understand that I am bound to do my duty. A murder has been committed. It must be solved. I am bound to expend every effort to discover the identity of the killer and bring him to justice. There are certain steps which I must, by law, take."

"We quite realize that, Chief Henri," said the Lord Admiral.

The Chief finished the rest of his brandy. "At the same time, we have no desire to hamper the Navy in any way nor to disclose information publicly that may be of benefit to our country's enemies."

"Naturally," the Lord Admiral agreed.

"But this case is a difficult one," Chief Henri went on. "We know—thanks to the evidence of the concierge—the time at which the crime was committed to within ten minutes. We know that Barbour stayed in that room all night, left this morning at about five minutes of ten, and came back at approximately twenty after. Everyone else in the house had left much earlier, since they are all working folk. There was no one in the building except Barbour and the concierge. All very fine so far as it goes.

"But this case is almost clueless. We do not know Barbour. We have no notion of whom he might have known, whom he might have met, or with whom he might have had dealings. We have no idea who might have owned the very common knife with which he was killed.

"When all that is added to the international ramifications of this affair, I am forced to admit that the case is beyond me. The law is clear upon that point; I must notify the Investigation Department of His Royal Highness at Rouen."

Admiral Brencourt nodded. "That's quite clear. Certainly, anyone from His Highness' offices would be of assistance. Is there any further way in which we can help you?"

"If it is possible, My Lord Admiral, there is. Presumably someone in London knows something about this fellow Barbour. If it would not be a violation of security, I should like to know as much about him as possible. I should like very much to have more information from London."

"I shall certainly see what can be done, Chief Henri," the Lord Admiral said. "Lord Ashley is returning to England within the hour. The Office of the Lord High Admiral must be informed of this development immediately, of course. I shall send a letter requesting the information you desire."

In spite of himself, Chief Henri grinned. "By the Blue! Lord Darcy is never wrong!"

"Darcy?" My Lord Admiral blinked. "I don't . . . Oh, yes. I recall now. Chief Investigator for His Highness. He cleared up that situation here in

Cherbourg last year—the 'Atlantic Curse' business
—didn't he?"

Chief Henri coughed delicately. "I may say that he
did, My Lord Admiral. I am not permitted to discuss
details."

"Of course, of course. But why do you say that he
is never wrong?"

"Well, I have never known him to be," Chief Henri said staunchly. "When I made my call to Rouen to
inform his lordship of the murder, he told me that he
would not be able to come immediately, that he was
sending down his second-in-command, Sir Eliot
Meredith, to take charge until he could get here. He
also said that you would undoubtedly be sending a
courier to London almost immediately and he wondered if I would be so good, as he put it, to ask My
Lord Admiral if the courier could carry a special
message for him."

Lord Admiral Brencourt chuckled. "An astute
gentleman, Lord Darcy. I dare say we can see our
way clear to that. What is the nature of the
message?"

"Lord Darcy's chief forensic sorcerer, Master Sean
O Lochlainn, is attending a convention in London at
the Royal Steward Arms. He would like you to convey the message that he is to return to Normandy, to
come straight here to Cherbourg, as soon as possible."

"Certainly," the Lord Admiral said agreeably. "If
you will write the letter, Lord Ashley will deliver it
upon his arrival. The Royal Steward is not far from
the Admiralty offices."

"Thank you," said Chief Henri. "The mail packet
will not leave Cherbourg until this evening, and the
letter wouldn't be delivered until late tomorrow af-

ternoon. This will save a great deal of time. May I borrow pen and paper?"

"Certainly; here you are."

Chief Henri dipped the Admiral's pen in the inkstand and began to write.

# 2

SEAN O LOCHLAINN, Master Sorcerer, Fellow of the
Royal Thaumaturgical Society, and Chief Forensic
Sorcerer to His Royal Highness, Richard, Duke of
Normandy, was excruciatingly angry and doing his
best not to show it. That his attempt to do so was
highly successful was due almost entirely to his years
of training as an officer of the law; had his Irish blood
been allowed to follow its natural bent, it would have
boiled over. But above all things, a sorcerer must
have control over his own emotions.

He was not angry at any person, least of all himself. He was furious with Fate, with Chance, with
Coincidence—poor targets upon which to vent one's
wrath even if one were to allow oneself to do so.
Therefore, Master Sean channeled his ire, converted
it, and allowed it to show as a pleasant smile and a
pleasant manner.

But that did not keep him from thinking more
about the paper he had spent six months in prepar-
ing, only to find that he had been anticipated, than in

listening to what his lordship the Bishop of Winchester was saying. His eyes wandered over the crowd in the Main Exhibit Hall while the voice of the Bishop—who was a fine thaumaturgist and Healer, but a crashing bore—droned on in his right ear, keeping just enough attention on the episcopal voice to enable him to murmur "Yes, my lord," or "Indeed, my lord," at appropriate intervals.

Most of the men and women in the hall were wearing the light-blue dress clothing appropriate to sorcerers and sorceresses, but there were many spots of clerical black, and several of episcopal purple. Over in one corner, four bearded Healers in rabbinical dress were conversing earnestly with the Archbishop of York, whose wispy white hair seemed to form a cloud around his purple skullcap. Over near the door, looking rather lost, was a Naval Commander in full dress uniform, complete with gold braid and a thin, narrow-bladed dress sword with a gilded hilt. Master Sean wondered briefly why a Naval officer was here. To give a paper, or as a guest?

His attention shifted to the botanical section of the exhibit. He thought he recognized the back of the man who was standing in front of a row of potted herbs.

"I wonder what *he's* doing here?" he muttered without thinking.

"Um-m-m?" said the Bishop of Winchester. "Who?"

"Oh. I beg your pardon. I thought I recognized a colleague of my master, Lord Darcy, but I couldn't be sure, since his back is turned."

"Where?" asked my lord the Bishop, turning his head.

"Over at the botanical display. Isn't that Lord

Bontriomphe, Chief Investigator for London? It looks like him from here."

"Yes, I believe it is. The Marquis of London, as you may know, makes a hobby of cultivating rare and exotic herbs. Very likely he sent Bontriomphe down here to look over the displays. My lord the Marquis leaves his palace but seldom, you know. Dear me! Look at the time! Why, it's after nine! I had no idea it was so late! I must deliver an address at ten this morning, and I promised Father Quinn, my Healer, that I'd have a short session with him before that. You must excuse me, Master Sean."

"Of course, my lord. It has been most pleasant." Master Sean took the outstretched hand, bowed, and kissed the ring.

"Indeed, I found it most enlightening, Master Sean. Good day."

"Good day, my lord."

*Physician, heal thyself,* Master Sean thought wryly. The phrase was archaic only in that Healers no longer relied on "physick" to heal their patients. When the brilliant genius, St. Hilary Robert, worked out the laws of magic in the Fourteenth Century, the "leech" and the "physician" might have heard their death knell ringing from the bell tower of the little English monastery at Walsingham, where St. Hilary lived. Not everyone could use the laws; only those who had the Talent. But the ceremony of healing by the Laying On of Hands had, from that time on, become as reliable as it had been erratic before. However, it was still easier to see—and to remove—the speck in one's brother's eye than to see the beam in one's own. Besides, my lord of Winchester was a very old man, and the two ailments still incurable by the finest Healers were old age and death.

Master Sean looked back at the botanical display, but Lord Bontriomphe had vanished while the Bishop was taking his leave, and, look as he might, the tubby little Irish sorcerer could not locate the Chief Investigator of London anywhere in the crowd.

The Triennial Convention of Healers and Sorcerers was an event which Master Sean always looked forward to with pleasure, but this time the pleasure had soured—badly. To find that a paper, which one had been researching for three years and writing on for six months, has been almost exactly paralleled by the work of another is not conducive to overwhelming joy. Still, there was no help for it, Sean thought, and, besides, Sir James Zwinge felt as upset about it as Sean O Lochlainn did.

"Ah! Good morning, Master Sean! You slept well last night, I trust?" The brisk, rather dry voice came from Master Sean's left.

He turned quickly and gave a medium bow. "Good morning, Grand Master," he said pleasantly. "I slept reasonably well, thank you. And you?"

Master Sean had *not* slept well, and the Grand Master not only knew he hadn't but knew *why* he hadn't. But not even Master Sean O Lochlainn would argue with Sir Lyon Gandolphus Grey, K.G.L., M.S., Th.D., F.R.T.S., Grand Master of the Most Ancient and Honorable Guild of Sorcerers.

"As well as yourself," said Sir Lyon. "But at my age, one must not expect to sleep well. I should like to introduce you to a promising young man."

The Grand Master was an imposing figure, tall, thin almost to the point of emaciation, yet with an aura of strength about him, both physical and psychical. His hair was silvery gray, as was the rather long beard which he affected. His eyes were deep-set and piercing, his nose thin and aquiline, his brows bushy and overshadowing.

But Master Sean had known the Grand Master so long that his face and figure were too familiar to be remarkable. The tubby little Irish sorcerer found his eyes drawn to the young man who stood next to Sir Lyon.

The man was of average height, taller than Master Sean but not nearly as tall as Sir Lyon Grey. The sleeves of his blue dress suit were slashed with white, denoting a Journeyman Sorcerer, instead of the silver of a Master. It was his face which drew Master Sean's attention. The skin was a dark reddish-brown, the nose broad and well shaped, the nearly black pupils of his eyes almost hidden beneath heavy lids. His mouth was pleasantly smiling and rather wide.

"Master Sean," said Sir Lyon, "may I present Journeyman Lord John Quetzal, fourth son of His Gracious Highness, the Duke of Mechicoe."

"A pleasure to meet your lordship," Master Sean said with a slight bow.

Lord John Quetzal's bow was much deeper, as befitted Journeyman to Master. "I have looked forward to this meeting, Master," he said in almost flawless Anglo-French. Master Sean could detect only the slightest trace of the accent of Mechicoe, one of the southern-most duchies of New England, not far north of the isthmus which connected the continent of New France. But then, one would expect a regional accent from a scion of the Moqtessuma family.

"Lord John Quetzal," said Sir Lyon, "has determined to take up the study of forensic sorcery, and I feel he will do admirably in that field. And now, if you will excuse me, I must see the Program Committee and check up on the agenda."

And Master Sean found himself left with Journeyman Lord John Quetzal. He gave the young man his best Irish smile. "Well, your lordship, I see that you're not only quite intelligent but that you have a powerful Talent."

The young Mechicain's face took on an expression of startled awe.

"You can tell that just by looking?" he asked in a hushed voice.

Master Sean's smile broadened. "No, I deduced it." *Lord Darcy should hear me now,* he thought.

"Deduced it? How?"

"Why, bless you," Master Sean said with a chuckle, "the introduction you got from Grand Master Sir Lyon was enough to tell me that. 'A promising young man,' he calls you. 'I feel he will do admirably,' he says. Why, Sir Lyon Grey wouldn't introduce the King himself that way, the King having no Talent to speak of. If you have impressed the Grand Master, you come highly recommended indeed. Further, I can deduce that you're not the kind of lad who'd let praise go to his head—else the Grand Master wouldn't have said such a thing in your hearing."

Master Sean could sense that there was an embarrassed blush rising up beneath the young man's smooth mahogany skin, and quickly changed the subject. "What's been your specialty so far?"

Lord John Quetzal swallowed. "Why . . . uh . . . black magic."

Master Sean stared, shocked. He could not have been more shocked if a Healer or chirurgeon had announced that he specialized in poisoning people.

The young Mechicain aristocrat looked even more
flustered for a second or two, but he regained control
quickly. "I don't mean I *practice* it! Good Heavens!"
He looked round as if he were afraid someone might
have overheard. Satisfied that no one had, he returned his attention to Master Sean. "I don't mean I
*practice* it," he repeated in a lower voice. "I've been
studying it with a view to its prevention, you see. I
know you haven't much of it here in Europe, but . . .
well, Mechicoe isn't the same. Even after four hundred years, there are still believers in the Old Re-
ligion—especially the worship of Huitsilopochtelie,
the old War God. Not in the cities, or even in most of
the rural farming areas, but in the remote places of
the mountains and the jungles."

"Ah, I see. What sort of a god was this Eight-
whatsisname?" asked Master Sean.

"Huitsilopochtelie. The sort of god that's quite
common among barbaric peoples, especially milita-
ristic ones. Rigid discipline, extreme asceticism, vol-
untary privation, and sacrifice were expected of his
followers. A typical Satanic exaggeration of the vir-
tues of chastity, poverty, and obedience. Sacrifice
meant cutting the hearts out of living human beings.
Huitsilopochtelie was a nasty, bloody devil."

"Human sacrifice—or, at least, the advocation of
it—is not unknown here," Master Sean pointed out.

Lord John Quetzal nodded. "I know to what you
refer. The so-called Ancient Society of Holy Albion.
Their ringleaders were cleaned up in May of 1965, as
I recall—or early June."

"Aye," said Master Sean, "and that hasn't got rid
of all of 'em by any means. Black magic isn't as un-
common as you might think, either. The story wasn't
released to the public, but as a Journeyman o' the

Guild, you may have read about the case of Laird
Duncan of Duncan, back in '63.''

"Oh, yes. I read your write-up of it in the *Journal*.
That was in connection with the mysterious death of
the late Count D'Evreux. I should have liked to have
been there when Lord Darcy solved that one!" There
was a light in his obsidian eyes.

"What has your interest in forensic sorcery got to
do with black magic?" asked the Irish sorcerer.

"Well, as I said, there is a lot of Huitsilopochtelie
worship in the remoter parts of the Duchy—in fact, it
gets worse farther south; my noble cousin, the Duke
of Eucatanne, is constantly troubled by it. If it were
just peasant supersitition, it wouldn't be so bad, but
some of those people have genuine Talent, and some
of the better educated among them have found ways
of applying the Laws of Magic to the rites and ceremonies of Huitsilopochtelie. And always for evil
purposes. It's black magic of the worst kind, and I
intend to do what I can to stamp it out. They don't
confine their activities to the remote places where
their temples are hidden; their agents come into the
villages and terrorize the peasants and into the cities
to try to disrupt the Government itself. That sort of
thing must be stopped, and I will see that it *is*
stopped!"

"A formidable ambition—and a laudable one. Do
you—"

"Ah! Master Sean!" said an oily voice from just to
the left and behind Lord John Quetzal.

Master Sean had noticed the approach of Master
Ewen MacAlister, hoping—in vain, as it turned out
—that Master Ewen would not notice him. He had
enough troubles as it was.

"Master Ewen," said Master Sean with a forced

smile. Before he could introduce Lord John Quetzal,
Master Ewen, who totally ignored the journeyman
sorcerer, began talking.

"Heard you had a bit of a set-to with Sir James
yesterday, Sean, eh? Heheh."

"Hardly a set-to. We—"

"Oh, I didn't mean a quarrel. What *were* you arguing about, though? Nobody seems to know."

"Because it is nobody's business," snapped Master Sean.

"Of course not, heheh. Of course not. Still, it must
have been something hot, or the Grand Master
wouldn't have broken it up."

"He didn't 'break it up', as you put it," Master
Sean said through set teeth that were wreathed in a
false smile. "He merely arbitrated our discussion."

"Yes. Heheh. Naturally." The lanky, sandy-
haired Scot smiled toothily. "But I don't blame you
for being angry at Sir James. He can be pretty stiff at
times. Heheh. Cutting, I mean. Sharp-tongued, he
is."

"Quite sharp-tongued," said Lord John Quetzal
in agreement. "I've felt the bite of it, myself."

Master Ewen MacAlister turned and looked at the
young Mechicain as if seeing him for the first time.
"It is not proper," he said chillingly, "for a Journeyman to interrupt the conversation of Masters, nor
for a Journeyman to criticize a Master. And one
would be wise in any case not to criticize the Chief
Forensic Sorcerer for the City of London."

Lord John Quetzal's face became wooden,
masklike. He gave a courteous bow. "I beg your pardon, Master. I have erred. If you will excuse me,
Masters, I have an appointment. I trust I may see
you again, Master Sean."

"Certainly. How about lunch? I have some things I'd like to talk over with you."

"Excellent. When?"

"Noon, sharp. In the dining room."

"I shall be there. Good day, Master Sean, Master Ewen." He turned and walked away, proudly, even a little stiffly.

"Good day, your lordship," Master Sean said to his retreating back.

Master Ewen blinked. " 'Your lordship,' you said? Who is the boy?"

"Lord John Quetzal," said Master Sean with a malicious smile, "is the son of His Gracious Highness, Netsualcoyotle, Duke of Mechicoe."

Master Ewen paled visibly. "Dear me," he said in a low voice, "I do hope he wasn't offended."

"Your ingratiating ways will eventually make you many friends in high places, *Master* Ewen. And now, if you'll excuse me, I, too, have an appointment." He walked away, leaving MacAlister staring after the Mechicain lad and worrying his lower lip with his long horsey upper teeth.

Master Ewen's snobbery, Sean thought, would keep him from ever getting anywhere, no matter how good a magician he was. A Master had a perfect right to tick off a Journeyman, but for important things, not trivial ones. On the other hand, if one does exercise that right, one shouldn't go all puddingy just because the one ticked off happens to have high-ranking relatives. Master Sean decided he needed something to take the bad taste out of his mouth.

He looked at his wrist watch. Nine twenty-two. He still had time for a cool, foamy beer before his appointment. He headed for the private saloon bar that had been reserved for the Convention members and their guests. Five minutes later, with a pint of good English beer firmly ensconced in his round Irish belly, Sean was climbing the stairs to the upper floor. Then he walked down the hall toward the room that had been assigned to Master Sir James Zwinge, Chief Forensic Sorcerer for the City of London.

At precisely half past nine, Sean rapped on the door. There was no answer, but he fancied he could hear someone moving about inside so he rapped again, more loudly.

This time, he got an answer, but certainly not the one he had been expecting.

The scream was hoarse and reverberating, and yet the words were clear enough. *"Master Sean! Help!"*

And then came another sound which Sean recognized as that of someone—or something—heavy falling to the floor of the room.

Sean grabbed the door handle and twisted. To no avail; the door was locked firmly.

Other doors, up and down the corridor, were popping open.

# 3

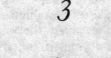

AT PRECISELY 7:03 that evening, Lord Darcy, Chief Investigator for His Royal Highness, Richard of Normandy, stepped out of a cab at the front door of the immense town house of my lord the Marquis of London. In Lord Darcy's hand was a large suitcase and in his eye was a purposeful gleam.

The soldier at the door, wearing the bright yellow uniform of the Marquis' Own Guard, asked him his business, and Lord Darcy informed the guard in a quiet, controlled voice that My Lord Marquis was expecting Lord Darcy from Rouen.

The guardsman looked at the tall, rather handsome man with the lean face and straight brown hair and wondered. In spite of the name and the city he gave as his residence, the gentleman spoke Anglo-French with a definite English accent. Then the guardsman saw the cold light that gleamed in the eyes and decided that it would be better to check with Lord Bontriomphe before he asked any questions.

Lord Bontriomphe was at the door in less than a

minute, ushering Lord Darcy in.

"Darcy! We weren't expecting you," he said with an affable smile.

"No?" Lord Darcy asked with a smile that had the hardness of chilled steel about it. "Am I to presume that you expected me to receive My Lord Marquis' message and then take off on a pilgrimage to Rome?"

Lord Bontriomphe noted the controlled anger. "We expected you to call us on the teleson from Dover," he said. "We would have had a carriage meet you at the station when the train pulled in."

"My Lord Marquis," said Lord Darcy coolly, "has not indicated that he was willing to pay for any expenses; therefore I assumed that such expenses would come out of my own pocket. Weighing the cost of a teleson message against the cost of a cab made me prefer the latter."

"Um-m-m. I see. Well, come on into the office. I think we'll find My Lord Marquis waiting for us." He led Lord Darcy down the corridor, opened a door and stood aside to allow Lord Darcy to pass.

The office was not immense, but it was roomy and well appointed. There were some comfortable-looking chairs and a large one covered with expensive red Moorish leather. There was a large globe of the world on a carved stand, two or three paintings— including a reproduction of a magnificent Vandenbosch which depicted a waterfall—and a pair of large desks.

Behind one of them sat my lord the Marquis de London.

The Marquis could only be described as immense. He was absolutely corpulent, but his massive face had a remarkable sharpness of expression, and his eyes had a thoughtful, introspective look. And in spite of a weight that was better than twenty stone, there was an air of firmness about him that gave him an almost regal air.

"Good evening, my lord," he said without rising, but extending a broad, fat hand that reminded one of the flipper of a seal.

"My lord Marquis," said Lord Darcy, gripping the hand and releasing it.

Then, before the Marquis could say anything more, Lord Darcy put one hand firmly on the desk, palm down, leaned over to look down at de London, and said: "And now, how much of this is flummery?"

"You mock me," said the Marquis heavily. "Sit down, if you please; I don't like to have to crane my neck to look up at you."

Lord Darcy took the red leather chair without taking his eyes off the Marquis.

"None of it is flummery," the Marquis said. "I admit I do not have the full roster of facts, but I feel I have enough to justify my actions. Would you care to hear Lord Bontriomphe's report?"

"I would," Lord Darcy said. He turned and looked at the second desk, behind which Lord Bontriomphe had seated himself. He was a fairly tall, rather good-looking, square-jawed man who was always well dressed and carried about him an air of competence.

"You may report, Bontriomphe," said the Marquis.

"Everything?"

"Everything. The conversation verbatim."

Lord Bontriomphe leaned back and closed his eyes for a moment. Lord Darcy prepared himself to listen closely. Bontriomphe had two things which made

him of tremendous value to the Marquis of London:
a flair for narrative and an eidetic memory.

Bontriomphe opened his eyes and looked at Darcy.

"At my lord's orders," he said, "I went to the
Sorcerers and Healers Convention to look at the herb
displays. He was especially interested in the spec-
imens of Polish devilwort, which he—"

The Marquis snorted. "Pah! That has nothing to
do with the murder."

"I haven't said it did. Where was I? Oh, yes.
Which he hasn't been able to grow from the seed,
only from cuttings. He wanted to find out how the
seed-grown plants had been cultivated.

"I went in to the Royal Steward a little after nine.
The place was packed with sorcerers of every size
and description and enough clergy to fill a church
from altar to narthex. I had to convince a couple of
guards at the door that I wasn't just some tourist
who wanted to gawk at the celebrities, but I made it
to the herb displays at about ten after. I took a good
long look at the Polish devilwort—it seemed to be
thriving well—and then took a survey of the rest of
the stuff. I took some notes on a few other rarities,
but that wouldn't interest you, so I'll omit the details.

"Then I wandered around and looked at the rest of
the displays, just to see if there was anything interesting. I didn't meet anyone I knew, which made me
just as happy, since I hadn't gone there for chitchat.
That is, I didn't meet any acquaintance until nine
twenty. That was when Commander Lord Ashley
tapped me on the shoulder.

"I turned around, and there he was, in full dress
Naval uniform, looking as uncomfortable as a Navy
officer at a magicians' convention.

" 'Bontriomphe,' he said, 'how good to see you again.'

" 'Good to see you,' I said, 'and how is the Imperial Navy? Have you become a Specialist in Sorcery?'

"That was a deliberate joke. Tony does have a touch of the Talent; he has what they call 'an intermittent and diffuse precognitive ability' that has helped him out of tight spots several times, and which, incidentally, is useful to him at the gaming tables. But in general he doesn't know any more about magic than an ostrich knows about icebergs.

"He laughed a little. 'Not yet and not ever,' he said. 'I'm here on Naval business. I'm looking for a friend of yours, but I don't know what he looks like.'

" 'Who are you looking for?' I asked.

" 'Master Sean O Lochlainn. I checked at the desk and got his room number, but he isn't in.'

" 'If he's around,' I said, 'I haven't seen him. But then I haven't been looking for him.'

"I stood there and looked around, but I couldn't spot him any place in that crowd. But I did happen to spot another face I knew.

" 'If anybody knows where Master Sean is,' I said, 'it will be Grand Master Sir Lyon Grey. Come along.'

"Sir Lyon was standing over near one of the doors talking to a man who was wearing the habit of one of the Flemish orders. The monk took his leave just as Lord Ashley and I approached Sir Lyon.

" 'Good morning, Sir Lyon,' I said. 'I think you've met Commander Ashley.'

" 'Good morning, Lord Bontriomphe,' the old sorcerer said. 'Yes, Commander Ashley and I have met. In what way may I be of assistance?'

" 'I have a message for Master Sean O Lochlainn, Sir Lyon,' said Ashley. 'Have you any idea where he is?'

"The Grand Master started to answer, but whatever he was going to say was lost. A scrawny little Master Sorcerer with a nose like a spike and rather bugged-out blue eyes suddenly popped from the door nearby, his hands fluttering about like a couple of drunken moths who had mistaken his head for a candle flame. He took a fast look around, saw Sir Lyon, and made a beeline for us, still flapping his hands.

" 'Grand Master! Grand Master! I must speak to you immediately!' he said in a low, excited voice.

" 'Compose yourself, Master Netly,' the Grand Master said. 'What is it?'

"Master Netly noticed Lord Ashley and me and said: 'It's . . . uh . . . confidential, Grand Master.'

"The Grand Master bent a little and cocked his head to one side while Master Netly, who is a good foot shorter than Sir Lyon, stood on tiptoe to whisper in his ear. I couldn't catch a word of what he said, but I saw Sir Lyon's eyes open wider as the skinny little sorcerer spoke. Then his eyes shifted and he looked straight at me.

"When he straightened up, he was still looking at me. And believe me when Grand Master Sir Lyon Gandolphus Grey fixes you with those eyes of his, you have an urge to search your conscience to see what particularly odious sins you have committed lately. Fortunately, my soul was reasonably pure.

" 'Will both of you gentlemen come with me, please?' he asked, shifting his gaze to Lord Ashley. 'Something of importance has come up. If you will be so good as to follow me . . .'

"He turned and went out the door, and Ashley

and I followed. As soon as we got out of the exhibition hall and into the corridor, I asked: 'What seems to be the trouble, Sir Lyon?'

" 'I am not certain yet. But apparently something has happened to Master Sir James Zwinge. We are fortunate that you, as an officer of the King's Justice, are on hand.'

"Then Lord Ashley said: 'Your pardon, Sir Lyon, but the delivery of this message to Master Sean is most important.'

" 'I am aware of that,' the old boy said rather testily. 'Master Sean is already at the scene. That is why I asked you to come along.'

" 'I see. I beg your pardon, Sir Lyon.'

"We followed him up the stairs and down the upper corridor without saying anything more. Netly pattered along with us, his hands still flitting about.

"There were three men and a woman standing in the hall outside the room that the management had assigned to Zwinge. Two of the men were wearing the light-blue dress clothing of sorcerers, and so was the woman. The third man was wearing ordinary merchant-class business clothes.

"One of the sorcerers was Master Sean. The second was a tall young man wearing the white slashes of a Journeyman, a Mechicain, by the look of him. The sorceress was one of the most beautiful honey blondes I have ever had the good fortune to meet in a hotel corridor, with a full-breasted, wide-shouldered, wide-hipped, narrow-waisted body and dark-blue eyes. She was only a couple of inches shorter than I am, and she—"

"Pfui—" For the second time, the Marquis of London interrupted the report of Lord Bontriomphe. "While you may enjoy dwelling upon the beauties of

women, there is no need to do it, much less to overdo
it. Darcy has already met Mary, Dowager Duchess of
Cumberland. Continue."

"Sorry," Lord Bontriomphe said blandly. "The
third man turned out to be Goodman Lewis Bolmer,
the manager of the Royal Steward Arms. He's about
an inch taller than Master Sean and looks as though
he had lost about fifty pounds too fast. His face and
jowls sag and give him a sort of floppy look, as if he
were made up of hounds' ears. He looked both wor-
ried and frightened.

"I asked what had happened as soon as I had identified myself.

"Master Sean said: 'I had an appointment with
Sir James at nine thirty, I knocked on the door and
no one answered. I knocked again. Then I heard a
scream and a sound as of a heavy body falling. Since
then, there's been nothing. The door is locked, and
we can't get in.'

"I looked at Goodman Lewis. 'Have you the key?'

" 'Yes, your lordship,' he said, nodding and jig-
gling his jowls. 'I brought it as soon as Master Netly
told me what had happened. But it won't turn the
bolt. It's stuck. Spell on it, I daresay.'

" 'It's a personalized lock spell,' Master Sean said.
'I'd say that only Sir James' key will open it. But I'm
afraid he may be badly injured. We'll have to get that
door down.'

"If you've ever been in the Royal Steward, you
know how thick those doors are. Very old fashioned
oak work—the building dates back to the Seven-
teenth Century.

" 'Can you take the spell off, Sean?' I asked.

" 'Sure and I can,' he said. 'But it would take time.
Half an hour if I'm lucky and get the psychic pattern

right away. Two or three hours if I'm not lucky.
That's not just an ordinary commercial spell; that's
a personal job put on there by Master Sir James himself.'

"I knelt down and took a peek through the keyhole. I couldn't see anything but the far wall of the
room. The keyhole is big enough, but the door is so
thick that it's like looking through a tunnel. Those
doors are two inches thick.

"I stood up again and turned to Goodman Lewis.
'Go get an ax. We'll have to chop through.'

"He looked as if he were about to object, but he
just said, 'Yes, your lordship. Right away,' and hur-
ried away.

"While he was gone, I asked some questions.
'What happened right after you heard the scream,
Sean?'

" 'Nothing for a few seconds,' he said. 'Then my
colleagues, here, came out of their rooms.'

" 'Which rooms?'

" 'Netly Dale has the room to the left of Sir James'
room, and Lord John Quetzal has the room to the
right, if I am not mistaken.'

"Netly clasped his hands together to keep from
fluttering them and nodded. 'That's right. Absolutely correct.'

"Lord John Quetzal just nodded his head in agreement.

" 'Lord John Quetzal,' I said. The name had
struck a bell. 'You are the fourth son of His Gracious
Highness, De Mechicoe, I think?'

"He bowed. 'The same, my lord.'

"Then I turned to the blond vision. I didn't know
who she was at the time, but she was wearing the De
Cumberland arms in full on her right breast instead

of just the crest on her shoulder, so I deduced—"

Lord Bontriomphe stopped his narrative again as he heard a snort from de London. "Yes, my lord?"

"It is not necessary to inform us of your deductions of the obvious," said the Marquis with heavy sarcasm. "Darcy wants facts, not the rather puerile thought processes by which you may have arrived at them."

"I sit corrected, my lord," said Lord Bontriomphe. "At any rate, I correctly identified the lady.

" 'Where is your room, Your Grace?' I asked.

" 'Just across the hall,' she said, pointing.

"The hallways in the Royal Steward are eight feet wide, and her room was directly opposite Zwinge's.

" 'Thank you,' I said. 'Now . . .' I looked at the others. . . . Why did you all come out of your rooms? What alarmed you?'

"They all said the same thing. The scream. None of them had heard Sean knocking; the doors are too thick for that to be noticed. I know; I tried it myself later. You can hear a knock on another door only if you listen carefully. That scream must have been a hell of a loud one. The only person to hear the body drop to the floor at that time was Sean. None of the others had opened their doors yet. I couldn't establish which one of the other three came out first; none of them noticed. There was evidently too much confusion at the time.

"When the manager, Goodman Lewis, came back with the ax, I glanced at my watch. It was twenty-three minutes of ten. Approximately seven minutes had passed since Sean had knocked on the door.

"I used the ax myself. Everyone else stood back, well away from the door. I cut a good-sized area out of the center without damaging either the frame or the lock. I kept everyone else out and squeezed through the hole I'd cut.

"It was an ordinary room, twelve by fifteen, with a bathroom. Across the room were two windows, both shuttered and bolted, but the shutters had been adjusted to let in the daylight. The glass panes were closed and unbroken.

"The body of our Chief Forensic Sorcerer was almost exactly in the middle of the room, more than six feet from the door. He was lying on his left side, in a pool of fresh blood, and there was so much blood on his jacket that it was hard for me to see at first what had happened. Then I saw that there was a rip in his jacket, high up on the left side of his chest, above the heart. I opened his jacket for a look. There was a vertical stab wound in the chest at that point.

"A couple of feet away, lying in the pool of blood, near the edge, was a knife. It was a heavy-handled one, with a black onyx hilt and a solid silver blade. I've seen knives like that before, Lord Darcy, and so have you. A sorcerer's knife, used in certain spells for symbolically cutting psychic linkages or something of the sort. But they can cut physically as well as psychically.

"About halfway between the body and the door was a key, the same kind of heavy brass key that the manager had tried to open the door with. I marked the spot with one of my own keys and then tried the key on the door. It worked; it turned the bolt, but no other key would. It was Sir James' key, all right.

"I searched the body. Nothing much there—his own key ring; two golden sovereigns, three silver sovereigns, and some odd change; a notebook full of magical symbols and equations which I don't understand; an ordinary small pocketknife; a cardfolder which contained his certificate as a Master Sorcerer, his license to practice magic—signed by the Bishop of London—his official identification as Chief Forensic Sorcerer, a card identifying him as a Fellow of the Royal Thaumaturgical Society, and a few personal cards. You can look at it all, Darcy; My Lord Marquis has it in an envelope in the wall safe.

"He had three other suits, all hanging neatly in the closet, with nothing in the pockets. There were some papers on the desk, all filled with thaumaturgical symbolism, and more like them in the wastebasket. I left them where they were. The only other thing in the room was his symbol-decorated carpetbag—the kind every sorcerer carries. I didn't try to open it or move it; it is not wise to meddle with the belongings of magicians, not even dead ones.

"The point is that there was nobody in that room but the dead man. I searched it carefully. There was no place to hide. I looked under the bed and in the closet and in the bathroom.

"Furthermore, nobody could have left by that door. It had been locked by the only key that would lock it, and that key was inside the room. Besides, there were four people in that corridor within seconds after Sir James screamed, and three of them were watching that door from that time until I cut it open.

"The windows were bolted shut from the inside. The glass and the laths in the shutters were solid. The windows look out on a small patio which is a part of the dining area. There were twelve people out there—all sorcerers—who were eating breakfast. None of them saw anything, although their attention was directed to the windows by the scream. Besides, the wall is sheer—a thirty-foot drop without ledges, handholds, or toeholds. No exit that way.

"There is no evidence that anyone went into that room or came out of it.

"By the time I had searched the room, the Chief Master-at-Arms and two of his men had arrived. You've met Chief Hennely Grayme—big, husky chap with a square face? Yes. Well, I told him to take over, to get a preservation spell cast over the body, and to touch nothing.

"Then I went back out in the hall and herded everybody out of there and into one of the empty rooms down the hall. The manager gave me the key and I told him to go on about his business.

"Commander Lord Ashley was a little impatient. He had already delivered his message to Master Sean and had to report back to the Lord Admiral's office, so I told him to go ahead. Sir Lyon, Master Sean, Master Netly, Journeyman Lord John Quetzal, and the Dowager Duchess of Cumberland all looked shocked at what they'd seen through the door, and none of them seemed to have much to say.

" 'Sir Lyon,' I said, 'that room was locked and sealed. Sir James was stabbed at a time when there was no one else in the room. What do you make of it?'

"He stroked his beard for a moment, then said: 'I understand your question. Yes, on first glance I should say that he was killed by Black Magic. But that is merely a supposition based upon the physical facts. I do not suppose you can detect it yourself, but this hotel is not at present equipped with just the ordinary commercial spells for privacy, to prevent unwarranted use of the clairvoyant Talent. Before the Convention started a special group of six sorcerers went through the entire building reinforcing those spells and adding others. They do not affect precognition, since there is no way to cast a spell into the future, but they prevent anyone from using his clairvoyant Talent to see into another's room, and they make it very difficult to understand or detect what is going on in someone else's mind. Before I can state flatly that Sir James was killed by Black Magic I should want further investigation into the facts.'

" 'There will be,' I told him. 'Next question, then: Who had reason to kill him? Had anyone quarreled with him?'

"So help me, Lord Darcy, every eye in the room turned to Master Sean. Except Master Sean's, of course.

"Naturally, I asked him what the quarrel was about.

" 'It wasn't a quarrel,' he said firmly. 'Both Sir James and I were angry, but not at each other.'

" 'Who were you angry with, then?"

" 'Not with anyone. We had both been working on a new thaumaturgical effect, and had discovered almost identical spells to produce that effect. It has happened before in the history of magic. We may have been growling and snapping at each other, but we weren't angry at anything but the coincidence.'

" 'How did the . . . er . . . discussion come about?' I asked him.

" 'Chance conversation in the committee room. We fell to talking and the subject came up. We compared notes, and . . . well, there it was. What we were really arguing about was who was to present his paper first. So we called Sir Lyon over to decide the problem.'

"I looked at Sir Lyon. He nodded. 'That's correct.

I decided that it would be best for them to pool their findings and present the paper jointly, under both their names, with a full explanation that the work had been done by both independently.'

" 'Tell me, Sir Lyon,' I said, 'this paper—or these papers—wouldn't be just a lot of thaumaturgical equations, would they?'

" 'Oh, no. They would have a full exposition of the effect. There would be equations, of course, but the text would be in Anglo-French. Naturally, there would be a lot of technical words, professional jargon, if you will, but—'

" 'Where is Sir James' paper, then?' I asked. 'It isn't in his room.'

" 'I have it,' said Sean. 'It was agreed between Sir James and myself that I should do a first collation between the two papers, and then we'd talk the thing over this morning at nine-thirty and do a second draft of our collaboration.'

" 'When was the last time you saw Sir James?' I asked.

" 'Last evening at about ten, it was,' Sean explained. 'I went with him to his room, so he could give me his manuscript. So far as I know, that's the last anyone saw of him. He was going to do a little further work he had in mind, and that he didn't want to be disturbed until half past nine.'

" 'Would he have been using a knife for that work?'

" 'Knife?' he said, looking puzzled.

" 'You know. One of those big, black-handled silver knives.'

" Oh. You mean a contact cutter. I wouldn't think so; he said he wanted to do some paper work, is all.

Not any actual experimentation. Still, I suppose it's possible.'

"I said, 'Master Sean, do you mind if I take a look at Sir James' manuscript?'

"I guess that must have fired his Irish temper up. 'I don't see what that has to do with this business,' he said peevishly. 'I've been working on this thing for three years. It was bad enough that Sir James was doing the same thing, but I'm not going to let out this information until I'm ready to present it myself!'

"Then Grand Master Sir Lyon spoke. 'I cannot insist that you show those papers to the Chief Investigator, Master Sean; I cannot ask you to reveal the process. But I feel that the subject may possibly have a bearing on the case.'

"Master Sean opened his mouth and then closed it again. After a second or so, he said: 'Well, that's already on the Program anyway. My paper was to have been called "A Method of Performing Surgery Upon Inaccessible Organs." Sir James called his "The Surgical Incision of Internal Organs Without Breaching the Abdominal Wall." '

"That was when Master Netly squeaked, 'You mean a method of controlling a blade within an enclosed space? Astounding!' Then he backed away from Sean a couple of steps. *That's* what he meant when he screamed!'

"That was the first I'd heard that Master Sir James had actually screamed words. The words were —and they all agreed on it—

" *'Master Sean! Help!'* "

The Marquis of London had been sitting during the entire narration with his eyes closed, but he was not asleep. "Satisfactory," he said. Then he opened his eyes, looking at Lord Darcy. "Now," he rumbled, "you understand why I felt constrained to order the arrest of Master Sean O Lochlainn on suspicion of murder."

# 4

LORD DARCY looked long and deeply into the eyes of My Lord Marquis, and the Marquis calmly returned that steady gaze. At last Lord Darcy said: "I see. Do you consider the evidence conclusive, then?"

"Oh, by no means," said the Marquis, patting the air with a heavy hand. "I certainly should not care to place the case before the Court of High Justice with the evidence now at hand. If I had that evidence, Master Sean would have already been charged with premeditated murder, not merely with suspicion."

"I see," Lord Darcy repeated, his voice icily polite. "Am I to presume that I will be expected to find that evidence?"

The Marquis de London lifted his massive shoulders perhaps a quarter of an inch and lowered them again. "It is a matter of indifference to me. However, understanding as I do your personal interest in the case, you may certainly count upon full co-operation from this office in any investigation you may care to undertake."

"Ahh. That's the way the wind blows, is it?" said

Lord Darcy. "Very well. I accept your hospitality and your co-operation. Will you release Master Sean on his own recognizance until such time as the remainder of the evidence is in?"

My Lord Marquis frowned, and for the first time there seemed to be a touch of discomfort in his manner. "You know as well as I that a man arrested for a capital crime cannot be released on his own recognizance. Such is the law; I am powerless to abrogate the King's Law."

"Of course," murmured Lord Darcy. "Of course. I trust, however, that I may speak to Master Sean?"

"Naturally. He is in the Tower, and I have given orders that he is to be made comfortable. You may see him at any time."

Lord Darcy rose to his feet. "My thanks, my lord. In that case, I shall go about my business. May I have your leave to go?"

"You have my leave, my lord. Lord Bontriomphe will see you to the door." The Marquis of London rose ponderously to his feet and walked out of his office without another word.

Lord Darcy said nothing to Lord Bontriomphe until both of them were standing at the front door. Then he said: "My Lord Marquis likes to play games, Bontriomphe."

"Hm-m-m. Yes. Yes, he does." Bontriomphe paused. "I am certain you can handle this, Darcy."

"I think so. Don't be surprised by anything."

"I shan't. Good evening, my lord."

"Good evening. I shall see you on the morrow."

\* \* \*

Master Sean O Lochlainn, in his comfortable room in that ancient fortress known as the Tower of London, was no longer angry—not even at Fate. The emotion that filled him now was a sort of determined patience. He knew Lord Darcy would come, and he knew that his imprisonment was purely nominal.

Earlier in the afternoon, when he had found himself charged with suspicion of murder, he had felt some small pique when he was told that he would not be allowed to bring his symbol-decorated carpetbag to the Tower with him. Locking up a sorcerer is difficult enough in itself; to allow him to have the tools of his trade would be foolish indeed.

But the Tower Wardens had erred in thinking that a sorcerer was helpless without his tools. They had not taken into account a certain spell that Master Sean had long since cast upon that symbol-decorated carpetbag. The effect of that spell can be expressed simply: The tools of a sorcerer cannot long be separated from their Master against his will. And the way the spell worked in practice was thus:

The carpetbag had been locked in Master Sean's room at the Royal Steward Arms, to remain there until such time as Master Sean's ultimate disposition should be decided. That had been ordered by the Chief Master-at-Arms at the time of Master Sean's arrest. Master Sean had delivered his key to the Chief Master-at-Arms in polite submission to the majesty of the law. But there had not been any special spell on the lock of Master Sean's room, such as there had been on the late Master James Zwinge's room. Therefore, when one of the hotel servants was making her cleaning rounds at one o'clock that afternoon, she had had with her a key to Master Sean's room—a key that would work.

Quite naturally, Bridget Courville took each room as she came to it. When she came to Master Sean's room, she went in and looked around.

"All's neat," she said to herself. "Bed unmade, but of course that's the way it always is. Ah, these sorcerers are neat enough, for sure. No bottles or trash scattered about. Not drinkers, much, I think. Which it shouldn't be for a sorcerer."

She tidied up—made the bed, laid out clean towels, put in new soap bars, and did all the other little things that needed to be done.

She noticed the symbol-decorated carpetbag, of course. There was one like it in almost every room during this convention. But she paid no attention to it consciously.

Her subconscious, however, whispered to her that "it didn't ought to be here."

It can be said that Bridget Courville really didn't think about what she was doing when she picked up the bag and set it out in the hall before she locked up the room and went on to the next one.

At one fifteen, a catering servant—a young lad in his late teens whose duty it was to see that drinks and food were brought to the guests when they were ordered—saw the bag sitting in the hall. It seemed out of place. Without bothering to think about it, he picked it up and took it downstairs. He left it on the luggage rack near the front entrance and promptly forgot about it.

Hennely Grayme, Chief Master-at-Arms for the City of London, having made all the notes he could on the scene of the crime, left the hotel at five minutes of two. He stopped near the door and saw the carpetbag on the luggage rack. He noticed the initials *S. O L.* on the handle. Automatically, he picked it up and took it with him. When he stopped by at the Tower, he said a few words to the Chief Warder and, without mentioning it, left the carpetbag behind.

The carpetbag remained unnoticed in the anteroom of the Chief Warder's office until fifteen minutes of three. During that time, many people went in and out of that anteroom without noticing the bag; none of them were going in the right direction.

At two forty-five, the Warder in charge of the cell in which Master Sean was incarcerated saw the bag. On his way out, after reporting to the Chief Warder, he picked up the bag.

Had he been going off duty, had he been going to the Middle Tower instead of St. Thomas' Tower, he would not even have noticed the symbol-decorated carpetbag. The spell was specific. But he did pick it up, and he did carry it up the spiral staircase to Master Sean's cell.

He unlocked the door to Master Sean's cell, then knocked politely.

"Master Sean, it is I, Warder Linsy."

"Come in, me boy, come in," said Master Sean jovially.

The door opened, and when Master Sean saw the carpetbag in the Warder's hand, he suppressed a smile and said: "What can I do for you, Warder?"

"I was to come up and see what you wanted for dinner, Master," Warder Linsy said deferentially. Absently he put the bag down inside the door.

"Ah, it's of no matter to me, my good Warder," said Master Sean. "Whatever the Chief Warder orders will be good enough for me."

Warder Linsy smiled. "That's good of you, Master." Then he lowered his voice. "Ain't none of us thinks you done it, Master Sean. We knows a sorcerer couldn't of killed a man. Not that way, I mean. Not by black magic."

"Thank you for your confidence, me boy," Master Sean said expansively. "I assure you it's not misplaced. Now, if you'll excuse me, I have some thinking to do."

"Of course, Master. Of course." And Warder Linsy closed the door, locked it carefully, and went on about his business.

\* \* \*

Lord Darcy's trip from the Palace du Marquis to the Tower of London was eventful. The cab clattered out of Mark Lane, swerved, and descended Tower Hill. In Water Lane, at the gate, it stopped. Lord Darcy stepped out.

A heavy, whitish fog drifted through the bars of the great iron fence and clung to the shadows of the Gothic archways. There was a fading sound of bells as the ships on the Thames moved through the mist-laden waters. The air was muggy, and a faint smell of marine decay drifted over the wall that formed one side of the fortress. Lord Darcy wrinkled his nostrils at the aroma that assailed them, and then walked over the stone bridge that led from the Middle Tower to another tower—larger and gray-black, with a few whitish stones here and there in its walls. There was another archway, then a short, straight path, and then Lord Darcy turned toward the right and entered St. Thomas' Tower.

Within a few minutes, the Warder was unlocking the door to Master Sean's cell. "Call me when you wants to leave, your lordship," he said. He left, closing the door and relocking it.

"Well, Master Sean," said Lord Darcy with a spark of humor in his gray eyes, "I trust you are enjoying this idyllic relaxation from your onerous duties, eh?"

"Hm-m-m—yes and no, my lord," said the tubby little sorcerer. He waved a hand at the small plain table on which his carpetbag sat. "I can't say I enjoy being locked up, but it has given me an opportunity to experiment and meditate."

"Indeed? Upon what?"

"Upon getting in and out of locked rooms, my lord."

"And what have you learned, my good Sean?" Lord Darcy asked.

"I've learned that the security system here is quite good, but not quite good enough. To hold *me* in, I mean. The spell on that lock took me ten minutes to solve." He picked up a small wand of gleaming brass and twirled it between thumb and forefinger. "I relocked it, of course, my lord. No need to disturb the Warder, who's a decent sort of fellow."

"I see you regained possession of your bag of equipment easily enough. Well, one could hardly expect an ordinary prison magician to compete with a Master Sorcerer of your capabilities. Now pray be seated and explain to me in detail how you came to be incarcerated in one of London's oldest landmarks. Omit no detail."

Lord Darcy did not interrupt while Master Sean told his story. He had worked with the little sorcerer for years; he knew that Sean's memory was accurate and complete.

"And then," Master Sean finished, "Lord Bontriomphe brought me here—with, I must say, sincere apologies. I can't for the life of me see why the Marquis should order me locked up, though. Surely a man of his abilities should be able to see that I had nothing to do with Sir James' death."

Lord Darcy scooped tobacco from a leathern

pouch and thumbed it into the gold-worked porcelain bowl of his favorite pipe. "Of course he knows you're innocent, my dear Sean," he said crisply. "My Lord Marquis is a parsimonious man and a lazy one. Bontriomphe is an excellent investigator, but he lacks the deductive faculty in its highest form. My Lord Marquis, on the other hand, is capable of brilliant reasoning, but he is both physically and mentally indolent. He leaves his own home but rarely, and never for the purpose of criminal investigation. When he is pressured into doing so, My Lord Marquis is perfectly capable of solving some of the most intricate and complex puzzles with nothing more to work with than the verbal reports given him by Lord Bontriomphe. His mind is—brilliant." Lord Darcy lit his pipe and surrounded himself with a cloud of fragrant smoke.

"Coming from you," said Master Sean, "that's quite a compliment."

"Not at all. It is merely a statement of fact. Perhaps it runs in the blood; we are cousins, you know."

Master Sean nodded. "At least the laziness doesn't run in the blood, my lord. But why lock me up because he's lazy?"

"Lazy *and* parsimonious, my good Sean," Lord Darcy corrected the sorcerer. "Both factors apply. He has already recognized that this case is far too complex for the relatively feeble powers of Lord Bontriomphe to cope with." Lord Darcy smiled and took the pipe from his lips. "You said a moment ago that I had complimented my lord's brilliancy. If that is so, then he has, in his own way, paid the same compliment to me. He is mentally lazy; therefore, he wishes to get someone else to do the work—someone competent to solve the problem with the same facility with which he would do it himself, were he to apply his mind. He has chosen me, and I flatter myself that he would not have chosen any other man."

"That still doesn't explain why he locked me up," Master Sean said. "He could have just asked you for assistance."

Lord Darcy sighed. "You have forgotten his parsimony again, my good Sean. Were he to ask His Royal Highness of Normandy to spare my services for a short while, he would be obligated to pay my salary from his own Privy Purse. But by incarcerating you, he deprives me of my most valued assistant. He knows I would not suffer you to be imprisoned one second longer than necessary. He knows that putting you in the Tower would force me to take a leave of absence, to solve the case on my own time, thereby saving himself a pretty penny."

"Blackmail," said Master Sean.

" 'Blackmail' is perhaps too strong a word," Lord Darcy said thoughtfully, "but I will admit that no other is quite strong enough. That problem, however, will be taken care of in its own time. At the moment, we are concerned with the death of Sir James.

"Now—what about the lock on Sir James' room?"

Master Sean settled himself deeper into his chair. "Well, my lord, as you know, most commercial spells are pretty simple, especially those where more than one key has to be used, as they have in a hotel."

Lord Darcy nodded patiently. Master Sean O Lochlainn had a rather pedagogical habit of framing his explanations as though they were lectures to be used in the training of apprentice sorcerers—which was not surprising, since the tubby little master magician had at one time taught in one of the Sorcerers'

Guild's schools and had written two textbooks and several monographs upon the subject. Lord Darcy had long ago formed the habit of listening, even though he had heard parts of each lecture before, for there was always something to be learned, something new to be stored away in the memory for future reference. Lord Darcy did not have the inborn Talent necessary to make use of the Laws of Magic directly, but one never knows when some esoteric bit of data might become pertinent and useful to a criminal investigator.

"The average commercial spell uses the Law of Contagion, so that every key which touches the lock during the casting of the spell will unlock and lock it," Master Sean continued. "But that means a relative weakening of the spell. An ordinary duplicate key won't work the lock, but any good apprentice o' the Guild could break the spell if he had such a duplicate. And any Master could break it *without* the key in a minute or two.

"But a personal spell by a Master uses the Law of Relevance to bind the whole lock-and-key mechanism together as a unit—one key, one lock. The spell is cast with the key in the lock, so that the binding considers the key simply as a detachable part of the mechanism, if you follow me, my lord. No other key will work, either to lock or to unlock the mechanism, even if it is so physically like the proper key that they couldn't be told apart."

"And Master Sir James' key-and-lock had that sort of spell on it, eh?" Lord Darcy asked.

"That it did, my lord."

"Could a Master Sorcerer have removed the spell?"

Master Sean nodded. "Aye, that he could—in half

an hour. But look what that would entail, my lord.

"The Unknown would have to stand in that corridor for at least half an hour, maybe more, going through the proper ritual. Anyone who came by during that time couldn't help but notice. Certainly Master Sir James would have noticed if he was inside the room.

"But let's say the Unknown actually does that. Now he opens the door with an ordinary duplicate, goes inside, and kills Master Sir James. Fine.

"Then he comes out, and casts *another* spell on the lock-and-key—with the key in the lock, as it must be. That takes him another half hour.

"And *then* . . ."

Master Sean held up his forefinger dramatically.

". . . And *then—he has to get that key back into the room!*"

Master Sean spread his hands, palms upward. "I submit that it isn't possible, my lord. Not even for a magician."

Lord Darcy puffed thoughtfully at his pipe for the space of two seconds. Then he said: "Is it not theoretically possible to move an object from one point in space to another without actually traversing the space between the two points?"

"Theoretically?" Master Sean made a wry grin. "Oh, yes, my lord. *Theoretically*, The Transmutation of metals is theoretically possible, too. But, like instantaneous transportation, no one has ever done it. If anyone did solve the rites and ceremonies necessary, it would be the biggest scientific breakthrough of the Twentieth Century. It couldn't be kept quiet. It is simply beyond our present stage of science, my lord.

"And when and if it is ever done, my lord, the process will not be used for such minor things as moving a big brass key a few feet."

"Very well, then," said his lordship, "we can eliminate that."

"The trouble is," said Master Sean, "that all those heavy privacy spells make it difficult for a man to do his work properly. If it weren't for them, your job would be simple."

"My dear Sean," said Lord Darcy with a smile, "if it were not for the privacy spells used in every hotel, private home, office building, and in public structures of all kinds, my job would not be simple, it would be nonexistent.

"Although the clairvoyant Talent is no doubt a useful one, its indiscriminate use leads to so much encroachment upon personal privacy and individual rights that we must protect ourselves from it. Imagine what a clairvoyant could do in a world where such protective spells were not used. There would be no need for investigators like myself. In such a world the police would have merely to bring the case to the attention of a clairvoyant, who would immediately inform them of how the crime was committed and who had committed it.

"On the other hand, think what opportunity there would be for a corrupt government to employ such clairvoyants to spy upon private citizens for their own nefarious purposes. Or think of the opportunities for criminal blackmail.

"We must be thankful that modern privacy spells protect us from such improper uses of the Talent, even though it makes physical investigation of a crime necessary. Even as it is, I am never called upon when something happens in the countryside. If a person is killed in a field or in a forest, a journeyman

sorcerer working for the local Armsmen can easily
take care of the job—as easily as he finds lost children and strayed animals. It is in the cities, towns
and villages where my ability to deduce facts from
physical and thaumaturgical evidence makes me useful.

"It is my job to find method, motive, and opportunity." He took a small, silver, ivory-handled
tool from his pocket and began tamping the ashes in
his pipe. "Method, motive and opportunity," he repeated thoughtfully. "So far we have no candidates
for the first two and entirely too many for the last."
He returned the tamper to his pocket and the pipe to
his mouth.

"Normally, my dear Sean," he continued, "when
a case appears to have magical elements in it, finding
the magician involved is a prime factor in the problem. You will recall the interesting behavior of Laird
Duncan at Castle D'Evreux, the curious habits of the
one-armed tinker at the Michaelmas Fair, the Polish
sorcerer in the Atlantic Curse problem, the missing
magician in the Canterbury blackmail case, and the
odd affair of Lady Overleigh's solid gold chamber
pot. In each case, only one sorcerer was directly involved.

"But what have we here?" Lord Darcy gestured
with his pipe in the general direction of the Royal
Steward Hotel. "We have nearly half the licensed
sorcerers of the Empire, a collection that includes
some seventy-five or eighty percent of the most powerful magicians on Earth.

"We are faced with a plenitude—indeed, a
plethora—of suspects, all of whom have the ability to
use black magic against Master Sir James Zwinge,

and had the opportunity of doing so."

Master Sean thoughtfully massaged his round Irish nose between the thumb and forefinger of his left hand. "I can't understand why any of 'em would do it, my lord. Every Guild member knows the danger of it. *'The mental state necessary to use the Talent for black sorcery is such that it invariably destroys the user.'* That's a quote from one of the basic textbooks, my lord, and every *grimoire* contains a variation of it. How could any sorcerer *be* so stupid?"

"Why do chirurgeons occasionally become addicts of the poppy distillates?" Lord Darcy asked.

"I know, my lord; I know," Master Sean said wearily. *"One* act of black magic isn't fatal; it doesn't even cause any detectable mental or moral change in many cases. But the operative word there is 'detectable.' And that's because the moral rot must already have set in before a man with the Talent would even *consider* practicing black magic."

\* \* \*

Even though it had happened before and would happen again, no member of the Guild of Sorcerers liked the idea that any single other member would resort to the perversion of his Art that constituted Black Magic.

Not that they were afraid to face it—oh, no! Face it they must, and face it they did—with a vengeance. Lord Darcy knew—although very few who were not high-ranking Masters of the Guild had that knowledge—exactly what happened to a member who was found guilty of using his Talent for evil.

*Destruction!*

The evil sorcerer, convicted by his own mind, convicted by the analysis of a true Jury of his true Peers, convicted by those who could really understand and sympathize with his motives and reasons, was condemned to have his Talent . . .

. . . Removed.

. . . Obliterated.

. . . Destroyed.

A Committee of Executors was appointed—a group of sorcerers large enough and powerful enough to overcome the Talent-power of the guilty man.

And when they were through, the convicted man had lost nothing but his Talent. His knowledge, his memory, his morals, his sanity—all remained the same. But his ability to perform magic was gone . . . never to return.

"Meanwhile," said Lord Darcy, "we have a problem of our own. Commander Lord Ashley gave you my message?"

"Indeed he did, my lord."

"I hate having to take you away from the Convention, my good Sean; I know what it means to you. But this is no ordinary murder; it concerns the security of the Empire."

"I know, my lord," said Master Sean, "duty is duty." But there was a touch of sadness in his voice. "I did rather want to present my paper, but it will be published in the Journal, which will be just as good."

"Hm-m-m," said Lord Darcy. "When were you scheduled to present your paper?"

"On Saturday, my lord. Master Sir James and I were going to combine our papers and present them jointly, but of course that is out of the question now. They'll have to be published separately."

"Saturday, eh?" said Lord Darcy. "Well, if we can get back to Cherbourg by tomorrow afternoon, I should say that most of the urgent work will be cleared up within twenty-four hours, say by Friday afternoon. You could take the evening boat back and be in time to present both your paper and the late Master Sir James'."

Master Sean brightened. "That's good of you, my lord! But you'll have to get me out o' this plush cell if we're to get the job done!"

*"Hah!"* Lord Darcy shot suddenly to his feet. "My dear Master Sean, *that* problem has, I think, already been solved—although it may take a little time to make the . . . er . . . proper arrangements. And now I shall bid you good night; I shall see you again tomorrow."

# 5

THE FOG had thickened in the courtyard below the high, embattled walls surrounding the Tower of London, and beyond the Water Lane gate the world seemed to have disappeared into a wall of impalpable cotton wool. The gas lamps in the courtyard and above the gate seemed to be shedding their light into nothingness.

"Had you no one waitin' for you, your lordship?" asked the Sergeant Warder as he stood on the steps with Lord Darcy.

"No," Lord Darcy admitted. "I came in a cab. I must confess I failed to check with the weather prognostication. How long is the fog to last?"

"According to the chief sorcerer at the Weather Office, your lordship, it isn't due to break up until five minutes after five o'clock in the morning. It's to turn to a light drizzle, which will clear at six twelve."

"Well, I certainly can't stay here until sun-up," Lord Darcy said ruefully.

"I'll have the man at the gate see if he can't whistle

you up a cab, your lordship; it's still fairly early. You
can wait in the outer—" He stopped. From somewhere in the fog that choked Water Lane came the
clatter of hooves and the rattle of wheels, becoming
increasingly louder.

"That may be a cab, now, your lordship!" He
raised his authoritative voice to a commanding
bellow: *"Warder Jason! Signal that cab!"*

*"Yes, Sergeant!"* came a fog-muffled voice from the
gate, followed immediately by the shrill *beep! beep!
beep!* of a cab whistle.

"I fear we are to be disappointed, Sergeant," Lord
Darcy said. "Your ears should tell you that the vehicle approaching is drawn by a pair; therefore, it is a
private town-carriage, not a public cab. There is no
cabman in the whole of London who would be so
profligate as to use two horses where one will do."

The Sergeant Warder cocked one ear toward the
sound. "Hm-m-m. Dare say you're right, your
lordship. It *do* sound like a pair, now I listen closer.
Still . . ."

"They are a well-trained pair," said his lordship.
"Almost perfectly in step. But since two hooves cannot possibly strike the paving stones at precisely the
same instant, there is a slight echo effect, clearly dis-
cernible to the trained ear."

The beeping sound of the whistle had stopped.
Evidently the Warder at the gate had realized that
the approaching vehicle was not a cab.

Nonetheless, the carriage could be heard to slow
and stop outside the gate. After a moment, the reins
snapped, and the horses started again. The carriage
was turning, coming in the gate. It loomed suddenly
out of the fog, seeming to coalesce into solidity out of
the very substance of the rolling mist itself. It came to

a halt at the curbing stone several yards away, still shadowy in the feeble yellow glow of the gas lamps.

Then a voice called out quite clearly from within it: "Lord Darcy! Is that you?"

It was plainly a feminine voice, and quite familiar, but because of the muffling effect of the fog and the distorting effect of the interior of the cab, Lord Darcy did not recognize it immediately. He knew that, standing almost directly under the gas lamp as he was, his own features stood out rather clearly at that distance.

"You have the advantage of me, my lady," he said.

There was a low laugh. "You mean you can't even read arms anymore?"

Lord Darcy had already noticed that a coat-of-arms was emblazoned on the door of the coach, but it was impossible to make it out in this light. There was no need to, however; Lord Darcy had recognized the voice upon the second hearing of it.

"Even the brilliancy of the arms of Cumberland can be dimmed beyond recognition in a London pea-soup," Lord Darcy said as he walked toward the vehicle. "Your Grace should have more than just the regulation night-lights and fog-lights if you want your arms to be recognized on a night like this."

He could see her clearly now; the beautiful face and the cloud of golden hair were only slightly dimmed by shadow and fog.

"I'm alone," she said very softly.

"Hullo, Mary," Lord Darcy said with equal softness. "What the deuce are you doing here?"

"Why, I came to fetch *you,* of course," said Mary, Dowager Duchess of Cumberland. "You dismissed your cab earlier because you didn't think about the fog coming, so now you're marooned. There isn't a cab to be had this side of St. Paul's. Get in, my dear, and let's leave this depressing prison."

Lord Darcy turned toward the Sergeant Warder, who still stood beneath the gas lamp. "Thank you for your efforts, Sergeant. I shan't need a cab. Her Grace has very kindly offered transportation."

"Very good, your lordship. Good night, your lordship. Good night, Your Grace."

They wished the Sergeant Warder a good night, Lord Darcy climbed into the carriage, and, at a word from Her Grace, the coachman snapped his reins and the carriage moved off into the swirling fog.

The Duchess pulled down the blinds and turned up the lamp in the top of the coach so that the two passengers could see each other clearly.

"You're looking well, my dear," she said.

"And you are as beautiful as ever," Lord Darcy replied. There was a mocking glint in his eyes that Her Grace of Cumberland could not quite fathom. "Where would you like to go?" she asked, trying to probe that look with her own startlingly dark-blue eyes.

"Anywhere you'd like, my sweet. We could just drive about London for a while—for however long it takes you to tell me about the important information you have regarding this morning's murder of Master Sir James Zwinge."

Her eyes widened. For a moment, she said nothing. Then: "Damn! How did you know?"

"I deduced it."

"Rot!"

"Not at all. You have a keen mind, my dear; you should be able to follow my reasoning."

Again there was a silence, this time for nearly a minute, as Mary de Cumberland looked unblinkingly at Lord Darcy, her mind working rapidly. Then she gave her head a quick shake. "You have some information I don't."

"I think not. Unless, perhaps, I know how your mind works better than you do. You have the delightful habit, my dear, of making a man feel as though he were terribly important to you—even when you have to tell small lies to do it."

She smiled. "You *are* important to me, darling. Furthermore, small lies are necessary to good manners and to diplomacy; there is no harm in them. And what, pray, does that have to do with your pretended deduction?"

"That was unworthy of you, my dear. You know I never pretend to mental abilities other than those I actually possess." His voice had an edge.

She smiled contritely and put out a hand to touch his arm. "I know. I apologize. Please explain."

Lord Darcy's smile returned. He put his hand on hers. "Apology accepted. Explanation—a simple one —as follows:

"You claimed that you had come to fetch me at the Tower. Now, I know that, aside from myself, the Warders at the Tower, Master Sean, and two other people, no one in London knew of my whereabouts or could have learned it by other than thaumaturgical means. No one but those even knew I was in London. You are a sorceress, true, but only journeyman, and we both know you are not prescient to any degree above normal. You might have deduced that I would come immediately I heard of Master Sean's arrest, but you could not possibly have known at exactly what time I would leave the Tower. Ergo, your arrival was a coincidence.

"However, as your coach approached the gate,

you heard the Warder whistling for a cab. You would not have stopped for that; you stopped to identify yourself to the Warder so that you could enter the courtyard. Therefore, your destination must have been the Tower itself; if it were not, you would have gone on by, ignoring the whistle.

"Then you came on in and saw me. The very tone of your voice when you hailed me showed that you had not expected to see me there.

"Your reasoning powers are well above average; it was hardly the work of a mental giant, however, to deduce from the whistle and my presence in the courtyard that it was I who desired a cab. Knowing, as you do, that I am not careless by habit, you further deduced that, having but recently arrived in London, I had failed to notice the fog prediction in the *Courier*, and had dismissed the cab that brought me. Thereupon, you spoke your flattering and entirely mendacious little piece about having come to get me."

Her laugh was soft and throaty. "It wasn't a lie intended to deceive you, my dear."

"I know. You wanted me to gasp in amazement and say: 'Goodness me! How*ever* did you know I was going to be here? Have you become a seer, then?' And you would have smiled and looked wise and said: 'Oh, I have my ways.'"

She laughed again. "You know me too well, my lord. But what has all that to do with your knowing I had information about the death of Master Sir James?"

"We return to the coincidence of your arrival at the Tower," Lord Darcy said. "If you had not come for me, then what was your purpose? It must have been important, else you would not have come out on so foggy a night. And yet, the moment you see *me*, you ask me to get in, and off we go. Whatever business you had at the Tower can be conducted with me, eh? Obviously, you went to tell Master Sean something, but not something strictly personal. Ergo—" He smiled, letting the conclusion go unsaid.

"One day," said the Dowager Duchess of Cumberland, "I shall learn not to try to beat you at your own game."

"But not, I pray, too soon," said Lord Darcy. "Few people of either sex bother to exercise their intellect; it is refreshing to know a woman who does."

"Alas!" Her voice was heavy with mock tragedy. "He loves me only for my mind!"

*"Mens sana in corpore sano,* my dear. Now let's get back to this information you have."

"Very well," she said, looking suddenly thoughtful. "I don't know whether it means anything or not; I'll give it to you for what it's worth and let you decide whether to follow it up."

Lord Darcy nodded. "Go ahead."

"It was something I saw—and heard," said Mary de Cumberland. "At seven minutes of eight this morning—I noticed the time particularly because I had an appointment for breakfast at eight-fifteen—I left my room at the hotel." She stopped and looked directly into his eyes. "I have the room directly across the hall from Master Sir James'. Did you know that?"

"Yes."

"Very well, then. I opened the door. I heard a voice coming through the door of the room opposite. As you know, the doors at the Royal Steward are quite thick; normal conversation won't carry through. But this was a woman's voice, not high in pitch, but quite strong and quite penetrating. Her words were very clear. She said—"

"Wait." Lord Darcy lifted a hand, interrupting her. "Can you repeat the words *exactly,* Mary?"

"I can; yes," the Duchess said firmly. "She said: 'By God, Sir James! You condemn him to death! I warn you! If *he* dies, *you* die!'"

There was a pause, a silence broken only by the clatter of hooves and the soft sussuration of pneumatic tires on the street.

"And the intonation that you have just reproduced," Lord Darcy said, "is that accurate? She sounded both angry and frightened?"

"More anger than fright, but there was certainly a touch of fear."

"Very good. Then what?"

"Then there was a very faint sound—as of someone speaking in a more normal tone of voice. It was hardly audible, much less recognizable or understandable."

"It could have been Sir James speaking?"

"It could have. It could have been anyone. I assumed, of course, at the time, that it *was* Sir James—but actually it could have been anyone."

"Or even no one?"

She thought for a second. "No. No, there was someone else in that room besides her."

"How do you know?"

"Because just then the door flew open and the girl came flouncing out. She slammed it shut behind her and went on down the hall without even noticing me —or, at least, not indicating it if she had. Then whoever was still in the room put a key in the lock and locked the door. Naturally, I had not intended to be a witness to such a scene; I ignored it and went on down to breakfast."

"Who was the girl?" Lord Darcy asked.

"To my knowledge, I had never seen her before," the Duchess said, "and she was certainly the kind of girl one would not easily forget. She is a tiny creature —not five feet tall,—but perfectly formed, a truly beautiful figure. Her hair is jet black and quite long, and was bound with a silver circlet in back, giving it a sort of horsetail appearance. Her face was as beautiful as the rest of her, with pixieish eyes and a rather sensuous mouth. She was wearing the costume of an apprentice—blue, with a white band at the sleeve— and that's odd, because, as you know, apprentices are allowed at the Convention only by special invitation, and such invitations are quite rare."

"It is even odder," Lord Darcy said musingly, "that an apprentice should use such speech towards a Master of the Art."

"Yes, it is," Her Grace agreed. "But, as I said, I really thought little of it at the time. After Master Sean was arrested, however, the incident came to mind again. I spent the rest of the morning and all afternoon trying to find out what I could about her."

"And yet you did not think it important enough to mention it either to Lord Bontriomphe or to the Chief Master-at-Arms?" Lord Darcy asked quietly.

"Important? Of course I thought it was important! I still do. But—mention it to the Armsmen? To what purpose, my dear? In the first place, I had no real information; at the time, I didn't even know her name. In the second place, that was an hour and a half before the murder actually took place. In the third place, if I had told either Bontriomphe or Chief Master Hennely about it, they would simply have bungled the whole thing by arresting her, too, and they would have had no more case against her than they do against Master Sean."

"And in the fourth place," Lord Darcy added, "you fancy yourself a detective. Go ahead. What did you find out?"

"Not much," she admitted. "I found her name easily enough in the Grand Register of the Convention. She's the only female apprentice listed. The name is Tia Einzig. T-I-A E-I-N-Z-I-G."

"Einzig?" Lord Darcy lifted an eyebrow. "Germanic, definitely. Possibly Prussian, which would, no doubt, make her a Polish subject."

"The name may be Prussian; she isn't," said Her Grace. "She is, however—or was—a subject of His Slavonic Majesty. She came from some little place on the eastern side of the Danube, a few hundred miles from the Adriatic coast—one of those towns with sixteen letters in its name, only three of which are vowels. K-D-J-A-something. She left in 1961 for the Grand Duchy of Venetia and lived in Belluno for about a year. Then she was in Milano for a couple of months, then went on to Torino. In 1963, she came to France, to live in Grenoble. All this came out last year, when her case was brought to Raymond's attention."

"Raymond?"

"His Grace, the Duke of Dauphine," Mary de Cumberland explained. "Naturally, a request for extradition would have to be brought to his personal attention."

"Naturally." The sardonic light had returned to

Lord Darcy's eyes, and now it gleamed dangerously.
"Mary."

"Yes?"

"I retract what I said about your being a woman
who uses her intellect. The rational mind marshals
its facts and reports them in a logical order. This is
the first I have heard of any extradition proceedings."

"Oh." She flashed him a brilliant smile. "I'm
sorry, my dear. I—"

He cut her off. "First, may I ask where you got this
information? You certainly didn't pop off to
Dauphine this afternoon and ask your old friend the
Duke to let you look at the Legal Proceedings Record
of the Duchy of Dauphine."

"How did you know he was an old friend?" the
Dowager Duchess asked. "I don't recall ever having
mentioned it to you before."

"You haven't. You are not a woman who parades
the names of influential friends. Neither would you
call an Imperial Governor by his Christian name
alone unless you were a close friend. That is neither
here nor there. I repeat: What is your source for this
history of Tia Einzig?"

"Father Dominique. The Reverend Father Dominique ap Tewdwr, O.S.B., who was the Sensitive in
charge of the clerical commission which the
Archbishop appointed to investigate the personality
of Tia Einzig. His Grace the Duke asked that the
commission be appointed to make the investigation
because of the charges that were made against her in
Belluno, Milano, and Torino—the requests for extradition, so that she could be tried locally on the
charges against her."

"What were those charges, specifically?"

"The same in all three cases. Practicing sorcery without a license, and . . ."

"And?"

"And black magic."

# PART TWO

CARLYLE HOUSE has been the property of the Dukes of Cumberland since it was built, although it is frequently and erroneously supposed that it is a part of the heritage of the Marquisate of Carlisle by those who do not recognize that the names are similar in pronunciation but not in spelling.

Mary, Dowager Duchess of Cumberland—formerly Duchess Consort, née Lady Mary de Beaufort—had been the second wife of the widowed Duke of Cumberland. The Duke, at the time of the marriage, was in his sixties, Lady Mary in her early twenties. But no one who knew them had thought of it as a May-December marriage, not even the Duke's son and heir by his late first wife. The old Duke, though only remotely related to the Royal Family, had the typically Plantagenet vigor, handsomeness, and longevity. His golden blond hair had lightened over the years, and his face had begun to show the deepening lines of age, but he was still as good as any man twenty years his junior, and he looked and behaved no older. But even a strong and powerful man may

have an accident with a horse, and His late Grace
was no exception.

Mary, who had loved her husband, not only for his
youthful vigor but for his mature wisdom, was a
widow before she was thirty.

Her stepson, Edwin—who, upon the death of his
father, followed by His Majesty's confirmation, had
become the present Duke of Cumberland—was rather a dull fellow. He was perfectly competent as an
Imperial Governor, but he lacked the Plantagenet
spark—however diluted—that his father had had.
He liked and respected his stepmother—who was
only six months his junior—but he did not understand her. Her vivaciousness, her quickness of mind,
and especially her touch of the Talent, made her a-
lien to him.

An agreement had been reached. De Cumberland
would take care of the duchy, remaining in Carlisle;
his stepmother would be given Carlyle House for life.
It was all His Grace could do for a stepmother he
loved but did not in the least understand.

When Lord Darcy and the Duchess entered the
front door of Carlyle House, the seneschal who held
it open for them murmured, "Good evening, Your
Grace, your lordship," and closed the door quickly to
block out the gray tendrils of fog that seemed to want
to follow them into the brightly lit hall.

"Good evening, Geffri," said Her Grace, turning
so that the seneschal could help her off with her
cloak. "Where is everyone?"

"My lords the Bishops of Winchester and Carlisle
have retired, Your Grace. The Benedictine Fathers
have gone to St. Paul's to chant Evensong with the
Chapter; they were so good as to inform me that because of the fog they will spend the night at the

Chapter House with their brethren. Sir Lyon Grey is remaining at his room in the Royal Steward tonight. Master Sean O Lochlainn has sent word that he is temporarily indisposed."

"Indisposed!" The Duchess laughed. "I should think so! He will spend the night in the Tower of London, Geffri."

"So I have been informed, Your Grace," said the imperturbable seneschal. "Sir Thomas Leseaux," he continued, taking Lord Darcy's cloak, "is in the salon. My Lord John Quetzal is upstairs donning his evening attire and should be down shortly. The selection of hot dishes which Your Grace ordered has been placed upon the buffet."

"Thank you, Geffri. Oh . . . I have sent the coach to the Palace du Marquis to fetch Lord Darcy's luggage. Let's see . . . where can we put my lord?"

"I should suggest the Lily Suite, Your Grace. It adjoins the Rose Suite and has a communicating door, making it suitable for the transfer thence of Master Sean's things, if that will be suitable and convenient for his lordship."

"Perfect, Geffri," said Lord Darcy. "When my things have been taken up, let me know, will you? I have not had an opportunity to freshen up since I arrived."

"I shall see that your lordship is notified immediately."

"Very good. Thank you, Geffri."

"A pleasure, your lordship."

"Come, my lord," said the Duchess, taking his arm, "we'll go in and have a drink with Sir Thomas to take the chill of the fog out of our bones."

As the two of them walked toward the salon, Lord Darcy said: "Who are your Benedictine guests?"

"The older one is a Father Quinn, from the north of Ireland."

"Father Quinn?" Lord Darcy said musingly. "I don't believe I know him. Who is the other?"

"A Father Patrique of Cherbourg," said Her Grace. "A remarkable Sensitive and Healer. You must meet him."

"Father Patrique and I have already met," said Lord Darcy, "and I must say I agree with your evaluation. It will be a pleasure to see him again."

They went into the large, high-ceilinged room which served as both salon and dining room. At the far end of the salon, in a large easy chair, his feet outstretched to the warmth of the blaze in the great fireplace, his hand holding a partly-filled goblet, sat a tall, lean man with pale features and with light brown hair brushed straight back from a broad, high forehead.

He rose to his feet as soon as he saw his hostess and Lord Darcy approaching.

"Good evening, Your Grace. Lord Darcy! How good to see you again!" His engaging smile seemed to make his blue-gray eyes sparkle.

Lord Darcy took his outstretched hand. "Good to see *you* again, Sir Thomas! You're looking as fit as ever."

"For a scholar, you mean," said Sir Thomas with a chuckle. "Here! May I be so bold as to offer you both a splash of our gracious hostess' excellent brandy?"

"Indeed you may, Sir Thomas," said the Duchess with a smile. "I feel as though I had fog in every vertebra."

Sir Thomas went to the sideboard and extracted the glass stopple from the brandy decanter with lean, agile fingers. As he poured the clear, red-brown liquid into two thin-walled brandy goblets, he said: "I was fairly certain you would be here as soon as I heard of Master Sean's arrest, but I hardly expected you so soon."

A trace of irony came into Lord Darcy's smile. "My Lord de London was good enough to send a special messenger across the Channel to relay the news, and I was able to make good train and boat connections."

Sir Thomas handed each of the others a goblet of brandy. "Is it your intention to put your brilliant brain to work to solve this murder in order to clear Master Sean?"

Lord Darcy laughed. "Far from it. My Lord Marquis would like me to do just that, but I shan't oblige him. The case is interesting, of course, but my duty lies in Normandy. Just among the three of us—and I ask you to let it go no further until after tomorrow— I intend to get Master Sean out by presenting my cousin de London with a dilemma. For that purpose, I have gathered enough facts to force him to release Master Sean. Then the two of us shall return to Normandy."

Mary de Cumberland looked at him with an expression that was both hurt and astonished. "You're returning and taking Master Sean with you? So soon? Shan't he be permitted to finish Convention Week?"

"I'm afraid not," Lord Darcy said. There was apology and contriteness in his manner and voice. "We have a murder of our own to solve, Sean and I. I can't reveal details, and I admit that the case is neither as spectacular nor as . . . er . . . notorious as this one, but duty is duty. If the matter can be resolved quickly, of course, Master Sean may be back before the week is out."

"But what about the paper he was to present?" the Duchess persisted.

"If it is at all possible," Lord Darcy promised firmly, "I shall see that he gets back. If nothing else, I shall see to it that he gets back Saturday to deliver his paper. That, after all, is a part of his duty as a sorcerer."

"And you'll just hand the case right back to Lord Bontriomphe, eh?" asked Sir Thomas.

"I don't need to hand it back," said Lord Darcy with a chuckle, "since I did not accept it in the first place. It's all his, and I wish him luck. He and the Marquis are perfectly capable of its solution, have no fear of that."

"Without a forensic sorcerer to aid them?" Sir Thomas said.

"They'll manage," said Lord Darcy. "The late Sir James Zwinge was not the only capable forensic sorcerer in London. Besides, it is apparent that My Lord Marquis does not feel the need for a good forensic sorcerer. As soon as the second best one was killed, he proceeded to lock up the best one. Hardly the act of a man who was desperate for first-class thaumaturgical advice."

As the other two laughed quietly, Lord Darcy took a sip from his brandy goblet.

A door at the other end of the room opened.

"Good evening, Your Grace; good evening, gentlemen," said a warm baritone voice. "I'm terribly sorry. Have I interrupted anything?"

Lord Darcy, too, had turned to look. The newcomer was a handsome young man in crimson and gold evening dress whose distinctive features marked him as Mechicain. This, then, was Lord John Quetzal du Moqtessuma de Mechicoe.

"Not at all, my lord," said the Duchess, "we have been expecting you. Come in and permit me to introduce our new guest."

The introductions were made in due form, and Lord John Quetzal's heavy-lidded eyes brightened as Lord Darcy's name was spoken.

"It's a very great pleasure to meet you, my lord," he said, "though, of course, I deplore the circumstances that bring you here. I do not for a moment believe Master Sean guilty of this terrible crime."

"Thank you, my lord," Lord Darcy replied. "And I thank you for Master Sean, too." Then he added smoothly, "I did not realize that Master Sean's guilelessness was so transparently obvious that it would be utterly convincing upon such short acquaintance."

The Mechicain looked rather self-conscious. "Well, it's not exactly that. Transparent? No, I shouldn't say that Master Sean is at all transparent. It's . . . er—" He hesitated in momentary confusion.

"My Lord John Quetzal's modesty does him credit," the Duchess cut in gently. "His is a Talent rare even among sorcerers. He is a witch-smeller."

"Indeed?" Lord Darcy looked at the young man with increased interest. "I confess that I have never met a sorcerer with that ability before. You can detect, then, the presence of a practitioner of black magic, even at a distance?"

Lord John Quetzal nodded. "Yes, my lord." He seemed embarrassed, like an adolescent lad who has just been told he is very handsome by a beautiful woman.

Sir Thomas chuckled. "Naturally, Lord Darcy, he

would know immediately that Master Sean does not dabble in black magic. To a witch-smeller, that would be instantly apparent." He turned his smile toward Lord John Quetzal. "When we have some free time together, I should like to discuss theory with you and see how it actually squares with practical results."

"That . . . that would be an honor and a pleasure, Sir Thomas," said the young nobleman. There was an awestruck note in his voice. "But . . . but I'm very weak in symbological theory. My math isn't exactly my strong point."

Sir Thomas laughed. "Don't worry, my lord; I promise not to smother you in analogy equations. Good Heavens, that's *work!* When I am away from my library, I do everything I can to avoid any heavy thinking."

That, Lord Darcy knew, was not true; Sir Thomas was merely putting the young man at ease. Sir Thomas Leseaux, in spite of his degree of Doctor of Thaumaturgy, was not a practicing sorcerer. He did not possess the Talent to any marked degree. He was a theoretical thaumaturgist who worked with the higher and more esoteric forms of the subjective algebrae, leaving it to others to test his theories in practice. His brilliant mind was capable of grasping symbological relationships that an ordinary sorcerer could only dimly perceive. There were very few Th. D.'s who could follow his abstruse and complex symbolic analogies through to their final conclusions; most Masters of the Art bogged down hopelessly after the first few similarities. Sir Thomas had not been so lacking in awareness as to suppose a mere journeyman could follow his mathematics. On the other hand, he immensely enjoyed discussing the Art with practicing magicians.

"May I ask you a question, my lord?" Lord Darcy asked thoughtfully. "Even though I am not officially involved in the investigation of the murder of Sir James Zwinge, a man in my profession has a certain natural curiosity. I should like to ask you what might be considered a professional question, and"—he smiled—"if you like you may send me a bill for services rendered."

Lord John Quetzal returned the smile. "If the question requires that I invoke a spell, I shall most certainly bill you—at the usual journeyman's rates, of course. To do otherwise would impair my standing in the Guild. But if you merely want a professional opinion, I am at your service."

"Then I shall leave the matter in your hands," said Lord Darcy. "The question is: Have you detected the presence of a black magician amongst the members of the Convention?"

There was a sudden silence, as if time itself were suspended for a moment. Both Sir Thomas and the Duchess seemed to be holding their breaths, awaiting the young Mechicain nobleman's answer.

But from Lord John Quetzal there was only a moment of hesitancy. When he spoke, his voice was firm.

"My lord, it is my ambition to study forensic sorcery under the tutelage of a Master. I have, as a matter of course, studied both law enforcement and criminal detection. May I counter your question with one of my own?"

"Certainly," said Lord Darcy.

Lord John Quetzal compressed his lips for a mo-

ment in thought before continuing. "Let us suppose
that you personally knew, through the exercise of
your own abilities, that a certain man was a criminal
—that he had committed a particular crime. But let
us further assume that, aside from your own personal
knowledge, there was not one shred of proof whatever of the fact. My counter-question is: Would you
denounce the man?"

"No," said Lord Darcy without hesitation. "Your
point is well taken. It is nugatory to accuse a man
without proof. But a word to the investigating of-
ficials, merely to give them a lead so they can discover proof if it exists, is certainly not a public ac-
cusation."

"Perhaps not," said the young sorcerer slowly. "I
shall certainly take your words under advisement.
But at the moment I feel that my unsupported word
alone is not sufficient evidence even for that."

"That, of course, is your decision," the investigator said evenly. "But keep it in mind that if
your Talent as a witch-smeller is widely known—if it
is known, for instance, to someone whose very life
might depend upon your silence—then I should ad-
vise you to be very careful that you are not silenced
permanently."

Before Lord John Quetzal could answer, the door
to the hall opened and Geffri appeared. "I trust you
will pardon the intrusion, Your Grace, but I was instructed to notify his lordship as soon as his
lordship's luggage had been taken to the Lily Suite."

"Oh, yes; thank you, Geffri," said Lord Darcy.

"I believe I shall put on my evening clothes, too,"
said Her Grace. "Will you excuse me, gentlemen?
And pray don't allow my absence to delay your own

supper; help yourselves from the array on the buffet."

\* \* \*

Fifteen minutes later, Lord Darcy, having bathed
and shaved, was feeling more human than he had for
hours. He took one last look at himself in the full-
length mirror that hung on the bedroom wall of the
Lily Suite. He made minor adjustments to the silver
lace at his throat and wrists, flicked an almost microscopic bit of dust from the coral satin of his dress
jacket, and decided he was ready to face the company in a better humor than when he had left them.

Downstairs, the door to the salon was open, and,
as he approached it, Lord Darcy could hear Sir
Thomas Leseaux's voice.

"The fact remains, my lord, that Sir James is, after
all, dead."

"Couldn't it have been suicide, Sir Thomas?"
asked Lord John Quetzal. "Or an accident?"

It was inevitable, Lord Darcy thought. Great and
brilliant men and women, whose usual conversations
were in the realm of ideas, would normally shun
gossip or sporting events or even crime—except in
the abstract—as topics for an evening's discourse.
But give them a murder—not a commonplace death
in a public house brawl, nor a shooting in a robbery,
nor a sordid killing in a fit of jealousy, nor an even
more sordid sex crime, but an inexplicable death surrounded by mystery—give them a nice, juicy, puzzle
of murder, and lo! they can speak of nothing else.

Sir Thomas Leseaux had said, less than half an
hour ago, that he wanted to get Lord John Quetzal
alone to discuss the theory of magic, with special em-
phasis on witch-smelling—and now he was saying:

"Accident or suicide? Why, as to that, I don't know, of course, but the authorities seem to be operating upon the assumption that it is murder."

"But why? I mean, what reason would anyone have for killing Master Sir James Zwinge? What is the motive?"

"A very good question," said Lord Darcy as he entered the salon. Only the two men were present. Obviously the Duchess had not yet finished dressing. "As a purely cerebral exercise, I have been pondering that question myself. But don't let me interrupt you. Pray continue your conversation whilst I sample the selection of goodies on the buffet table."

"Lord John Quetzal," said Sir Thomas, "seems to be at a loss for discovering a motive for the murder."

Lord Darcy looked at the row of copper bowls, each with its small alcohol flame flickering brightly beneath, and lifted the cover of the first. "Ah! Ham!" he said. "Very well, Sir Thomas. What about motive? Who might have wanted him dead?" He put a slice of ham on his plate and opened the next bowl.

Sir Thomas frowned. "No one that I know of," he said slowly. "He could be quite acerb at times, but he would not willingly have harmed anyone, I think."

Darcy ladled some hot cherry sauce over his ham. "You know of no threats to kill him? No violent arguments with anyone?"

"Aside from his so-called argument with Master Sean, you mean? Yes, come to think of it, there was one such. Master Ewen MacAlister said some rather bitter things about him a month ago. Master Ewen had made application to get on the Naval Research Staff, and Sir James—who had certain connections with Naval Research—recommended that Master Ewen's application not be approved."

"A revenge motive, then?" Lord Darcy poured himself a generous glass of claret and seated himself in a chair facing the other two, his tray on his lap. "I have never had the pleasure of meeting Master Ewen MacAlister, but from what Master Sean tells me, the pleasure would be doubtful. Is he the kind of man who would kill for revenge?"

"I . . . don't . . . know," said Sir Thomas slowly. "I can imagine his killing someone to prevent that person from harming him, but I hesitate to say he would bother to do so after the harm was done."

Lord Darcy made a mental note to tell Lord Bontriomphe about that in the morning. It might be wise for Bontriomphe to make inquiries to find out whether Master Ewen had made or intended to make application for some other position that Sir James Zwinge had "certain connections" with.

"Anyone else?" Darcy asked, looking down at his plate.

"No," said Sir Thomas after a moment. "No one that I know of, my lord."

"Do you know a Demoselle Tia Einzig?" Darcy asked in the same quiet tone of voice.

Sir Thomas' smile vanished. After several seconds, he said: "I know her, yes, my lord. Why?"

"She seems to have got herself charged with black magic. And it appears that Sir James was killed by black magic."

Sir Thomas' normally pale features darkened. "See here! You're not accusing Tia of this murder, are you?"

"Accuse? Not at all, Sir Thomas. I merely point out a possible connection."

"Well, there's nothing to it! Nothing, d'you understand! Tia is no more a witch than *you* are! I'll not have you making such insinuations, do you hear?"

"Do calm yourself, Sir Thomas," Darcy said mildly. "Relax. Get a grip on your emotions. Tell yourself a joke—or think of some refreshing equation."

The color in Sir Thomas' face subsided, but he did not smile at Lord Darcy's sally. "My deepest apologies, my lord. I . . . I hardly know what to say. I'm . . . I'm not myself. It's a . . . a touchy subject, my lord."

"Think nothing of it, Sir Thomas. I had no desire to upset you, but I am not at all offended. Murder is a touchy subject when it strikes as closely as this one has. Perhaps we had best discuss something else."

"No, no, please. Not on my account, I beg you."

"My dear Sir Thomas, I insist. All evening, I have been wanting to ask Lord John Quetzal questions about Mechicoe, and you have given me the perfect excuse for doing so. Murder is my business, but if I am not engaged in solving a given crime, discussing it begins to pall. So—

"My lord, if my memory of history has not betrayed me, the first Anglo-French ships touched the shores of Mechicoe in the year 1569, and the members of that expedition were the first Europeans your ancestors had ever seen. What was the cause of the superstitious awe with which the Europeans were regarded?"

"Ah! That's an interesting thing, my lord," the young man said with enthusiasm. "First you must understand the legend or myth of Quetzalcoatle . . ."

The first few minutes were a bit awkward, but the young Mechicain's enthusiasm was so genuine that both Sir Thomas and Lord Darcy were actually caught up in the discussion, and it was going full blast when the Dowager Duchess came down. An hour after that, all four of them were still discussing Mechicoe.

Lord Darcy did not get to bed until late, and he did not get to sleep until even later.

# 7

LORD DARCY'S resolve to keep his hands off the Zwinge case, to allow—or rather force—his cousin the Marquis of London to use his own resources to solve it, was a firm one. He had no intention of getting himself involved, even if that required that he bottle up his own intrinsic curiosity, seal the bottle, and sit on the cork. It was fortunate that he was not forced to do that, for Lord Darcy's curiosity was capable of generating a great deal of pressure. Any resolve, no matter how firm, can be dissipated, abolished, negated, removed, by changing circumstances, and the circumstances were to change drastically on the following morning.

On that morning, Thursday, Lord Darcy lay in his bed, drowsing, his mind still in a semi-dreamy state, his thoughts wandering. There was a quiet knock on the door of his bedroom.

"Yes?" he said without opening his eyes.

"Your caffe, my lord, as you ordered," said a low voice.

"Just leave it in the sitting room," Lord Darcy said

drowsily. "I shall be out in a few minutes."

But he wasn't. He drifted off to sleep again. He did not hear the bedroom door open; he did not hear the nearly silent footsteps that crossed the thick carpet from the door to his bed.

Suddenly, someone touched his shoulder. His eyes came open instantly, and he was wide awake.

"Mary!"

The Dowager Duchess curtsied. "Your servant, my lord. Shall I bring your caffe in, my lord?"

Lord Darcy sat up. "Ah! Capital! A Duchess for a serving wench! Indeed, yes! Bring the caffe in immediately! Hop to it, Your Grace!" He chuckled softly as the Duchess went out again, a soft smile on her lips. "And by the by!" he called after her, "will you have My Lord Marquis polish my boots?"

She came back in, pushing a wheeled serving cart upon which sat a silver caffe pot, a spoon, and a single caffe cup with saucer.

"Your boots are already polished, my lord," she said, still keeping her voice in the proper deferential tone. "I took the liberty, my lord, of having your lordship's clothing brushed and pressed, and hung in the clothes cupboard in the sitting room." She poured his caffe.

"Oh, indeed?" Lord Darcy said, reaching for his cup. "All done by a Bishop, I presume?"

"My Lord Bishop," said the Duchess, "had other, more pressing, business. However, His Imperial Majesty the King is prepared to take you for your morning drive."

Lord Darcy paused suddenly, the cup not yet touching his lips.

Bantering is all well enough, but one must draw the line somewhere.

One does not jest about His Most Sovereign Majesty the King.

And then Lord Darcy realized that his brain was not as completely awake as he had thought. He took a sip of the caffe and then returned the cup to its saucer before he spoke again.

"Who is His Majesty's agent?" he asked quietly.

"He's waiting in the hall. Shall I bring him in?"

"Yes. Wait! What o'clock is it, anyway?"

"Just on seven."

"Ask him to wait a minute or so. I'll dress. Fetch my clothes."

\* \* \*

Seven minutes and some odd seconds later, Lord Darcy, fully dressed in proper morning costume, opened the door to his sitting room. Mary, Dowager Duchess of Cumberland, was nowhere in sight. A short, spare, melancholy-looking man, wearing the usual blue-gray drab of a cabman, was sitting on one of the chairs. When he saw Lord Darcy, he came politely to his feet, his square cabman's hat in his hand.

"Lord Darcy?"

"The same. And you?"

From his cap, the smallish man took a silver badge engraved with the Royal Arms. Near the top a stone, polished but not faceted and looking like a quarter-inch bit of translucent gray glass, was inset in the metal.

"King's Messenger, my lord," said the man. He slid his right thumb forward and touched the stone. Immediately, it ceased to be a small lump of dull gray glass.

In the light, it gleamed with the reddish glow of a ruby!

There was no mistaking it. The stone was magically attuned to one man and one man only—the man whose touch would cause that red color to shine within it. A Royal Badge could be stolen, of course, but no thief could give that gray, drab stone its ruby glow.

The brilliant Sir Edward Elmer, Th.D., had designed that spell more than thirty years before, and no one had solved it yet; it was a perfect identification for Personal Agents of His Most Dread and Sovereign Majesty, John IV. The late Sir Edward had been Grand Master of the Sorcerers Guild, and it was accepted that he had outranked even Sir Lyon Gandolphus Grey as a sorcerer.

"Very well," said Lord Darcy. He did not ask the man's name; a King's Messenger remains anonymous. "The message?"

The Messenger bowed his head. "You are to accompany me, my lord. By His Majesty's request."

Lord Darcy frowned. "That's all?"

Again the Messenger bowed. "I have delivered His Majesty's message, my lord. I can say no more, my lord."

"I see. Will there be any objections if I come armed?"

A wide smile broke over the face of the King's Messenger. "If I may say so, my lord, it would be most expedient. His Majesty gave me a further message to your lordship, to be delivered only in case your lordship should ask that question. A message to be delivered in His Majesty's own words, my lord. If I may?"

"Proceed," said Lord Darcy.

Closing his eyes, the Messenger concentrated for a

moment. When he spoke, the voice was cultured and clear; it had none of the patois of the Londoner of the lower middle class. The timbre and intonation had changed, too.

The voice was that of the King.

"My dear Darcy. The last time we met, you came armed. I should not expect a man of your caliber to break a precedent. The matter is most urgent. Come with all haste."

Lord Darcy suppressed a desire to bow low to the Messenger and say: "Immediately, Sire." The Messenger was, after all, only an instrument. He was completely trustworthy, else he would not carry a Silver Badge; even his ordinary messages were to be honored. But when he delivered a message in His Majesty's Own Voice, even he, the Messenger, did not know what he said. When he murmured the key spell to himself, the message in the Royal Voice was delivered. The Messenger had no memory of it either before or after the delivery. He had submitted willingly to the recording of that message, and he had submitted willingly to its delivery and erasure. No sorcerer on Earth could pry that information out of him once it had been delivered, since, in his mind, it no longer existed.

Before it had been delivered, of course, it could be pried out, but not from a King's Messenger. Any attempt to get such a message from the mind of a King's Messenger without authority would result in the immediate death of the Messenger—a fact which the Messenger realized and accepted as a part of his duty to Sovereign and Empire.

After a moment, the King's Messenger opened his eyes. "All right, your lordship?"

"Perfectly, my good fellow. Are you a good cab-man?"

"The best in London, my lord—though I say it who shouldn't."

"Excellent! We must go without delay!"

During the ride, Lord Darcy mused upon the King's words. When he had asked the Messenger whether or not he should go armed, it had been a simple question that any Officer of His Majesty's Peace might have asked. Lord Darcy had had no notion that the Messenger was actually taking him to the Royal Presence; he had asked about arming himself purely in the interests of his official duties. And now, as a result of a perfectly ordinary question, he found himself among the small handful of men who were permitted to be armed in the Royal Presence.

Traditionally, only the Great Lords of State were permitted to remain armed in the King's presence— and they only with swords.

In so far as he knew, Lord Darcy was the only person who, in all of history, had been given Royal permission—which amounted to a command—to appear before His Majesty armed with a gun. It was a singular, a unique, honor—and Lord Darcy was well aware of it.

But those thoughts did not distract his mind for long; of far more importance at the moment was the reason for the King's message. Why should His Majesty be personally interested in an affair which, although it had its outré elements, was, after all, a rather ordinary murder? At least, on the surface of it, it seemed to have no connection with Affairs of State. However . . .

Suddenly Lord Darcy smote his forehead with the

palm of his hand. "Fool!" he muttered sharply to himself. "Dolt! Moron! Idiot! Cherbourg, of course!" This, he thought, is what comes of allowing one's emotions to be distracted by Master Sean's plight when one should have them under full control for analyzing the problem at hand. The thing was as plain as a pikestaff once a competent mind came to focus on it.

Therefore, Lord Darcy was not in the least surprised, after the cab had swept through the gates of Westminster Palace, past the armed guard who recognized the vehicle and driver immediately, to find that a Naval officer wearing the uniform of a Commander was waiting for him in the courtyard. In fact, the lack of such a person would indeed have surprised him.

The Commander opened the door of the cab, and, as Lord Darcy stepped out, the Commander said: "Lord Darcy? I am Commander Lord Ashley and your servant, my lord."

"And I yours, my lord," said Lord Darcy. "Your presence here, by the by, confirms my suspicions."

"Suspicions?" The Commander looked startled.

"That there is presumed to be a connection between the murder of a certain Georges Barbour in Cherbourg two days ago, and the murder of Master Sir James Zwinge yesterday in the Royal Steward. At least, Naval Intelligence presumes a connection."

"We are almost certain there is a connection," said Lord Ashley. "Will you come this way? There is to be a meeting in Queen Anette's Parlor immediately. Just through this door, down the hall to the stairway and— But perhaps I am taking a liberty, my lord. Do you know your way about the Palace?"

"I have made it a point, my lord, to study the floor

plans of the great palaces and castles of the Empire. Queen Anette's Parlor, where the Treaty of Kobenhavn was revised and signed in 1891, is directly above the Chapel of St. Edward the Confessor—consecrated in 1633, during the reign of Edward VII. Thus, it would be up this stairway, left turn, down the hall, through the gascon Door, right turn, fifth door on the right, easily recognizable by the fact that it still bears the gilt-and-polychromed personal arms of Anette of Flanders, consort to Harold II." Lord Darcy gave Commander Lord Ashley a broad smile. "But to answer the question as you meant it: No, I have never been in Westminster Palace before."

The Commander smiled back. "Nor have I." He chuckled. "If I may say so, I find myself somewhat taken aback by this sudden soaring into a rather rarified atmosphere. Two men whom I had never met are done in—something which happens all too frequently in Intelligence work—and then, without warning, what seemed a rather routine killing is suddenly catapulted to the importance of an Affair of State." He lowered his voice a little. "His Majesty himself will attend the meeting." They went up the stairway and turned left, toward the Gascon Door.

"Tell me," Lord Darcy said, "have you any theory?"

"As to who killed them? Polish agents, of course," the Commander said. "But if you mean do I have any theory as to who the agents may be, then—no, I don't. Could be anyone, you know. Some little shopkeeper or tradesman or something of the sort, a perfectly ordinary appearing man, is one day told by his Polish superiors, 'Go to such-and-such a place, where you will find a man named thus-and-so. Kill him.' He does it, and an hour later is back at his regular business. No connection between him and the dead man. No motive that can be linked personally to the killer. No clue of any kind." They passed through the doorway and turned right.

"I trust," said Lord Darcy with a smile, "that your pessimism is not generally shared by the Naval Intelligence Corps."

"Well, as a matter of fact," said the Commander in a slightly apologetic tone, "I believe it is. If the killers can be found, so much the better, of course, but that will be merely a by-product of the real business, you see."

"Then the Navy feels that there is something more dangerous going on than murder?" The two men stopped before the door with the gilt-and-polychrome arms that marked Queen Anette's Parlor.

"Indeed we do. The King views it with greatest consternation. He'll give you any further information."

Lord Ashley opened the ornate door, and the two men went in.

# 8

THE THREE MEN seated at the long table were immediately recognizable to Lord Darcy, although he had met only one of them before. Lord Bontriomphe was looking his usual calm, affable self.

The erect, silver-bearded old man with the piercing eyes and the magnificent blade of a nose could only be Sir Lyon Grey, in spite of the fact that he wore ordinary morning clothing instead of the formal pale-blue and silver of a Master Sorcerer.

The third man had a highly distinctive face. He appeared to be in his late forties or early fifties, although his dark, curly, slightly disarrayed hair showed only a few threads of gray, and then only when one looked closely. His forehead was high and craggy, giving his head a rather squared-off appearance; his eyes were heavy-lidded and deep-set beneath thick, bushy eyebrows; his nose was as large as Sir Lyon's, but instead of being thin and bladelike, it was wide and slightly twisted, as though it had been broken at least once and allowed to heal without the services of a Healer. His mouth was wide and straight, and the moustache above it was thick and busy, spreading out to either side like a cat's whiskers, each hair curling separately upwards at the end. His heavy beard was full, but was cut fairly short, and was as wiry and curly as his hair, moustache, and eyebrows.

At first glance, one got the impression of forbidding ruthlessness and remorseless purpose; it required a second, closer look to see that those qualities were modified by both wisdom and humor. It was the face of a man with tremendous inner power and the ability to control and use it both wisely and well.

Lord Darcy had heard the man described, and the uniform of royal blue heavily encrusted with gold merely clinched the identification of Peter de Valera ap Smith, Lord High Admiral of the Imperial Navy, Commander of the Combined Fleets, Knight Commander of the Order of the Golden Leopard, and Chief of Staff for Naval Operations.

A fourth man, standing near the Lord High Admiral, seemed about the same age, but his hair was noticeably gray, and his features were so commonplace that they paled into insignificance in comparison. Lord Darcy did not recognize him, but the uniform he wore was that of a Naval Captain, which suggested that he was connected with Naval Intelligence.

When Commander Lord Ashley performed the necessary introductions, all of Lord Darcy's tentative identifications had proved correct, including the last; the man was Captain Percy Smollett, Chief of Naval Intelligence, European Branch.

Of the three Navy men, Lord Darcy noticed, only the Lord High Admiral wore his dress sword; he alone of the three was so permitted in the Royal Pres-

ence. Lord Darcy was suddenly intensely aware of
the pistol on his right hip, concealed though it was by
his morning coat.

Hardly had the introductions been completed
when a door to an adjoining room opened suddenly,
and a man wearing the livery of the Major Domo of
the Royal Household entered.

"My lords and gentlemen!" he said firmly. "His
Imperial Majesty the King!"

The six men were on their feet. As the King entered, they bowed low rather than genuflecting. This
was a nice point of etiquette often misunderstood.
His Majesty was dressed in the uniform of the
Commander-in-Chief of the Imperial Navy. Had he
worn full regalia or ordinary street clothes, a genuflection would have been in order; but in Army or
Navy uniform he was wearing the *persona* of a military
officer—an officer of the most exalted rank, true, but
an officer, nonetheless, and no military officer rates a
genuflection.

"My lords and gentlemen, please be seated," said
His Majesty.

John IV, by the Grace of God, King and Emperor
of England, France, Scotland, Ireland, New England, and New France; Defender of the Faith, et
cetera, was the perfect model of a Plantagenet King.
Tall, broad of shoulder, blue of eye, and blondly
handsome, John of England was a direct descendant
of Henry II, the first Plantagenet King, through
Henry's grandson, King Arthur. Like his predeces-
sors, King John IV showed all the strength, ability,
and wisdom that was typical of the oldest ruling family in Europe. In no way but physically did he re-
semble the members of the wild, spendthrift, un-
stable cadet branch of the family—now fortunately

extinct—which had descended from the youngest son of Henry II, the unhappy Prince John Lackland who had died in exile three years before the death of King Richard the Lion Hearted in 1219.

The King sat at the head of the table. To his left sat, in order, the Lord High Admiral, Captain Smollett, and Lord Bontriomphe. To his right were Sir Lyon, Commander Lord Ashley, and Lord Darcy.

"My lords, gentlemen, I think we all understand the reason for this meeting, but in order to get the facts straight in our minds, I will ask My Lord High Admiral to explain what we are up against. If you will, my lord."

"Certainly, Sire." My Lord High Admiral's voice was a faintly rasping baritone which, even when it was muted, sounded as though it should be bellowing orders from the quarterdeck instead of holding a quiet discussion at Westminster Palace. He looked round the table with his piercing seaman's gaze. "This concerns a weapon," he said bluntly. "That is, *I* call it a weapon. Sir Lyon doesn't. But I'm only a Navy man, not a sorcerer. We all know that sorcery has its limitations, eh? That's why magic can't be used in warfare; if a sorcerer uses magic to destroy an enemy ship, he has to use Black Magic, and no sane sorcerer wants to do that. Besides, Black Magic isn't that effective. The Polish Royal Navy tried to use it back in '39, and our counter-spells nullified it easily. We blasted 'em out of the water with cannon while they were trying to make their spells work. But, as I understand it, this is *not* Black Magic." He looked over at the Grand Master. "Perhaps you'd better explain, Sir Lyon."

"Very well, my lord," said the Master Sorcerer.

"Perhaps, to begin with, I had best make it clear to you that the line between what we call 'Black' magic and what we call 'White' magic is not as clearly defined as many people suppose. We say, for instance, that the practice of the Healing Art is White Magic, and that the use of curses to cause illness or death is Black Magic. But, one may ask, is it White Magic to cure a homicidal maniac of a broken leg so that he may go out and kill again? Or, contrariwise, is it Black Magic to curse that same maniac so that he dies and kills no more? Well, in both cases—yes. It can be so proven by the symbological mathematics of the Theory of Ethics. I won't bore you with the analogy equations themselves; suffice it to say that, in such widely diverse cases, the Theory of Ethics is quite clear.

"This is summed up in the aphorism that every first-year apprentice sorcerer knows by heart: *Black Magic is a matter of symbolism and intent.*"

Sir Lyon smiled and turned his right palm up in a gesture of admission. "So, of course, is White Magic —but it is the Black against which we must warn."

"Quite understandable," said Captain Smollett.

"I shan't go into this further," said Sir Lyon, "except to say that the Theory of Ethics *does* allow one to *interfere* with the actions of another, when that other is bent upon destruction. As a result, we have perfected the . . . er . . . 'weapon' which my lord the High Admiral has mentioned." Sir Lyon glanced round the table again, his deep-set brilliant eyes looking at each man in turn. Then he bent over and took an object from beneath the table and placed it on the polished oaken surface for all to see.

"This is it, my lords and gentlemen."

It was an odd-looking device. The main bulk was

a brass cylinder eight inches in diameter and eighteen inches long. This cylinder was mounted on a short tripod which held it horizontally four inches off the table top. On one end of the cylinder, there were two handles, fitted so that the cylinder could be aimed by gripping with both hands. From the other end there projected a smaller cylinder, some three inches in diameter and ten inches long. The last four inches flared out to a diameter of six inches, making a bell-like muzzle.

Lord Bontriomphe smiled. "That's a very oddly shaped gun, Sir Lyon."

The Grand Master chuckled dryly. "Your lordship perceives, of course, that the device is *not* a gun—but, in a way, the analogy is an apt one. I cannot demonstrate its operation here, of course, but the explanation of its operation—"

"One moment, Sir Lyon." The King's voice cut in smoothly.

"Sire?" The Grand Master Sorcerer's eyebrows lifted. He had not expected His Majesty to interrupt at that point.

"Can the device be operated against a single man?" His Majesty asked.

"Of course, Sire," said Sir Lyon. "But Your Majesty must understand that it works to inhibit only a single type of operation, and we have not the facilities here to—"

"Bear with me, Sir Sorcerer," said the King. "I think we *do* have the facilities you mention. Could you use Lord Darcy as your target?"

"I could, Sire," said Sir Lyon, a speculative gleam in his deep-set eyes.

"Excellent." The King looked at Lord Darcy.

"Would you consent to an experiment involving yourself, my lord?"

"Your Majesty has but to ask," said Lord Darcy.

"Very good." His Majesty held out his right hand. "Would you be so good as to give me the pistol you carry at your hip, my lord?"

It was as though a silent lightning bolt had struck every man at the table. Heads jerked round. Every eye focused in startled surprise on Lord Darcy's face. The Lord High Admiral grasped the hilt of his narrow-bladed Naval dress sword and withdrew it half an inch from its scabbard.

The shock was obvious. How *dare* any man come into the King's Sovereign Presence armed with a pistol?

"Peace, My Lord Admiral!" said the King. "My lord of Arcy comes armed by Our request and permission. Your pistol, Lord Darcy."

Coolly, Lord Darcy performed an act that would have turned the stomach of every right-thinking man in the Empire. He drew a gun in the presence of His Dread and Sovereign Majesty the King.

Then he rose, leaned across the table, and presented the pistol to the King, butt first. "As Your Majesty bids," he said calmly.

"Thank you, my lord. Ah! An excellent weapon! I have always considered the .40 caliber MacGregor to be the finest handgun yet built. Are you ready, Sir Lyon?"

Sir Lyon Grey had obviously already fathomed the King's intentions. He smiled and swiveled the gleaming metal device around so that the bell-like muzzle pointed directly at Lord Darcy. "I am ready, Sire," he said.

The King, meanwhile, had unloaded the Mac-Gregor, taking all seven of the .40 caliber cartridges out and placing them on the table in front of him while five pairs of eyes watched him in fascination.

"My lord," said the King, looking up, "I shall ask you to ignore what Sir Lyon is doing."

"I understand, Sire," said Lord Darcy.

"Excellent, my lord." His Majesty's eyes moved upwards, along the wall opposite. "Hm-m-m. Yes. My lord, I call your attention to the stained glass in yonder window—particularly to that area which depicts King Arthur holding the scroll, the scene which symbolizes the establishment of the Most Ancient and Noble Order of the Round Table."

Lord Darcy looked at the window. "I see the section to which Your Majesty refers," he said.

"Good. That window, my lord, is a priceless work of art. Nonetheless, it offends me."

Lord Darcy looked back at the King. His Majesty pushed the unloaded pistol, and it slid across the polished surface to come to rest in front of Lord Darcy. Then he flipped a finger, and a single cartridge spun across the table to come to rest beside the gun. "I repeat, my lord," said the King, "that bit of glass offends me. Would you do me the favor of putting a bullet through it?"

"As you command, Sire," said Lord Darcy.

Had he not known that he was the subject of a scientific experiment, the scene that followed would have been one of the most humiliating in Lord Darcy's career. It was only afterwards that he realized that a single snicker or chuckle from any of the other six men at the table would have snapped his temper. For a man who normally had such magnificent control over his emotions, such an explosion of wrath would have been almost the final humiliation. But no one laughed, for which Lord Darcy was afterward deeply thankful.

The task was a simple one. Pick up the cartridge, place it in the chamber, close the lock, aim, and fire.

Lord Darcy reached for the pistol with his right hand and for the cartridge with his left. Somehow, he caught the handgun wrong, so that he gripped it upside down, with the muzzle facing him. At the same time, his fingers closed on the cartridge wrong, so that it slipped from his grasp and skittered across the table. He reached out again, grabbed at it, and it slid away. Then, angry, he slammed his palm down on it and finally caught it.

Then there was a loud clatter. In focusing his attention on the cartridge, he had allowed the pistol to slip from the grasp of his other hand.

He set his teeth and clenched his left hand around the wayward cartridge. Then he reached out with great determination and picked up the pistol with his right hand. Fine.

Now to open the lock. His right thumb found the stud and pushed it, but his other fingers missed their grip at that point, and the gun was suddenly hanging from his forefinger, swinging by the trigger guard. He tried to swing it round so that he could grasp the butt but it slipped from his forefinger and banged to the table top again.

Lord Darcy took a deep breath. Then, with calm deliberation, he reached out and picked up the gun. This time, he used his left thumb to open the lock, but in doing so he dropped the cartridge again.

The next few minutes were a nightmare. The cartridge persisted in slipping from his grasp when he tried to pick it up, and when he did manage to pick it up it refused to go into the chamber. And just as it seemed about to slide in properly, he would drop the gun again.

Lord Darcy set his teeth; the muscles in the sides of his jaw stood out in hard relief. Moving his hands slowly and carefully, he finally managed—after many fumbles, slips, and errors—to get the cartridge into the chamber and close the lock.

His feeling of relief at having achieved this was so great that his fingers relaxed and the gun fell to the table again. Angry, he reached out, snatched it up, aimed in the general direction of the window, and—

The gun went off with a crash, long before he had intended it to.

King Arthur and his scroll remained serenely undamaged while the slug slammed into the stone wall two feet away, chipping off a large flake of stone and ricocheting up to the ceiling, where it buried itself in an oak beam.

After what seemed like an interminably long silence, Sir Lyon Gandolphus Grey said softly: "Magnificent! Your Majesty, in all our tests, no one has ever managed to load the gun, much less come that close to hitting the target. We are fortunate in knowing that we shall not find many minds so superbly disciplined—especially in the ranks of the Polish Royal Navy."

His Majesty spun the remaining six cartridges down the table. "Reload and reholster your weapon, my lord. Please accept my apologies for any . . . ah . . . inconveniences this experiment may have caused."

"Not at all, Sire. It has been a most educational experience." He scooped up the six cartridges and reloaded his MacGregor with expert ease. Although the belled muzzle of the device was still pointed in his direction, Sir Lyon's hands were no longer upon the grips.

"I congratulate you, my lord," said the King. "All of us here, with the exception of Lord Bontriomphe and yourself, have seen this device in operation before. As Sir Lyon says, you are the first ever to succeed in loading a weapon while under its spell." Then he looked at Sir Lyon. "Have you anything further to add, Sir Sorcerer?"

"Nothing, Sire . . . unless there are any questions."

Lord Bontriomphe raised a hand. "One question, Sir Lyon."

"Certainly, my lord."

Lord Bontriomphe gestured toward the device. "Is this gadget one that can be operated by anyone—by any layman, I mean—or does it require a sorcerer as operator?"

Sir Lyon smiled. "Fortunately, my lord, the device cannot be operated by one without a trained Talent. It does not, however, require the services of a Master; an apprentice of three years standing can operate the device."

"Then, Sir Lyon," said Lord Darcy, cutting off whatever it was that Lord Bontriomphe had to say, "the secret of its operation is divided into two parts. Am I correct?"

"My lord," said Sir Lyon after a moment, "your lack of the Talent is a great loss to the Sorcerers Guild. As you have correctly deduced, there are two parts to the spell. The first—and most important—part is built into this device here." He pointed toward the golden-gleaming brass instrument. "The symbolism built into this . . . er . . . 'gadget' I think you called it, Lord Bontriomphe—is most important. Within this brass cylinder are the invariables—what we call the 'hardware' of the spell. But this, by itself, is of no use. It can only be used by a sorcerer who can use the proper verbal spells to activate it. These spells we call the 'software'—if you follow me, my lord."

Lord Bontriomphe nodded, grinning. "Between the two of you," he said, "you and Lord Darcy have answered my question. Do proceed, Sir Lyon."

"I think there is no need to," said Sir Lyon. "I shall turn the rest of the discussion over to the Lord High Admiral."

"I think we can all see," said the Lord High Admiral without waiting for Sir Lyon to sit down, "what this device could do to an enemy ship in the hands of a sorcerer who knew the spells. It does not prevent them from steering the ship—that, as I understand it, would be Black Magic—but any attempt to load and fire their batteries would result in chaos. We have seen what happens when *one* man attempts it. You should see what it does to a *team!* Each man is not only fumbling his own job, but is continually getting in the way of others. As I said—chaos.

"With this device, my lords and gentlemen, the Imperial Navy can keep the Slavonic Royal Navy bottled up in the Baltic for as long as necessary. Provided, of course, that *we* have it and *they* don't.

"And that, sirs, is the crux of our problem. The secret of this device must not be allowed to fall into Polish hands!"

*The crux indeed!* thought Lord Darcy, suppressing a smile of satisfaction. The King had already taken out his pipe and was filling it; Lord Darcy, the Lord High Admiral, and Captain Smollett had immediate-

ly reached for their own smoking equipment. But
Lord Darcy was watching Captain Smollett. He
could have predicted almost to the word what the
Lord High Admiral's next words would be.

"We are faced, then," said my lord the High Admiral, "with a problem of espionage. Captain
Smollett, the details, if you please."

"Aye, aye, my lord." The Chief of Naval Intelligence puffed solemnly on his pipe for a second.
Then: "Problem's very simple, m'luds. Answer's difficult. Someone's been tryin' to sell the secret of this
device to the Poles, d'you see. Here's what's happened:

"We had a double agent in Cherbourg—name's
Barbour, Georges Barbour. Not Anglo-French, ac-
tually. Pole. Did damn' good work for us, though.
Trustworthiness high."

Smollett took his pipe from his mouth and
gestured with the stem. "Now"—he stabbed the air
with the pipestem—"a few weeks ago, Barbour got a
letter—anonymous, untraceable—saying that the secret of the device was for sale. Description of exterior
and of effect of device quite accurate, you understand, m'luds. Very well. Barbour contacted his su-
perior—chap known to him only by code name 'Zed'
—and asked for instructions. Zed came to me; I went
to My Lord High Admiral. Amongst the three of us,
we set a trap."

"Your pardon, Captain Smollett," said Lord
Darcy, taking advantage of a pause in the captain's
narrative.

"Certainly, m'lud."

"No one knew of this trap save yourself, my lord
the High Admiral, and Zed?"

"No one, m'lud," Captain Smollett said emphatically. "Absolutely no one."

"Thank you. Pardon the interruption, Captain."

"Certainly, m'lud. At any rate." He took a puff from his pipe. "At any rate, we set it up. Barbour was to make further contact. Asking price for details of secret—five thousand golden sovereigns."

*And worth it, too,* Lord Darcy thought to himself. One golden sovereign was worth fifty silver sovereigns, and a "twelfth-bit"—one twelfth of a silver sovereign—would buy a cup of caffe in a public house. One can buy an awesome amount of caffe for a quarter of a million silver sovereigns.

"Negotiations took time," Captain Smollett continued. "Barbour couldn't appear too eager. Look suspicious, eh? Yes. Well, 't'any rate, negotiations went on. Barbour, you must understand, was not working through Intelligence in Cherbourg. Worked through Zed. Had to be careful of contacts with us, you see. Always watched by Polish agents in Cherbourg." Captain Smollett gave a short, sharp, barking laugh. "While we watched Poles, of course. Devilish job.

"Didn't dare break Barbour's cover, d'you see; too damn' valuable a man. Now—during the negotiations, the man who was trying to sell the secret came twice to see Barbour. Barbour described him. Black hair, black beard and moustache, straight nose, fairly tall. Wore blue-tinted glasses, spoke with a hoarse, whispery voice in a Provence accent. Fairly tall. Dressed like a member of the well-to-do merchant class."

Lord Darcy caught Lord Bontriomphe's eyes, and the two investigators exchanged quick grins. The description was such that neither of the two men needed Captain Smollett's next statement.

"Obviously a disguise," said Captain Smollett.

"A question, Captain," said Lord Bontriomphe.

"Yes, m'lud?"

"This bloke made two appointments with Barbour. Since you must have known about 'em before hand, why didn't you grab him then—when he kept the appointments?"

"Couldn't, m'lud," Captain Smollett said firmly. "Not without breaking Barbour's cover. Too many Polish agents in Cherbourg keeping an eye on Barbour. *They* knew Barbour was dealing with this chap—called himself Goodman FitzJean, by the way. Any attempt to grab FitzJean would have meant that we'd've had to grab Barbour, too, d'you see. If we didn't, the Polish agents would've known that we knew about Barbour. *Not*, p'raps, that he was a double agent, but—at least—that we knew of 'im, eh? Would've broken his cover, rendered him useless to His Slavonic Majesty. Couldn't afford that, d'you see."

"You could have had this FitzJean followed after the appointments," Lord Bontriomphe pointed out.

"We *did*, m'lud," the captain said with some acerbity. "Naturally. Both times." Captain Smollett frowned in chagrin. "Unfortunately, I am forced to admit that the man eluded our agents both times." He took a deep breath. "Our Goodman FitzJean, m'luds and gentlemen, is no amateur." He looked around at each of the others. "Damn' sharp man. Don't know whether he knew he was being followed or not. But he likely suspected Polish agents following him, even if he didn't suspect Imperial agents. Managed to get away both times, and I make no apologies, m'luds."

Captain Smollett paused to take a breath, and the

Lord High Admiral cut in—this time addressing His
Majesty.

"With your permission, Sire, I stand behind Captain Smollett. No agent or group of agents can follow
a suspect for very long if the suspect is aware that he
is being followed and is trained in evasion techniques."

"I am aware of that, my lord," said King John
calmly. "Please continue, Captain Smollett."

"Yes, Sire," said the captain. He cleared his
throat. "As I was saying, m'luds, we failed to follow
the so-called FitzJean. But Barbour had—with our
connivance—baited the trap. He agreed, d'you see,
that the information FitzJean had was worth the five
thousand golden sovereigns. He told FitzJean that
His Slavonic Majesty's Government had agreed to
the price. *Provided* . . ." Captain Smollett gestured
vaguely with his pipe, and cleared his throat again.

"*Provided* . . . ahum . . . that he prove to Barbour
that he—FitzJean, that is—prove that he was a person who had access to the secret."

Captain Smollett put his pipe back in his mouth
and surveyed the others with his eyes. "I trust you
follow, m'luds," he said, clenching the pipe in his
molars and speaking round it. "FitzJean wouldn't
divulge the plans of the device without cash in hand.
But how were the Polish agents to know that the secret was worth anything? Eh?"

Captain Smollett held up a finger. "*That*, m'luds,
is what our double agent Barbour told FitzJean. Not
the truth, of course. Barbour had to give a cover story
to His Slavonic Majesty's agents. Told them, as a
matter of fact, that he had contacted an Imperial
Naval officer who was willing to give him the plans
for the deployment of Imperial and Scandinavian

ships in the North Sea and the Baltic. Price, according to what Barbour told his Polish superiors, was two hundred golden sovereigns." Captain Smollett spread his hands in a gesture of disgust. "Most they'd pay, of course, since fleet deployment can be changed rather quickly. But still useful.

"Evidently, the Poles agreed. But they wouldn't pay until they'd received the information. On the other hand, FitzJean demanded a hundred gold sovereigns just to prove that he was in earnest.

"We agreed. Barbour was to pretend that the money was coming from Poland. Said that, upon proof of FitzJean's bona fides, he'd give FitzJean a hundred sovereigns and then get the other forty-nine hundred and pay them when the details of the secret were delivered. Trouble was, FitzJean wouldn't make a definite appointment. Clever of him, you know. Kept Barbour on tenterhooks, as it were. D'you follow, m'luds?"

"I follow," said Lord Bontriomphe. "This Fitz-Jean was actually trapped into giving away his identity for five thousand silver sovereigns. Right? But he didn't do so, did he? That is, your organization never paid the hundred gold sovereigns, did they?"

"No, m'lud," said Captain Smollett. "The hundred sovereigns were never paid." He looked across the table. "Explain, Commander," he said to Lord Ashley.

Commander Lord Ashley nodded. "Aye, sir." He looked at Lord Darcy, then at Lord Bontriomphe. "I was supposed to bring the money to him yesterday morning. He was dead when I arrived; stabbed only minutes before, evidently."

He went on to explain exactly what he had done following his examination of the body, including the

conversation with Chief Henri and Lord Admiral
Brencourt.

Lord Bontriomphe listened without asking questions until the commander's narrative was finished;
then he looked at the Lord High Admiral and waited
expectantly.

"Huhum!" The Lord High Admiral gave a rum-
bling chuckle. "Yes, my lords. The connection, of
course. It was this: Sir James Zwinge, Master
Sorcerer and Chief Forensic Sorcerer for the City of
London, was also the head of our counterespionage
branch—operating under the code name of 'Zed.' "

# 9

"AND NOW," said Lord Darcy an hour later, "I am prepared to make an arrest for the murder of Master Sir James Zwinge."

My lord the Marquis of London remained all but motionless behind his desk. Only the slight narrowing of his eyes gave any indication that he had heard what the Chief Investigator of Normandy had said.

Lord Darcy and Lord Bontriomphe had returned to de London's office immediately after His Majesty had dismissed the meeting at Westminster Palace. Lord Darcy could still hear the King's last orders: "Then we are agreed, my lords. Our civilian investigators will proceed to investigate these murders as though they were in no way connected with the Navy, as though they were merely seeking a murderer. No connection must be made between the killing of Barbour and the killing of Sir James, as far as the public is concerned. Meanwhile, the Naval Intelligence Corps will be working to uncover the other contacts of Barbour, and make a minute investigation of the reports he filed with 'Zed' and the reports

'Zed' filed with the London office. There may be more evidence than we realize in those report files. Finally, we must all do our best to see that His Slavonic Majesty's secret agents remain at least as much in the dark as we are."

For a moment, Lord Darcy had thought that last bit of heavy sarcasm from the King had made Lord High Admiral Peter de Valera ap Smith angry. Then he had realized that the Lord High Admiral's choked expression came from a valiant and successful attempt to smother a laugh.

*By Heaven*, Lord Darcy had thought, *I must get to know that old pirate better.*

My Lord of London had been seated behind his desk reading a book when Lord Darcy and Lord Bontriomphe had entered the office. The Marquis had picked up a thin golden bookmark, put it carefully between the pages of the book, closed the book and placed it on the desktop before him. "Good morning, my lords," he had rumbled, inclining his head perhaps an eighth of an inch. "There is a letter for you, Lord Darcy." He had pushed a white envelope across the desk with a fat forefinger. "Delivered this morning by special courier."

"Thank you," Lord Darcy had murmured politely, picking up the envelope. He had broken the seal, read the three sheets of closely written paper, refolded them, replaced them in the envelope, and smiled.

"A very informative letter from—as you no doubt noticed from the seal, My Lord Marquis—Sir Eliot Meredith, my Assistant Chief Investigator. And now, I am prepared to make an arrest for the murder of Master Sir James Zwinge."

"Indeed?" said my lord the Marquis after a moment. "You have solved the case? Without checking the evidence personally? Without questioning a witness? How extraordinarily astute—even for you, my dear cousin."

"You are hardly one to cavil at lack of personal investigation," Lord Darcy said mildly, seating himself comfortably in the red leather chair. "As for my witness, there is no need to question him any further. The information is before us; we have but to examine it."

The Marquis put his palms flat on his desktop, inhaled four pecks of air, and let it out slowly through his nose. "All right. Let's hear it."

"It is simplicity itself. So obvious, in fact, that one tends to overlook it because of the very obviousness of the killer. Consider: A man is killed inside a locked and sealed room—in a hotel full of magicians. Naturally, we are led to believe that it is black magic. Obvious. In fact, *too* obvious. That is exactly what we are supposed to believe."

"How *was* it done, then?" asked the Marquis, becoming interested.

"Zwinge was stabbed to death right in front of the very witnesses who were there to testify that the room was locked and sealed," Lord Darcy said calmly.

My lord the Marquis closed his eyes. "I see. That's the way the wind blows, eh?" He opened his eyes again and looked at Lord Bontriomphe. Lord Bontriomphe looked back at him, steadily, expressionlessly. "Continue, Lord Darcy," the Marquis said. "I should like to hear all of it."

"As you have deduced, dear cousin," Lord Darcy continued, "only Bontriomphe could have done it. It was he who broke the door down. He was the first one in the room. He ordered the others to stay out, to

stay back. Then he bent over the unconscious body of
Sir James, and, concealing his actions with his own
body, sank a knife into the Master Sorcerer's heart.''

"How did he know Sir James would be unconscious? Why did Sir James scream? What motive
did Bontriomphe have?" The three questions were
deliberate, almost emotionless. "You have explanations, I presume?"

"Naturally. There are several drugs in the *materia
medica* of the adept herbalist which will cause unconsciousness and coma. Bontriomphe, knowing that
Sir James intended to lock himself into his room yesterday morning, managed to slip some such drug
into the sorcerer's morning caffe—a simple job for an
expert. After that, all he had to do was wait. Eventually, Sir James would be missed. Someone would
wonder why he had not kept an appointment. Someone would check his room and find it locked. At last,
someone would ask the management to see if something could be wrong. When the manager found he
could not open the door, he would ask for official
help. And, fortuitously, Lord Bontriomphe, Chief Investigator for My Lord Marquis of London, just happens to be right on the spot. He calls for an ax
and . . ." Lord Darcy turned one hand palm up as
though he were handing the Marquis the whole case
on a platter, and left the sentence unfinished.

"Go on." There was a dangerous note in the Marquis' voice.

"The scream is easily explained," Lord Darcy
said. "Sir James was not completely comatose. He
heard Master Sean knock. Now, Sean had an appointment at that time; Sir James knew it was he at
the door. Aroused by the knock, he called out: 'Master Sean! Help!' And then he collapsed back into his

drugged coma. Bontriomphe, of course, could not have known that would happen, but it was certainly a stroke of luck, even though it was completely unnecessary to his plan. If there had been no scream, Sean would certainly have known something was amiss and notified the manager. After that, everything would have followed naturally."

Lord Darcy folded his arms, slumped back in the chair, rested his chin on his chest, and looked at the speechless, glowering de London from beneath his brows. "The motive is quite clear. Jealousy."

"*Pah!*" the Marquis exploded. "Now I have you! Up to now, you have been clever. But now you show that your wits are addled. A woman? *Pfui!* Lord Bontriomphe may occasionally play the fool, but he is not a fool about women. I will not go so far as to say that the woman does not live whom Lord Bontriomphe could not get if he wanted her, but I will say that his ego is such that he would have no desire for a woman who did not want him or who had rejected him for another. He would not go out of his way to snap his fingers at such a woman, much less kill because of her."

"Agreed," said Lord Darcy complacently. "I mentioned no woman. And I was not speaking of *his* jealousy."

"Of whose, then?"

"Of yours."

"Hah! This is fatuous."

"Not at all. Your hobby of herb cultivation, my lord, is one of the strongest passions of your life. You are an acknowledged expert and are proud of that fact. Zwinge, too, was a herbalist, but not quite in your league. Still, if you ever had any real rival in the field, it was Master Sir James Zwinge. Recently, Sir

James succeeded in growing Polish devilwort from the seed instead of from cuttings, as is normally done. You have failed to do so. Therefore, out of pique, you asked Bontriomphe to remove your rival; he, out of loyalty, proceeded to do so. And there you have it, my lord: Method, Motive, and Opportunity. *Quod erat demonstrandum.*"

My Lord Marquis swiveled his head and glared at Lord Bontriomphe. "Are you an accessory to this imbecilic tomfoolery?"

Lord Bontriomphe shook his head once, left to right. "No, my lord. But it does look as though he has us dead to rights, doesn't it?"

"Buffoon!" the Marquis snorted. He looked back at Lord Darcy. "Very well. I know when I am being gulled as well as you do. I regret having jailed Master Sean; it was frivolous. And you are well aware that I would just as soon go to the Tower myself as to lose the services of Lord Bontriomphe for any extended length of time. Outside this building, he is my eyes and ears. I will sign an order for Master Sean's release immediately. Since you have been assigned to this case by the King, you will, of course, be remunerated from the Royal Privy Purse?"

"Beginning today, yes," said Lord Darcy. "But there is the little matter of yesterday—including cross-Channel transportation, train ticket, and cab fare."

"Done," the Marquis growled. He signed a release form, poured melted sealing wax on it, and stamped it with the seal of the Marquisate of London, all without a word. Then he heaved his massive bulk out of the chair. "Lord Bontriomphe, give my lord cousin what is owed him. Open the wall safe and take it out of petty cash. I am going upstairs to the plant rooms." He did not quite slam the door as he left.

Lord Bontriomphe looked at Lord Darcy. "Look here—you don't really think . . ."

"*Chah!* Don't be ridiculous. I know perfectly well that every word of your narrative was accurate and truthful. And the Marquis is quite aware that I know it." Lord Darcy was not one to err in a matter of judgment like that, and, as it turned out, he did not. Lord Bontriomphe's recital was correct and precise in every detail.

"Let's get to the Tower," said Lord Darcy.

Lord Bontriomphe was at his desk taking a pistol out of a drawer. "Just a second, my lord," he said, "I once resolved never to go out on a murder case unarmed. By the way, don't you think it would be best to set up an auxiliary headquarters in the Royal Steward? That way we can keep in touch with each other and with Chief Hennely's plainclothes investigators."

"An excellent idea," said Lord Darcy, "and speaking of plainclothes investigators, did you get statements from everyone concerned yesterday?"

"As many as possible, my lord. Of course, we couldn't get everyone, but I think the reports we have now are fairly complete."

"Good. Bring them along, will you? I should like to look them over on our way to the Tower. Are you ready to go?"

"Ready, my lord," said Lord Bontriomphe.

"Very well, then," said Lord Darcy. "Come, let's get Master Sean out of durance vile."

# 10

AS THE OFFICIAL CARRIAGE, bearing the London arms, moved through the streets toward the Royal Steward Hotel, its pneumatic tires jouncing briskly on their spring suspensions as a soft accompaniment to the clopping of the horses' hooves, Sean O Lochlainn, Master Sorcerer, leaned back in the seat, clutching his symbol-decorated carpetbag to his round paunch.

"Ah, my lords," he said to the two men on the seat opposite, "a relief it is, indeed, to be free again. Twenty-four hours of sitting in the Tower is not my notion of a grand time, and you may be sure of that. Not that I object to being alone in a comfortable room for a while; any sorcerer who doesn't take a week or so off every year for a Contemplation Retreat will find his power deserting him. But when there's work to be done . . ." He paused. "My lord, you didn't get me out of the Tower by *solving* this case, did you?"

Lord Darcy laughed. "No fear, my good Sean. You haven't missed any of the excitement yet."

"His lordship," said Lord Bontriomphe, "got you out by simple but effective blackmail."

"*Counter*-blackmail, if you please," Lord Darcy

corrected. "I merely showed de London that Lord Bontriomphe could be jailed on the same sort of flimsy evidence that the Marquis used to jail you."

"Now wait a moment," said Lord Bontriomphe. "The evidence wasn't all *that* flimsy. There was certainly enough—in both cases—to permit holding a man for questioning."

"Certainly," Lord Darcy agreed. "But My Lord Marquis had no intention of questioning Master Sean. He was adhering to the letter of the law rather than to its spirit. It is a matter of family rivalry; we have, the Marquis and I, similar although not identical abilities, and therefore a basically friendly but at times emotionally charged antagonism. He would not dare have locked up an ordinary subject of His Majesty on such evidence unless he honestly believed that the suspect had actually committed the crime. Indeed, I will go further; he would never even have considered such an act."

"I'm glad to hear you say that," said Lord Bontriomphe, "since it happens to be true. But once in a while, this rivalry goes a little too far. Normally, I keep out of it, but then—"

"Permit me to correct you," Lord Darcy said with a smile. "Normally, you do *not* keep out of it. To the contrary, you are normally rigidly loyal to My Lord Marquis; you normally take *his* side, forcing me to outwit both of you—an admittedly difficult job. This time, however, you felt that imprisoning Master Sean in order to get at me was just a little too much. I am well aware that, had it been *I* who went to the Tower, the matter would have been quite different."

Lord Bontriomphe gazed dreamily at the roof of the carriage. "Now *there's* a thought," he said in a speculative tone.

"Don't think on it too hard, my lord," said Master
Sean with gentle menace. "Not too hard at all, at
all."

Lord Bontriomphe brought his eyes down sharply
and started to say something, but his words were for-
ever lost as the carriage slowed suddenly and the
driver opened the trapdoor in the roof and said:

"The Royal Steward, my lords."

Half a minute later, the footman opened the door,
and the three men got out. Lord Bontriomphe quietly slipped a couple of large coins into the footman's
hand. "Wait for us, Barney. See that the carriage
and horses are taken care of, and then you and Denys
wait in the pub across the street. We may be quite
some time, so have a few beers and relax. I'll send
word if we need you."

"Very good, my lord," Goodman Barney said
warmly. "Thank you."

Then Lord Bontriomphe followed Lord Darcy and
Master Sean into the Royal Steward.

Lord Darcy was standing alone just inside the
foyer, looking through the glass-paned doors at the
crowd in the lobby.

"Where's Master Sean?" Bontriomphe asked.

"In there. I sent him on ahead. As you will observe, there are at least a dozen well-wishers and possibly two dozen who are merely curious, all of whom
are crowded around Sean, congratulating him upon
his release, saying they knew all along he was innocent, and pumping him for information about the
murder of Sir James Zwinge. While their attention is
thus distracted, my lord, you and I will make a quiet
entrance and go directly to the murder room.
Come."

* * *

They did not attract attention as they went in.

This was Visitors' Day at the Sorcerers Convention, and the lobby was filled with folk who had come to see the displays and the sorcerers themselves. They were just two more sightseers.

At one of the display booths, a journeyman sorcerer was demonstrating a children's toy to two wide-eyed children and a fondly patronizing father. It consisted of a six-inch black wand with one white tip, five differently-colored pith balls an inch in diameter, and a foot-long board with six holes in it, five of which were ringed with colors to match the balls and the fifth one ringed with white.

"Now you'll notice, my lads," said the journeyman sorcerer, "that the balls aren't in their proper holes; the colors don't match. The object of the game is to put 'em right, you see. The rule is that you move one ball at a time, like this:" He aimed the wand at the board, which was several feet away, and one of the balls floated smoothly up and across, to drop into the extra hole. Then another moved into the vacated hole to match colors. The process was repeated until all the balls were in the proper holes. "You see? Now, I'll just mix these balls up again and let you try it, lad. Just point the white tip of the wand and think of which color ball you want to come up; then, when it's in the air, think of the color hole you want it to go to. There, now. That's it—"

It was more than just a toy, Lord Darcy knew; it was a testing and teaching device. With the spell it now had on it, anyone could do the trick; but the spell was timed to fade slowly over a period of a few months. By that time, most children were thoroughly tired of it, anyway. But if a rare child with the Talent got hold of one, his interest usually did not wane. Furthermore, he began to get the feel of the spell itself, aided by the simple ritual and ceremony of the game. If that happened, the child would still be able to do the trick a year later, though none of his un-Talented friends would. The original spell had worn off and had been replaced by the child's own simple version. A booklet went with the game which explained all that to the parents, urging them to have the child given further tests if he succeeded in preserving the activity of the toy.

At another booth, a priest in clerical black with white lace at collar and cuffs was distributing booklets describing the new building being erected at Oxford to house the Royal Thaumaturgical Laboratories at Edward's College. The display was a scale model of the proposed structure.

Directly in their path, the two men saw what looked like an ordinary door frame. An illusion sign floated in its center, translucent blue letters that said: PLEASE STEP THROUGH.

As they did, the illusion sign vanished and they could feel what seemed to be a slight wind tugging at their clothing. On the other side, another illusion sign appeared.

THANK YOU

*If you will examine your clothing, you will see that every speck of loose dust and lint has been removed. This is a prototype device, still in the experimental stage. Eventually, no home will be without one.*

*Wells & Sons*
*Thaumaturgical Home Appliances*

"Quite a gadget," said Lord Bontriomphe. "Look; even our boots are shiny," he added as they walked through the second sign and it dissolved around them.

"Useful," Lord Darcy agreed, "but quite impracticable. Sean told me they had it at the last Convention. It makes a good advertisement for the company, but that 'no home will be without one' is visionary. Far too expensive, since the spell has to be renewed by a Master Sorcerer at least once a week. With this mob in here, they'll be lucky if they get through the day with it."

"Hm-m-m. Like that 'See London From the Air' device they had a few years back," said Bontriomphe. "Remember that?"

"I read something about it. I don't recall the details," Lord Darcy said.

"It looked quite impressive. They had a crystal ball about"—he held his hands in front of him as though he were grasping an imaginary sphere—"oh, ten inches in diameter, I guess. It was mounted on a pedestal, and you looked into it from above. It gave you the weird feeling that you were looking down from a great height, from a point just above Admiral Buckingham Hall, where the exhibit was. You could actually see people walking about, and carriages moving through the streets, as though you were up in a cathedral spire looking down. There was a magic mirror suspended a couple of hundred feet above the building, you see, which projected the scene into the crystal by psychic reflection."

"Ah, I see. Whatever happened to it? I've heard no more about it," Lord Darcy said.

"Well, right off the bat, the War Office was interested. You can imagine what sort of reconnaissance you'd have, with a magic mirror floating high over enemy lines and an observer safe behind your own lines watching everything they were doing. Anyway, the War Office thaumaturgists are still working on it, but it hasn't come to anything. In the first place, it takes three Masters to run it: One to levitate the mirror, one to keep the mirror activated, and one to keep the receiving crystal activated. And they have to be specially trained for the job and then train together as a team. In the second place, the sorcerers controlling the mirror have to be within sight of the mirror, and the plane of the surface has to be perpendicular to a radius of the crystal ball. Don't ask me why; I'm no sorcerer and I don't know a thing about the theory. At any rate, the thing hasn't been made practical for long distance transmission of images yet."

They left the lobby and started upstairs toward the late Sir James Zwinge's room.

"So far," said Lord Darcy, "aside from such things as the semaphore and the heliotelegraph—both of which require line-of-sight towers for transmission—the only practical means of long distance communication we have is the teleson. And the mathematical thaumaturgists still have not come up with a satisfactory theory to explain its functioning. Ah! I see that your Armsmen are on duty." They had reached the top of the stairway. Down the hall, directly in front of the door to the murder room were two black-clad Armsmen of the King's Peace.

"Good morning, Jeffers, Dubois," said Lord Bontriomphe as he and Lord Darcy approached the door.

The Armsmen saluted. "Good morning, my lord," said the older of the two.

"Everything all right? No disturbances?"

"None, my lord. Quiet as a tomb."

"Jeffers," said Lord Bontriomphe with a smile, "with a wit like that, you will either rise rapidly to Master-at-Arms or you will remain a foot patrolman all your life."

"My ambition is modest, my lord," said Jeffers with a straight face. "I only wish to become a Sergeant-at-Arms. For that, I need only to be a half-wit."

"Foot patrolman," Lord Darcy said sadly. "Forever." He looked at the door to the murder room. "I see they have covered the hole in the door."

"Yes, my lord," said Jeffers. "They just tacked this panel over the hole. Otherwise, the door's untouched. Would you be wanting to look in, my lords?" He took a large, thick, heavy brass key from the pouch at his belt. "This is Sir James' key," he said. "You can open the door, but Grand Master Sir Lyon has put a spell on the room itself, my lords."

Lord Darcy took the key, fitted it into the long, narrow keyhole, turned the bolt, and opened the door. He and Lord Bontriomphe stopped at the threshold.

There was no tangible barrier at the door. There was nothing they could see or touch. But the barrier was almost palpably there, nonetheless. Lord Darcy found that he had no desire to enter the room at all. Quite the contrary; he felt a distinct aversion to the room, a sense of wanting to avoid, at all costs, going into that room for any reason whatever. There was nothing in that room that interested him, no reason at all why he should enter it. It was taboo—a forbidden place. To look from without was both necessary and desirable; to enter was neither necessary nor desirable.

Lord Darcy surveyed the room with his eyes.

Master Sir James Zwinge still lay where he had fallen, looking as though he had died only minutes before, thanks to the preservative spell which had been cast over the corpse.

Footsteps came down the hall. Lord Darcy turned

to see Master Sean approaching.

"Sorry to be so long, my lord," said the sorcerer as he neared the door. He stopped at the threshold. "Now what have we here? Hm-m-m. An aversion spell, eh? Hm-m-m. And cast by a Master, too, I'll be bound. It would take quite a time to solve that one." He stood looking through the door.

"It was cast by Grand Master Sir Lyon himself," said Lord Darcy.

"Then I'll go fetch him to take it off," said Master Sean. "I wouldn't waste time trying to take it off meself."

"Pardon me, Master Sorcerer," said Armsman Jeffers deferentially, "are you Master Sean O Lochlainn?"

"That I am."

The Armsman took an envelope from an inside jacket pocket. "The Grand Master," he said, "told me to be sure and give this to you when you came, Master Sean."

Master Sean placed his symbol-decorated carpet-bag on the floor, took the envelope, opened it, extracted a single sheet of paper, and read it carefully.

"Ah!" he said, his round Irish face beaming. "I see! Ingenious! I shall most certainly have to remember that one!" He looked at Lord Darcy with the smile still wreathing his face. "Sir Lyon has given me the key. He expected me to be here this morning. Now, if you'll excuse me for a few minutes—"

The tubby little Irish sorcerer knelt down and opened his carpetbag. He fished around inside and took out a gold-and-ebony wand, a small brazen bowl, an iron tripod with six-inch legs, two silver phials, and an oddly constructed flint-and-steel firestriker.

The others stepped back respectfully. One does not disturb a magician at work.

Master Sean placed the tripod on the floor just in front of the open door and set the small brazen bowl on top of it. Then he put in a few lumps of charcoal from his carpetbag. Within two minutes, he had the coals glowing redly. Then he added a large pinch of powder from each of the two silver phials, and a dense column of aromatic blue-gray smoke arose from the small brazier. Master Sean traced a series of symbols in the air with his wand while he murmured something the others could not hear. Then he carefully folded, in an intricate and complex manner, the letter from Sir Lyon Grey. When it was properly folded, he dropped it on the coals. As it burst into flame, he traced more symbols and murmured further words.

"There," he said. "You can go in now, my lords."

The two investigators walked across the threshold. Their aversion to doing so had completely vanished. Master Sean took a small bronze lid from his carpetbag and fitted it tightly over the mouth of the little brazier.

"Just leave it there, lads," he said to the two Armsmen. "It will cool off in a few minutes. Mind you don't knock it over, now." Then he joined Lord Darcy and Lord Bontriomphe inside the murder room.

Lord Darcy closed the door and looked at it. From the inside, the damage done by Lord Bontriomphe's ax work was plainly visible. Otherwise, there was nothing unusual about the door. A rapid but thorough inspection of the doors and windows convinced Lord Darcy that Lord Bontriomphe had been absolutely right when he said the room was sealed.

There were no secret panels, no trapdoors. The windows were firmly bolted, and there was no way they could have been bolted from the outside by other than magical means.

With difficulty, Lord Darcy slid back the bolt on one of the windows and opened it. It creaked gently as it swung outward.

Lord Darcy looked out the window. There was a thirty-foot drop of smooth stone beneath him. The window opened onto a small courtyard, where several chair-surrounded tables formed a part of the dining facilities of the Royal Steward Hotel.

Some of the tables were occupied. Five sorcerers, three priests, and a bishop had all heard the window open and were looking up at him.

Lord Darcy craned his neck around and looked up. Ten feet above were the windows of the next floor. Lord Darcy pulled his head back in and closed the window.

"No one went out that way," he said firmly. "For an ordinary man to have done so would have required a rope. He would have had either to slide down thirty feet or to climb up ten feet hand over hand."

"An *ordinary* man," said Lord Bontriomphe, emphasizing the word. "But levitation is not too difficult a trick for a Master Sorcerer."

"What say you, Master Sean?" Lord Darcy asked the tubby little sorcerer.

"It could have been done that way," Master Sean admitted.

"Furthermore," said Lord Bontriomphe, "those bolts could have been thrown from the outside by magic."

"Indeed they could," Master Sean agreed.

Lord Bontriomphe looked expectantly at Lord Darcy.

"Very well," said Lord Darcy with a smile, "let us proceed to try that theory by what the geometers call, I believe, the *reductio ad absurdum*. Imagine the scene. What happens?"

He gestured toward the body on the floor. "Sir James is stabbed. Our sorcerer-murderer—if you'll pardon the double entendre—goes to the window. He opens it. Then he steps up to the sill and steps out into empty air, levitating himself as he does so. Then he closes the window and proceeds to cast a spell which slides the bolts into their sockets. When that is done, he floats off somewhere—up or down, it matters not which." He looked at Master Sean. "How long would that take?"

"Five or six minutes at the least. If he could do it at all. Levitation causes a tremendous psychic drain; the spell can only be held for a matter of minutes. In addition, you're asking him to cast a second spell while he's holding the first. A spell of the type that was cast on this room is what we call a *static* spell, my lord. It imposes a *condition*, you see. But levitating and the moving of bolts are *kinetic* spells; you have to keep them moving. To use two kinetic spells at the same time requires tremendous concentration, power, and precision. I would hesitate, myself, to try casting a window-locking spell with a thirty-foot drop beneath me. Certainly not if I were in a hurry or distracted."

"And even if it could be done, it would take five or six minutes," Lord Darcy said. "Bontriomphe, would you mind opening the *other* window? We haven't tested it yet."

The London investigator drew back the bolt and

pushed the window open. It groaned audibly.

"What do you see out there?" Lord Darcy asked.

"About nine pairs of eyes staring up at me," Lord Bontriomphe said.

"Exactly. Both windows make a slight noise when they are opened. That noise is quite audible in the courtyard below. Yesterday morning, Sir James' scream was clearly audible through that window, but even if it had not been—even if Sir James had not screamed at all when he was stabbed—the killer could not have gone out through that window without being seen, much less hovered there for five or six minutes."

Lord Bontriomphe pulled the window closed again. "What if he were invisible?" he asked, looking at the little Irish sorcerer.

"The Tarnhelm Effect?" asked Master Sean. He chuckled. "My lord, regardless of what the layman may think, the Tarnhelm Effect is extremely difficult to use in practice. Besides, 'invisibility' is a layman's term. Spells using the Tarnhelm Effect are very similar in structure to the aversion spell you met at the door to this room. If a sorcerer were to cast such a spell about himself, your eyes would avoid looking directly at him. You wouldn't realize it yourself, but you would simply keep your eyes averted from him at all times. He could stand in the middle of a crowd and no one could later swear that he was there because no one would have seen him except out of the corner of the eye, if you follow me.

"Even if he were alone, you wouldn't see him because you'd never look at him. You would subconsciously assume that whatever it was you were seeing out of the corner of your eye was a cabinet or a hatrack or an umbrella stand or a lamppost—

whatever was most likely under the circumstances. Your mind would explain him away as something that *ought* to be there, as a part of the normal background and therefore unnoticeable.

"But he wouldn't actually be invisible. You could see him, for instance, in a mirror or other reflecting surface simply because the spell wouldn't keep your eyes away from the mirror."

"He could cast a sight-avoidance spell on the mirror, couldn't he?" Lord Bontriomphe asked. "That's a static spell, I believe."

"Certainly," said Master Sean. "He could cast a sight-avoidance spell on every reflecting surface in the place. But a man has to look *somewhere,* and even a layman would get suspicious under circumstances like that. Besides, to anyone with even a half-trained Talent, he'd be detectable immediately.

"And even supposing he did make himself invisible outside that window, do you realize what he would have to do? Now you have him juggling three spells at once: he's levitating himself; he's making himself 'invisible'; and he's closing that window.

"No, my lord; it won't do. It just isn't humanly possible."

Lord Darcy let his gaze wander over the room. "That's settled, then. Our killer did not go out those windows either by thaumaturgical or by ordinary physical means. Therefore, we—"

"Wait a minute!" said Lord Bontriomphe, his eyes widening. He pointed a finger at Master Sean. "Look here; suppose it happened this way. The killer stabs Master Sir James. His victim screams. The killer knows that you are outside the door. He knows he can't get out through the door. The windows are out, too, for the reasons you've just given. What can he do? He uses the Tarnhelm Effect. When I come busting in here with an ax, I don't see him. As far as I'm concerned, the room is empty except for the corpse. I wouldn't be able to see him, would I? Then, when the door's open, he walks out as cool as an oyster, with nobody noticing him."

Master Sean shook his head. "*You* wouldn't notice him; that's so. But *I* would have. And so would Grand Master Sir Lyon. We were both looking in through that hole in the door, and a man can see the whole room from there—even the bathroom, when the door to it is open."

Lord Bontriomphe looked at the bathroom through the open door. "No, you can't. Take a look. Suppose he were lying down in the tub. You couldn't even see him from in here."

"True. But I distinctly recall your looking down directly into the tub. You couldn't have done that if a killer using the Tarnhelm Effect were in it."

Lord Bontriomphe frowned thoughtfully. "Yes. I did. Hm-m-m. Well, that eliminates that. He wasn't in the room, and he didn't leave the room." He looked at Lord Darcy. "What does that leave?"

"We don't know yet, my dear fellow. We need more data." He stepped over to where the body lay and knelt down, being careful not to disturb anything.

* * *

Master Sir James Zwinge had been a short, lean man, with receding gray hair and a small gray beard and moustache. He was wearing a neat, fairly expensive gentleman's suit, rather than the formal sorcerer's costume to which he was entitled. As Bontriomphe had said, it was difficult to see the stab wound at first glance. It was small, barely an inch long, and had not opened widely. It was further obscured by the blood which covered the front of the dead magician's clothing. Nearby, a black-handled, silver-bladed knife lay in the pool of blood on the floor, its gleaming blade splashed with red.

"This blood—" Lord Darcy gestured with his hand. "Are you absolutely certain, Bontriomphe, that it was fresh when you broke into this room?"

"Absolutely certain," Bontriomphe said. "It was bright red and still liquid. There was still a slight flow of blood from the wound itself. I'll admit I am not a chirurgeon, but I am certainly no amateur when it comes to knowing something about *that* particular subject. He couldn't have been dead more than a few minutes when I first saw his body."

Lord Darcy nodded. "Indeed. The condition of the blood even now, under the preservation spell, shows a certain freshness."

He gestured toward a key that lay a few feet away from the body. "Is that your key, my lord?"

Lord Bontriomphe nodded. "Yes. I put it there to mark the spot when I picked up Sir James' key."

"It is still where you put it?"

"Yes."

Lord Darcy measured the distance between the key and the door with his eye. "Four and a half feet," he murmured. He stood up. "Give me Sir James' key. Thank you. An experiment is in order."

"An experiment, my lord?" Master Sean repeated. His face brightened.

"Not of the thaumaturgical variety, my good Sean. That will come in good time." He walked over to the door and opened it, ignoring the two Armsmen who stood at attention outside. He looked down at his feet. "Master Sean, would you be so good as to remove this brazier?"

The tubby little Irish sorcerer bent over and put

his hand near the brazen bowl. "It's still a little hot. I'll put it on the table." He picked up the tripod by one leg and carried it into the room.

"I don't see what you're getting at," said Lord Bontriomphe.

"Surely you have noticed the clearance between the bottom of the door and the floor?" Lord Darcy said. "Is it possible that the murderer simply stabbed Sir James, came out, locked the door behind him, and slid the key back under the door?"

Master Sean blinked. "With me standing outside the door all the time?" he said in surprise. "Why, that's impossible, me lord!"

"Once we have eliminated the impossible," Lord Darcy said calmly, "we shall be able to concentrate on the merely improbable."

He knelt down and looked at the floor beneath the door. "As you see, the space is somewhat wider than it appears to be from the inside. The carpeting does not extend under the door. Close the door, if you will, Master Sean."

The sorcerer pushed the door shut and waited patiently on the other side. Lord Darcy put the heavy brass key on the floor and attempted to push it under the door. "I thought not," he said, almost to himself. "The key is much too large and thick. It can be forced under—" He pushed hard at the key. "But it wedges tight. And the thickness of the carpet would stop it on the other side." He pulled the key out. "Open the door again, Master Sean."

The door swung inward. "Observe," Lord Darcy continued, "how the attempt to push it under has scored the wood at that point. It would be impossible even to make the attempt without leaving traces, much less—" He paused, cutting off his own words abruptly. "What is this?" he said, leaning over to peer more closely at a spot on the carpet inside the room.

"What's *what?*" asked Lord Bontriomphe.

Lord Darcy ignored him. He was looking at a spot on the carpet near the right-hand doorpost, on the side away from the hinges, and approximately eight inches in from the edge of the carpet itself.

"May I borrow your magnifying glass, Master Sean?" Lord Darcy said without looking up.

"Certainly." Master Sean went over to the table, opened his symbol-decorated carpetbag, took out a large bone-handled lens, and handed it to his lordship.

"What is it?" he asked, echoing Lord Bontriomphe's question. He knelt down to look, as Lord Darcy continued to study a small spot on the carpet without answering.

The mark, Master Sean saw, was a dark stain in the shape of a half circle, with the straight side running parallel to the door and the arc curving in toward the interior of the room. It was small, about half the size of a man's thumbnail.

"Is it blood?" asked Master Sean.

"It is difficult to tell on this dark green carpet," said Lord Darcy. "It might be blood; it might be some other dark substance. Whatever it is, it has soaked into the fibers of the pile, although not down to the backing. Interesting." He stood up.

"May I?" said Lord Bontriomphe, holding out his hand for the glass.

"Certainly." He handed over the lens, and while the London investigator knelt to look at the stain, Lord Darcy said to Master Sean: "I would be much obliged, my dear Sean, if you would make a simi-

larity test on that stain. I should like to know if it is
blood, and, if so, whether it is Sir James' blood." He
narrowed his eyes thoughtfully. "And while you're at
it, do a thorough check of the bloodstain around the
body. I should like to be certain that all of the blood
is actually Sir James Zwinge's."

"Very good, my lord. Would you want any other
tests besides the usual ones?"

"Yes. First: Was there, *in fact,* anyone at all in this
room when Sir James Zwinge died? Second: If there
was any black magical effect directed at this room, of
what sort was it?"

"I shall endeavor to give satisfaction, my Lord,"
Master Sean said doubtfully, "but it won't be easy."

Lord Bontriomphe rose to his feet and handed
Master Sean the magnifying glass. "What would be
difficult about it?" he asked. "I know those tests
aren't exactly routine, but I've seen journeyman
sorcerers perform them."

"My dear Bontriomphe," said Lord Darcy, "consider the circumstances. If, as we assume, this act of
murder was committed by a magician, then he was
most certainly a master magician. Knowing, as he
must have, that this hotel abounds in master magicians, he would have taken every precaution to cover his tracks and hide his identity—precautions that
no ordinary criminal would ever think of and could
not take even if he *had* thought of them. Since Master
Sir James was killed rather early yesterday morning,
it is likely that the murderer had all of the preceding
night for the casting of his spells. Can we, then, expect Master Sean to unravel in a few moments what
another master may have taken all night to ac-
complish?"

He put his hand into an inside jacket pocket and

took out the envelope which de London had handed him earlier. "Besides, I have further evidence that the killer or killers are quite capable of covering their tracks. This morning's communication from Sir Eliot Meredith, my Chief Assistant, is a report of what he has thus far discovered in regard to the murder of the double agent Georges Barbour in Cherbourg. It contains two apparently conflicting pieces of information." He looked at Master Sean.

"My good Sean. Would you give me your professional opinion of the journeyman who is the forensic sorcerer for Chief Master-at-Arms Henri Vert in Cherbourg?"

"Goodman Juseppy?" Master Sean pursed his lips, then said: "Competent, I should say; quite competent. He's not a Master, of course, but—"

"Would you consider him capable of bungling the two tests which I have just asked you to perform?"

"We are all capable of error, my lord. But . . . no. In an ordinary case, I should say that Goodman Juseppy's testimony as to his results would be quite reliable."

"In an ordinary case. Just so. But what if he were pitted against the machinations of a Master Sorcerer?"

Master Sean shrugged. "Then it's certainly possible that his results might be in error. Goodman Juseppy simply isn't of that caliber."

"Then that may account for the conflicting evidence," Lord Darcy said. "I hesitate to say definitely that it does, but it may."

"All right," said Lord Bontriomphe impatiently, "just what *is* this conflicting evidence?"

"According to Goodman Juseppy's official report, there was no one in Barbour's room at the time he was killed. Furthermore, there had not been anyone but himself in the room for several hours before."

"Very well," said Lord Bontriomphe, "but where is the conflict?"

"The second test," said Lord Darcy calmly. "Goodman Juseppy could detect no trace whatever of black magic—or, indeed, of any kind of sorcery at all."

In the silence that followed, Lord Darcy returned the envelope to his jacket pocket.

Master Sean O Lochlainn sighed. "Well, my lords, I'll perform the tests. However, I should like to call in another sorcerer to help. That way—"

"No!" Lord Darcy interrupted firmly. "Under no circumstances! As of this moment, Master Sean, you are the only sorcerer in this world in whom I can unhesitatingly place complete trust."

The little Irish sorcerer turned, took a deep breath, and looked up into Lord Darcy's eyes. "My lord," he said in a low, solemn voice, "in all humility I wish to point out that while yours is undoubtedly the finest deductive mind upon the face of this Earth, *I* am a Master Sorcerer." He paused. "We have worked together for a long time, my lord. During that time I have used sorcery to discover the facts, and you have taken those facts and made a cogent case of them. You cannot do the one, my lord, and I cannot do the other. Thus far there has been a tacit agreement between us, my lord, that I do not attempt to do your job, and you do not attempt to do mine. Has that agreement been abrogated?"

Lord Darcy was silent for a moment, trying to put his thoughts into words. Then, in a startlingly similar low voice, he said: "Master Sean, I should like to express my most humble apologies. I am an expert in my field. You are an expert on sorcery and sorcerers. Let it be so. The agreement has *not* been abrogated— nor, I trust, shall it ever be."

He paused for a moment, then, after a deep breath, said, in a more normal tone of voice, "Of course, Master Sean. You may choose any kind of consultation you wish."

During the moment of tension between the two friends, Lord Bontriomphe had quietly turned away, walked over to the corpse, and looked down at it without actually seeing it.

"Well, my lord—" There was just the slightest touch of embarrassment in Master Sean's voice. He cleared his throat and began again. "Well, my lord, it wasn't exactly consultation I was thinking of. What I really need is a good assistant. With your permission, I should like to ask Lord John Quetzal to help me. He's only a journeyman, but he wants to become a forensic sorcerer and the experience will be good for him."

"Of course, Master Sean, an excellent choice I should say. Now let me see—" He looked across at the body again. "I shan't disturb the evidence any more than is necessary. Those ceremonial knives are all constructed to the same pattern, are they not?"

"Yes, my lord. Every sorcerer must make his own, with his own hands, but they are built to rigid specifications. That's one of the things an apprentice has to learn right off, to build his own tools. You can't use another man's tools in this business, nor tools made by an ordinary craftsman. It's the making of them that attunes them to the individual who uses them. They must be generally similar and individually different."

"So I understand. Would you permit me to examine your own, so that I need not disturb Sir James'?"

"Of course." He got the knife from his carpetbag and handed it to his lordship. "Mind you don't cut yourself; that blade is razor sharp."

Lord Darcy eased the onyx-handled knife from its black couirbouilli sheath. The gleaming blade was a perfect isosceles triangle, five inches from handguard to point and two inches wide at the handguard. Lord Darcy turned it and looked at the base of the pommel. "This is your monogram and symbol. I presume Sir James' knife is identified in the same way?"

"Yes, my lord."

"Would you mind looking at that knife and telling me whether you can positively identify it as his?"

"Oh, that's the first thing I looked at. Many's the time I've seen it, and it's his knife, all right."

"Excellent. That accounts for its being here." He slid the deadly-looking blade back into its sheath and handed it back to the little sorcerer.

"That blade is pure silver, Master Sean?" Lord Bontriomphe asked.

"Pure silver, my lord."

"Tell me: how do you keep a razor edge on anything that soft?"

Master Sean smiled broadly. "Well, I'll admit it's a hard job getting the edge on it in the first place. It has to be finished with jeweler's rouge and very soft kidskin. But it's only used as a symbolical knife, d'ye see. We never actually cut anything material with it, so it never needs to be sharpened again if a man's careful."

"But if you never cut anything with it," said Lord Bontriomphe, "then why sharpen it at all? Wouldn't it work as well if its edges were as dull as, say, a letter opener?"

Master Sean gave the London investigator a rather pained look. "My lord," he said with infinite patience, "this is a symbol of a *sharp* knife. I also have a slightly different one with blunt edges; it is a symbol for a *dull* knife. Your lordship should realize that, for many purposes, the best symbol for a thing is the thing itself."

Lord Bontriomphe grinned and raised one hand, palm outward. "Sorry, Master Sorcerer; my apologies. But please don't give me any lectures on advanced symbolic theory. I never could get it through my head."

"Is there anything else you wanted to look at, Bontriomphe?" Lord Darcy asked briskly. "If not, I suggest we be on our way, and permit Master Sean to go about his work. We will instruct the guards at the door that you are not to be disturbed, Master Sean. When you have finished, notify Chief Master-at-Arms Hennely Grayme that we should like an autopsy performed upon the body immediately. And I should appreciate it very much if you would go to the morgue and personally supervise the chirurgeon's work."

"Very well. I'll see to it. I'll get the report to My Lord Marquis' office as soon as possible."

"Excellent. Come, Bontriomphe; there is work to be done."

# 11

AS LORD BONTRIOMPHE gave instructions to the Armsmen outside the late Master Sir James Zwinge's room, Lord Darcy walked across the hall to the door facing the murder room and rapped briskly on it at a point just above the keyhole.

"Are you decent, Your Grace?"

There was a muffled flurry of movement inside, and the door flew open. "Lord Darcy!" said the Dowager Duchess of Cumberland, flashing him a brilliant smile. "You startled me, my lord."

Lord Darcy pitched his own voice low enough so that the Armsmen and Lord Bontriomphe could not hear. "There is an old adage to the effect that people who listen at keyholes often hear things that startle them."

Raising his voice to a normal speaking tone, he went on. "I should like to speak to Your Grace privately for a moment, if I may."

"Certainly, my lord." She stepped back to let him in the room, and he closed the door behind him.

"What is it?" she asked.

"A few quick questions, Mary. I need your help."

"I thought you were going back to Cherbourg as soon as you got Master Sean out of the Tower."

"Circumstances have changed," he cut in. "Bontriomphe and I are working together on the case. But never mind that now. When you told me about the Damoselle Tia last night, the one thing you failed to mention was her connection with Sir Thomas Leseaux."

Her Grace's blue eyes widened. "But—aside from the fact that he was among those who recommended her for apprenticeship in the Guild, I don't know of any connection. Why?"

Lord Darcy frowned in thought. "Unless I am very much mistaken, the connection goes a great deal deeper than that. Sir Thomas is in love with the girl —or thinks he is. He is also afraid that she might be mixed up in something illegal, something criminal— and he is afraid to admit the possibility to himself."

"Criminal? Do you mean Black Magic or . . ." she hesitated, "the actual murder of Sir James?"

"I don't know. It might be either or both—or something completely different. But I am not so much interested in what Sir Thomas suspects as I am in what the girl was and is actually doing that may be connected with the murder. At the same time, I do not want her to know that she is suspected in any way. Therefore, I would rather not question her myself. She has already undergone the routine questioning by a plainclothes Sergeant-at-Arms; to subject her to any further questioning would indicate that we have singled her out for special treatment. So far, she does not know that she was seen leaving Sir James' room, and I am not ready for her to know yet."

"You want me to question her, then?" asked the

Duchess, her eyes almost sparkling with animation.

"Precisely. I know you, Mary; you are going to snoop anyway, and I would prefer that all the snoopers in this case have their activities co-ordinated as much as possible. So your job will be the Damoselle Tia. Question her—but not directly. Use indirectness and subtlety. Get to know her; gain her confidence if you can. Certainly there would be nothing suspicious about the two of you discussing the murder. I dare say everyone in the hotel is discussing it."

She laughed. "Discussing it? Haven't you felt the psychic tension in this place?"

"To a certain extent, but not, obviously, to the degree that you can sense it."

"Well, it's there, all right. There have been enough protective spells cast, enough amulets charged, enough charms and countercharms worked in the past twenty-four hours to ward off a full phalanx of the Legions of Hell." Her smile faded. "They're not only talking about it, my dear; they're doing something about it. The Guild is a damn sight more disturbed than it would appear upon the surface. There is a Black Sorcerer around with enough power to kill Master Sir James Zwinge. That's enough to make a Master edgy; what do you think it's doing to us journeymen? We've *got* to find him—and yet the counterspells in this hotel have obfuscated any trace of the kind of evil malignancy that should be hanging like swamp fog over the place. It has all of us in a tizzy."

"I shouldn't wonder," Lord Darcy said. "But at least that will allow you to bring up the subject at any time without arousing suspicion."

"True. But there's another factor we'll have to consider. It will soon be all over the place, if it isn't already, that you are working on this case, and it is certainly no secret that you and I are friends. If the Damoselle Tia knows that, *she* may try to pump *me* for information."

"Let her try, my dear. Find out what kind of information she's looking for. If she just asks questions that would be normal under the circumstances, that tells us one thing. If the questions seem a little too urgent or a trifle off-key, that tells us another. But don't give her any information except what is common knowledge. Tell her that I am reticent, that I am dull, that I am a bore—anything you like, so long as you make it clear to her that I tell you nothing.

"And try to keep a close watch on the girl, if you can do it without being too conspicuous about it.

"Will you do that for me, Mary?"

"I'll do my best, my lord."

"Excellent. Lord Bontriomphe and I will be setting up a temporary headquarters here in the hotel. There will be a Sergeant-at-Arms on duty there at all times. If you have any messages for me, let him know, or leave a sealed envelope with my name on it."

"Very well," said Her Grace, "I'll take the job. Be on about your snooping, and I shall be on about mine."

Lord Bontriomphe was waiting patiently in the hall outside.

"Where now?" he asked.

"Down to see the General Manager, Goodman Lewie," said Lord Darcy. "We may as well make arrangements for our temporary headquarters." They walked on down the hall. "Do you have three good Sergeants-at-Arms to spare for this duty, so we can have someone there twenty-four hours a day?"

"Easily," Lord Bontriomphe said. "Plainclothes or uniformed?"

"Uniformed, by all means. Everyone will know they are Armsmen anyway, and Armsmen in uniform will draw attention away from any plainclothes operatives we may need to use."

"Right. I'll arrange it with Chief Hennely."

Downstairs at the desk, Lord Bontriomphe asked to speak to Goodman Lewie Bolmer. The clerk disappeared and returned a minute later and said: "Goodman Lewie asks if you would be so good as to come back to his office, my lords."

The two investigators followed the clerk back to an office at the rear of the registration desk. Lewie Bolmer stood up as they were shown in.

The general manager looked haggard. Except for the dark pouches beneath his eyes, his saggy face looked pale and sallow, as though the folds and bags of translucent skin that made up his face were filled with soft suet instead of flesh. His smile seemed genuine, but it was as tired as the rest of of him.

"Good afternoon, your lordships," he said. "How may I help you?"

Lord Bontriomphe introduced Lord Darcy, and then explained their need for a temporary headquarters.

"I think . . . yes, we have just the thing," said the manager after a moment's thought. "I can put you in the night manager's office. He can double up with the afternoon manager if . . . uh . . . when he comes back to work. I'll clean out his desk and . . . uh . . . put his stuff in the other office. It's a fairly good-sized office—just a little smaller than this one. Will that do?"

"We'd like to take a look at it, if we may," said Bontriomphe.

"Certainly. If your lordships will come this way—"

He led them to a corridor that ran from the lobby to the rear of the building, just to one side of the registration desk. There were two doors leading off it to the right, just a few yards from the lobby. Further back, more doors led off on either side. Goodman Lewie opened the second of the two doors.

"The first one is the afternoon manager's office," he explained. "This is what I had in mind, your lordships." He waved his hand in a gesture that took in the fifteen-by-fifteen room.

"It looks fine to me," said Lord Bontriomphe. "What do you think, Darcy?"

"Perfectly satisfactory, I should say." He looked down the corridor toward the rear of the building. "Where does this corridor lead, Goodman Lewie?"

"Those are the service rooms back there, your lordship. Lumber rooms, furniture repair workshop, laundry, janitors' supplies—that sort of thing. The door at the far end is the back entrance. It opens into Potsmoke Alley, which is an extension of Upper Swandham Lane."

"Can it be opened from the outside?"

"Only with a key. It has a night lock on it. Anyone could go out, but one needs a key to get back in."

"I have an idea," said Lord Bontriomphe. "We can station an Armsman back there to make sure no unauthorized person comes in, then we'll unlock the door. That way, the Armsmen can come and go as necessary without tromping through your lobby and disturbing your guests. Would that be all right?"

"Of course, your lordship!"

"Good. I'll have a Sergeant-at-Arms down here to take charge of the office."

"Very well, your lordship. I'll have the desk cleared out. Will there be anything else?"

"Yes," said Lord Darcy. "One other thing. Yesterday, the hotel was closed to all except members of the Healers' and Sorcerers' Convention, was it not?"

"And their guests, yes. Only those who had business here were allowed in. The doormen had explicit orders about that."

"I see. Is any record kept?"

"Oh, yes. There is a register book kept at the door at all times. Not today, of course, since this is Visitor's Day, but during those times when the Convention is closed."

"I should like to see it, if I may," Lord Darcy said.

"You certainly may, your lordship. Shall we return to my office? I'll fetch the register book for you."

A minute or so later, the three men were looking at a clothbound register book which lay open on Bolmer's desk.

"That's the page for Wednesday," Lewie Bolmer said. "From midnight to midnight."

Lord Darcy and Lord Bontriomphe looked down the list. There were four columns, marked *Time Arrived*, *Name*, *Business*, and *Time Departed*.

There were not many entries; the first one was for half past six, when a man from the Royal Postal Service had delivered the mail; he had left again at 6:35. At twelve minutes of nine Commander Lord Ashley had arrived, giving as his business "Official message for Master Sorcerer Sean O Lochlainn." He had left at 9:55. At two minutes after nine, Lord Bontriomphe had come in, on "Personal business of the

Marquis de London." No time of departure was
noted. The next entry was for 9:51. It simply said
"Chief Master-at-Arms Hennely Grayme, and four
Men-at-Arms. On the King's Business."

"No help there," said Lord Bontriomphe. "But
then, I didn't expect there would be."

Lord Darcy grinned. "What kind of entry were
you expecting? '9:20 a.m.; Master Sorcerer Lucifer
S. Beelzebub. Business: To murder Master Sir James
Zwinge. Exit time: 9:31' I suppose?"

"That would have been helpful," admitted Lord
Bontriomphe.

"I notice there's no exit time down for you or for
the Armsmen." He looked up at Goodman Lewie.
"Why is that?"

The hotel manager was stifling a yawn. "Eh?
What, your lordship? The time of leaving? Well,
there were so many Armsmen in and out that I simply gave the doormen orders to allow any Officer of
the King's Peace to come and go as he pleased." He
stifled another yawn. "Pardon me. Lack of sleep. My
night manager, who has the midnight-to-nine shift,
didn't show up for work last night, so I had to take
over."

"Perfectly all right," said Lord Darcy, still looking
at the register book. There were more entries in the
afternoon, mostly merchants and manufacturers who
used sorcery or employed sorcerers in the course of
their business. One entry caught his eye.

"What's this?" he said, tapping it with his finger.

Lord Bontriomphe read it aloud: " '2:54; Commander Lord Ashley; official business with Manager
Bolmer.' No exit time marked."

"Wuh . . . well, your lordships, there were several
Navy men in and out. Official business, you know."

"Official business? Why did they want to talk to you?" Darcy asked.

"Not to me. To . . . to Paul Nichols, my night manager."

"About what?"

"I . . . I'm not at liberty to say, your lordship. Strict instructions from the Admiralty. In the King's Name."

"I see," said Lord Darcy in a hard voice. "Thank you, Goodman Lewie. There will be a Sergeant-at-Arms around later to take over that office. Come on, Bontriomphe." He turned and strode out of the office, with Lord Bontriomphe at his heels.

They were halfway across the lobby, threading their way through the crowded exhibits, before Lord Bontriomphe spoke. "Do I detect blood in your eye?"

"Damn right you do," snapped Darcy. "How far is the Admiralty Office from here?"

"Ten minutes if we walk, or we can take the coach and get there in three."

"The coach, by all means," said Lord Darcy.

* * *

Barney, the footman, was standing near the coach, which was drawn up alongside the curb a few yards from the front door of the Royal Steward.

"Barney," Lord Bontriomphe shouted. "Where's Denys?"

"Still in the pub, my lord." the footman called back.

"Get ready to go, I'll fetch him." He ran across the street to the pub and was out again thirty seconds later with the coachman running alongside him.

"To the Admiralty Office!" Lord Bontriomphe ordered as Denys climbed into his seat. "As fast as you can." He climbed inside with Lord Darcy.

"So Smollett is holding out on us," he said, as the coach started forward with a jerk.

"He knows something we don't, that's for certain," said Lord Darcy.

"Keep in mind that those orders to keep quiet were given to Bolmer yesterday, before the King ordered us to work together."

"True," said Lord Darcy, "but considering the fact that the Navy is all in a pother about a man who has suddenly turned up missing, and that Goodman Lewie Bolmer shows by his behavior that he is convinced that his night manager will not return, doesn't it seem odd to you that neither Smollett nor Ashley mentioned it to us this morning?"

"More than odd," Lord Bontriomphe agreed. "That's what I said: Smollett is holding out on us. You want to hold him while I poke him in the eye, or the other way around?"

"Neither," said Lord Darcy. "We'll each take an arm and twist."

# PART THREE

# 12

LORD BONTRIOMPHE had not misjudged the time very much; it was less than four minutes later when Darcy and Bontriomphe climbed out of the coach in front of the big, bulky, old building that housed the Admiralty offices of the Imperial Navy. They went up the steps and through the wide doors into a large anteroom that was almost the size of a hotel lobby. They were heading towards a desk marked *Information* when Lord Darcy suddenly spotted a familiar figure.

"There's our pigeon," he murmured to Lord Bontriomphe, then raised his voice:

"Ah, Commander Ashley."

Lord Ashley turned, recognized them, and gave them an affable smile. "Good afternoon, my lords. Can I do anything for you?"

"I certainly hope so," said Lord Darcy.

Lord Ashley's smile disappeared. "What's the trouble? Has anything happened?"

"I don't know. That's what I want you to tell me. Why is the Navy so interested in a certain Paul Nichols, the night manager at the Royal Steward?"

Lord Ashley blinked. "Didn't Captain Smollett tell you?"

"Sure he did," said Lord Bontriomphe. "He told us all about it. But we forgot. That's why we're here asking questions."

Commander Lord Ashley ignored the London investigator's sarcasm. There was a vaguely troubled look in his seaman's eyes. Abruptly he came to a decision. "That information will have to come from Captain Smollett. I'll take you to his office. May I tell him that you have come to get the information directly from him?"

"So," said Lord Darcy with a dry smile, "Captain Smollett prefers that his subordinates keep silent, eh?"

Lord Ashley grinned lopsidedly. "I have my orders. And there are good reasons for them. The Naval Intelligence Corps, after all, does not make a habit of broadcasting its information to the four winds."

"I'm aware of that," said Lord Darcy, "and I am not suggesting that the corps acquire such habits. Nonetheless, His Majesty's instructions were, I think, explicit."

"I'm certain it was merely an oversight on the captain's part. This affair has the whole Intelligence Corps in an uproar, and Captain Smollett and his staff, as I told you this morning, do not have any high hopes that the killers will be found."

"And frankly don't much care, I presume," said Lord Darcy.

"I wouldn't go so far as to say that, my lord; it is simply that we don't feel that the tracking down of hired Polish assassins is our job. We're not equipped for it. Our job is the impossible one of finding out everything that King Casimir's Navy is up to and keeping him from finding out anything at all about ours. You people are equipped and trained to catch murderers, and we—very rightly, I think—leave the job in your hands."

"We can't do it without the pertinent information," said Lord Darcy, "and that's what we're here to get."

"Well, I don't know whether the information is pertinent or not, but come along; I'll take you to Captain Smollett."

The two investigators followed the commander down a corridor, up a flight of stairs, and down another corridor toward the rear of the building.

There was a middle-aged petty officer sitting behind a desk in the outer office who looked up from his work as the three men entered. He did not even bother to look at the two civilians.

"Yes, My Lord Commander?" he said.

"Would you tell Captain Smollett that Lord Darcy and Lord Bontriomphe are here to see him. He will know what their business is."

"Aye, my lord." The petty officer got up from behind the desk, went into an inner office, and came out again a minute or so later. "Compliments of the Captain, my lords. He would like to see all three of you in his office immediately."

*There are three ways of doing things,* Lord Darcy thought to himself, *the right way, the wrong way, and the Navy way.*

Captain Smollett was standing behind his desk when they went into the room, a pipe clenched firmly between his teeth, his gray-fringed bald head gleaming in the afternoon sunlight that streamed through the windows at his back.

"Good afternoon, m'luds," he said briskly. "Didn't expect to see you again so soon. Trust you have some information for me."

"I was rather hoping you had some information for us, Captain," Lord Darcy said.

Smollett's eyebrows lifted. "Eh? Not much, I'm afraid," he said, speaking through his teeth and around his pipestem. "Nothing new has happened since this morning. That's why I was hoping that you had some information."

"It is not new information I want, Captain Smollett. By now, indeed, it may be rather stale.

"Yesterday afternoon at 2:54 your agent, Commander Lord Ashley, returned to the Royal Steward Hotel. After that, several other of your agents came and went. The General Manager, Goodman Lewie Bolmer, has informed us that he is under strict instructions from the Navy, in the King's Name, to give information to no one, including, presumably, duly authorized Officers of the King's Peace, operating under a special warrant which also permits them to act and speak in the King's Name.

"I could have forced the information from him but he was acting in good faith and he had enough troubles as it is. I felt that you could give me all the information he has and a great deal more besides. We met My Lord Commander downstairs, but doubtless he, too, is under orders, so, as with Goodman Lewie, it would not be worth my time to pry the information out of him when I can get it from you.

"This much we know: Goodman Paul Nichols, the night manager, failed to show up for work at midnight last night. This, apparently, is important; and yet, your agents were asking questions about him some nine hours before. What we want to know is why. I shall not ask you why we were not given this information this morning; I shall merely ask that we be given it now."

Captain Smollett was silent for the space of several seconds, his cold gray eyes looking with unblinking directness into Darcy's own. "Um," he said finally, "I suppose I deserve that. Should have mentioned it this morning. I admit it. Thing is, it just isn't in your jurisdiction—that is, normally it wouldn't be. We have men looking everywhere for Nichols, but he hasn't done a thing we can prove."

"What do you think he's done?"

"Stolen something," said Captain Smollett. "Trouble is, we can't prove the thing we think he's stolen ever existed. And if it did exist, we're not certain of its value."

"Very mysterious," said Lord Bontriomphe. "At least, to me. Does this have a beginning somewhere?"

"Hm-m-m. Beg your pardon. Don't mean to sound mysterious. Here, will you be seated? Brandy on the table over there. Pour them some brandy, Commander. Make yourselves comfortable. It's a rather longish story."

He sat down behind his desk, reached out toward a pile of file folders, and took an envelope out of the top one.

"Here's the picture: Zwinge was a busy man. Had a great many things to keep an eye on. Being Chief Forensic Sorcerer for the City of London would be a full-time job for an ordinary man." He looked at Lord Bontriomphe. "Be frank, m'lud. Did you ever suspect that he was working for the Naval Intelligence Corps?"

"Never," Bontriomphe admitted, "though Heaven

knows he worked hard enough. He was always busy, and he was one of those men who think that anything more than five hours sleep a night is an indication of sloth. Tell me, Captain, did My Lord Marquis know?"

"He was never told," said Captain Smollett. "Zwinge did say that he suspected that My Lord de London was aware of his Navy work, but if so he never mentioned it."

"He wouldn't," said Lord Bontriomphe.

"No, of course not. At any rate, Zwinge had a great many irons in the fire. More things going on in Europe than just this one affair, I can assure you. Nonetheless, he felt it necessary to go to this Healers and Sorcerers Convention. Look odd if he didn't, he said, what with his being right here in London and all. But of course he kept right on working, even there."

"That is undoubtedly why he put the special spell on the lock of his hotel room," said Lord Darcy.

"No doubt, no doubt," agreed Captain Smollett. "At any rate, yesterday morning he sent this letter to me by messenger from the hotel." He handed the envelope to Lord Darcy. "You'll notice it is stamped 7:45 a.m."

Lord Darcy looked at the outside of the envelope. It was addressed to Captain Percy Smollett and was marked "Personal." Darcy opened it and took out the single sheet of paper. "This is in code," said Lord Darcy.

"Of course," said Captain Smollett. He took another sheet from the file and handed it over. "Here is the clear," he said. Lord Darcy read the message aloud:

" 'Sir: I have a special packet for you containing

information of the utmost importance which I have just received. It is impossible for me to leave the hotel at this time, and I do not wish to entrust this information to a common messenger. Accordingly, I have given the envelope with my seal upon it to the hotel manager, Goodman Paul Nichols. He has placed it in the hotel safe and has been instructed to hand it over to your courier.' "

The note was signed with the single letter "Z."

Lord Darcy handed the papers back to the captain. "I see, Captain. Pray continue."

"As I said, the message arrived at 7:45. It was placed on my desk with the rest of my morning mail. Now—I didn't arrive here at the office until a few minutes before ten. Hadn't had time to even glance at my mail when Commander Ashley came in, bringing the news from Cherbourg that Barbour had been murdered—which was bad enough—and the further intelligence that Master Sir James had been stabbed to death only half an hour before. Since you already know of the importance we've attached to this affair, you'll understand that for the next few hours I was a very busy man. Didn't have a chance to look at my mail until well after two o'clock. When I decoded the letter, I sent Ashley, here, over to fetch the packet." He looked at the Commander. "You'd better take it from there, Commander. I'm sure Lord Darcy prefers to get his facts as directly as possible."

"Aye, sir." He turned to face Lord Darcy. "I went directly to the hotel and asked to see Goodman Lewie, and told him that Sir James had left an envelope addressed to Captain Smollett in the safe, to be delivered to the Navy.

"He said he knew nothing of it, and I told him that it had been left with Goodman Paul.

"He informed me that Goodman Paul had made no mention of it when he went off duty at nine, but he agreed to open the safe and get the envelope out.

"I was standing by him when he opened the safe. It's a small one and there wasn't much inside it. Certainly there was no envelope addressed to Captain Smollett, nor any sign that there had ever been one. Bolmer swore that he had not opened the safe that morning, and both of the desk clerks substantiated that. Bolmer and his two assistant managers are the only ones who know the combination, and the security spell only allows the assistant managers to open the safe during the time they are on duty, that is, from three p.m. till midnight for the afternoon manager and from midnight to nine a.m. for the night manager."

Lord Darcy nodded. "That does rather narrow it down to Goodman Paul. Only he could have removed that packet from the safe."

"My thought exactly," said Commander Lord Ashley. "Naturally, I insisted upon speaking to Paul Nichols immediately, and asked for his home address. It turns out that he lived there in the hotel; he has a room up on the top floor. Bolmer took me up and I knocked on Nichols' door, got no answer, and Bolmer let us in with a pass key. Nichols wasn't in. His bed was made and certainly didn't look as though it had been slept in. Bolmer said that was odd because usually Nichols goes out to have a bite to eat after he gets off work, then comes back to the hotel and sleeps until around six o'clock."

"Did you find out whether Nichols took advantage of the hotel's maid service?" Lord Darcy asked.

The Commander nodded. "He did. Nichols quite often went out of an evening, and the maid had orders to make up his room between 7:30 and 8:30. I looked the room over and checked through his things. He didn't seem to have packed anything. His suitcase, empty, was in the closet, and Bolmer said that as far as he knew it was the only suitcase Nichols owned."

"That's the advantage of being a counterspy," said Lord Bontriomphe with a sigh. "If an officer of the King's Peace tried searching a man's room without a warrant he'd find himself in the Court of the King's Bench trying to explain to My Lord Justice how he had come to make such a mistake."

"Well, I didn't really search the place," Ashley said. "I was just taking a look around."

"So," said Lord Darcy, "you found that Nichols was not there and apparently had not been to bed since the bed was made on the previous evening."

"Right. I questioned some of the hotel servants. No one had seen him come back from his breakfast— or perhaps for him it was supper—so I instructed Bolmer to say nothing but to let us know as soon as Nichols returned. Then I came back here and reported to Captain Smollett."

Lord Darcy nodded and looked back at the captain.

"Been looking for him ever since. Sent men over to the hotel, to wait for him to come to work at midnight; he didn't show up. Still no sign of him. Not a trace."

"You suspect then," said Lord Darcy, "that the disappearance of the packet and the disappearance of Nichols are linked. I agree with you. The contents of that envelope would have been in code, would they not, Captain?"

"Yes indeed. And not the simple code used for that

note, either. Furthermore, Zwinge always used ink and paper with a special spell on it. If an unauthorized person broke the seal, the writing would vanish before he could get the paper out of the envelope."

"Obviously, then, Nichols did not remove it from the safe, read it over, and decide that it was valuable on the spur of the moment."

"Obviously not," agreed Captain Smollett. "Furthermore, Zwinge was no fool. Wouldn't have given it to. Nichols unless he trusted him. Also, since the envelope had that protective spell on it, the only way to read the contents would be to get it to a magician who is clever enough and powerful enough to analyze and nullify Master Sir James Zwinge's spell."

"Do you have any idea what sort of information might have been in that envelope, Captain Smollett?" Lord Darcy asked.

"None. None whatsoever. Can't have been terribly urgent—that is, not requiring immediate action—or Zwinge would have brought it here himself, in spite of everything. But it was certainly important enough to drive King Casimir's agents to murder to get it."

"How do you think this ties in with the murder of Barbour, then? And with the Navy's new secret weapon?"

The captain scowled and puffed at his pipe for a few seconds. "Now there we're on shaky ground. Obviously it was discovered that Barbour was a double agent; otherwise he wouldn't have been killed."

"I agree with you there," said Lord Darcy.

"Very well. But that leaves us several possible speculations about FitzJean and about the Poles' knowledge of the confusion projector.

"If, as we hope, they know nothing of the device,

then they knew nothing about FitzJean except the purely mendacious material which Barbour had passed on to them. When they discovered he was a double agent, they simply killed him and ignored FitzJean. Information on fleet disposition isn't worth taking any great pains over.

"However, I am afraid that we would be unrealistically optimistic to put any faith in the notion that the Polish Government is entirely unaware of the existence of the confusion projector.

"Much more likely, they are sparing no effort to find out what it is and how it works—which would still indicate that they know nothing whatever about FitzJean. If they did, they would certainly not have killed Barbour until they could get their hands on FitzJean—which, of course, they may have done. Or again they may already have the secret and not give two hoots in Hell about FitzJean.

"And finally, there is the possibility that FitzJean was himself a Polish agent sent in to test Barbour. When they discovered that Barbour's output to them differed drastically from what they knew the input to be, his death warrant was sealed."

Captain Smollett spread his hands. "But these are mere speculations; they tell us nothing. Important thing right now's to get our hands on Paul Nichols. Would have given you this before, but, as I said, there's actually nothing we can hold Nichols on. Can't prove that envelope ever existed, much less that he stole it. So how could we turn the matter over to Officers of the King's Justice?"

"My dear Captain, you should study something besides Admiralty law. Fleeing the scene of a crime is always enough evidence to warrant asking for a man's arrest and detention for questioning. Now the first question any investigator asks himself is: Where would the suspect go? To the Polish Embassy?"

Smollett shook his head. "No. There's a twenty-four hour watch on everyone entering or leaving the Polish Embassy."

"Exactly. I know that. So do the Poles. But the local headquarters for this Polish espionage ring is somewhere in the City. Where?"

"Wish I knew," said the captain. "Give half a year's pay for that information. We have reason to believe that there are at least three separate rings operating here in London, each unknown to the others, or at least known only to a select few. We know some of the agents, of course. We keep an eye on 'em; I've had my men watching every known agent in London for the past eighteen hours. So far, no news. But what we do *not* know is where any of their headquarters might be. Hate to admit it, but it's true. We have no hint, no suggestion, no clue of any kind."

"Then the only way to find Nichols," Lord Darcy said, "is to comb London for him. And that requires legwork. While your men are searching for him covertly, Lord Bontriomphe and the Armsmen of London can be looking for him for questioning on the charge of fleeing the scene of a crime."

Bontriomphe nodded. "We can have a net out for him within an hour. If we find anything, Captain, I'll let you know immediately."

"Very good, m'lud."

"I'd better get started on it," Bontriomphe said, getting to his feet. "The quicker the better. If you need to contact me for any reason, Captain, send word to the Royal Steward. We have set up our headquarters there; there will be a Sergeant-at-Arms on duty at all times, and I shall be checking in there regularly."

"Excellent. Thank you, m'lud."

"I shall see you later, gentlemen. Good day." Lord Bontriomphe walked out the door as if he were pleased at the prospect of finally having something he could sink his teeth into.

* * *

"As for me, Captain," said Lord Darcy, "I should like to ask your indulgence in what I know may be a touchy matter."

"What might that be?"

"I should like to have a look at your secret files, most especially at the letters from Barbour concerning FitzJean and the confusion projector."

"M'lud," said Captain Smollett with a wintery smile, "any Intelligence organization is justly jealous of its secret files and our Corps is no exception. Until now, these files have been classified *Most Secret*. Barbour's existence as a double agent was known only to the high echelons of the Admiralty. But you've taken me to task once for withholding information. Won't happen again. I shall have the pertinent files brought in so that both you and Commander Ashley can study them. And may *I* ask *your* indulgence?"

"Certainly, Captain, what is it?"

"With your permission, I'd like to make Commander Lord Ashley the liaison officer between the civilian investigators and the Navy. To be more specific, between you and me. He knows the Navy, he knows Intelligence work, and he knows something about criminal investigation. He was in the Naval C.I.D. before he was transferred to this Corps. His orders will be to assist you in every possible way. You agree, m'lud?"

"Of course, Captain. A splendid idea."

"Very well, Commander; those are your orders then."

"Aye, aye, Captain." He smiled at Lord Darcy. "I'll keep out from underfoot as much as possible, my lord."

"That's settled, then," said Captain Smollett, getting to his feet. "Now I'll go get those files."

* * *

Master Sean O Lochlainn stood near the closed door of the murder room and surveyed its entire contents. Then he turned to Journeyman Sorcerer Lord John Quetzal who stood next to him. "Now, d'ye understand what we have to be careful of? We are not yet ready to take the preservative spell off the body, so we have to be careful that none of the spells that we're working with inside the room interfere with it. D'ye understand?"

Lord John Quetzal nodded. "Yes, Master, I think I do."

Master Sean smiled at him. "I think you do, too, my lad. You followed through on the blood tests beautifully." He paused. "By the bye, d'ye think you could do them by yourself next time, should you happen to be called upon to perform them?"

Lord John Quetzal glanced sideways at the little sorcerer. "The blood tests? Yes, Master Sorcerer, I think I could," he said firmly.

"Ah, good." Master Sean nodded with satisfaction. "*But*"—he raised a warning finger—"this next one's a little tougher.

"We're dealing here with psychic shock. Now, whenever a man's hurt, or when he dies, there's psychic shock—unless, of course, he just fades away in his sleep or something like that.

"But *here* we're talking about violence."

"I understand," said Lord John Quetzal.

"All right. Now, you're going to be my thurifer. The ingredients are laid out on the table. Now I'll ask *you* to prepare the thurible, seeing as how it's you that's got to use it."

"Very well, Master," said the young Mechicain nobleman, with the tiniest trace of uneasiness in his voice.

On the table near the door sat the instrument which Master Sean had taken from his symbol-decorated carpetbag. It was a brazen pot with a perforated brazen cap, which, when assembled, would swing from the end of a clutch of chains some three feet long. Now, it was open, on the table.

Lord John Quetzal took several tools from his own carpetbag. Under the watchful eye and sharp ear of Master Sean O Lochlainn, the young sorcerer prepared the contents of the thurible.

After placing the brazen pot on an iron tripod, he fired up several lumps of charcoal in the bottom of it. Then, from the row of jars and bottles which had been lined up on the table, he took various ingredients and put them into his special golden mixing bowl, using a small golden spoon. With his own pencil-sized golden wand, he cast a spell over each ingredient as he added it, stirring it into the mixture.

There was frankincense and sweet balsam, samonyl and fenogreek, turmeric and taelesin, sandalwood and cedarwood, and four other lesser known but even more powerful ingredients—added in a precise order, each with its unique and individual spell.

And when he had finished the mixing, and cast the final spell, the journeyman sorcerer lifted his head and turned his dark eyes to the tubby little Master.

Sean O Lochlainn nodded his head. "Very well done. *Very* well done." He smiled. "Now I'll not ask you if you know what you've done. It's a habit of mine to assume that a student lacks knowledge. Being, as it were, a student meself, I know how much knowledge I lack. And besides," he chuckled, "as Lord Darcy would tell you, I'm a man who's fond of lecturing.

"The spell we're about to perform is a dynamic spell, and must be warded off by a dynamic spell—which means that in order to protect the body I'll have to be working while you are censing the room. D'ye understand, my lad?"

"I do, Master."

"Very well. Now, when you place that mixture into the thurible, there will be given off a smoke, which is composed of many different kinds of small particles. Because of the spell you've cast on them, these particles will tend to be attracted to, and adhere to, the walls and the furniture in this room in a particular manner.

"They will form what we call hologram patterns upon the surfaces they touch. Each of the different kinds of smoke particles forms its own pattern according to the psychic influences which have been impressed upon those surfaces. And by understanding the totality of those patterns we may identify definitely those psychic impressions."

He folded his arms on his chest, looked up at the tall young Mechicain, and gave him his best Irish grin. "Ah, lad, you're the kind of student a man looks for. You listen when the old master talks, and you don't get bored by what you already know, because you're waiting for more information."

Again, that almost invisible flush colored John Quetzal's dark skin. "Yes, Master Sean," he said carefully, "I have learned pattern theory."

"Aye—pattern *theory* you've learned. But you're wise enough to admit that you know only theory, not practice." He nodded his head in satisfaction. "You'll make a fine forensic sorcerer, lad. A *fine* forensic sorcerer!" Then his smile twisted slightly. "That is, you have the right attitude, me lad. Now we'll see if you have the technique."

He turned away from Lord John Quetzal and looked again at the walls. "If you do this thing right, Lord John Quetzal, there will be, upon those walls, patterns in smoke particles, each individual pattern distinguished by the spell cast on the various substances, and the hologram patterns distinguished by the combination of those spells. No man without the Talent will see anything but slightly smudgy walls— if that. You and I will see the patterns, and I'll do my best to show you how to interpret them."

He turned again.

"Are you ready, my lad?"

Lord John Quetzal set his lips. "I'm ready, Master."

"Very well, then."

Master Sean took two wands from his symbol-decorated carpetbag, walked over to the corpse which lay near the edge of the desk, and stood over it. "I'm ready, lad. Go ahead. Watch your spells."

The young Mechicain blew gently on the lumps of charcoal in the bottom of the thurible until they flared red-orange, then, his lips muttering a special spell, he poured the aromatic contents of the golden

cup over the glowing coals. Immediately a dense
cloud of white smoke rose toward the ceiling. Lord
John Quetzal quickly fitted the perforated cap down
over the bowl, locked it in place, and picked up the
thurible by its clutch of chains. His left hand held the
end of the chains, his right hand held them about
halfway down, allowing the thurible to swing free.
He moved over to the nearest wall, swinging the
censer in a long arc, allowing the dense smoke to drift
toward it.

He moved along the wall step by step, swinging
the thurible rhythmically, his lips moving in time
with it, and the dense smoke drifted along the walls
and billowed upwards, spreading a clinging, heavy
fragrance through the room.

While his assistant performed the censing, the
Master Sorcerer stood immobile over the body, a
long wand of glittering crystal in each hand, his arms
flung wide to provide the psychic umbrella which
would protect the corpse from being affected by the
magical ritual that John Quetzal was enacting.

The Irish sorcerer's pose did not seem strained.
There was an aura of strength about him; he seemed
taller, somehow; and his thick torso had an appearance of hardness about it. The light from the gas
lamp glittered and flickered in the depths of the two
crystal wands, flashing sparkling rainbows about the
room.

The smoke from the censer avoided the area under
Master Sean's control. It billowed in great clouds,
but there seemed to be an invisible force that kept
that portion of the room totally clear of the tiny particles. Those microscopic bits of fragrant ash moved
toward walls, furniture and ceiling, each clinging in
its individual way—but none came near the powerful

figure of the Master Sorcerer who shielded one area of evidence from their effect.

Three times, the young sorcerer made the circuit of the room with his swinging thurible, and except for that one specially protected area, the air grew dimly blue with smoke.

Then, while Master Sean still remained unmoving, he went back to the table, placed the hot, smoking thurible on the iron tripod, removed the perforated cap, and replaced it with a solid cap which cut off the flow of smoke and smothered the burning coals.

From his own symbol-decorated carpetbag, he took a silver wand with a knoblike thickening at one end. Grasping it by the other end, he turned and traced symbols in the air toward each wall in turn.

As he did so, the fog of smoke moved even more strongly toward the walls, and the air quickly cleared.

After a moment, Lord John Quetzal softly said: "It is finished, Master."

Master Sean looked around the room, lowered his arms, walked over and put the two crystal wands back in his carpetbag. Then he surveyed the room once more.

"A fine job, my lad," he said. "Indeed a fine job. Now, can you tell me what happened here?"

Lord John Quetzal looked. Although both sorcerers were using their eyes, it was not their eyes with which they saw. To a man without the Talent, the psychic patterns wrought by the acts which had taken place within the room, and brought out by the censing process, would have been totally invisible. To a man with the Talent they were quite clear.

But while Lord John Quetzal could perceive the patterns, he had not yet had enough training to interpret them. Master Sean sensed his hesitation. "Go ahead, lad," he said. "Rely on your hunches. Make a guess. 'Tis the only way you can check on your perceptions, and thereby progress from supposition to certainty."

"Well," Lord John Quetzal began uncertainly, "it looks like—" He stopped, then said: "But of course that's ridiculous. It just couldn't be that way."

Master Sean let out his breath in an exasperated manner. "Oh, lad, lad! You're trying to second-guess yourself. You're trying to make a *logical* interpretation before you've subjectively absorbed the data. Now I'll ask you again. What does it seem to you happened?"

Lord John Quetzal took another look. This time he pivoted slowly, turning a full three hundred and sixty degrees, taking in every bit of his surroundings. Then, carefully, he said: "There was no one else in this room but Sir James . . ." He hesitated.

"That's correct, absolutely correct," said Master Sean. "Go on. You still haven't said what it is that looks paradoxical."

Lord John Quetzal said, in a faintly puzzled voice, "Master, it looks to me as though Sir James Zwinge were killed twice. Several minutes—perhaps as much as half an hour—intervened between the murders."

Master Sean smiled and nodded. "You almost have it, lad. I think the results of the autopsy will bear you out. But you haven't analyzed the full significance of what is there." He made a broad sweeping gesture with his arm. "Take a good look at what the patterns show. There are two strong patterns superimposed chronologically. Two successive psychic shocks occurred while our late colleague was alone in this room. And, as you've pointed out, they were separated in time by half an hour. The first, d'you see, was when he was *killed;* the second occurred when he *died*."

# 13

THE BROAD DOORS that led from the lobby of the Royal Steward Hotel to the main ballroom were closed but not locked. There was no sign upon the door that said *Convention Members Only;* at a Sorcerers Convention such signs were unnecessary. The spell on those doors was such that none of the lay visitors who were so eagerly thronging to the displays in the lobby would ever have thought of entering them—or, if the thought did occur to them, it would be dismissed in a matter of seconds.

Sir Thomas Leseaux and the Dowager Duchess of Cumberland pushed through the swinging doors. A few feet inside the ballroom Lady de Cumberland stopped and took a deep breath.

"Trouble, Your Grace?"

"Good Heavens, what a mob!" said Mary de Cumberland. "I feel as though they're breathing up all the fresh air in London."

The ballroom presented a picture that was both peaceful and relaxed in comparison with the lobby. The room was almost the same size but contained only a tenth as many people. And instead of the kaleidoscopic variety of color in the costumes displayed in the lobby, the costumes in the ballroom were of a few basic colors. There was the dominating pale blue of the Sorcerers, modified by the stark black-and-white of the priestly Healers, and the additional touch of episcopal purple. The dark rabbinical dress of the occasional Jewish Healer was hardly distinguishable from that of a priest, but an occasional flash of bright color showed the presence of a very few *Hakime,* Healers who were part of the entourages of various Ambassadors from the Islamic countries.

"Visitors Day," said Sir Thomas, "is simply something we must put up with, Your Grace. The people have a right to know what the Guild is doing; the Guild has the duty to inform the people."

Mary turned her bright blue eyes up to Sir Thomas' face. "My dear Sir Thomas, there are many acts that human beings must perform which are utterly necessary. That does not necessarily mean that they are enjoyable. Now, where is this lovely creature of yours?"

"A moment, Your Grace, let me look." Sir Thomas, who was a good two inches taller than the average, surveyed the ballroom. "Ah, there she is. Come, Your Grace."

The Dowager Duchess followed Sir Thomas across the floor. The Damoselle Tia was surrounded by a group of young, handsome journeymen. Mary of Cumberland smiled to herself. It was obvious that the young journeymen were not discussing the Art with the beautiful apprentice. Her 'prentice's smock was plain pale blue, and was not designed to be alluring, but on the Damoselle Tia . . .

And then the Dowager Duchess noticed something that had escaped her attention before: the Damoselle Tia was wearing arms which declared her to be an apprentice of His Grace, Charles Archbishop of York.

To Mary of Cumberland, the Damoselle Tia appeared somewhat taller than she had when the Duchess saw her leaving Master Sir James' room on the previous morning. Then she saw the reason. Tia was wearing shoes of fashion that had arisen in the southern part of the Polish Hegemony and had not yet been accepted in the fashion centers either of Poland or of the Empire. They were like ordinary slippers except that the toes came to a point and the heels were lifted above the floor by a spike some two-and-a-half inches long. *Good Heavens*, thought Mary to herself, *how can a woman wear such high heels without ruining her feet?*

Was it, she wondered, some psychological quirk? Tia was a tiny girl, a good inch less than five feet tall without those outré heels, and a good foot shorter than the Dowager Duchess of Cumberland. Did she wear those heels simply to increase her physical height?

No. Mary decided; Tia had too much self-assurance, too much confidence in her own abilities, to need the false prop of those little stilts. She wore them simply because they were the fashion she had become used to. They were "native costume," nothing more.

"Excuse me," said Sir Thomas Leseaux, pushing his way through the crowd that surrounded Tia. Every one of the journeymen looked thrice at Sir Thomas. Their first look told them that he did not wear the blue of a sorcerer. *A layman, then?* Their second look encompassed the ribbons on his left breast which proclaimed him a Doctor of Thaumaturgy and a Fellow of the Royal Thaumaturgical Society. *No, not a layman.* Their third look took in his unmistakable features, which identified him immediately as the brilliant theoretical sorcerer whose portrait was known to every apprentice of a week's standing. They stepped back, fading away from Tia in awe at the appearance of Sir Thomas.

\* \* \*

Tia had noticed that the handsome young sorcerers who were paying court to her seemed to be vanishing, and she looked up to discover the cause of the dispersion. Mary de Cumberland noticed that Tia's eyes lit up and a smile came to her pixieish face when she saw the tall figure of Sir Thomas Leseaux.

*Well, well,* she thought, *so Tia reciprocates Sir Thomas' feelings.* She remembered that Lord Darcy had said "Sir Thomas is in love with the girl—or thinks he is." But Lord Darcy was not a Sensitive. Since she herself was sensitive to a minor degree, she knew that there was no question about the feeling between the two.

Before Sir Thomas could speak the Damoselle Tia bowed her head. "Good afternoon, Sir Thomas."

"Good afternoon, Tia. I'm sorry to have dispersed your court.

"Your Grace," continued Sir Thomas, "may I present to you the Damoselle Tia. Tia, I should like you to know my friend, Mary, Duchess of Cumberland."

Tia curtsied. "It is an honor to meet Your Grace."

Then Sir Thomas looked at his watch and said, "Good Heavens! It's time for the meeting of the Royal Thaumaturgical Society." He gave both women a quick, brief smile. "I trust you ladies will forgive me. I shall see you later on."

Mary de Cumberland's smile was only partly directed towards Tia. The rest of it was self-congratulatory. Lord Darcy, she thought, would approve of her timing; by carefully checking the meeting time of the R.T.S., she had obtained an introduction by Sir Thomas and his immediate disappearance thereafter.

"Tia," she said, "have you tasted our English beer? Or our French wines?"

The girl's eyes sparkled. "The wines, yes, Your Grace. English beer? No." She hesitated. "I have heard they compare well with German beers."

Her Grace sniffed. "My dear Tia, that is like saying that claret compares with vinegar." She grinned. "Come on, let's get out of this solemn conclave and I'll introduce you to English beer."

The Sword Room of the Royal Steward was, like the lobby, thronged with visitors. In one of its booths, the Dowager Duchess of Cumberland lifted the chilled pewter mug.

"Tia, my dear," she said, "there are many drinks in this world. There are wines for the gourmet, there are whiskies and brandies for the men, there are sweet cordials for the women, and there are milk and lemonade for children—but for good friendly drinking, there is nothing that can compare with the honest beer of England."

Tia picked up her own mug and touched it to Mary's. "Your Grace," she said, "with an introduction like that, the brew of England shall be given its every opportunity."

She drank, draining half the mug. Then she looked

at Mary with her sparkling pixie eyes. "It *is* good, Your Grace!"

"Better than our French wines?" asked Mary, setting down her own mug half empty.

Tia laughed. "Right now, much better, Your Grace; I was thirsty."

Mary smiled back at her. "You're quite right, my dear. Wine is for the palate—beer is for the thirst."

Tia drank again from her mug. "You know, Your Grace, where I come from, it would be terribly presumptuous for a girl of my class even to sit down in the presence of a duchess, much less to sit down and have a beer with her in a public house."

"Fiddle!" said Mary de Cumberland. "I'm not a Peer of the Realm; I'm as much a commoner as you are."

Tia shook her head with a soft laugh. "It would make no difference, Your Grace. *Anyone* with a title is considered infinitely far above a common person like myself—at least, in the province of Banat, which, I confess, is all of the Polish Hegemony I have ever seen. So when I hear the title 'Duchess', I automatically give a start."

"I noticed," said Mary, "and I point out to you that anyone who aspires to a degree in Sorcery had better learn to handle symbols better than that."

"I know," the girl said softly. "I intend to try very hard, Your Grace."

"I'm sure you will, my dear." Then, changing the subject quickly: "Tell me, where did you learn Anglo-French? You speak it beautifully."

"My accent is terrible," Tia objected.

"Not at all! If you want to hear how the language *can* be butchered, you should hear some of our Londoners. Whoever taught you did very well."

"My Uncle Neapeler, my father's brother, taught me," Tia said. "He is a merchant who spent a part of his youth in the Angevin Empire. And Sir Thomas has been helping me a great deal—correcting my speech and teaching me the proper manners, according to the ways things are done here."

The Duchess nodded and then gave Tia a quick smile. "Speaking of Sir Thomas—I hope his title doesn't make you frightened of him."

The sparkle returned to Tia's eyes. "Frightened of Sir Thomas? Oh, Your Grace, *no!* He's been so good to me. Much better than I deserve, I'm sure.

"But, then, everyone has been so good to me since I came here. Everyone. Nowhere does one find the friendliness, the *good*ness that one finds in the realm of His Majesty King John."

"Not even in Italy?" The Dowager Duchess asked casually.

Tia's expression darkened. "They might have hanged me in Italy."

"Hanged you? My dear, what on earth for?"

After a moment's silence, the girl said: "It's no secret, I suppose. I was charged with practicing the Black Art in Italy."

The Dowager Duchess of Cumberland nodded gravely. "Yes. Go on. What happened?"

"Your Grace, I have never been able to stand by and watch people suffer. I think it is because I watched both my parents die when I was very young —within a few months of each other. I wanted so very much for them both to live, and there was nothing I could do. I was—helpless to do anything for them. All children experience that terrible feeling of helplessness at times, Your Grace—but this was a very special thing." There was a heavy somberness in her dark eyes.

Mary de Cumberland said nothing, but her sympathy was apparent.

"I was brought up by Uncle Neapeler—a kind and wondrous man. He has the Healing Talent, too, you see, but it is untrained." Tia was looking back down at her beer mug, running one tiny, dainty finger around and around its rim. "He had no opportunity to train it. He might never have known that he possessed it if he had not spent so many years of his life in the Angevin Empire, where such things are searched out. He found that I had it, and taught me all he knew—which was small enough.

"In the Slavonic States, a man's right to become a Healer is judged by his political connections and by his ability to pay. And the right to have the services of a trained Healer is judged in the same way. Uncle Neapeler is—*was*—a merchant, a hard man of business. But he was never rich except in comparison to the villagers, and he was politically suspect because of the time he had spent in the Imperial domains.

"He used his Talent, untrained as it was, to help the villagers and the peasants when they were ill. They all knew they could rely on him for help, no matter who they were, and they loved him for it. He brought me up in that tradition, Your Grace."

She stopped, compressed her lips, and took another drink from her mug. "Then—something happened. The Count's officers . . ." She stopped again. "I don't want to talk about that," she said after a moment. "I . . . I got away. To Italy. And there were sick people there. People who needed help. I helped them, and they gave me food and shelter. I had no money to support myself. I had nothing after . . . but

never mind. The poor helped me, for the help I could
give them. For the children.

"But those who did not know called it Black
Magic.

"First in Belluno. Then in Milano. Then in
Torino. Each time, the whisper went around that I
was practicing the Black Art. And each time, I had to
go on. Finally, I had to flee the Italian States alto-
gether.

"I got across the Imperial border and went to
Grenoble. I thought I would be safe. I thought I
could get a job of some kind—apprentice myself as a
lady's personal maid, perhaps, since it is an honored
profession. But the Grand Duke of Piemonte had
sent word ahead, and I was arrested by the Armsmen
in Grenoble.

"I was frightened. I had broken no Imperial law,
but the Piemontese wanted to extradite me. I was
brought before my lord the Marquis of Grenoble,
who heard my plea and turned the case over to the
Court of Justice of His Grace the Duke of Dauphine.
I was afraid they would just hand me over to the
Piemontese authorities as soon as they heard the
charge. Why should anyone listen to a nobody?"

"Things just aren't done that way under the
King's Justice," said the Dowager Duchess.

"I know," said Tia. "I found that out. I was
turned over to a special ecclesiastical commission for
examination." She drank again from the mug and
then looked straight into Mary of Cumberland's
eyes. "The commission cleared me," she said. "I had
practiced magic without a license, that was true. But
they said that that was not an extraditable offense
under the law. And the Sensitives of the commission

found that I had not practiced Black Magic in my
healing. They warned me, however, that I must not
practice magic in the Empire without a license to do
so.

"Father Dominique, the head of the commission,
told me that a Talent such as mine should be trained.
He introduced me to Sir Thomas, who was lecturing
at a seminar for Master Sorcerers in Grenoble, and
Sir Thomas brought me to England and introduced
me to His Grace the Archbishop of York.

"Do you know the Archbishop, Your Grace? He is
a saint, a perfect saint."

"I'm sure he'd be embarrassed to hear you say
so," said the Duchess with a smile, "but just between
us, I agree with you. He is a marvelous Sensitive.
And obviously"—she gestured toward the archiepis-
copal arms on Tia's shoulder—"His Grace's decision
was favorable. Quite favorable, I should say."

Tia nodded. "Yes. It was through the recommen-
dation of His Grace that I was accepted as an apprentice of the Guild."

Mary de Cumberland could sense the aura of dark
foreboding that hung like a pall around the girl.
"Well, now that your future is assured," she said
warmly, "you have nothing to worry about."

"No," said Tia with a little smile. "No. Nothing to
worry about." But there was bleakness in her eyes,
and the pall of darkness did not dissipate.

At that moment, the waiter reappeared and
coughed politely. "Your pardon, Your Grace." He
looked at Tia. "Your pardon, Damoselle. Are you
Apprentice Sorcerer Tia . . . uh . . . Einzig?" He hit
the final *g* a little too hard.

Tia smiled up at him. "Yes, I am. What is it?"

"Well, Damoselle, there's a man at the bar who would like to speak to you. He says you'll know him."

"Really?" Tia did not turn to look. She raised an eyebrow. "Which one?"

The waiter did not turn, either. He kept his voice low. "The chap at the bar, Damoselle, on the third stool from the right; the merchant in the mauve jacket."

Casually, Tia shifted her eyes toward the bar. So did the Dowager Duchess. She saw a dark man with bristling eyebrows, a heavy drooping moustache, and deep-set eyes that darted about like a ferret's. The jacket he wore was of the oddly-cut "Douglas style," which was a strong indication that he was a Manx-man, since the style was very little favored except on the Isle of Man.

She heard Tia gasp, "I . . . I'll speak to him. Would you excuse me, Your Grace?"

"Of course, my dear. Waiter, would you refill our mugs?"

Mary watched as Tia rose and walked over to the bar. She could see the stranger's face and Tia's back, but in the hash of emotion that was washing back and forth through the room, it was impossible to interpret Tia's emotions. As for the stranger, there was no way for her to catch his words. His face seemed immobile, his lips seemed hardly to move, and what movements they did make were covered by the heavy moustache. The entire conversation took less than two minutes. Then the stranger bowed his head to Tia, rose, and walked out of the Sword Room.

Tia stood where she was for perhaps another thirty seconds. Then she turned and came back to the booth where the Dowager Duchess of Cumberland waited. On her face was a look which Mary could only interpret as grim joy.

"Excuse me, Your Grace," she said. "A friend. We had not seen each other for some time." She sat down and picked up her tankard.

Then she said suddenly, "Pardon me, Your Grace. What o'clock is it?"

Mary looked at the watch on her wrist. "Twelve after six."

"Oh, dear," said Tia, "Sir Thomas told me specifically that I should wear evening costume after six."

Mary laughed. "He's right, of course. We should both have changed before this."

Tia leaned forward. "Your Grace," she said confidingly, "I must admit something. I'm not used to Angevin styles. Sir Thomas was good enough to buy me some evening dresses, and there is one in particular I have never worn before. I should like to wear it tonight, but"—her voice sank even lower—"I don't know how to wear the thing properly. Would Your Grace be so good as to come up and help me with it?"

"Surely, my dear," Mary said with a laugh, "under one condition."

"What's that, Your Grace?"

"The dress I have to wear normally requires a battalion of assistants to get it on. Do you think you can substitute for a battalion?"

The statement was untrue; the Duchess was perfectly capable of dressing herself, but Lord Darcy had asked her to keep an eye on this girl and, even though she was not certain that it was still necessary, she would obey his orders.

"I can certainly try, Your Grace," said Tia, smiling. "My room is two flights up."

"Good, we'll go up and strap you into your finery, then go down one flight and strap me into mine. Between the two of us we'll have every sorcerer in the place groveling at our feet."

The Duchess signed the bill that the waiter presented, and the two women left the Sword Room.

* * *

Tia turned the key in the door to her room. She pushed open the door and stopped. On the floor, just beyond the door, was an envelope. She picked it up and smiled at the Duchess. "Excuse me, Your Grace," she said, "The dress I was telling you about is in the closet over there. I would like Your Grace to give me your opinion on it. It's the blue one."

Mary walked over to the closet, opened it, and looked at the array of dresses, but before she could say anything she heard Tia's voice behind her. She could not understand the words of the girl's short expletive, but she could feel the anger in them. Slowly she turned around and said, "What seems to be the trouble?"

"Trouble?" the girl's eyes flashed fire. Her right hand crumpled the envelope and then with a convulsive gesture threw it into the wastebasket nearby. "No trouble, Your Grace, no trouble at all." Her smile was forced. She walked over to the closet and looked at the dress. She stared at it without saying anything.

Mary of Cumberland stepped back. "It's a lovely dress, Tia," she said quietly. "You'll look magnificent in it." With one lightning-like movement she reached out to the wastebasket, grabbed the piece of paper Tia had thrown away, and slipped it into her pocket. "Yes," she said, "a very beautiful dress."

Mary could sense the girl's hesitation and confusion. Something in that note had upset her, had changed her plans, and now she was trying to think of what to do next.

Tia turned, a pained look on her face. "Your Grace, I don't . . . I don't feel well. I should like to lie down for a few minutes." For a moment, Mary de Cumberland thought she should offer her services as a Healer. Then she realized that that would simply add to the confusion. Tia had no headache. She simply wanted to get rid of her guest. There was nothing Mary could do.

"Of course, my dear. I understand. I shall," she smiled, realizing she was repeating Sir Thomas' words, "see you later on, then. Good evening, my dear."

She went out into the hall and heard the door close behind her. *What now?* she thought. There was no way of intruding on Tia without making her intrusion obvious. What to do next?

She went down the stairs. Halfway down she took out the note that had been under Tia's door, the note she had retrieved from the wastebasket. She opened it and looked at it.

It was in a language she could not identify. Not a single word of it was understandable. The only thing that stood out was a number that was easily recognizable.

*7:00.*

Nothing else was comprehensible.

## 14

LORD DARCY LEANED BACK in the hard, straight-backed chair that apparently epitomized Admiralty furniture and stretched his back muscles. "Ahhh-h-h . . ." he exhaled audibly. He felt as though weariness had settled into every cell of his body.

Then he leaned forward again, closed the folder on the table in front of him, and looked across the table at Lord Ashley.

"Doesn't tell us much, does it, my lord?"

Lord Ashley shook his head. "No, my lord. None of them do. The mysterious FitzJean remains as mysterious as ever."

Lord Darcy pushed the folder away from him. "Agreed." He drummed his fingers on the tabletop. "We have no clue from Barbour as to FitzJean's identity. The Admiralty staff at Cherbourg Naval Base did not even know of Barbour's existence. Unless something unexpected turns up, we will get no further information about FitzJean from that end."

"Do you see any clues at this end, my lord?"

"Well, look at the data." Lord Darcy gestured toward the pile of folders. "Only three men, presumably, know how to build and how to activate the confusion projector: Sir Lyon Grey, Sir Thomas Leseaux, and the late Sir James Zwinge. Of course, it is possible that that information was stolen from them, but let us explore the first possibility that suggests itself: Could it have been one of them?"

The Commander frowned. "It's hard to imagine that such respected and trusted men could betray the Empire."

"Indeed," said Lord Darcy. "It is difficult to imagine why *any* highly-placed officer could betray the Empire. But it has happened before, and we must consider the possibility.

"What about Sir Thomas, for instance? He worked out the theory and the mathematics for this device. What about Sir Lyon, or Sir James? They collaborated on working out the thaumaturgical engineering technique which made the device a working reality.

"If you had to pick one of the three, my lord, which would it be?"

The Commander leaned back in his chair and looked up, away from the low-hanging gas lamp, at the shadowed beams of the high ceiling.

"Well," he said after a moment, "first off, I'd eliminate Sir Thomas. Since the basic discovery was his, it would have been much simpler all around for him to have sold it directly to His Slavonic Majesty's Government in the first place, if he needed money that badly."

"Agreed," said Lord Darcy tonelessly.

"Sir Lyon," Commander Ashley continued, "has

plenty of money in his own right. I don't say that a quarter of a million silver sovereigns would mean nothing to him, but it hardly seems enough to entice a man in his position to commit treason."

"Agreed," Lord Darcy repeated.

"Sir James?" Ashley paused. "I don't know. Certainly he was not a wealthy man."

He stared at the ceiling for another twenty seconds, then lowered his head and looked at Darcy. "Here's a suggestion for you, my lord. I don't know how good it is, but we can try it for size."

"Proceed," said Lord Darcy. "I should be grateful for any light you may shed upon the subject."

"All right; suppose that Zwinge and Barbour were in this together. Naturally, to cover themselves, they would have to invent the mysterious FitzJean. No one ever saw FitzJean and Barbour together. Our agents saw him enter Barbour's place, and they saw him leave it. He came from nowhere and vanished into nowhere. What could be simpler than for Barbour himself to personate this mysterious being? Barbour, after all, actually did have contacts with Polish agents."

"Barbour wasn't Zwinge's only contact," Lord Darcy pointed out. "Why not use one of the others, and quietly sell the secret without all this play-acting?"

The Commander put his hand on the table, palm up. "What would happen if he did? As soon as the Royal Polish Navy was equipped with this device, we would find it out. We would know that one of those three men had sold it. Our first suspicion would naturally fall on Zwinge, because, of the three, only he was known to have had any contacts with Polish agents.

"After all, an ordinary man with a secret to sell can't simply say to himself, 'Well, I guess I'll just dot out and peddle it to a Polish agent.' Polish agents aren't that easy to find."

"True," Lord Darcy said thoughtfully. "It is difficult to sell something if you don't know how to get in contact with your customers. Pray continue."

"Very well then. In order to divert suspicion from himself, he sets up this little playlet with Barbour. Everyone is looking for the mysterious FitzJean. A trap is laid for him. Meanwhile, Barbour is actually dealing with the Poles, giving them the same story about FitzJean."

"How was the playlet to end, then?" Lord Darcy asked.

"Well, let's see. The secret is given to the Poles. The Poles pay off Barbour. I imagine Zwinge would have found some excuse to be there at the same time. I doubt if he would have trusted Barbour with five thousand golden sovereigns.

"The trap for the mysterious FitzJean fails, of course, since there is no FitzJean, and—after we find that the Polish Navy has the confusion projector— Zwinge's excuse is: 'FitzJean must have become suspicious of Barbour and peddled the secret elsewhere.'

"Zwinge may have intended to pay off Barbour, to split the money with him, or he may have intended to kill him. We can't know which."

"Interesting," said Lord Darcy. "There is certainly nothing impossible about just such a plan having been conceived, but, if so, the plan did not come off. What, then, are your theories as to what actually *did* happen?"

"Personally," said the Commander, "I believe that the Poles discovered that Barbour was working for Zed, and that Zed was Sir James. Now then, if my hypothesis is anywhere close to the truth, there are at least two possible explanations for what happened.

"One: The Poles decided that the whole business about the confusion projector was mere bait for some kind of trap, a hoax cooked up for some reason by Sir James; so they sent out agents to eliminate both.

"Or, two: They had reason to believe that Sir James actually was a traitor and was ready to negotiate with them. They would know that Sir James wouldn't give the plans and specifications for the device to Barbour unless all the arrangements were made. But they would also know that he would have had to have those plans in a place where he could lay his hands on them quickly. He must have had them already drawn up and hidden somewhere; he could hardly have expected to be able to sit down and draw them from memory at the snap of a finger.

"So, while one group of agents is dealing with Barbour in Cherbourg, another is watching Zwinge in London. Arrangements for the payoff are made in Cherbourg, and Barbour sends this information to Zwinge. Zwinge, not knowing he is being watched by Polish agents, fetches the plans to send them to Barbour. But now, the Poles know where those plans are because Zwinge has taken them from their hiding place. They send orders to Cherbourg to dispose of Barbour, and the agents here kill Zwinge and grab the plans, thereby saving themselves five thousand golden sovereigns."

"I must admit," said Lord Darcy slowly, "that my lack of knowledge of international intelligence networks has hampered me. That theory would never have occurred to me. What about the actual mechanism of Sir James' murder? How did the Polish agents actually go about killing him?"

Commander Lord Ashley shrugged eloquently. "Now there you have me, my lord. My knowledge of black magic is nil, and, in spite of Captain Smollett's statement of my qualifications, I am forced to admit that my experience in the Naval C.I.D. never included a murder investigation."

Lord Darcy laughed. "Well, that is honest enough, anyway. I hope this investigation will allow you to see how we poor benighted civilians go about it. What o'clock is it?" He looked at the watch at his wrist. "Heavens! It's after six. I thought the Admiralty closed at six o'clock."

The Commander grinned. "I daresay Captain Smollett left word for us not to be disturbed."

"Of course," said Lord Darcy. "All right. Let's put these folders back in their files and go to the hotel. I want to ask Sir Lyon Grey some questions if we can get hold of him, and also I should like to speak to His Grace the Archbishop of York. We need to know more about a girl named Tia Einzig."

"Tia Einzig?" Lord Ashley blinked. The name was totally new to him.

"I'll tell you what little I know about her on the way over to the hotel. Will the Admiralty have transportation for us? Or will we have to find a cab?"

"I'm afraid the Admiralty coaches are all locked up at six, my lord," said the Commander. "We'll have to take a cab—if we can find one."

"If not, we can walk," said Lord Darcy. "It's not as if the Royal Steward were halfway across the city."

A few minutes later, they walked down the darkened corridors of the Admiralty offices. In the lobby, an armed Petty Officer let them out through the front door. "Awfully foggy out tonight, my lords," he said. "Trust you have a good ride. Captain Smollett left orders that a coach be waiting for you."

"Let us thank God for small favors," said Lord Darcy.

The fog was even heavier than it had been the night before. At the curb, barely visible in the dim glow of the gas lamp above the doors of the Admiralty Building, stood a coach bearing the Admiralty arms. The two men went down the steps to the curb. Commander Lord Ashley said:

"Petty Officer Hosquins, is that you?"

"Yes, My Lord Commander," came a voice from the driver's seat, "Captain Smollett told us to wait for you."

"Excellent. Take us to the Royal Steward, then." And the two men climbed into the coach.

* * *

It took longer to make the trip than it had earlier that afternoon. Most of the visitors, anticipating the fog, had gone home. Lord Darcy and Lord Ashley found the lobby almost deserted. A man wearing the silver-slashed blue of a Master Sorcerer was looking at one of the displays. Lord Darcy and Lord Ashley went over to him and Lord Darcy tapped him on the shoulder.

"Your pardon, Master Sorcerer," he said formally. "I am Lord Darcy, special investigator under a King's Warrant, and I would appreciate it if you could tell me where I might find Sir Lyon Gandolphus Grey."

The master sorcerer turned, an obsequious smile

on his face. "Ah, Lord Darcy," he said. "It is indeed a pleasure to meet your lordship. I am Master Ewen MacAlister. My very good friend Master Sean O Lochlainn has told me a great deal about you, your lordship." Then his face fell in sudden gloom. "I am sorry to say, your lordship, that Grand Master Sir Lyon is unavailable at the moment. He is attending a Special Executive Session of the top officers of the Royal Thaumaturgical Society and the Sorcerers Guild. Can I do anything else to help your lordships?"

Lord Darcy refrained from pointing out that thus far he had done nothing at all to help their lordships. "Ah, that is too bad. But no matter. Tell me, is His Grace the Archbishop of York also attending that meeting?"

"Oh no, your lordship. His Grace is not a member of the Executive Committee. His ecclesiastical ties are much too onerous to permit him to take on the added burden. As a matter of fact, I saw His Grace only a few moments ago. He is taking his evening tea in the restaurant—in the Buckler Room, your lordship."

He lifted his hand and took a quick glance at his wristwatch. "Yes, that was only a few minutes ago, your lordships. His Grace should still be there.

"Tell me, is there anything else I can do to help your lordships?" Before either of them could answer, he went on, "Can I do anything that will aid you in apprehending the fiendish criminal who perpetrated the heinous murder of"—he suddenly looked very sad—"our good friend Master Sir James? A deplorable thing. Is your lordship prepared to make an arrest?"

"We shall do our best, Master Ewen," said Lord Darcy briskly.

"We thank you for your information. Good evening, Master Ewen, and thank you again."

He and Lord Ashley turned and walked toward the restaurant, leaving Master Ewen MacAlister looking blankly after them.

"Master Ewen MacAlister, eh?" said Lord Ashley. "Oily little bastard, isn't he?"

"I should have known him, from Master Sean's description, even if he had not introduced himself."

"Is there any possibility, my lord," Lord Ashley said thoughtfully, "that Master Ewen is involved in the matter?"

Lord Darcy took two more steps before he answered the question. "I shall be honest with you," he said then. "Although I have no evidence, I feel it highly probable that Master Ewen MacAlister is one of the prime movers in the mystery which surrounds Sir James' death."

Lord Ashley looked surprised. "You didn't seem disposed to question him any further."

"I have read the statement he made to Lord Bontriomphe yesterday. He was in his room all that morning until ten or fifteen minutes after nine. He is not sure of the time. After that, he was down in the lobby. Master Sean corroborates a part of his testimony. The interesting thing, however, is that Master Ewen's room is on the floor above, and directly over, the room in which Sir James was killed."

"That *is* food for thought," said Ashley as they approached the door of the Buckler Room.

Lord Darcy pushed the door open and the two men went in. The courtyard outside, which had been visible that morning from Sir James' room, was now shrouded in fog, but the gas lamps gave bright illumination to the restaurant itself. The two men stopped and surveyed the room. At one table an elderly man in episcopal purple sat by himself, sipping tea.

Lord Darcy said, "That, I believe, is His Grace of York." They walked toward the table.

The Archbishop appeared to be deep in thought. He had a notebook on the table and was carefully marking down symbols upon its open pages.

"My apologies for this interruption, Your Grace," said Lord Darcy politely. "I would not willingly disturb your cogitations, but I come upon the King's Business."

The old man looked up with a smile, the light from the gas lamps making a halo of the silver hair that surrounded his purple skullcap. Without rising he extended his hand. "You do not interrupt, my lord," he said gently. "My time is yours. You are Lord Darcy from Rouen, I believe?"

"I am, Your Grace," said Lord Darcy, "and this is Commander Lord Ashley of the Imperial Naval Intelligence Corps."

"Very good," said the wise old Sensitive. "Please be seated, my lords. Thank you. You come then to discuss the problem propounded by the death of Sir James Zwinge."

"We do, Your Grace," said Lord Darcy, settling himself in his chair. His Grace of York folded his hands upon the table.

"I am at your service. Anything that may be done to clear this matter up . . ."

"Your Grace is most kind," said Lord Darcy. "I

am not, as you know a Talented man," he began, "and there are, therefore, certain data which you may possess that I do not."

"Very probably. Such as what?"

"As I understand it, it would be difficult for a sorcerer to perform a rite of Black Magic within this hotel without giving himself away. Furthermore, every sorcerer here has been examined for orthodoxy of practice and carries a license signed by his diocesan bishop attesting to that examination."

"And so your question is," the Archbishop interjected smoothly, "how is it such a person could have escaped our notice."

"Precisely."

"Very well, I shall attempt an explanation. Let us begin with the license to practice. This license is given to an individual sorcerer when, upon completing his apprenticeship, he becomes qualified, according to the rules of the Guild, to practice his Art. Each three years thereafter he is reexamined and his license renewed if he passes the qualifications. You are aware of this?"

Lord Darcy nodded. "Yes, Your Grace."

"Very well," said the Archbishop, "but what would disqualify a sorcerer? What would prevent the Church from renewing his license? Well, there are many things, but chief among them would certainly be the practice of Black Magic. Unfortunately, except for a very few peculiarly qualified Sensitives it is not possible to detect when a man has practiced what is technically known as Black Magic if the spells are minor, if the harm they have done is relatively small, if the practitioner has not been too greatly corrupted by the practice. Do you follow?"

"I think so," said Lord Darcy.

"Then," continued the Archbishop, raising a finger, "you will see how it is that a man may get away with practicing Black Magic for some time before it has such an effect upon his psyche that it becomes obvious to a Board of Examiners that he can no longer be certified as practicing orthodox sorcery.

"Now a major crime, such as murder, would, of course, instantly be detectable to a certifying commission assembled for the purpose. The sorcerer in question would be required to undergo certain tests which he would automatically fail if he had used his Art to commit so heinous a crime as murder."

He turned a hand palm upward. "But you can see that it would be impossible to give every sorcerer here such a test. The Guild must assume that a member is orthodox unless there is sufficient evidence to warrant testing his orthodoxy."

"I quite understand that," said Lord Darcy, "but I also know that you are one of the most delicate Sensitives and one of the most powerful Healers in Christendom." He looked directly into the Archbishop's eyes. "I knew Lord Seiger of Yorkshire."

His Grace's eyes showed sadness. "Ah, yes, poor Seiger. A troubled soul. I did for him what I could, and yet I knew . . . yes, I knew . . . that in spite of everything he would not live long."

"Your Grace recognized him as a psychopathic killer," said Lord Darcy. "If we have such a killer in our midst now, would he not be as easily recognizable as was Lord Seiger?"

The Archbishop's troubled eyes looked first at Lord Darcy and then at Lord Ashley. "My lords," he said carefully, "the realm of magic is not that easily divisible into stark white and deadly black, nor can human souls be so easily judged. Lord Seiger was an extreme case, and, therefore, easily perceived and easily isolated, even though he was difficult to treat. But one cannot say 'this man is capable of killing,' and 'this man has killed,' and for that reason alone isolate him from society. For these traits are not necessarily evil. The ability to kill is a necessary survival characteristic of the human animal. To do away with it by fiat would be in essence to destroy our humanity. For instance, as a Sensitive I can detect that both of you are capable of killing; further, that both of you have killed other human beings. But that does not tell me whether or not these killings were justified. We Sensitives are not angels, my lords. We do not presume to the powers of God Himself. Only when there is true, deep-seated evil intent does it become so blatantly obvious that it is instantly detectable. I find, for instance, no such evil in either of you."

There was a long moment of silence and finally Lord Darcy said, "I believe I understand. Am I correct, however, in saying that, if every sorcerer here were to be given the standard tests for orthodoxy, anyone who had committed a murder by Black Magic would be detectable through these tests?"

"Oh, indeed," said the Archbishop, "indeed. Rest assured that if the secular arm cannot discover the culprit these tests *will* be given. But"—he emphasized his point with a long, thin finger—"as yet neither the Church nor the Guild has any evidence whatever that such black sorcery has been practiced. That is why we hold off."

"I see," said Lord Darcy. "One other thing, with Your Grace's permission. What do you know of a Damoselle Tia Einzig?"

"Damoselle Tia?" the saintly old man chuckled. "Ah, there is one, my lord, whom you may dismiss immediately from your mind if you suspect her of any complicity in this affair. In the past few months she has been examined twice by competent Boards and Examiners. She has never in her life practiced Black Magic."

"I disagree with you that that alone absolves her of complicity," said Lord Darcy. "A person could certainly be involved in a murder without having been the actual practitioner of Black Magic. Correct me if I am wrong."

The Archbishop looked thoughtful. "Well, you are right, of course. It would be possible . . . yes, yes, it *would* be possible . . . for Damoselle Tia to have committed a crime, so long as it was not the crime of Black Magic we would not necessarily have detected it." He smiled. "I assure you there is no harm in her, no harm at all."

His attention was distracted by someone who was approaching the table. Lord Darcy looked up. Mary of Cumberland was excited, but she was doing her best to keep from showing it.

"Your Grace," she said. She curtsied quickly, and then looked at Lord Darcy. "I"—she stopped and glanced at Lord Ashley and then at the Archbishop before looking back at Lord Darcy—"Is it all right to talk, my lord?"

"About your assignment?" Lord Darcy asked.

"Yes."

"We have just been discussing Tia. What new intelligence do you have for us?"

"Pray be seated, Your Grace," said the Archbishop. "I should like to hear anything you have to say about Tia."

In a low voice the Dowager Duchess of Cumberland told of her conversation with Tia Einzig, of Tia's short meeting with the man in the bar, and of the incident concerning the note in Tia's room, with an attention to detail and accuracy that not even Lord Bontriomphe could have surpassed.

"I have been looking all over for you," she finished up. "I went to the office; the Sergeant-at-Arms said he hadn't seen you. It was just lucky that I walked in here."

Lord Darcy held out his hand. "Let me see that piece of paper," he snapped. She handed it to him.

"That's why I was in such a hurry to find you. All I can read on it are the numbers."

"It is in Polish," said Lord Darcy. " 'Be at the *Dog and Hare* at seven o'clock,' " he translated. "There is no signature."

He glanced at his watch. "Three minutes of seven! Where the Devil is the *Dog and Hare?*"

"Could that be *'Hound and Hare'?*" said Lord Ashley. "That's a pub on Upper Swandhan Lane. We can just make it."

"You know of no *'Dog and Hare'?* No? Then we'll have to take a chance," Lord Darcy said. He turned to the Dowager Duchess. "Mary, you've done a magnificent job. I haven't time to thank you further just now. I must leave you in the company of the Archbishop. Your Grace must excuse us. Come on, Ashley. Where is this *Hound and Hare?*"

They walked out of the Buckler Room into the lobby of the hotel. Lord Ashley gestured. "There's a corridor that runs off the lobby here and opens into Potsmoke Alley. A turn to our right puts us on Upper Swandham Lane. No more than a minute and a half."

The two men pulled their cloaks about them and put up their hoods to guard against the chill of the fog outside. Ignoring the looks of several sorcerers who wondered why two men were charging across the lobby at high speed, they went down the corridor to the rear door. A Man-at-Arms was standing by the door.

"I'm Lord Darcy," snapped the investigator. "Tell Lord Bontriomphe that we are going to the *Hound and Hare;* that we shall return as soon as possible."

# 15

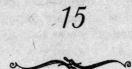

IN POTSMOKE ALLEY the fog closed about the two men, and when the rear door to the Royal Steward was closed behind them they were surrounded by darkness.

"This way," said Ashley. They turned right, feeling their way down Potsmoke Alley to the end of the block of buildings to where St. Swithin's Street crossed the narrow alley and widened it to become Upper Swandham Lane. Here there were a few gas lanterns glowing dimly in the fog, but even so it was difficult to see more than a few feet ahead.

As he and Ashley emerged from Potsmoke Alley, Lord Darcy could hear a distant *click! . . . click! . . . click! . . .* approaching through the fog to their right, on St. Swithin's Street. It sounded like someone wearing shoes with steel taps. To the left he could hear two pairs of leather-shod boots retreating, one fairly close by, the other farther down the street. Somewhere ahead, far down Upper Swandham Lane, he could hear a coach and pair clattering slowly across the cobblestones.

The two men crossed St. Swithin's Street and went down Upper Swandham Lane. "I think that's it ahead," said Lord Ashley, after a minute. "Yes. Yes, that's it."

The sign underneath the gas lantern depicted a bright blue gaze-hound in hot pursuit of an equally blue hare.

"All right, let's go in," said Lord Darcy. "Keep your hood up and your cloak closed. I shouldn't want anyone to see that Naval uniform. This way, we might be ordinary middle-class merchants."

"Right," said Lord Ashley, "I hope we can spot the girl. Do you know her when you see her?"

"I think so. Her Grace's description was quite detailed; there can't be many girls of her size and appearance wandering about London." He pushed open the door.

There was a long bar stretching along the full length of the wall to Darcy's left. Along the wall to his right was a series of booths that also stretched to the back of the room. In the rear there were several tables in the center of the floor, between the bar and the booths. Some men at one were playing cards, and a dart board on the back wall was responding with the *thunk!* . . . *thunk!* . . . *thunk!* . . . of darts thrown by a patron whose arm was as strong as his aim was weak.

Darcy and Ashley moved quickly to an empty spot at the bar. In spite of the number of customers the big room was not crowded.

"See anybody we know?" murmured Lord Ashley.

"Not from here," Lord Darcy said. "She could be in one of those rear booths. Or possibly she hasn't arrived yet."

"I think your second guess was correct," Ashley

said. "Take a look in the mirror behind the bar."

The mirror reflected the front door perfectly, and Lord Darcy easily recognized the tiny figure and beautiful face of Tia Einzig. As she walked across the room toward the back the identification was complete in Darcy's mind. "That's the girl," he said. "Notice the high heels that Her Grace mentioned."

And, he realized, those heels also explained those clicking footsteps he had heard on St. Swithin's Street. She hadn't been more than thirty seconds behind Ashley and himself.

\* \* \*

Tia did not look around. She walked straight toward the rear as if she knew exactly where the person she was to meet would be waiting. She went directly to the last booth, near the back door of the pub, and slid in on the far side, facing the front door.

"I wonder," said Lord Darcy, "is there somebody already in that booth? Or is she waiting for the person who sent her the note?"

"Let's just stroll back and see," said Lord Ashley.

"Good, but don't get too close. I don't want either of them to see our faces."

"We could watch the dart game," said Lord Ashley, "that might be interesting."

"Yes, let's," said Lord Darcy. They walked slowly back to the far end of the bar.

There was someone in the booth, seated directly across from Tia Einzig. It was obviously a man, but the hood of the cloak completely concealed his face, and he kept his head bent low over the table.

Lord Darcy said: "Let's move over to that table. I want to see if I can hear their conversation. But move carefully. Keep your face concealed without being obvious about it."

The nearest table was further toward the front of

the room than the booth that the two men were watching. They could no longer see the hooded man at all. His back was to them now and he kept his voice low, so that, while it was audible, it was not intelligible. Tia, however, was facing them, and, as Mary de Cumberland had told Lard Darcy the previous evening, the girl's voice had abnormal carrying power, even when she did not speak loudly.

For several seconds all they could hear was the low mutter of the man's voice, then Tia said, "If you didn't want him dead, why did you kill him?" Her expression was hard and cold, with an undertone of anger.

More muttering, then Tia again: "You discovered that Zed, the much-feared head of Imperial Naval Intelligence in Europe, was actually Master Sir James Zwinge, and you mean to sit there and tell me that King Casimir's Secret Service didn't want him dead."

A couple of angry words from the hooded man.

"I'll talk any way I please," said Tia. "*You* keep a civil tongue in *your* head."

She said nothing more for nearly a minute, as she listened to the hooded man with that unchanging stony expression of cold anger on her beautiful face. Then an icy smile came across her lips.

"No, I will not," she said. "I won't ask him. Not for you, not for Poland, not for King Casimir's whole damned army!"

A short phrase from the hooded man. Tia's cold smile widened just a trifle. "No, damn you, not for *him* either. And do you know why? Because I know *now* that you *lied* to me! Because I know *now* that he's safe from the torture chambers of the Polish Secret Service!"

The hooded man said something more. "Signing

his death warrant?" She laughed sharply, without humor. "Oh no. You've harassed me long enough. You've tried to force me to betray a country that has been good to me, and a man who loves me. I've lived in constant fear and terror because of you, but no longer. Oh, I'm going to sign a death warrant all right—yours! I'm going to blow this whole plot sky high. I'm going to tell the Imperial authorities everything I know, and I hope they hang you, you vicious, miserable little . . ."

She stopped suddenly and blinked. "What? She blinked again.

Lord Darcy, watching Tia's face covertly from beneath his hood, saw her expression change. Where before it had been stony, now it became wooden. The cold expression became no expression at all.

The Commander suddenly reached over and grabbed Darcy's wrist.

"Watch it!" he whispered harshly. "They're going to leave by the back door!"

Lord Darcy smiled inwardly. Lord Bontriomphe had mentioned that Ashley had occasional flashes of precognition, and here was an example of it. Such flashes came to an untrained Talent in moments of personal stress.

As Ashley had predicted, Tia rose to her feet, as did the hooded man, his back still toward the watchers. The hooded man did not turn. Tia did, and the two of them walked directly out the back door, only a few feet away.

Darcy and the Commander were on their feet, heading toward the back door. Then Lord Darcy stopped, his hand on the doorknob.

"What are you waiting for?" Ashley asked.

"I want them to get far enough ahead so that they

won't notice the light when I open this door."

"But we'll lose them in this fog!"

"Not with those high heels of hers. You can hear them ten yards away."

He eased the door open a trifle. "Hear that? They're moving away toward our right. What street is this?"

"This would be Old Barnegat Road," said Lord Ashley.

"All right, let's go." Lord Darcy swung open the door and the two men stepped out into the billowing fog. The steady clicking of Tia's heels was still clearly audible.

"Let's close up the distance," Lord Darcy said as they walked steadily through the shrouded darkness. "If we walk quietly, they won't notice our footsteps over the sound of hers."

The two men said nothing for several minutes as they followed the beacon of sound that came from Tia's heels. Then, in a low voice, Lord Ashley said, "You know, I didn't understand much of that conversation back at the pub—but I guess I should be thankful I could understand any of it at all."

"Why?" asked Lord Darcy.

"I had rather assumed it would be in Polish. We know the Einzig girl speaks Polish and the note indicates that the man does, too."

"Quite the contrary," said Lord Darcy. "The note indicates that the man has a slight acquaintance with the Polish tongue, but hardly enough to carry on a lengthy conversation in it. The Poles differentiate between a 'hound' and a 'dog' just as we do. Yet in translating *'Hound and Hare'* into Polish, he used the Polish word for 'dog,' which no one who was conversant with the language would have done. And that tells us a great deal more about the man we are following."

"In what way, my lord?"

"That he is vain, pretentious, and has an overdeveloped sense of the melodramatic. He could quite as easily have written the note in Anglo-French, yet he did not. Why?"

"Perhaps because he felt that it would not be understood by anyone else who happened to see it."

"Precisely; and you have fallen into the same error he did. Only a man who is unfamiliar with a language thinks of it as a kind of secret writing. Do you think of Anglo-French as a cryptic language with which to conceal your thoughts from others?"

"Hardly," said Lord Ashley with a smile.

"But even so," Lord Darcy said softly, "only a vain, pretentious man would attempt to show off his patently poor knowledge of a language to a person whose native tongue it is."

At a corner ahead of them, the sound of Tia's heels turned again to the right. "Where are we now?" Lord Darcy asked.

"If I haven't lost my bearings, we just passed Great Harlow House; that means they turned on Thames Street, heading roughly south."

Lord Darcy wished, not for the first time, that he knew more about the geography of London. "Have you any idea where they're going?" he asked.

"Well, if we keep on this way," said Lord Ashley, "we'll pass St. Martin's Church and end up smack in the middle of Westminster Palace."

"Don't tell me they're going to see the King," said Lord Darcy. "I really don't believe I could swallow that."

"Wait, they're turning left."

"Where would that be?"

"Somerset Bridge," Lord Ashley said. "They're crossing the river. We'd better drop back a little. There are lights on the bridge."

"I think not," said Lord Darcy. "We'll take our chances."

"How much longer are they going to keep walking?" Lord Ashley muttered. "Are they out on a pleasant evening stroll to Croydon or something?"

The lights on the bridge did not hamper them in any way. They were widely spaced, and the fog was so dense, especially here over the Thames, that someone standing directly under a gas lamp could not be seen from fifteen feet away. They kept walking at a steady pace.

Suddenly the clicking stopped, somewhere near the middle of the bridge. Automatically the two men also stopped. Then they heard a single sentence, muffled but clearly intelligible: "Now climb up on the balustrade."

"Good God!" said Darcy. "Let's go!"

The two men broke into a run. Caution now was out of the question. The hooded man came suddenly into sight, through the veil of fog. He was standing near one of the gas lamps. Tia Einzig was nowhere to be seen. From the river below came the sound of a muffled splash.

At the sound of footsteps the hooded man turned, his face still hidden, shadowed from the overhead light by the hood of his cloak. He froze for a second as if deciding whether or not to run. Then he realized it was too late, that his pursuers were too close for him to escape. His right hand dived beneath his cloak and came out again with a smallsword. Its needlelike blade gleamed in the foggy light.

The Imperial Navy's training was such that Commander Lord Ashley's reaction was almost instinctive. His own narrow-bladed sword came from its scabbard and into position before the hooded man could attack.

"Take care of him!" Lord Darcy shouted. "I'll get the girl!" He was already racing across the bridge to the downstream side, opening his cloak and dropping it behind him as he ran. He vaulted to the top of the broad stone balustrade, stood for a moment, then took a long clean dive into the impenetrable blackness below.

# 16

COMMANDER LORD ASHLEY did not see Lord Darcy's dive from the bridge. His eyes had not for a second left the hooded figure that faced him in the tiny area of mist-filled light beneath the gas lamp. He felt confident, sure of himself. The way the other man had drawn his sword proclaimed him an amateur.

Then, as his opponent came in suddenly, he felt an odd surge of fear. The sword in the other man's hand seemed to flicker and vanish as it moved!

It was only by instinct and pure luck that he managed to avoid the point of the other's sword and parry the thrust with his own blade. And still his eyes could not find that slim, deadly shaft of steel. It was as if his eyes refused to focus on it, refused to look directly at it.

The next few seconds brought him close to panic as thrust after thrust narrowly missed their mark, and his own thrusts were parried easily by a blade he could not see, a blade he could not find.

Wherever he looked, it was always somewhere else, moving in hard and fast, with strikes that would have been deadly, had his own sword not somehow managed to ward them off each time. His own thrusts were parried again and again, for each time the other blade neared his own, his eyes would uncontrollably look away.

He did not need to be told that this was sorcery. It was all too apparent that he was faced with an enchanted blade in the hands of a deadly killer.

And then the Commander's own latent, untrained Talent came to the fore. It was a Talent that was rare even in the Sorcerers Guild. It was an ability to see a very short time into the future, usually only for seconds, and—very rarely—for whole minutes.

The Guild could train most men with that Talent; these were the sorcerers who predicted the weather, warned of earthquakes, and foresaw other natural phenomena that were not subject to the actions of men. But, as yet, not even the greatest thaumaturgical scientists had devised a method of training the Commander's peculiar ability. For that ability was the rarest of all—the ability to predict the results of the actions of men. And since the thaumaturgical laws of time symmetry had not yet been fathomed, that kind of Talent still could not be brought to the peak of reliability that others had been.

The Commander had occasional flashes of precognition, but he never knew when they would come nor how long he could sustain their flow. But, like any other intelligent man who has what he knows is an accurate hunch, Commander Lord Ashley was capable of acting upon it.

Quite suddenly, he realized that he had known instinctively, with each thrust, where that ensorcelled blade was going to be. The black sorcerer who sought to kill him might have trained Talent on his side, but he could not possibly cope with Commander Lord Ashley's hunches.

Once he realized that, Ashley's eyes no longer sought the enemy's blade, or the arm that held it. They watched the body of his opponent. It moved from one position to another as though posing for sketches in a beginner's textbook. But he could have kept his eyes closed and still known.

For a little while, Ashley did nothing but ward off the other's attacks, getting the feel of the black sorcerer's sword work. But he was no longer retreating.

He began to move in. Step by step he forced his opponent back. Now they were directly beneath the gas lamp again. Lord Ashley could tell that the other man was beginning to lose his confidence. His thrusts and parries were less certain. Now the panic and fear were all on the other side.

With careful deliberation, Commander Lord Ashley plotted out his own course of action. He did not want this man dead; this sorcerer and spy must be arrested, tried, and hanged, either for the actual murder of Sir James Zwinge, or for having ordered it done. There was no doubt in Lord Ashley's mind as to the guilt of this black sorcerer, but it would be folly to kill him, to take the King's Justice into his own hands.

He knew, now, that it would be easy to take his opponent alive. It would require only two quick moves: a thrust between elbow and wrist to disarm the man, and then a quick blow to the side of his head with the flat of the blade to knock him senseless.

Lord Ashley made two more feints to move his opponent back and get him in just the right position to receive the final thrust. The sorcerer retreated as though he were obeying orders—which, indeed, he was: the orders of the lightning-swift sword in the Commander's hand.

Now the gas lamp was at Ashley's back, and for the first time the light fell full upon the face beneath the hood.

Lord Ashley smiled grimly as he recognized those features. Taking *this* man in would be a pleasure indeed!

Then the moment came. Ashley began his lunge toward the sorcerer's momentarily unprotected forearm.

It was at that moment that he felt his Talent desert him. He had become overconfident, and the psychic tension, which had sustained his steady flow of accurate hunches, had fallen below the critical threshold.

His left foot slipped on the fog-damp pavement of the bridge.

He tried to regain his balance but it was too late. In that moment, he could almost feel death.

But he had already thrown the fear of death so deeply into his opponent that the sorcerer did not see the opening as a chance to kill. He only saw that, for a moment, the deadly Naval sword no longer threatened him. His cloak swirled around him as he turned and ran, vanishing into the surrounding fog as though he had never been.

Lord Ashley kept himself from falling flat on his face by catching his weight on his outstretched left arm. Then he was back on his feet, and a stab of pain went through his right ankle. He could hear the running steps of the sorcerer fading into the distance, but he knew he could never catch him trying to run on a twisted ankle.

He braced himself against the balustrade for a moment and gave in to the laughter that had been welling up ever since he had seen that twisted, frightened face. The laughter was at himself, basically. To think that, for a few seconds, he had actually been deathly afraid of that obsequious little worm, Master Ewen MacAlister!

It took half a minute or so for the laughter to subside. Then he pulled a deep breath of fog-laden air into his lungs, and wiped the perspiration from his forehead with the back of his left hand. Deftly, he slid his sword back into its sheath.

It was too bad, he thought, that a spot of slippery pavement had prevented him from capturing Master Ewen, but at least the identity of the black sorcerer was now known, and Lord Darcy could—

*Lord Darcy!*

The haze of excitement cleared from his brain, and he limped across the bridge to the balustrade on the downstream side.

Black as pitch down there. He could see nothing.

*"Darcy!"* the Commander's voice rang out across the water, but the dense fog that brooded over the river seemed to distort and disperse the sound before it traveled far. There was no answer.

Twice more he called, and still there was no answer.

He heard rapid footsteps coming from his right and turned to face them, his hand on the hilt of his narrow-bladed sword.

MacAlister returning? It couldn't be! And yet . . .

Damn the fog! He felt as though he were isolated in a little world of his own, whose boundaries were a bank of cotton wool a dozen feet away, and which was surrounded by invisible beings that were nothing but disembodied footsteps.

Then he saw a glow of light, and out of the cotton wool came a friendly figure, carrying a pressure-gas lantern. Lord Ashley didn't know the big, heavy man, but the black uniform of a London Armsman made him a friend. The Armsman slowed, stopped, and put his hand on the hilt of his own smallsword. "May I ask what's going on here, sir?" he inquired politely. But his eyes were wary.

Lord Ashley carefully took his hand off the hilt of his own sword. The Armsman kept his where it was. "I heard a disturbance on the bridge, sir," he said stolidly. "A noise of swords clashing, it sounded like, sir. Then somebody from off the bridge ran past me in the fog. And just now . . ." He paused. "Were that you shouting, sir?"

It came suddenly to Lord Ashley what a forbidding figure he must be. In his long black Naval cloak, with the hood up, and his back to the lamp, his shadowed face was as invisible as MacAlister's had been. He reached up with one hand and pulled back the hood, and then pushed the cloak back over his shoulders so that the Armsman could see his uniform.

"I am Commander Lord Ashley," he said. "Yes Armsman, there has been trouble. The man you heard running is a criminal wanted for murder."

"Murder, your lordship?" said the Armsman blankly. "Who was he?"

"I'm afraid he did not give me his name," said Lord Ashley. The statement was perfectly true, he thought, and he wanted to tell Darcy about MacAlister before he told anyone else. "The point is that a short time ago he pushed a young girl off the bridge. My companion dived in after her."

"Dived in after her? That were a foolish thing to do on a night like this. Likely we've lost two people instead of one, your lordship."

"That may well be," Lord Ashley admitted. "I've called him and he doesn't answer. But he's a powerful man, and although the chances are against his having found the girl, there's a good chance he can make it to shore by himself."

"All right, your lordship, we'll start looking for both of them right away." He took out his whistle and blew a series of shrill, high, keening notes into the murk-filled air—the "Assistance" call of the King's Armsmen. A second or two later, they heard distant whistles from both sides of the river blowing the answer: "Coming." After several more seconds, the Armsman repeated the call, to give his hearers a bearing.

"There'll be help along in a few minutes. Nothing we can do till then," the Armsman said briskly. He took a notebook from his jacket pocket. "Now, your lordship, if I might have your name again and the names of the other people involved."

The Commander repeated his own name, then he said, "The girl's name is Tia Einzig." He spelled it. "She is an important witness in a murder case, which is why the killer tried to do away with her. The man who went in after her is Lord Darcy, the—"

"Lord Darcy, did you say?" The Armsman lifted his head suddenly from the notebook. "Lord Darcy, the famous investigator from Rouen?"

"That's right," said Lord Ashley.

"The same Lord Darcy," persisted the Armsman, who seemed to want to make absolutely sure of the identification, "who came over from Normandy to help Lord Bontriomphe solve the Royal Steward Hotel Murder?"

"The same," Lord Ashley said wearily.

"And he's gone and jumped in the *river*?"

"Yes, that's what I said. He jumped in the river. He was trying to save this girl. By now he's had time to swim clear to the Nore. If we wait a little longer, he may be on his way back."

The Armsman looked miffed. "No need to get impatient, your lordship. We'll get things done as fast as we can." He put his whistle to his lips again and sent out the distress call a third time. Then, after a moment, a fourth.

Then they could hear hoofbeats clattering on the distant street and the sound changed to a hollow thunder as the horse galloped onto the bridge. They could see a glow of light approaching through the fog; the Armsman signaled with his own lantern. "Here comes the sergeant now, your lordship."

The mounted Sergeant-at-Arms was suddenly upon them, pulling his big bay gelding to a halt, as the Armsman came to attention. "What seems to be the trouble, Armsman Arthur?"

"This gentleman here, Sergeant, is Commander Lord Ashley of the Imperial Navy." Referring to his notebook, he went on to report quickly and concisely what Lord Ashley had told him. By that time, they could hear the thud of heavy boots and the clatter of hoofbeats from both ends of the bridge, as more Armsmen approached.

"All right, My Lord Commander," said the sergeant, "we'll take care of it. Likely he swam for the right bank since it's the nearer, but we'll cover both sides. Arthur, you go to the Thames Street River Patrol Station. Tell them to get their boats out, and to send a message to the other patrol stations downriver. We'll want everything covered from here to Chelsea."

"Right away, Sergeant." Armsman Arthur disappeared into the fog.

"I'd like to ask a favor if I may, Sergeant," said Lord Ashley.

"What might that be, My Lord Commander?"

"Send a horseman to the Royal Steward Hotel, if you would. Have him report exactly what happened to the Sergeant-at-Arms on duty there. Also, there is an official Admiralty coach waiting for me there, Petty Officer Hosquins in charge. Have your man tell Hosquins that Commander Lord Ashley wants him to bring the coach to Thames Street and Somerset Bridge immediately. I'm going to assume that Lord Darcy made for the right bank, and help your men search that side."

"Very good, My Lord Commander. I'll send a man right along."

* * *

Mary de Cumberland walked across the almost deserted lobby of the Royal Steward, doing her best to suppress her nervous impatience.

She felt she ought to be doing something, but what?

She would like to have talked to someone but there was no one to talk to.

Sir Lyon and Sir Thomas were still in conclave with the highest ranking sorcerers of the Empire.

Master Sean was at the morgue attending to the autopsy of Sir James Zwinge. Lord Bontriomphe, according to the Sergeant-at-Arms who was on duty in the temporary office, was out prowling the city in search of a missing man named Paul Nichols. (She knew that the Sergeant-at-Arms would not have given her even that much information except that Lord Bontriomphe had told him that Her Grace of Cumberland would be bringing in information. The sergeant apparently assumed that her status in the investigation was a great deal more official than it actually was.)

And Lord Darcy was in a low dive down the street, keeping an eye on Tia.

Which left the Duchess with nothing to do.

Part way across the lobby, she turned and headed down the hall that led back to the temporary office. Maybe some information had come in. Even if none had, it was better to be talking to the sergeant than to be pointlessly pacing the hotel lobby.

If this had been a normal convention, she could have found plenty of convivial companionship in the Sword Room, but the murder had stilled the thirst of every sorcerer in the hotel. She went through the open door of the little office. "Anything new, Sergeant Peter?"

"Not a thing, Your Grace," said the Sergeant-at-Arms, rising to his feet. "Lord Bontriomphe's not back yet and neither is Lord Darcy."

"You look as though you're as bored as I am, Sergeant. Do you mind if I sit down?"

"It would be an honor, Your Grace. Here, take this chair. Not too comfortable, I'm afraid. They didn't exactly give their night manager their best furniture."

They were interrupted by another Sergeant-at-Arms who walked in the door. He gave the Duchess a quick nod, said, "Evening, mum," and then addressed Sergeant Peter. "Are you in charge here, Sergeant?"

"Until Lord Bontriomphe or Lord Darcy gets back, I am. Sergeant Peter O Sechnaill."

"Sergeant Michael Coeur-Terre, River Detail. Lord Darcy might not *be* back. Girl named Tia Einzig got pushed off Somerset Bridge, and Lord Darcy jumped off the bridge after her. They're putting out patrol boats and search parties on both sides of the river from Somerset Bridge to Chelsea, but personally I don't think there's much chance. A Commander Lord Ashley asked us to report to you. He said Lord Bontriomphe would want the information."

Sergeant Peter nodded. "Right," he said briskly. "I'll tell his lordship as soon as he comes in. Anything else?"

"Yes. Do you know where an Admiralty coach is parked around here with a Petty Officer Hosquins in charge of it? Commander Lord Ashley says he wants it at Thames Street and Somerset Bridge immediately. He wants transportation for Lord Darcy when they find him, though it's my opinion that his lordship is done for."

Mary de Cumberland had already risen to her feet. Now she said, in a very quiet voice, "He is not dead. I should know it if he were dead."

"I beg your pardon, mum?" said Sergeant Michael.

"Nothing, Sergeant," she said calmly. "At Thames Street and Somerset Bridge, you said? I

know where the Admiralty coach is. I shall tell Petty
Officer Hosquins."

Sergeant Michael noticed, for the first time, the
Cumberland arms on Mary's dress. Simultaneously,
Sergeant Peter said, "Her Grace is working with us
on this case."

"That's . . . that's very good of Your Grace, I'm
sure," said Sergeant Michael.

"Not at all, Sergeant." She swept out of the room,
walked rapidly down the hall, across the lobby, and
out the front door of the Royal Steward. She hadn't
the dimmest notion of where the Admiralty coach
might be parked, but this was no time to quibble over
details.

It didn't take her long to find it. It was waiting half
a block away, toward St. Swithin's Street. There was
no mistaking the Admiralty arms emblazoned on its
door. The coachman and the footman were sitting up
in the driver's seat, their greatcoats wrapped around
them and a blanket over their legs, quietly smoking
their pipes and talking.

"Petty Officer Hosquins?" Mary said author-
itatively. "I'm the Duchess of Cumberland. Lord
Ashley has sent word that the coach is wanted immediately at Thames Street and Somerset Bridge.
I'm going with you." Before the footman had even
had a chance to climb down she had opened the door
and was inside the coach. Petty Officer Hosquins
opened the trap door in the roof and looked down at
her.

"But Your Grace," he began.

"Lord Ashley," the Duchess cut in coldly, "said
'immediately.' This is an emergency. Now, dammit,
get a move on, man."

Petty Officer Hosquins blinked. "Yes, Your Grace," he said. He closed the trap. The coach moved on.

# PART FOUR

# 17

THERE WAS A CHILLING SHOCK as Lord Darcy's body cut into the inky waters of the Thames. For long seconds it seemed as if he would keep on going down until he buried himself in the mud and muck at the bottom; then he was fighting his way up again, tearing off his jacket. His head broke the surface, he took one deep breath, and then doubled over to pull off his boots.

And all the while Lord Darcy was telling himself that he was a fool—a bloody, stupid, harebrained fool. The girl had allowed herself to be pushed in without a struggle, and she had fallen without a sound. What chance was there of finding her in a world of darkness and watery death, better than a hundred yards from the nearest bank? A heaviness at his hip reminded him of something else. He could have drawn his pistol, but he would never have shot a man armed only with a sword, and the time it would have taken to force the man to drop his weapon and then turn him over to Ashley would have been precious seconds wasted. His chances of finding the girl were small now; they would have been in-finitesimal if there had been any delay.

At least, he told himself, he could have drawn his gun and dropped it on the bridge as he had his cloak. Its added weight now was only a hindrance. Regret-fully he drew it from its holster and consigned it for-ever to the muddy depths of the mighty river. He sur-faced again and looked around. It was not as dark as he had thought. Dimly, he could still see the lights on the bridge.

"Tia!" he shouted. "Tia Einzig! Where are you? Can you hear me?"

She should have been borne downstream, beneath Somerset Bridge, but how far beneath the surface? Had she already taken her last gasp and filled her lungs with water?

And then he heard a noise.

There was a soft, spluttering, sobbing sound and a faint splash.

"Tia Einzig!" he shouted again. "Say something! Where are you?"

There was no answer except that faint sound again, coming from upstream, between himself and the bridge. His sprint across the bridge and his long dive had put him downstream from her, as he had hoped.

Lord Darcy swam toward the sound, his powerful arms fighting against the current of the Thames. The sound came closer, a sort of mewing sob that hardly sounded human.

And then he touched her.

She was struggling, but not much. Just enough, apparently, to keep her head above water. He put his left arm around her, holding them both up with pow-erful strokes of his right, and her struggles stopped.

Her cloak, he noticed, was gone—probably torn off when she struck the water. The whimpering sounds had ceased, and her body was completely relaxed but she was still breathing. He kept her face above water and began swimming toward the right bank, towing her through the chilling water. Thank God she was small and light, he thought. She didn't weigh more than seven stone, sopping wet.

The joke struck him as funny but he couldn't waste his breath now in laughing. *It would be like laughing at my own funeral,* he thought, and this second joke was grim enough to preclude any desire to laugh.

Where was the damned bank, anyway? How long does it take to cover a hundred-odd yards of water? He felt as though he had been swimming for hours, and the muscles of his right shoulder were beginning to feel the strain. Treading water, carefully holding the girl's head above the surface, he changed about, letting his right arm keep her up, and swimming with his left.

Hours more seemed to pass, and now there was nothing but blackness around him. The lights of the bridge had long since faded away, and the lights on the river bank—if there *was* any river bank!—were not yet visible.

Had he lost his bearings? Was he swimming downstream instead of across it? There was no way of knowing; his body was moving with the water and there was nothing visible to judge by.

Then, as he reached out for another in a seemingly endless series of strokes, his fingers slammed into something hard and sent a stinging pain into his hand and wrist. He reached out again, more carefully this time.

It was a shelf of stone, one of the steps leading down to the water's edge from the bank above. He levered the girl's body up onto the step, then climbed out of the water himself. She was all right, as far as he could tell; she was still breathing.

He realized suddenly that he was too weak and exhausted even to climb the steps to the embankment by himself, much less carry the girl up. But he couldn't just let her lie there on the cold stone. He lifted her up and held her in his arms, trying to warm her body with his, and then for a long time he just sat there—motionless, cold, and wet, his mind almost as blank as the endless darkness that surrounded them.

\* \* \*

After what might have been minutes or hours of mental and physical numbness, a slight, almost imperceptible change in Lord Darcy's surroundings forced his sluggish mind to function again.

What was it that was different? Something to his left. Something he could see out of the corner of his eye. He turned his head to look. It was nothing; just a light—a dim glow in the distance that seemed to shift back and forth a little and grow steadily brighter. No, not just one light, there were two . . . three . . .

Then a voice said, "Hallooo . . . Lord Darcy! Can you hear us, my lord?"

Lord Darcy's mind snapped into full wakefulness. The fog must have thinned somewhat, he realized. He could tell from the voice that they were still some distance away, but the lights were easily visible. "Halloo," he shouted. His voice sounded weak, even to his own ears. He tried again. "Halloo."

"Who's that?" called the voice.

Lord Darcy grinned in spite of his weariness.

"Lord Darcy here," he shouted. "You were calling me, I believe?"

Then somebody yelled: "We've found him; he's here!" Somebody else blew on a whistle. Lord Darcy felt himself beginning to shiver.

*Reaction,* he thought, trying to keep his teeth from chattering. *I feel weak as a kitten.* His muscles felt as though they had been jelled by the cold; the only warm spot in his body was his chest, against which he had been holding Tia. She was still breathing— quietly, regularly. But she was limp in his arms, completely relaxed; she wasn't even shivering. *That's all right,* Lord Darcy thought, *I'm shivering enough for both of us.* There were more whistles and more lights and footfalls all over the place. He wondered vaguely whether they had decided to call out the Army. And then a Man-at-Arms with a lantern was beside him, saying, "Are you all right, Lord Darcy?"

"I'm all right, just cold."

"Good Heavens, my lord, you've got the girl." He shouted up the embankment, "He's got the girl!"

But Lord Darcy hardly heard the words. The light from the man's lantern was shining directly into Tia's face, and her eyes were wide open, staring blankly, unseeingly, into nothing. He would have thought her dead, but the dead do not breathe.

There were more men around him now.

"Give his lordship more light."

"Let me help you up, my lord."

Then: "Darcy! Thank Heaven you're safe! And the girl, too! It's a miracle!"

"Hullo, Ashley," said Darcy. "Thanks for calling out the troops."

Lord Ashley grinned. "Here's your cloak. You shouldn't go around leaving things on bridges." And then he was taking off his own cloak to wrap it around Tia. He took her from Darcy's arms and carried her up the steps, carefully, tenderly.

Lord Darcy wrapped his cloak tightly around himself, but it didn't help the shivering.

"We'll have to get you some place warm, my lord, or you'll catch your death of dampness," said an Armsman.

Lord Darcy started up the steps. Then a voice from the top said, "Did you find him?"

"We found both of them, Your Grace," said another Armsman.

Darcy said, "Mary. What the deuce are you doing here?"

"As I told you last night," she said, "when you asked that same question, I came to fetch you."

"This time," Lord Darcy said, "I believe you."

\* \* \*

When he reached the top and had climbed over the retaining wall, he saw Lord Ashley standing solidly, holding Tia in his arms. Several Armsmen were shining their lanterns on her, and Mary, not a Duchess now but a trained nurse, was looking at the girl and touching her with her Sensitive's fingers.

"How is she?" he asked. "What's the matter with her?"

"You're shivering," said Mary without looking up. "There's brandy in the coach, go get yourself some." She looked up at Lord Ashley. "Put her in the coach. We'll take her directly to Carlyle House. Father Patrique is there; she couldn't get better care in a hospital."

Two good swallows of brandy had calmed Lord Darcy's shivering. "What's the matter with her?" he asked again.

"Shock and cold, of course," she said. "There may be some internal injuries. Nothing serious. But she's under a spell, one I can't break. We'll have to get her to Father Patrique as soon as possible."

They stretched the girl out on one of the coach seats.

"Will she be all right?" asked Lord Ashley.

"I think so," said the Duchess.

Then Lord Ashley said, "Lord Darcy, may I speak to you a moment?"

"Surely; what is it?"

They stepped out of earshot of the others.

"The man on the bridge," Lord Ashley began.

"Oh, yes," said Lord Darcy. "I should have asked about him. I see you're not hurt. I hope you didn't have to kill him."

"No, I'm ashamed to say I didn't even capture him. My foot slipped on the pavement and he got away. But I got a good look at his face."

"Did you recognize him?"

"Yes. It was our oily friend, Master Ewen MacAlister."

Lord Darcy nodded. "I thought I recognized something familiar in his voice when he told Tia to climb up on the balustrade. He had her under a spell, as Her Grace just said."

"That wasn't the only Black Magic the little swine was working," Lord Ashley said. He told Lord Darcy about the ensorcelled sword.

"Then you need not apologize for letting him escape," Darcy said. "I am thankful that you're still alive."

"So am I," said Lord Ashley. "Look here; there's not going to be room for all of us in that coach with Tia taking up one whole seat. And I shan't be needed any more tonight anyway. You two go ahead." He stepped back. "Petty Officer Hosquins," he called. "Her Grace and Lord Darcy are going to Carlyle House. One of the Armsmen will get a cab to take me home."

"Very well, My Lord Commander," answered Hosquins.

"Thank you," said Lord Darcy. "Would you do me one favor? Would you go to the Royal Steward and report everything to Lord Bontriomphe? If Master Ewen knows you recognized him, he won't show up at the hotel, of course. Tell Lord Bontriomphe to notify Sir Lyon. All right?"

"Certainly. I'll get down there right away. Good night, my lord. Good night, Your Grace," he said, raising his voice.

Lord Darcy opened the door of the coach. "To Carlyle House, Hosquins," he said, and climbed in.

* * *

It was more than an hour later before Lord Darcy really felt good again. A hot bath had taken the smell of the Thames from him, and some of the chill out of his blood. A short session with Father Patrique had removed any susceptibility to catching cold. Mary de Cumberland and the good Father had both insisted that he go to bed, so now he found himself in his silken night clothes, propped up on four or five pillows, with a couple of warm woolen blankets over his legs, a heavy shawl around his shoulders, a hot water bottle at his feet, and two bowlsful of hot, nourishing soup inside him.

The door opened and Mary de Cumberland came in, bearing a large steaming mug on a tray. "How do you feel?" she asked.

"Quite fit, really. How is Tia?"

"Father Patrique says she'll be all right. He put her to sleep. He says that she won't be able to talk to anyone until tomorrow." She put the mug down on the bedside table. "Here, this is for you."

"What is it?" Lord Darcy asked, eyeing the mug suspiciously.

"Medicine. It's good for what ails you."

"What's in it?"

"If you must know, it contains brandy, Oporto, honey, hot water, and a couple of herbs that Father Patrique prescribed."

"Humph," said Lord Darcy. "You made it sound good until you mentioned that last." He picked up the mug and sipped. "Not bad at all," he admitted.

"Do you feel strong enough to see visitors?" she asked solicitously.

"No," he said. "I'm on my deathbed. I'm in a coma. My breathing is shallow, my pulse weak and threadlike. Who wants to see me?"

"Well, Sir Thomas wanted to see you; he just wanted to thank you for saving Tia's life, but the poor man seems on the verge of collapse himself and I told him he could thank you tomorrow. Lord John Quetzal said that he could wait to speak to you until tomorrow, too. But Sir Lyon Grey arrived just a few minutes ago, and I strongly suggest that you see him."

"And where, may I ask, is Master Sean?"

"I have no doubt that he would be here, my lord, if anyone had thought to tell him of your desire for an invigorating cold bath. He is still at the morgue."

"Poor chap," said Darcy, "he's had a hard day's work."

"And what have *you* been doing?" said Her Grace. "Tatting?"

Lord Darcy ignored her. "I presume that he is making absolutely sure, one way or another, whether drugs or poisons were administered," he said thoughtfully. "I am strongly inclined to doubt that they were, but when Sean has finished with his work we shall know for certain."

"Yes," agreed Her Grace. "Will you see Sir Lyon?"

"Of course, of course. Show him in, will you?"

The Dowager Duchess of Cumberland went out and returned a minute later accompanied by the tall, stately, silver-bearded figure of Sir Lyon Gandolphus Grey. "I understand you have had quite an adventurous evening, my lord," he said gravely.

"All in the day's work for an Officer of the King's Justice, Sir Lyon. Pray be seated."

"Thank you," said Sir Lyon. Then, as the Duchess started to leave the room, "Please, Your Grace—if you would be so good as to remain? This concerns every member of the Guild, as well as the King's Officers."

"Certainly, Grand Master."

Sir Lyon looked back at Lord Darcy. "Commander Lord Ashley has informed me of his identification of Master Ewen MacAlister. He and Lord Bontriomphe have sent out word to the Armsmen all over the city to be on the watch for him. I have sent out every available Master Sorcerer in London to accompany the Armsmen, to make certain he does not use his Art to escape."

"Very good," said Lord Darcy.

"Lord Ashley's unsupported word," continued the Grand Master, "would not be sufficient in itself to bring charges against Master Ewen before the Special Executive Commission of the Guild. But it was enough to make us take immediate action to procure further evidence."

"Indeed?" said Lord Darcy with interest. "You have found this evidence, of course."

Sir Lyon nodded gravely. "We have. You are perhaps aware that a sorcerer casts certain protective and precautionary spells upon the bag in which he carries the tools of his trade?"

"I am," said Lord Darcy, remembering how easily Master Sean had regained possession of his own symbol-decorated carpetbag.

"Then you will understand why we asked Lord Bontriomphe to procure a search warrant from a magistrate immediately, and then went directly to Master Ewen's room. He, too, had put a special spell on the lock, as Sir James had done, but we solved it within fifteen minutes. Then we solved and removed the protective spells from his bag. The evidence was there—a bottle of graveyard dirt, two mummified bats, human bones, fire powder containing sulphur —and other things which no sorcerer should have in his possession without a special research permit from the Guild and special authority from the Church."

Lord Darcy nodded. " 'Black Magic is a matter of symbolism and intent,' " he quoted.

"Precisely," said Sir Lyon. "Then, in addition, I have Father Patrique's testimony concerning the black spell that Ewen cast upon Tia this evening. We have, then, my lord, quite sufficient evidence to convict him of Black Magic. Whether or not you can obtain enough evidence to convict him of his other crimes is, of course, another matter. But rest assured that the Guild will do everything in its power to help you obtain it. You have but to ask, my lord."

"I thank you, Sir Lyon. A question, merely to satisfy my curiosity: Lord Ashley told you, did he not, of the swordplay on Somerset Bridge?"

"He did."

"Am I correct in assuming that the spell Master Ewen had cast upon his own blade was in some manner a utilization of the Tarnhelm Effect?"

"It was indeed," Sir Lyon said with a rather puzzled smile. "It was astute of you to recognize it from Lord Ashley's description alone."

"Not at all," Lord Darcy said. "It is simply that Sean is an excellent teacher."

"It's more than astute, Grand Master," said the Dowager Duchess. "To me, it's irritating. I know what the Tarnhelm Effect is, of course, since I have come across mention of it in my studies, but its utilization and theory are quite beyond me."

"You should not find it irritating, but gratifying," Sir Lyon said in a firm voice. "One of the troubles with the world is that so few laymen take an interest in science. If more people were like Lord Darcy, we could eliminate the superstitions that still cling to the minds of ninety-nine people out of a hundred." He smiled. "I realize you spoke in jest, but it behooves all of us to educate the layman whenever we can. It is only because of ignorance and superstition that hedge magicians and witches and other unlicensed practitioners can operate. It is only because of ignorance and superstition that so many people believe that only Black Magic can overcome Black Magic, that the only way to destroy evil is by using more evil. It is only because of ignorance and superstition that quacks and mountebanks who have no trace of the Talent can peddle their useless medallions and charms."

He sighed then, and Lord Darcy thought he

looked somehow older and wearier. "Of course, education of that kind will not eliminate the Master Ewens of this world. Modern science has given us an advantage over earlier ages, in that it has enabled us to keep our Government, our Church and our Courts more nearly uncorrupt and incorruptible than was ever before possible. But not even science is infallible. There are still quirks in the human mind that we cannot detect until it is too late, and Ewen MacAlister is a perfect example of our failure to do so."

"Sir Lyon," said Lord Darcy, "I should like to suggest that Master Ewen is more than that. In our own history, and in certain countries even today, we find organizations that attempt to hide and gloss over the wrongdoings of their own members. There was a time when the Church, the Government, and the Courts would ignore or conceal the peculations of a priest, a governor, or a judge rather than admit to the public that they were not infallible. Any group which makes a claim to infallibility must be very careful not to make any mistakes, and the mistakes that will inevitably occur must be kept secret or explained away —by lies, subterfuges and distortions. And that will eventually cause the collapse of the entire edifice. Anyone who has power in the Empire today—be it spiritual, temporal, or thaumaturgical—is trusted by the little man who has no power, precisely because he knows that we do our best to uncover the occasional Master Ewen and remove his power, rather than hiding him and pretending he does not exist. Master Ewen then becomes in himself the embodiment of the failure which may be converted to a symbol of success."

"Of course," said Sir Lyon. "But it is still unpleasant when it does happen. The last time was back in '39, when Sir Edward Elmer was Grand Master. I was on the Special Executive Commission then, and I had rather hoped it would not happen again in my lifetime. However, we shall do what must be done."

He rose. "Is there anything further I can do for you?"

"I think not, Sir Lyon, not at the moment. Thank you very much for your information.

"Oh, yes. One thing. Would you tell the sorcerers who are searching for him that if Master Ewen is taken during the night I am to be notified immediately, no matter what o'clock it is. I have several questions which I wish to put to him."

"I have already given such instructions in regard to myself," said Sir Lyon. "I shall see that you are notified. Good night, my lord. Good night, Your Grace. I shall be in my room if there is any word."

When the silvery-bearded old sorcerer had left, the Dowager Duchess said, "Well, I hope they don't catch him until morning; you need a good night's sleep. But at least this horrible mess is almost over."

"Don't be too optimistic," said Lord Darcy. "There are far too many questions which remain unanswered. As you implied, they have not yet caught Master Ewen, and Paul Nichols has managed to remain hidden wherever he is for more than thirty-six hours. We still do not have the results of Master Sean's Herculean labors. There are still too many knots in this tangled string to say that the end is in sight."

He looked down at his empty mug. "Would you mind bringing me another one of those? Without the good Father's additional flavorings this time, if you please."

"Certainly."

But when she returned, Lord Darcy was fast asleep, and the hot mug became her own nightcap instead of his.

# 18

"I TRUST you are feeling fit, my lord."

The always punctilious Geffri put the caffe urn and the cup on the bedside table.

"Quite fit, Geffri; thank you," said Lord Darcy. "Ah! the caffe smells delicious. Brewed by your own hand as usual, I trust? Carlyle House is, except for my own home, the only place in the Empire where one can get one's morning caffe at exactly the right temperature and brewed to perfection."

"It is most gratifying to hear you say so, my lord," said Geffri, pouring the caffe. "By the bye, I have taken the liberty, my lord, of bringing up this morning's *Courier*. There is, however, another communication which your lordship might prefer to peruse previous to perusal of the news." He produced an envelope, ten inches wide by fourteen long. Lord Darcy immediately recognized Master Sean's personal seal upon the flap.

"Master Sean," said Geffri, "arrived late last night —after your lordship had retired. He requested that

I deliver this to your lordship immediately upon your lordship's awakening."

Lord Darcy took the envelope. It was quite obviously the report on the tubby little Irish sorcerer's thaumaturgical investigation and the autopsy report on the body of Sir James Zwinge.

Lord Darcy glanced at his watch on the bedside table. "Thank you, Geffri. Would you be so good as to waken Master Sean in forty-five minutes and tell him that I should like to have him join me for breakfast at ten o'clock?"

"Of course, my lord. Is there anything else, my lord?"

"Not at the moment, I think."

"It is a pleasure to serve you, my lord," said Geffri. Then he was gone.

By the time an hour had passed, Lord Darcy had read both Master Sean's report and the London *Courier,* and was awaiting the knock on the door that came at precisely ten o'clock. By that time, Lord Darcy was dressed and ready for the day's work, and the hot breakfast for two had been brought in and laid out on the table in the sitting room.

"Come in, my good Sean," Lord Darcy said. "The bacon and eggs are waiting."

The sorcerer entered with a smile on his face, but it was quite evident to Lord Darcy that the smile was rather forced.

"Good morning, my lord," he said pleasantly. "You've read my report?" He seated himself at the table.

"I have," Lord Darcy said, "but I see nothing in it to account for that dour look. We'll discuss it after breakfast. Have you seen this morning's *Courier?*"

"No, my lord, I have not." Master Sean seated

himself and began to dig into the bacon and eggs. "Is there something of interest there?"

"Not particularly," said Lord Darcy. "Except for some rather flattering references to myself, and some even more flattering references to you, there is little of interest. You may peruse it at your leisure. The only offering of any consequence is the fact that there will be no fog tonight."

\* \* \*

The next quarter of an hour was spent in relative silence. Master Sean, usually quite loquacious, seemed to have little to say.

Finally, with some irritation, Lord Darcy pushed his plate aside and said: "All pleasantries aside, Master Sean, you are not your usual ebullient self. If there is anything I should know besides what is contained in your report, I'd like to hear it."

Master Sean smiled across his caffe cup. "Oh, no, it's all there. I have nothing to add to it. Don't mean to disturb you. Perhaps I'm a bit sleepy."

Lord Darcy frowned, reached over, picked up the carefully written report and flipped it open. "Very well. I do have a question or two, merely as a matter of clarification. First, as to the wound."

"Yes, my lord?"

"According to your report, the blade entered the chest vertically, between the third and fourth ribs, making a wound some five inches deep. It nicked the wall of the pulmonic aorta and made a small gash in the heart itself, and this wound was definitely the cause of death?"

"Definitely, my lord."

"Very well." He stood up. "If you will, Master Sean, take that spoon and assume that it is a knife.

Yes. Now, would you be so good as to stab me at the precise angle which would cause exactly such a wound as you discovered in Sir James's chest."

Master Sean grasped the handle of the spoon, lifted it high over his head, and brought it down slowly in a long arc to touch his lordship's chest. "Very good, Master Sean, thank you. The wound, if extended, then, would have gone well down into the bowels?"

"Well, my lord, if a bullet had entered at that angle, it would have come out the small of the back."

Lord Darcy nodded, and looked back down at the report. "And," he mused, "as could be surmised from the exterior aspect of the wound, the blade actually did slice into the ribs above and below the cut itself."

He looked up from the report. "Master Sean, if you were going to stab a man, how would you do it?"

Master Sean reversed the spoon in his hand so that his thumb was pointing toward the bowl. He moved his hand forward to touch Lord Darcy. "This way, of course, my lord."

Lord Darcy nodded. "And in that position, the flat of the knife is parallel to the ribs instead of perpendicular to them."

"Well, of course, my lord," said Master Sean. "With the blade up and down you're likely to get your blade stuck between the ribs."

"Precisely," Lord Darcy agreed. "Now, according to the autopsy report which Sir Eliot sent us yesterday from Cherbourg, Goodman Georges Barbour was stabbed in the efficient manner you have just demonstrated, and yet Sir James was stabbed in a manner which no efficient knifesman would use."

"That's true, my lord. Nobody who knew how to use a knife would come in with a high overhand stab like that."

"Why should the same man stab with two such completely different techniques?"

"If it *was* the same man, my lord."

"Very well, assuming that there were two different killers, which is the Navy's hypothesis, the blow that killed Sir James was still inefficient, was it not? Would a professional hired killer have deliberately used a thrust like that?"

Master Sean chuckled. "Well, if it were up to me to hire him, my lord, I don't think he'd pass my employment specifications."

"Neatly put," Lord Darcy said with a smile. "And by the way, did you examine the knife closely?"

"Sir James's contact cutter? I did."

"So did I, when it was on the floor of Sir James's hotel room yesterday. I should like to call your attention to the peculiar condition of that knife."

Master Sean frowned. "But . . . there was nothing peculiar about the condition of that knife."

"Precisely. That was the peculiar condition."

While Master Sean thought that over, Lord Darcy said: "Now to another matter." He sat down and turned over a page of the report. Master Sean settled himself in his chair and put the spoon back on his plate.

"You say here that Sir James died between 9:25 and 9:35, eh?"

"That's according to the chirurgical and thaumaturgical evidence. Since I meself heard him cry out at precisely half past nine—give or take half a minute—I can say that Sir James died between 9:30 and 9:35."

"Very well," Lord Darcy said. "But he was stabbed at approximately five minutes of nine. Now, as I understand it, the psychic patterns show both the time of the stabbing and the time of death." He flipped over a page of the report. "And the death thrust cut down and into the wall of the pulmonic aorta, but did not actually open that great blood vessel itself. There was a thin integument of the arterial wall still intact. The wound was, however, severe enough to cause him to fall into shock. He was mortally wounded, then, at that time."

"Well, my lord," Master Sean said. "It might not have been a mortal wound. It is possible that a good Healer, if he had arrived in time, might have saved Sir James's life."

"Because the pulmonic aorta was not actually cut into, eh?"

"That's right. If that artery had actually been severed at that time, Master Sir James would have been dead before he struck the floor. When that artery is cut open the drop in blood pressure and the loss of blood cause unconsciousness in a fraction of a second. The heart goes into fibrillation and death occurs very shortly thereafter."

Lord Darcy nodded. "I see. But the wall was not breached. It was cut almost through but not completely. Then, after lying on the floor for half an hour or better, Sir James heard your knock, which brought him out of his shock-induced stupor. He tried to lift himself from the floor, grabbing at his desk, upon which lay, among other things, his key." He paused and frowned. "Obviously his shout to you was a shout for help, and he wanted to get his key to unlock the door for you." He tapped a finger on the report. "This exertion caused the final rupture of the aorta wall. His life's blood gushed forth upon the floor, he dropped the key, and died. Is that your interpretation of it, Master Sean?"

Master Sean nodded. "That's the way it seems to me, my lord. Both the thaumaturgical and the chirurgical evidence corroborate each other."

"I agree completely, Master Sean," Lord Darcy said. He flipped over a few more pages. "No drugs or poisons, then."

"Not unless somebody used a substance that is unknown to the Official Pharmacopoeia. I performed a test for every one of 'em, and unless God Himself has repealed the Law of Similarity, Master Sir James was neither poisoned nor drugged."

Lord Darcy flipped over another page. "And the brain and skull were both undamaged . . . no bruises . . . no fractures . . . yes." He turned to another section of the report. "Now, we come to the thaumaturgical section. According to your tests, all the blood in the room was Master Sir James's?"

"It was, my lord."

"And what of that curious half-moon stain near the door?"

"It was definitely Sir James's blood."

Lord Darcy nodded. "As I suspected," he said. "Now, according to the thaumaturgical tests, there was no one in the room except Sir James at the time he was stabbed. This corresponds to the information on Georges Barbour that we have from Cherbourg." He smiled. "Master Sean, I well understand that you can only put scientifically provable facts in a report like this, but do you have any suggestion, any guess, anything that will help me?"

"I shall try, my lord," said Master Sean slowly. "Well, as I told you yesterday, I should be able to detect the operation of a black sorcerer. As you are aware, the *ankh* is almost infallible as a detector of evil." He took a deep breath. "And now that we know the culpability of Master Ewen MacAlister, his operations should be easy to detect."

Then Master Sean pointed at the sheaf of paper in front of Lord Darcy. "But I will not—I cannot—go back on what I said there." He took another deep breath. "My lord, I can find no trace of any kind of magic—black *or* white—associated with the murder of Master Sir James Zwinge. There was no . . ."

He was interrupted by a rap on the door. "Yes," Lord Darcy said with a touch of impatience in his voice, "who is it?"

"Father Patrique," came the voice from the other side of the door.

Lord Darcy's irritation vanished. "Ah, come in, Reverend Sir."

The door opened and a tall, rather pale man in Benedictine habit entered the room. "Good morning, my lord; good morning, Master Sean," he said with a smile. "I see you are well this morning, my lord."

"In your hands, Reverend Father, how could I be otherwise? Can I be of service to you?"

"I believe you can—and be of service to yourself at the same time, if I may say so."

"In what way, Father?"

The priest looked gravely thoughtful. "Under ordinary conditions," he said carefully, "I cannot, as you know, discuss a penitent's confession with anyone. But in this case I have been specifically requested by the penitent to speak to you."

"The Damoselle Tia, I presume," said Lord Darcy.

"Of course. She has told her story twice—once to

me, and once to Sir Thomas Leseaux." He looked at Master Sean, who was solemnly nodding his head up and down. "Ah, you follow me, Master Sorcerer."

"Oh, certainly, Your Reverence. The classic trilogy. Once to the Church, once to the loved one, and"—he gestured respectfully toward Lord Darcy —"once to the temporal authorities."

"Exactly," said the priest. "It will complete the Healing." He looked back at Lord Darcy, who had already risen from his chair. "I will give you no further details, my lord; it is best that you hear them for yourself. But she is well aware that it was you who saved her life last night, and you must understand that you must not depreciate your part in the matter."

"I think I understand, Reverend Father. May I ask you a couple of questions before we go in?"

"Certainly. As long as they do not require me to violate my vows, I shall answer them."

"They have merely to do with the spell that was cast over her last evening. Does she remember anything that happened after Master Ewen cast his black enchantment upon her?"

Father Patrique shook his head. "She does not. She will explain to you."

"Yes, but what bothers me, Reverend Father, is the speed and ease with which it was done. I was watching. One moment she was coherent, in full possession of her senses, the next she was an automaton, obeying his every word. I was not aware that sorcerers had such power over others."

"Oh, good Heavens, it can't be done that quickly," said Master Sean. "Not at all, my lord! Not even the most powerful of black sorcerers could take over another's mind just by waving his hand that way."

"Not even Satan himself can take over a human mind without some preparation, my lord," said Father Patrique. "Master Ewen must have prepared preliminary spells before that time. He would have had to, for the spell to have been as effective as it was."

"I seem to recall," said Lord Darcy, "that at the last Triennial Convention, a footpad made the foolish mistake of attacking a Master Sorcerer on the street during the last night of the Convention. The sorcerer informed the Armsmen shortly thereafter what had happened. He himself was unharmed, but the footpad was paralyzed from the neck down, completely unable to move. It was a brilliant piece of work, I admit; the spell was such that it could not be removed until the criminal made a full and complete confession of his crime—which meant, of course, that the sorcerer need not appear in Court against him. But that spell must have been cast in a matter of seconds."

"That is a somewhat different matter, my lord," said Father Patrique. "In that case, when there is evil intent on the part of the attacker, the evil itself can be reflected back upon its generator to cause the paralysis you spoke of. Any Master Sorcerer can use that as a defensive technique. But to cast a spell over a human being who has no evil intent requires the use of the sorcerer's own power; he cannot use the psychic force of his attacker, since he is not being attacked. Therefore, his own spells require much more time to be set up and to become effective."

"I see. Thank you, Father," Lord Darcy said. "That clears up the matter. Well, let's get along then and see the young lady."

"With your permission, my lord," said Master

Sean, "I'll go on to the Royal Steward. Likely Lord Bontriomphe will be wanting to take a look at my report."

Lord Darcy smiled. "And likely you'd be wanting to get back to the Convention, eh?"

Master Sean grinned back. "Well, yes, my lord, I would."

"All right. I'll be along later."

* * *

Sir Thomas Leseaux, tall, lean and grim-faced, was standing outside the Gardenia Suite, which the Duchess of Cumberland had given to Tia Einzig. "Good morning, my lord," he said. "I . . . I want to thank you for what you did last night, but I know of no way to do so."

"My dear Sir Thomas, I did nothing that you would not have done had you been there. And there is no need for the grim look."

"Grim?" Sir Thomas forced a smile. "Was I grim?"

"Of course you were grim, Sir Thomas. Why shouldn't you be? You have heard Tia's story and you are greatly afraid that I shall arrest her on a charge of espionage."

Sir Thomas blinked and said nothing.

"Come, come, my dear fellow," said Lord Darcy. "She cannot have betrayed the Empire to any great extent, else you would be as eager for her arrest as anyone. You are not a man to allow love to blind you. Further, may I remind you of the laws concerning King's Evidence. Ah, that's better, Sir Thomas, now your smile looks more genuine. And now, if you gentlemen will excuse me, I shall allow you to pace this hallway at your leisure." He opened the door and went in.

Lord Darcy walked through the sitting room of the Gardenia Suite toward the bedroom, and halfway there heard a girl's voice.

"My Lord Darcy? Is that you?"

Lord Darcy went to the bedroom door. "Yes, Damoselle, I am Lord Darcy."

She was in bed, covered by warm blankets up to her shoulders. Her lips curved in a soft smile. "You are handsome, my lord. I am very glad. I don't think I should care to owe my life to an ugly man."

"My dear Tia, so long as beauty such as yours has been saved, the beauty of he who saved it is immaterial." He walked over and sat down in the chair by her bed.

"I won't ask you how you came to be there when you were so sorely needed, my lord," she said softly. "I merely want to say again that I am glad you were."

"So am I, Damoselle. But the question, as you have said, does not concern how *I* happened to be upon that bridge, but how *you* did. Tell me about Master Ewen MacAlister."

For a moment her mouth was set in grim, hard lines; then she smiled again. "I'll have to go back a little; back to my home in Banat."

The story she told him was essentially the same as the one she had told Mary of Cumberland—with added details. Her Uncle Neapeler had been denounced for practicing his Healing Art by a business rival, and because his political sympathies were already suspect, the Secret Police of King Casimir IX had come to their home to arrest them both. But Neapeler Einzig had been prepared for just such an eventuality, and his strong—although untrained— Talent had warned him in time. Only a few minutes

ahead of the dread Secret Police, they had both
headed toward the Italian border. But the Secret Police, too, had sources of sorcery, and the fleeing pair
had almost been caught in a trap, less than a hundred yards from the frontier. Neapeler had told his
niece to run while he stood off the Secret Police.

And that was the last she had seen of him.

The story she told of her movements through Italy
and of her extradition hearing in Dauphine was a
familiar one to Lord Darcy, but he listened with care.
Then she came to the part he had been waiting for.

"I thought I was safe when Sir Thomas brought
me here to England," she said, "and then Master
Ewen came to me. I didn't know who he was then; he
didn't tell me his name. But he told me that Uncle
Neapeler had been captured and imprisoned by the
Polish Secret Police. My uncle was being treated
well, he said, but his continued well-being would depend entirely upon my cooperation.

"Master Ewen told me that Sir Thomas knew the
secret of a weapon that had been developed for the
Angevin Imperial Navy. He didn't know what the
weapon was, but the Polish Secret Service had somehow discovered its existence and knew that Sir
Thomas had highly valuable information concerning
it. Since he knew that Sir Thomas trusted me, he
asked me to get this information for him. He threatened to torture—to kill—Uncle Neapeler unless I did
as he asked." She turned her head back suddenly
and looked straight at Lord Darcy. "But I didn't.
You must understand that I *didn't*. Sir Thomas will
tell you, I never once asked him about any of his secret work—*never!*"

Lord Darcy thought of Sir Thomas' face as he had
last seen it. "I believe you, Damoselle. Go on."

"I didn't know what to do. I didn't want to tell them anything, and I didn't want to betray Sir Thomas, either. I told them that I was trying. I told them that I was working my way into his confidence. I told them"—she paused for a moment, biting at her lower lip—"I told Master Ewen anything and everything I could to keep my uncle alive."

"Of course," said Lord Darcy gently. "No one can blame you for that."

"And then came the Convention," she said. "MacAlister said I had to attend, that I had to be there. I tried to stay away. I pointed out to him that even though I had been admitted to the Guild as an apprentice, the Convention does not normally accept apprentices as members. But he said that I had influence—with Sir Thomas, with His Grace the Archbishop—and that if I did not do my best to get in, he would see that I was sent one of Uncle Neapeler's fingers for every day of the Convention I missed. I had to do something, you understand that, don't you, my lord?"

"I understand," said Lord Darcy.

"Ewen MacAlister," she went one, "had warned me specifically to stay away from Master Sir James Zwinge. He said that Sir James was a top counterspy, that he was head of the Imperial Intelligence apparatus for Europe. So I thought perhaps Sir James could help me. I went to his room Wednesday morning. I met him just as he was leaving the lobby, and asked if I could speak to him. I told him that I had important information for him." She smiled a little. "He was very grouchy, but he asked me to come to his room. I told him everything—about my uncle, about Master Ewen—everything.

"And he just *sat* there!

"I told him *surely* the Imperial agents could get my uncle out of a Polish prison.

"He told me that he knew nothing about spy work, that he was merely a forensic sorcerer, working for the Marquis de London. He said he knew no way of getting my uncle out of a Polish prison or any other prison for that matter.

"I was furious. I don't really know what I said to him but it was—vicious. I wish now that I had not said it. I left his room and he locked the door after me. I may have been the last person to see Sir James Zwinge alive." Then she added hurriedly, "That is, aside from his murderer."

"Damoselle Tia," said Lord Darcy in his most gentle voice, "at this point I must tell you something, and I must ask you to reveal it to no one else until I give you leave. Agreed?"

"Agreed, of course, my lord."

"It is this. I believe that you *were* the last person to see him alive. The evidence I have thus far indicates that. But I want you to know that I do not believe you are in any way responsible for his death."

"Thank you, my lord," she said, and suddenly there were tears in her eyes.

Lord Darcy took her hand. "Come, my dear, this is a poor time to cry. Come now, no more tears."

She smiled in spite of her tears. "You're very kind, my lord."

"Oh, no, my dear Tia, I'm not kind at all. I am cruel and vicious and I have ulterior motives."

She laughed. "Most men do."

"I didn't mean it quite that way," said Lord Darcy dryly. "What I intended to convey was that I *do* have another question to ask."

She brushed tears from her eyes with one hand,

and gave him her impish smile. "No ulterior motives, then. That's a shame." Then she became serious again. "What is the question?"

"Why did Master Ewen decide to kill you?" Lord Darcy was quite certain that he knew the answer, but he did not want to disclose to the girl how he knew it.

This time her smile had the same cold, vengeful quality that he had seen the night before. "Because I learned the truth," she said. "Yesterday evening I was approached by a friend of my uncle's—a Goodman Colin MacDavid—a Manxman whom I remembered from when I was a very little girl. Goodman Colin told me the truth.

"My Uncle Neapeler escaped from the trap that I told you of. Goodman Colin helped him escape, and my uncle has been working with him on the Isle of Man ever since. He is safe. But he has been in hiding all this time, because he is afraid the Poles will kill him. He thought *I* was dead—until he saw my name in the London *Courier,* in the list of those attending the Convention; then he sent Goodman Colin straight away to find me.

"But Goodman Colin also explained that when my uncle escaped he left behind evidence indicating that he had been killed. He did this to protect me. All the time Master Ewen was using my uncle's life as a weapon against me, he and the Polish Secret Police actually thought he was dead. Do you wonder that I was furious when I finally found out the truth?"

"Of course not," said Lord Darcy. "That was yesterday evening."

"Yes," she said. "Then I got a note from Master Ewen telling me to meet him in a pub called the *Hound and Hare.* Do you know of it?"

"I know where it is," said Lord Darcy. "Go on."

"I suppose I lost my temper again," she said. "I suppose I said the wrong things, just as I did with Sir James." Her eyes hardened. "But I'm not sorry for what I said to Master Ewen! I told him what I thought of him, I told him I would report everything to the Imperial authorities, I told him I wanted to see him hanged, I—" She stopped suddenly and gave Lord Darcy a puzzled frown. "I'm not quite sure what happened after that. He raised his hand," she said slowly, "and traced a symbol in the air, and . . . and after that I remember nothing, that is . . . nothing until this morning, when I woke up here and saw Father Patrique."

She reached out suddenly and grasped Lord Darcy's right hand in both of her own. "I know I have done wrong, my lord. Will I . . . will I have to appear before His Majesty's Court of High Justice?"

Lord Darcy smiled and stood up. "I rather think that you will, my dear—you will be our most important witness against Master Ewen MacAlister. I think I can assure you that you will not appear before the Court in any other capacity."

The girl was still holding Lord Darcy's hand. With a sudden movement she brought it to her lips, kissed it and then let it go.

"Thank you, my lord," she said.

"It is I who must thank you," said Lord Darcy with a bow. "If I may do you any further service, Damoselle, you have but to ask."

He went out the door of the Gardenia Suite expecting to see two men waiting for him in the hall. Instead, there were three. Father Patrique and Sir Thomas looked at him as he closed the door behind him.

"How is she?" asked Father Patrique.

"Quite well, I think." Then he glanced at the third man, a uniformed Sergeant-at-Arms.

"Sergeant Peter has news for you," Father Patrique said, "but I would not allow him to interrupt. Now, if you'll excuse me, I'll see my patient." The door closed behind him as he went into the Gardenia Suite.

Lord Darcy smiled at Sir Thomas. "All is well, my friend. Neither of you has anything to fear."

Then he looked back at the Sergeant-at-Arms. "You have information for me, Sergeant?"

"Yes, my lord. Lord Bontriomphe said it was most important. We have found Goodman Paul Nichols."

"Oh, indeed?" said Lord Darcy. "Where did you find him? Has he anything to say for himself?"

"I'm afraid not," said Sergeant Peter. "He was found in a lumber room at the hotel. And he was dead, my lord. Quite dead."

# 19

LORD DARCY STRODE across the lobby of the Royal
Steward Hotel, closely followed by the Sergeant-at-
Arms. He went down the hallway, past the offices,
toward the rear door. Sergeant Peter had already
told him where the room in question was, but the
information proved unnecessary, since there were
two Armsmen on guard before it. It led off to the left
from the narrow hallway, about halfway between the
temporary headquarters office and the rear door.
The room was a workshop, set up for furniture repair. There were worktables and tools around the
walls, and several pieces of half-finished furniture
scattered about. Towards the rear of the room was
an open door, beyond which Lord Darcy could see
only darkness.

Near the door stood Lord Bontriomphe and Master Sean O Lochlainn. They both looked around as
Lord Darcy walked across the room toward them.

"Hullo, Darcy," said Lord Bontriomphe. "We've
got another one." He gestured past the open door

which, Lord Darcy now saw, opened into a small closet filled with odds and ends of wood and pieces of broken furniture. Beyond the door, just inside the closet, lay a man's body.

It was not a pleasant sight. The face was blackened and the tongue protruded. Around the throat, set deep into the flesh, was a knotted cord.

Lord Darcy looked at Lord Bontriomphe. "What happened?"

Lord Bontriomphe did not take his eyes off the corpse. "I think I shall go out and beat my head against a wall. I've been looking for this man ever since yesterday afternoon. I've combed London for him. I've asked every employee in this hotel every question I could think of." Then he looked up at Lord Darcy. "I had finally arrived at what I thought was the ridiculous conclusion that Goodman Paul Nichols had never left the hotel." He gave Lord Darcy a rather lopsided smile. "And then, half an hour ago, one of the hotel's employees, a joiner and carpenter whose job it is to keep the hotel's furniture in repair, came in here and opened that door." He gestured toward the closet. "He needed a piece of wood. He found—*that*. He came running out into the hall in a screaming fit. Fortunately I was in the office. Master Sean had just shown up, so we came back to take a look."

"He has definitely been identified as Paul Nichols?" Lord Darcy asked.

"Oh, yes, no question of that."

Lord Darcy looked at Master Sean. "There is no rest for the weary, eh, Master Sean? What do you find?"

Master Sean sighed. "Well, I won't know for sure

until after the chirurgeon has performed the autopsy, but it's my opinion the man's been dead for at least forty-eight hours. There's a bruise on his right temple—hard to see because of the coagulation of the blood in the face, but it's there all right—which indicates that he was knocked unconscious before he was killed. Someone hit him on the side of the head, and then took that bit of upholsterer's cord and tightened it around his throat to strangle him."

"Forty-eight hours," said Lord Darcy thoughtfully. He looked at his watch. "That would be, give or take an hour or so, at approximately the same time Master Sir James was killed. Interesting."

"There's one thing, my lord," said Master Sean, "which you might find even more interesting." He knelt down and pointed at some bits of material lying on the corpse's shirt front. "What does that look like to you?"

Lord Darcy knelt and looked. "Sealing wax," he said softly. "Bits of blue sealing wax."

Master Sean nodded. "That's what they looked like to me, my lord."

Lord Darcy stood up. "I hate to put you through another session of such grueling work, Sean, but it must be done. I must know the time of his death, and—"

Master Sean took one more look at the dead man's shirt front, and then stood up himself. "And something more about those bits of blue sealing wax, eh, my lord?"

"Exactly."

"Well," said Lord Bontriomphe, "at least this time we know who killed him."

"Yes, I know *who* killed him, all right," Lord

Darcy said. "What I don't understand is *why*."

"You mean, the motive?" Lord Bontriomphe asked.

"Oh, I know the motive. What I want to know is the motive behind the motive, if you follow me."

Lord Bontriomphe didn't.

**\* \* \***

Another half hour of meticulous investigation revealed nothing of further interest. The murder of Paul Nichols appeared to be as simple as that of Sir James had been complex. There was no locked door, no indication of Black Magic, no question as to the method of death. By the time he was finished looking the area over, Lord Darcy was convinced that his mental reconstruction of the murder was reasonably accurate. Paul Nichols had been enticed into the workshop, knocked unconscious, strangled with a handy piece of upholsterer's cord, and dumped into the small lumber room. Exactly what had happened after that was not quite as clear, but Lord Darcy felt that subsequent data would not drastically change his hypothesis.

Satisfied, Lord Darcy left the remainder of the investigation to Lord Bontriomphe and Master Sean. *Now*, he thought to himself, *what to do next?* Go to the Palace du Marquis first and pick up a gun, he decided. He had mentioned to Lord Bontriomphe that he had lost his own weapon in the Thames, and Bontriomphe had said, "I have another in my desk, a Heron .36. You can use that if you want; it's a good weapon." Lord Darcy decided that one good stiff drink would probably stand him in good stead before he took a cab to the Palace du Marquis. He went to the Sword Room and ordered a brandy and soda.

There was still a state of tension in the hotel, and the Convention seemed to have been held in abeyance. Of all the sorcerers he had seen that morning, with the exception of Master Sean himself, not one had been wearing the silver slashes of a Master. Lord Darcy saw a familiar face further down the bar, a young man who was giving his full attention to a pint of good English beer. With a slight frown, Lord Darcy picked up his glass and walked down to where the other man was sitting.

"Good morning, my lord," he said. "I should have thought you would be out on the chase."

Journeyman Sorcerer Lord John Quetzal looked up, a little startled. "Lord Darcy! I've been wanting to talk to you," he said. The smile on his face looked a little sad. "They didn't ask me to help find Master Ewen," he said. "They're afraid a journeyman couldn't hold his own against a Master."

"And you think you could?" Lord Darcy asked.

"No!" Lord John Quetzal said excitedly. "That's not the point, don't you see? Master Ewen may be a more powerful sorcerer than I am, I don't argue with that. But *I* don't have to face him down. If he uses magic when he's cornered, another, more powerful sorcerer can take care of him then. The point is that I can *find* Master Ewen. I can find out where he is. But nobody listens to a journeyman sorcerer."

Lord Darcy looked at him. "Now let me understand you," he said carefully. "You think you can find where Master Ewen is hiding now?"

"Not just *think; I know!* I am positive I can find him. When you brought the Damoselle Tia in last night, she stank to high Heaven of Black Magic." He looked apologetic. "I don't mean a real smell, you understand, not the way you'd smell tobacco smoke or"—he gestured towards Lord Darcy's glass—"brandy, or something like that."

"I understand," said Lord Darcy. "It is merely a psychic analogy to the physical sense which it most nearly resembles. That is why people with your particular kind of Talent are called witch-smellers."

"Yes, my lord; exactly. And any given act of black sorcery has its characteristic 'aroma'—a stink that identifies the sorcerer who performed it. You asked me Wednesday night if I suspected anyone, and I refused to tell you. But it was Master Ewen. I could detect the taint on him even then. But now, with an example of his work to go on, I could smell him out anywhere in London."

He smiled rather sheepishly. "I was just sitting here trying to make up my mind whether I should go out on my own or not."

"You could detect the stink of Black Magic on the Damoselle Tia," Lord Darcy said. "How did you know that it was not she who was practicing the Black Art?"

"My lord," said Lord John Quetzal, "there is a great deal of difference between a dirty finger and a dirty finger-mark."

Lord Darcy contemplated his drink in silence for a full minute. Then he picked it up and finished it in two swallows.

"My Lord John Quetzal," he said briskly. "Lord Bontriomphe and his Armsmen are searching for Master Ewen. So are Sir Lyon and the Masters of the Guild. So are Commander Lord Ashley and the Naval Intelligence Corps. And do you know what?"

"No, my lord," said Lord John Quetzal, putting

down his empty beer mug, "what?"

"You and I are going to make them all look foolish. Come with me. We must fetch a cab. First to the Palace du Marquis, and then, my lord—wherever your nose leads us."

# 20

IT TOOK HOURS.

In a little pub far to the north of the river, Journeyman Sorcerer Lord John Quetzal stared blankly at a mug of beer that he had no intention of drinking.

"I think I have him, my lord," he said dully. "I think I have him."

"Very good," said Lord Darcy.

He dared say nothing further. During all this time he had followed Lord John Quetzal's leads, making marks on the map as the young Mechicain witch-smeller came ever closer to the black sorcerer who was his prey.

"It's not as easy as I thought," said Lord John Quetzal.

Lord Darcy nodded grimly. Witch-smelling—the detection of psychic evil—was not the same as clairvoyance, but even so the privacy spells in London had dimmed the young Mechicain's perceptions.

"Not easy, perhaps," he said, "but just as certain, just as sure." His lordship realized that the young journeyman had not yet perfected his innate ability to its utmost. That, of course, would come with time and further training. "Let's go through it again. Tell me the clues as you picked them up."

"Yes, my lord," said the young Mechicain. After a moment he began: "He's surrounded by those who will help him—Master Ewen is, I mean. But they will not risk their own lives for him.

"There is a tremendous amount of psychic tension surrounding him," Lord John Quetzal continued, "but it has nothing to do with him personally. They don't know that he exists."

"I understand, my lord," said Lord Darcy. "From the descriptions you have given me, it appears to me that Master Ewen is surrounded by generally un-Talented people who are attempting to use the Talent." He spread his map of London out on the table. "Now, let's see if we can get a fix." He tapped a spot on the map. "From here"—he moved his finger—"in that direction, eh?"

"Yes, my lord," said Lord John Quetzal.

"Now," Lord Darcy moved his finger further down the map. "From here"—he moved his finger again—"to there. Eh?"

"Yes."

Lord John Quetzal knew direction and magnitude, but he seemed unable to give any further information. Time after time Lord Darcy had gone through this same routine—so many times that it seemed monotonous, repetitive.

And yet, each time, more information came to the fore. At last, Lord Darcy was able to draw a circle on the map of London, and tap it with the point of his pencil.

"He is somewhere within that area. There is no other possible answer." Then he reached out and put his hand on the young journeyman's shoulder. "I know you're tired. Fatigue is the normal condition of an Investigator for the King."

Lord John Quetzal straightened his shoulders and looked up suddenly. "I know. But"—he tapped the spot that Lord Darcy had circled—"that's quite a bit of area. I thought that I could locate him precisely, exactly." He took a deep breath. "And now I find that . . ."

"Oh, come," Lord Darcy said. "You give in too easily. We have him located; it is simply that you do not realize how closely we have surrounded our quarry. We know the general area, but we do not have the exact description of his immediate surroundings."

"But there I cannot help," Lord John Quetzal said, the dullness coming back into his voice.

"I think you can," said Lord Darcy. "I ask you to put your attention upon the symbols surrounding Master Ewen MacAlister—not his actual physical surroundings but his symbolic surroundings."

And then Lord Darcy waited.

Suddenly Lord John Quetzal looked up. "I have an intuition. I see . . ." Lord John Quetzal began again. "It is the blazon of a coat of arms, my lord: *Argent, in saltire, five fusils gules.*"

"Go on," said Lord Darcy urgently, making a rapid notation on the margin of the map.

Lord John Quetzal looked out into nothing. *"Argent,"* he said *"in pale, three trefoils sable, the lower-most inverted."*

Lord Darcy made another note, and then put his hand very carefully on the top of the table, palm down. "I ask you to give me one more, my lord—just one more."

"*Argent,*" said Lord John Quetzal, "*a heart gules.*"

Lord Darcy leaned back in the booth, took a deep breath and said, "We have it, my lord, we have it. Thanks to you. Come, we must get back to Carlyle House."

* * *

Half an hour after that, Her Grace, Mary, the Dowager Duchess of Cumberland, was looking at the same map. "Yes, yes, of course," she said. She looked at the young Mechicain. "Of course. *Argent, in saltire, five fusils gules.*" She looked up at Lord Darcy. "The five of diamonds."

"Right," said Lord Darcy.

"And the second is the three of clubs. And the third, the ace of hearts."

"Exactly. Do you doubt now that Master Ewen is hiding there?"

She looked back down at the map. "No, of course not. Of course he's there." She looked up at him. "You went no further, my lord?" Then she glanced at Lord John Quetzal and corrected herself. "My lords?"

"Was there any need?" Lord Darcy asked. "My Lord du Moqtessuma has assured me that if Master Ewen leaves his hiding place he shall know it. Right, my lord?"

"Right." Then he added, "That is, I cannot guarantee his future movements, but if he should go very far from there I should know it."

"One thing I do not understand," Her Grace said frankly, "is why my lord John Quetzal did not immediately recognize the symbolism." She looked at the young Mechicain nobleman with a smile. "I do not mean this as a reflection upon your abilities. You *did* visualize the symbols—and yet you translated them in terms of heraldry rather than in terms of playing cards. Undoubtedly you could explain why, but with your permission I should like to know how Lord Darcy knew."

"It was information you did not have," Lord Darcy said with a smile. "The night before last when we were discussing Mechicoe, while you were dressing, we had a short discussion of gambling and recreation in Mechicoe. I observed that not once did Lord John Quetzal mention playing cards—from which I gathered that they are very little used."

"In Mechicoe," said Lord John Quetzal, "a deck of cards is generally considered to be a fortune-telling device, used by unlicensed wizards and black sorcerers. I am not familiar with the card deck as a gambling device, although I have heard, of course, that it can be used as such."

"Of course," said Lord Darcy. "Therefore, you translated the symbols you saw in terms of heraldry, a field of knowledge with which you are familiar. But your description is quite clear." He looked at the Duchess. "And, therefore, we came to you." He smiled. "If anyone knows the gambling clubs of London, it is you."

She looked back down at the map. "Yes," she said. "There's only one such club in that area. He must be there. It's the *Manzana de Oro*."

"Ah," said Lord Darcy. "The *Golden Apple,* eh? What do you know of it?"

"It is owned by a Moor from Granada."

"Indeed?" said Lord Darcy. "Describe him to me."

"Oh, he's an absolutely fascinating creature," said Her Grace. "He's tall—as tall as you are—and quite devilishly handsome. He has dark skin—almost

black—flashing eyes, and a small pointed beard. He
dresses magnificently in the Oriental fashion.
There's an enormous emerald on his left ring finger,
and a great ruby—or perhaps it is a spinel—in his
turban. He carries at his waist a jewelled Persian
dagger that is probably worth a fortune. For all I
know he is an unmitigated scoundrel, but in his
manners and bearing he is unquestionably a gentleman. He calls himself the Sidi al-Nasir."

Lord Darcy leaned back and laughed.

"May I ask," the Duchess said acidly, "what is so
funny, my lord?"

"My apologies," said Lord Darcy, smothering his
laughter. "I wasn't trying to be funny. You must
credit it to our Moorish friend. 'Sidi al-Nasir' indeed! How lovely. I have a feeling I shall like this
gentleman."

"Would it be too much," Her Grace said pleasantly, "for you to let us in on the joke?"

"It is the felicitous choice of name and title," Lord
Darcy said. "Translating broadly, *Sidi al-Nasir*
means 'My Lord the Winner.' How magnificently he
has informed the upper class gamblers of London
that the advantage is with the house. Yes, indeed, I
think I shall like My Lord al-Nasir." He looked at
the Duchess. "Do you have entry into his club?"

"You know I do," she said. "You would never
have mentioned it to me otherwise."

"True," said Lord Darcy blandly. "But now that
you are in on our little trap, I shall not deny you the
further enjoyment of helping us close it solidly upon
our quarry." He looked at Lord John Quetzal. "My
lord," he said, "the quarry is cornered. We now have
but to devise the trap itself."

Lord John Quetzal nodded smilingly. "Indeed, my lord. Oh, yes indeed. Now, to begin with . . ."

\* \* \*

The night was clear. Each star in the sky above shone like a separate brilliant jewel in the black velvet of the heavens. A magnificent carriage bearing the Cumberland arms pulled up in front of the *Manzana de Oro*, the footman opened and bowed low before the polychrome and gilt door, and four people descended. The first to alight was no less than Her Grace the Dowager Duchess of Cumberland. She was followed by a tall, lean, handsome man in impeccable evening clothes. The third passenger was equally tall—a dark-faced man wearing the arms of the ducal house of Moqtessuma. All three bowed low as the fourth passenger stepped out.

His Highness the Prince of Vladistov was a short, round gentleman, with a dark, bushy, heavy beard and an eyeglass screwed into his right eye. He descended from the coach in silence with great dignity, and acknowledged his companions' bows with a patronizing tilt of his head.

Her Grace of Cumberland nodded to the brace of doormen who stood at rigid attention at either side of the entrance to the *Manzana de Oro*, and the four of them marched inside. At the inner door, Her Grace's escort spoke to the majordomo. "You may announce to My Lord al-Nasir—Her Grace, Mary, Dowager Duchess of Cumberland; Lord John Quetzal du Moqtessuma de Mechicoe; His Most Serene Highness, Jehan, Prince of Vladistov; and myself, the Lord of Arcy."

The majordomo bowed low before this magnificent company and said. "His lordship shall be so

informed." Then he glanced at the Dowager
Duchess. "Your pardon ... uh ... Your Grace
vouches for these gentlemen?"

"Of course, Goodman Abdul," said Her Grace im-
periously, and the party of four swept across the
threshold.

Lord Darcy held back and, as Lord John Quetzal
caught up with him, whispered, "Is he here?"

"He's here," said Lord John Quetzal. "I can place
him within ten feet now."

"Good. Keep smiling and follow my lead. But if he
moves, let me know immediately."

They followed Her Grace and the magnificently
attired Prince of Vladistov into the interior.

The anteroom was large—some thirty feet broad
by twenty feet deep—and gave no hint that the *Manzana de Oro* was a gambling club. The decor was
Moorish, and—to Lord Darcy, who had seen Southern Spain, North Africa, and Arabia—far too
Moorish. The decor was not that of a public place in
the Islamic countries, but that of the *hareem*. The
walls were hung with cloth-of-gold—or what passed
for it; the archways which led off it were—embroidered was the only word—embroidered with
quotations from the *Qu'ran*—quotations which, while
very decorative because of the Arabic script, were essentially meaningless in the context.

The floor was inlaid with Moorish tile, and exotic
flowers set in brazen pots of earth were tastefully
placed around the walls. In the center of the room, a
golden fountain played. The water moved in fantastic patterns, always shifting, never repeating,
forming weird and unusual shapes in the air. The
fountain was lined with lights whose colors changed
and moved with the waving patterns. The water

flowed down over a series of baffles that produced a shifting musical note in the air.

Well-dressed people in evening clothes stood around exchanging pleasantries.

Her Grace turned and smiled. "Shall we go to the gaming rooms, gentle sirs?"

The Prince of Vladistov glanced at Lord Darcy. Lord Darcy said, "Of course, Your Grace."

She gestured toward one of the side doors that led off the anteroom and said, "Will you accompany me?" and led them through the arched doorway to their right. The gaming room was even more flamboyant than the anteroom. The hangings were of gold, embroidered with purple and red, decorated with scenes from ancient Islamic myth. But their beauty formed only a background to the Oriental magnificence of the room itself, and the brilliant evening dress of the people who played at the gaming tables stood out glitteringly against that background.

A number of sharp-eyed men moved unobtrusively among the gaming tables, observing the play. Lord Darcy knew they were journeymen sorcerers hired to spot any player's attempt to use a trained Talent to affect his chances. Their job was not to overcome any such magic, but merely to report it and expel the offender. The effect of any untrained Talent present in the players could be expected to cancel out.

The Prince of Vladistov smiled broadly at Lord Darcy and said, in a very low tone, "I've twigged to Master Ewen meself, my lord—thanks to Lord John Quetzal's aid. Sure and we have him now. He's in the room to the right, just beyond that arch with the purple scribblings about it."

Lord Darcy bowed. "Your Highness is most astute," he said. "But where the Devil is Sidi al-

Nasir?" It was a rhetorical question to which he did not expect an answer. Mary of Cumberland had assured him that al-Nasir invariably greeted members of the nobility when they came to his club, and yet there had been no sign of the Moor.

The Prince of Vladistov answered Lord Darcy's rhetorical question. "He seems to be in his office. We can't be sure, Lord John Quetzal and I, but we both agree that that's where he seems to be."

Lord Darcy nodded. "All right, we'll work it that way." He moved up and smiled at the Dowager Duchess of Cumberland. "Your Grace," he said very softly, "I observe that the gentleman who was at the door has followed us in."

She did not turn her head. "Goodman Abdul? Yes. By this time he is probably wondering why we have not gone to the gaming tables."

"A good question, from his point of view. We shall take advantage of it. Go over and ask him where Sidi al-Nasir is. Insist upon speaking to the Sidi. You have brought, after all, a most important guest, the Prince of the distant Russian principality of Vladistov, and you see no reason why el Sidi should not greet him as he deserves. Pour it on thick. But make sure his back is toward us."

She nodded and moved across the room toward el Sidi's minion, leaving her three companions clustered in a group around the door that was their target.

As soon as the Duchess had distracted Abdul's attention, Lord Darcy whispered, "All right. This is it. Move in."

Lord John Quetzal turned and faced the crowd, watching every movement. Lord Darcy and the Prince of Vladistov moved toward the door.

"No spell on the lock," said the short, round man with the beard. "Too many people moving in and out."

"Very good." Lord Darcy reached out, turned the knob, pulled open the door, and within the space of half a second he and his companion were inside, the door closed behind them.

Sidi al-Nasir conformed precisely to the description that the Duchess had given them. When he saw the two strangers enter his office, one hand reached for a drawer—then stopped. His black eyes looked down the equally black muzzle of the Heron .36 that stared at him. Then they lifted to the face of the man who carried the weapon. "With your permission, my lord," he said coolly, "I shall put my empty hand back on top of my desk."

"I suggest that you do so," said Lord Darcy. He glanced at the man who sat across from Sidi al-Nasir's desk. "Good evening, my lord. I see that you are here before me."

Commander Lord Ashley smiled calmly. "It was inevitable," he said in a cool, constrained voice. "I am glad to see you." He looked toward Sidi al-Nasir. "My Lord al-Nasir," he said, "has just proposed that I go to work for the Government of Poland."

Lord Darcy looked at the dark-complexioned man. "Have you now, My Lord the Winner?"

Sidi al-Nasir spread his hands on the surface of the desk and smiled. "Ah, then you understand Arabic, most noble lord?" he said in that language.

"While I do not, perhaps, have your liquid fluency in the Tongue of Tongues," Lord Darcy said in return, "my poor knowledge of the language of the Prophet is adequate for most purposes."

Sidi al-Nasir's finely-chiseled lips wreathed in a

smile. "I am not one to contradict, most noble," he said. "But, except that your enunciation betrays the fact that your mentor was a subject of the Shah of Shahs, your command of the speech of the *Qu'ran* is most flowing."

Lord Darcy allowed a half-smile to touch his lips. "It is true that my instructor in the noble language of the Prophet of Islam came from the Court of the Shadow of God on Earth, the Shah of Persia, but—would you prefer that I spoke in the debased fashion of Northwest Africa and Southern Spain?"

The sudden shift in Lord Darcy's accent made Sidi al-Nasir blink. Then he raised his eyebrows and his smile broadened even further. "Ah, most wise one, your knowledge betrays you. But few people of your Frankish Empire have such a command of the Tongue of Tongues. You are, then, the renowned Sidi of Arcy. It is indeed a pleasure to meet you, my lord."

"I hope that events may prove that it was a pleasure to meet you, my lord," said Lord Darcy. Then, shifting, "But you have guests, my lord. Shall we continue in Anglo-French?"

"Of course," said Sidi al-Nasir. He glanced at Lord Ashley. "So it was all a trap then?"

Lord Ashley nodded. "All a trap, my dear al-Nasir."

"A poor one, I think," said Sidi al-Nasir with a smile. "Poorly planned and poorly executed." He chuckled softly. "I need not even deny the truth."

"Well, we shall see," said Lord Darcy. "What *is* the truth?"

Sidi al-Nasir's smile did not vanish. He merely looked at Commander Lord Ashley.

Lord Ashley gave him one glance and then looked up at Lord Darcy with a smile. "Sorry to have pulled this on you. Didn't know you'd be here. We have long suspected that the *Manzana de Oro* was the headquarters of a spy ring working for His Slavonic Majesty. In order to prove our case I ran up a debt here of . . ." He looked at Sidi al-Nasir.

The Moor, still smiling, sighed. "Of some one hundred and fifty golden sovereigns, my lord. More than you could earn in a year."

Lord Ashley nodded calmly. "Exactly. And tonight you offered me two alternatives. You would either report my debt to the Admiralty, in which case —so you assumed—I would be ruined, or I could become a spy for His Slavonic Majesty."

Sidi al-Nasir's smile broadened. "That was why I said the trap was poorly laid, My Lord Commander. I deny that I made you any such offer, and you have no witnesses to prove it."

Lord Darcy, still holding his pistol level, allowed a smile to come over his own face. "My Lord al-Nasir," he said, "for your information, I shall say that I am quite confident that you *have* just made such an offer to my lord the Commander."

Sidi al-Nasir showed his white teeth in a broad smile. "Ah, my lord, *you* may be certain." He laughed. "Perhaps even *I* am certain, no? And of course Commander Lord Ashley is certain. But"— he spread his hands—"is this evidence? Would it stand up in court?" He looked suddenly very sad. "Ah, you might, of course, deport me. The evidence of my lord Ashley may be strong enough for that. There is, certainly, enough suspicion here to force me to return to my native Spain. I must close down the

*Manzana de Oro.* What a pity it will be to leave the chill and fog of London for the warmth, the color, the beauty of Granada . . ." Then he directed his smile at Lord Darcy. "But I am afraid that you cannot imprison me."

"As to that," said Lord Darcy, "possibly you are right. But we shall see."

"Is it necessary, my lord, that you keep the muzzle of that weapon pointing at me?" said Sidi al-Nasir. "I find it distinctly ungentlemanly."

"Of course, my lord," said Lord Darcy, not deviating the aim of his weapon one iota. "If you would be so good as to remove—no! no! . . . not just the gun . . . the whole drawer from your desk. There may be more than one gun in it."

Sidi al-Nasir very carefully pulled out the drawer and placed it on the desk top. "Only one, my lord, and I shouldn't think of touching it in your presence."

Lord Darcy looked at the weapon that lay by itself in the drawer. "Ah," he said, "a Toledo .39. A very good weapon, my lord. I shall see to it that it is returned to you, if the law so allows."

The Sidi al-Nasir's obsidian eyes suddenly flickered as his gaze moved across Lord Darcy's face. In that instant he realized that Darcy's information covered a great deal more territory than a mere suspicion of espionage. The Sidi knew that this trap was more dangerous than it had at first appeared.

"It is possible, my lord," he said smoothly, "that Lord Ashley's losses were due to the machinations of a certain Master Sorcerer, whom I have decided to release from my employ. The Commander's winnings up until a short time ago were considerable.

The Master Sorcerer of whom I spoke may have decided to correct that. If so, of course, I am not personally responsible . . ."

"Ah," said Lord Darcy. "So Commander Lord Ashley's slight precognitive ability was overcome by Master Ewen." He addressed the Commander without taking his eyes off Sidi al-Nasir. "What did you usually play, Ashley?"

"Rouge-et-Or," said the Commander.

"I see. Then the precognition would be of little use at that game if a Master Sorcerer were working against you. If you made a bet on any given number, the sorcerer could almost always make certain that the little ivory ball did not land in the proper slot—even if he were operating from another room."

His eyes gazed directly at those of Sidi al-Nasir. "A deliberate plot, then," he said. "You tried to enlist the Commander by having your sorcerer force the game to go against him."

"We suspected something of the sort," Lord Ashley said cheerfully, "so we decided to let Sidi al-Nasir run it as he would and see what developed."

The Sidi al-Nasir shrugged, still keeping his hands well above the table. "Whatever may have happened," he said, "I assure you that this sorcerer is no longer in my employ. However, my information leads me to believe that you are rather eager to locate him. It is possible I may be of some assistance to you in your search. I might be in a position to inform you as to Master Ewen's present whereabouts. After all, we are all of us reasonable men, are we not?"

"I am afraid your information is superfluous, my lord . . ." Lord Darcy began.

At that point the door of the office was flung open

and Lord John Quetzal burst in. "Look out! He's moving! He knows he's being betrayed!" he shouted.

Even as he spoke, the rear door was swinging open. Master Ewen MacAlister ran out, heading for the door that led to freedom. Only Lord John Quetzal stood between him and that door. The black sorcerer gestured with one hand toward the young Mechicain.

Lord John Quetzal threw up his hand to ward off the spell that had been cast, but his journeyman's powers were not the equal of those of a Master. His own shielding spell softened the blow, but could not completely stop it. He staggered and fell to his knees. He did not collapse, but his eyes glazed over and he remained in his kneeling position, unmoving.

But his moment of resistance, slight though it was, was enough to slow Master Ewen's flight. The bogus Prince of Vladistov was already in action. Master Sean O Lochlainn ripped off his false beard and allowed his eyeglass to drop to the floor.

Lord Darcy did not move. It took every ounce of his self-control to keep his pistol fixed firmly on the Sidi al-Nasir. The Moor also remained motionless. He did not even glance away from the muzzle of Lord Darcy's pistol.

The black sorcerer spun around to face Master Sean and gestured with one hand, describing an intricate symbol in the air with a flourish of his fingers, his features contorted in strained grimace.

Lord Darcy and everyone else in the room felt the psychic blast of that hastily conjured spell. Master Ewen's hours in hiding had obviously been spent in conjuring up the spells he would need to defend himself when the time came.

Master Sean O Lochlainn, toward whom the spell was directed, seemed to freeze for perhaps half a second. But he, too, had prepared himself, and he had the further advantage of having known the identity of his prey, while Master Ewen had no way of knowing —except by conjecture—who would come after him.

Master Sean's hand moved, creating a symbol in the air.

Master Ewen blinked, gritted his teeth and, from somewhere beneath his cloak, drew a long white wand.

No one else in the room, not even Lord Darcy, could move. They held their positions partly because of the psychic tension in the air around them, partly because they wanted to see the outcome of this duel between two master magicians, but primarily because the undirected corona effects of the spells themselves held them enthralled.

Except for Master Sean, no one there recognized the white wand that Master Ewen drew. But Master Sean saw it, recognized it as having been made from a human thigh bone, and in an instant had prepared a counterspell. The thighbone-wand was thrust out, and Master Ewen's lips moved malevolently.

The corona effect of the spell went beyond the immediate area. Outside in the gaming rooms, the players seemed to freeze for a moment. Then, for no apparent reason, the heavy bettors put their money on odds-on bets. One young scion of a wealthy family put fifty golden sovereigns on a bet that would have netted him a single silver sovereign if he had won.

And in al-Nasir's office, Lord John Quetzal suddenly blinked his eyes and looked away, Lord Ashley started to draw his sword, Sidi al-Nasir himself moved groggily away from his desk; and Lord

Darcy's hand quivered on the grip of the Heron .36, keeping it aligned on the Sidi, but not firing.

But Master Sean had warded off the effectiveness of even that spell, which was designed to make him take a stupid chance.

With great determination, he stalked toward Master Ewen, and his voice was hard and cold as he said, "In the Name of the Guild, Master Ewen—*yield!* Otherwise I shall not be responsible for what happens."

Master Ewen's reply contained three words— words which were furious, foul, and filthy.

Again that whitened thighbone-wand stabbed out.

And again Master Sean stood the brunt of that terrible psychic shock. Without a wand, without anything save his own hand, Master Sean made the final effective gesture of the battle.

But not the final gesture, for Master Ewen repeated himself. He stepped forward, and again jabbed with his chalk-white wand.

Then he stepped forward once more.

Another jab.

Another step.

Another jab.

Another step.

Master Sean moved to one side, watching Master Ewen.

The jabs of the black sorcerer's wand were no longer directed toward the tubby little Irish sorcerer but toward the point in space where he had been.

Master Sean took a deep breath. "I'd better catch him before he runs into the wall."

Lord Darcy did not move the muzzle of his weapon from Sidi al-Nasir. "What is he doing?" he asked.

"He's trapped in a time cycle, my lord. I've tied

his thought processes in a knot. They go round and round through their contortions and end up where they started. He'll keep repeating the same useless notions again and again until I pull him out of it."

In spite of Master Ewen MacAlister's apparently thaumaturgical gestures, everyone could feel that the corona effect was gone. Whatever was going on in the repeating cycle inside Master Ewen's mind, it had no magical effect.

"How is Lord John Quetzal?" Lord Darcy asked.

"Oh, he'll be all right as soon as I release him from that daze spell."

"Magnificently done, Master Sean," said Lord Darcy. "My Lord Ashley," he said to the Naval Commander, "will you be so good as to go to the nearest window, identify yourself, and shout for help? The place is completely surrounded by the Armsmen of London."

# 21

SIR FREDERIQUE BRULEUR, the seneschal of the Palace du Marquis, brought three cups of caffe into my lord de London's office. The first was placed on the center of My Lord Marquis' desk, the second on the center of Lord Bontriomphe's desk, the third on the corner of Lord Bontriomphe's desk near the red leather chair where Lord Darcy was seated. Then Sir Frederique withdrew silently.

My Lord Marquis sipped at his cup, then glowered at Lord Darcy. "You insist upon this confrontation, my lord cousin?"

"Can you see any other way of getting the evidence we need?" Lord Darcy asked blandly. He had wanted to discuss the problem earlier with the Marquis of London, but the Marquis insisted that no business should be discussed during dinner.

The Marquis took another sip at his cup. "No, I suppose not," he agreed. He focused his gaze upon Lord Bontriomphe. "You now have Master Ewen locked up. Securely, I presume?"

"We have three Master Sorcerers keeping an eye on him," Lord Bontriomphe said. "Master Sean has put a spell on him that will keep him in a total daze until we get around to taking it off. I don't know what more you want."

The Marquis of London snorted. "I want to make certain he doesn't get away, of course." He glanced at the clock on the wall. "It has now been three hours since you made your arrests at the *Manzana de Oro*. If Master Ewen is still in his cell I will concede that you have him properly guarded. Now: What information did you get?"

Lord Bontriomphe turned a hand palm up. "Master Ewen admits almost everything. He knows we have him on an espionage charge; he knows that we have him on a charge of Black Magic; he knows that we have him on a charge of thaumaturgical assault and attempted murder against the person of the Damoselle Tia Einzig.

"He admits to all that, but refuses to admit to a charge of murder. Until Master Sean put him under a quieting spell, he was talking his head off—admitting everything, as long as it would not put his neck in a noose."

"*Pah!* Naturally he would attempt to save his miserable skin. Very well. What happened? I have your reports and Lord Darcy's reports. From the facts, the conclusions are obvious. What do you say?" He looked straight into Bontriomphe's eyes.

Lord Bontriomphe shrugged. "I'm not the genius around here. I'll tell you what Chief Hennely thinks. I'll give you *his* theory for what it's worth. But mind you, I don't consider that it is accurate in every detail. But Chief Master-at-Arms Hennely has discussed this with Commander Lord Ashley and with

Captain Smollett, so I give you their theory for what *it's* worth."

The Marquis glanced at Lord Darcy, then looked back at Lord Bontriomphe. "Very well. Proceed."

"All right. To begin with, we needn't worry about the murder in Cherbourg. It was committed by a Polish agent detailed for the purpose, simply because they discovered that Barbour was a double agent— and our chances of finding the killer are small.

"The killer of Master Sir James is another matter. Here, we know who the killer is, and we know the tool he used.

"We know that the Damoselle Tia was being blackmailed, that Master Ewen threatened to have her uncle tortured and killed if she did not obey orders. Defying those orders, she went to Sir James Zwinge, and told him everything—including everything she knew about Master Ewen. Naturally, MacAlister had to dispose of Sir James, even though that would mean that a new head of the European Intelligence network would be appointed, and that the Poles would have to repeat all the work of discovering the identity of his successor as soon as the Navy appointed one."

He looked over at Lord Darcy. "As to *how* it was done, the important clue was that half-moon bloodstain that you pointed out to me." He looked back at the Marquis. "You see that, don't you? It was a heel print. And there was only one pair of shoes in the hotel that could have made such a print—the high-heeled shoes of Tia Einzig.

"Look at the evidence. We know, from Master Sean O Lochlainn's report, that Master Sir James was stabbed—not at 9:30 when he screamed—but at approximately nine o'clock, half an hour before. The wound was not immediately fatal."

He glanced back at Lord Darcy. "Sir James lay there, unconscious, for half an hour—and then, when he heard Master Sean's knock, he came out of his coma long enough to shout to Master Sean for help. He lifted himself up, but this last effort finished him. He dropped and died. Do you agree?"

"Most certainly," said Lord Darcy. "It could not have happened in any other way. He was stabbed at nine—or thereabouts—but did not die until half past.

"The chirurgical evidence of the blood, and the thaumaturgical evidence of the time of psychic shock demonstrate that clearly.

"But you have yet to explain how he was stabbed inside a locked room at nine o'clock—or at any other time. The evidence shows that there was no one else in that room when he was stabbed. What is your explanation for that?"

"I hate to say it," said Lord Bontriomphe, "but it appears to me that Master Sean's testimony is faulty. With another master sorcerer at work here, the evidence could have been fudged. Here's what happened: Master Ewen, knowing that he had to get rid of the Damoselle Tia, decided to use her to get rid of Master Sir James at the same time. He put her under a spell. She talked her way into Master Sir James's room, used his own knife on him when he least suspected it, and walked out, leaving that half-moon heel print near the door."

Lord Bontriomphe leaned back in his chair. "As a matter of cold fact, if it were not for that heel print, I would say that Master Ewen put Master Sir James under a spell which forced him to stab himself with that contact cutter.

"Naturally, he would fumble the job. Even under the most powerful magic spell it is difficult to force anyone to commit suicide."

He glanced at Lord Darcy. "As you yourself noticed with the Damoselle Tia, my lord; although she was induced to jump off the bridge, she nevertheless fought to keep herself afloat after she struck the water."

"Yes, she did," Lord Darcy agreed. "Go on."

"As I said," Lord Bontriomphe continued, "if it weren't for that heel print, I would say that Sir James was forced to suicide by Black Magic." He shrugged. "That still may be possible, but I'd like to account for that heel print. So, I say that the Damoselle Tia stabbed him and walked out, and that Master Ewen used sorcery to relock the door from the room above. I don't say that she is technically guilty of murder, but certainly she was a tool in Master Ewen's hands."

The Marquis of London snorted loudly and opened his mouth to say something, but Lord Darcy held up a warning hand. "Please, my lord cousin," he said mildly. "I think it incumbent upon us to listen to the rest of Lord Bontriomphe's theories. Pray continue, my lord," he said, addressing the London investigator.

Lord Bontriomphe looked at him bitterly. "All right; so you two geniuses have worked everything out. I am just a legman; I've never claimed to be anything else. But—if you don't like those theories, here's another."

He took a deep breath and went on. "We arrested Master Sean in the first place on the rather flimsy evidence that he and Sir James had both worked out a way to manipulate a knife by thaumaturgical means. Now suppose that was done? Suppose that is the way Sir James was killed? Who could have done it?" He spread a hand.

"I won't say Sir James did—although he could have. But, to assume that he took such a roundabout way of committing suicide would be, in the words of my lord the Marquis, fatuous. To think that it happened by accident would be even more fatuous.

"Or my lord may think of another adjective; I won't quibble.

"We know that Master Sean did not do it, because it would have taken at least three quarters of an hour to prepare the spell, and, according to Grand Master Sir Lyon, there could not be more than one wall, or other material barrier, between the sorcerer and his victim—and certainly Master Sean could not have stood out in that hall, going through an intricate spell like that for half an hour or more, without being noticed. Besides, he wasn't even in that hall at that time." He waved a hand. "Forget Master Sean."

"Good of you," murmured Lord Darcy.

"Who is left? Nobody that we know of. But couldn't Master Ewen have figured out the process? After all, if two Master magicians can figure it out separately, why not a third? Or maybe he stole it; I don't know. But isn't it possible that Master Ewen forced the weapon into Master Sir James's chest?"

Lord Darcy started to say something, but this time it was the Marquis of London who interrupted.

"Great God!" he rumbled. "And it was I who trained this man!" He swiveled his massive head and looked at Lord Bontriomphe. "And pray, would you explain what happened to the weapon? Where did it disappear to?"

Lord Bontriomphe blinked, said nothing, and

turned his eyes to Lord Darcy.

"Surely you see," said Lord Darcy calmly, "that the contact cutter which lay beside Sir James's body —and which, by the bye, was the only edged weapon in the room—could not possibly have been the murder weapon. You *did* read the autopsy report, did you not?"

"Why, yes, but—"

"Then surely you see that a blade in the shape of an isosceles triangle—two inches wide at the base, and five inches long—could not have made a stab wound five inches deep if the cut it made was less than an inch wide.

"Even more important—as I pointed out to Master Sean earlier today—a knife of pure silver, while harder than pure gold, is softer than pure lead. Its edges would certainly have been noticeably blunted if it had cut into two ribs. And yet, the knife retained its razor edge.

"It follows that Master Sir James was not killed by his own contact cutter—further, that the weapon which killed him was not in the room in which he died."

Lord Bontriomphe stared at Lord Darcy for a long second, then he turned and looked at the Marquis of London. "All right. As I said, I didn't like those hypotheses, because they don't explain away the heel print—and now they don't explain the missing knife. So I'll stick to my original theory, with one small change: Tia brought her own knife and took it away with her."

The Marquis of London did not even bother to look up from his desk. "Most unsatisfactory, my lord," he said, "most unsatisfactory." Then he glanced at Lord Bontriomphe. "And you intend to put the blame on the Damoselle Tia? Hah! Upon what evidence?"

"Why—upon the evidence of her heel print." Lord Bontriomphe leaned forward. "It *was* Master Sir James's blood, wasn't it? And how could she have got it on her heel except after Master Sir James bled all over the middle of the floor?"

The Marquis of London looked up toward the ceiling. "Were I a lesser man," he said ponderously, "this would be more than I could bear. Your deductions would be perfectly correct, Bontriomphe—*if* that were the Damoselle Tia's heel print. But, of course, it was not."

"Whose else could it have been?" Bontriomphe snapped. "Who else could have made a half-moon print in blood like that?"

My lord the Marquis closed his eyes and, obviously addressing Lord Darcy, said: "I intend to discuss this no further. I shall be perfectly happy to preside over this evening's discussion—especially since we have obtained official permission for it. I shall return when our guests arrive." He rose and headed toward the rear door, then he stopped and turned. "In the meantime, would you be so good as to dispel Lord Bontriomphe's fantasy about the Damoselle Tia's heel print?" And then he was gone.

Lord Bontriomphe took a deep breath and held it. It seemed a good three minutes before he let it out again—slowly.

"All right," he said at last, "I told you I wasn't the genius around here. Obviously you have observed a great deal more in this case than I have. We'll do as my lord of London has agreed. We'll get them all up here and talk to them."

Then, abruptly, he slammed the flat of his hand

down upon the top of his desk. "But—by *Heaven,* there's one thing I want to know before we go on with this! Why do you say that that heel print did not belong to Damoselle Tia?"

"Because, my dear Bontriomphe," said Lord Darcy carefully, "it was not a heel print." He paused.

"If it had been, the weight of the person wearing the heel would have pressed the blood down into the fiber of the rug; and yet—you will agree that it did not? That the blood touched only the top of the fibers, and soaked only a little way down?"

Lord Bontriomphe closed his eyes and let his exceptional memory bring up a mental picture of the bloodstain. Then he opened his eyes. "All right. So I was wrong. The bloodstain was not a heel print. Then where did I make my mistake?"

"Your error lay in assuming that it was a bloodstain," said Lord Darcy.

Lord Bontriomphe's scowl grew deeper. "Don't tell me it *wasn't* a bloodstain!"

"Not exactly," said Lord Darcy. "It was only *half* a bloodstain."

THERE WERE NINE GUESTS in the office of my lord the
Marquis of London that night. Sir Frederique
Bruleur had brought in enough of the yellow chairs
to seat eight. Lord Bontriomphe and the Marquis sat
behind their desks. Lord Darcy sat to the left of
Bontriomphe's desk, in the red leather chair, which
had been swiveled around to face the rest of the company. From left to right, Lord Darcy saw, in the first
row, Grand Master Sir Lyon Gandolphus Grey,
Mary of Cumberland, Captain Percy Smollett, and
Commander Lord Ashley. And in the second row,
Sir Thomas Leseaux, Lord John Quetzal, Father Patrique, and Master Sean O Lochlainn. Behind them,
near the door, stood Chief Master-at-Arms Hennely
Grayme, who had told Sir Frederique that he pre-
ferred to stand.

Sir Frederique had served drinks all around, then
had quietly retired.

My Lord the Marquis of London looked them all
over once and then said: "My lords, Your Grace,
gentlemen." He paused and looked them all over

once again. "I will not say that it was very good of
you to come. You are not here by invitation, but by
fiat. Nonetheless, all but one of you have been asked
merely as witnesses to help us discover the truth, and
all but that one may consider themselves my guests."
He paused again, took a deep breath, and let it out
slowly. "It is my duty to inform you that you are all
here to answer questions if they are put to you—not
simply because I, as Lord of London, have requested
your cooperation, but, more important, because you
are here by order of our Most Dread Sovereign, His
Majesty the King. Is that understood?"

Nine heads nodded silently.

"This is, then," my lord Marquis continued, "a
Court of Inquiry, presided over by myself as Justice
of the King's Court. Lord Bontriomphe is here as
Clerk of the King's Court. This may seem irregular
but it is quite in accord with the law. Is all of *that*
understood?" Again, there were nine silent nods of
assent. "Very well. I hardly think I need say—although by law I must—that anything anyone of you
says here will be taken down by Lord Bontriomphe
in writing, and may be used in evidence.

"The Reverend Father Patrique, O.B.S., is here in
the official capacity of *amicus curia,* as a registered
Sensitive of Holy Mother Church.

"As official Sergeant-at-Arms, we have Chief
Master-at-Arms Hennely Grayme of this City.

"Presenting the case for the Crown is Lord Darcy,
at present of Rouen, Chief Investigator for His Royal
Highness, Prince Richard, Duke of Normandy.

"Although this Court has the power to make a rec-
ommendation, it is understood that anyone accused
may appeal without prejudice, and may be repre-

sented in such Court as our Most Dread Sovereign His Majesty the King may appoint, by any counsel such accused may choose."

My lord Marquis took another deep breath and cleared his throat. "Is all of *that* quite clear? You will answer by voice." And a ragged chorus of voices said, "Yes, my lord."

"Very well." He heaved his massive bulk up from his chair, and everyone else stood. "Will you administer the oath, Reverend Father," he said to the Benedictine. When the oath had been administered to everyone there, my lord the Marquis sat down again with a sigh of comfort. "Now, before we proceed, are there any questions?"

There were none.

The Marquis of London lifted his head a fraction of an inch and looked at Lord Darcy from beneath his brows. "Very well, my Lord Advocate. You may proceed."

Lord Darcy stood up from the red leather chair, bowed in the direction of the Court, and said, "Thank you, my Lord Justice. Do I have the Court's permission to be seated during the presentation of the Crown's case?"

"You do, my lord. Pray be seated."

"Thank you, my lord." Lord Darcy settled himself again in the red leather chair.

His eyes searched each of the nine in turn, then he said, "We are faced here with a case of treason and murder.

"Although I am aware that most of you know the facts, legally I must assume that you do not. Therefore, I shall have to discuss each of those facts in turn. You must understand that the evidence proving these facts will be produced after my preliminary presentation.

"Three days ago, shortly before eleven o'clock on the morning of Tuesday, October 25, Anno Domini One Thousand Nine Hundred and Sixty-Six, a man named Georges Barbour was stabbed to death in a cheap rooming house in Cherbourg. Evidence which will be produced before this Court will show that Goodman Georges was a double agent; that is, he was a man who, while pretending to work for the Secret Service of His Slavonic Majesty King Casimir IX, was also in the pay of our own Naval Intelligence, and was, as far as the evidence shows, loyal to the Empire. Will you testify to that, Captain Smollett?" he asked, looking at the second chair from his right.

"I will, m'lud Advocate."

"Very shortly after he was killed," Lord Darcy went on, "Commander Lord Ashley of the Naval Intelligence Corps reported the discovery of Goodman Georges' body to the Armsmen of Cherbourg. He also reported that he had been ordered to give one hundred golden sovereigns to Goodman Georges because the double agent in question needed it to pay off a certain Goodman Fitz-Jean."

Bit by bit, item by item, Lord Darcy outlined the case to those present, omitting no detail except the precise nature and function of the confusion projector. Lord Darcy described it simply as a "highly important Naval secret."

He described the discovery of the murder of Sir James Zwinge, the attack upon the Damoselle Tia, the fight upon the bridge, the Damoselle Tia's statement, the discovery of the body of Goodman

Paul Nichols, and the search for and arrest of Master Ewen MacAlister.

"The questions before this Court," Lord Darcy said, "are: Who killed those three men: And why? It is the contention of the Crown that one person, and one only, is responsible for all three deaths."

He looked over the nine faces before him, trying to assess the expressions on their faces. Not one betrayed any sign of guilt, not even the one whom Lord Darcy knew was guilty.

"I see you have a question, Captain Smollett. Would you ask it, please? No, don't bother to rise."

Captain Smollett cleared his throat. "M'lud." He paused, cleared his throat again. "Since we already have the guilty man under arrest, may I ask why this inquiry is necessary?"

"Because we do not have the guilty man under arrest, Captain. Master Ewen, no matter what his actual crimes, is not guilty of a single murder—much less a triple one."

Captain Smollett said "Um," and nothing more.

"You have before you, my lords, Your Grace, gentlemen, every bit of pertinent evidence. It is now the duty of myself as Advocate of the Crown to link up that evidence into a coherent chain. First, let us dismiss the theory that Master Ewen MacAlister was more than remotely connected with these murders. Master Ewen was, it is true, an agent of His Slavonic Majesty, working with the owner of the *Manzana de Oro,* the Sidi al-Nasir. This evidence can be produced later; let us merely accept these facts as true."

He turned to the Chief of Naval Intelligence. "Captain Smollett."

"Yes, m'lud?"

"I wish to put to you a hypothetical question, and for the sake of security let us keep it hypothetical. *If* . . . I say, *if* . . . you were aware of the identity of the Polish Chief of Intelligence for France and the British Isles, would you order him assassinated?"

Captain Smollett's eyes narrowed. "No, m'lud, never."

"Why not, Captain?"

"It would be stupid, m'lud. Yes. As long as we know who he is . . . uh . . . if we knew who he was . . . it would be much more to our advantage to keep an eye on him, to watch him; to see to it, in fact, that he got the information that we wanted him to have, rather than the information he wants. Also, our knowing the Chief of Polish Intelligence would lead us to his agents. It is much easier to keep the body under surveillance when one can identify the head, m'lud."

"Then would you say, Captain, that it would be very stupid of Polish Intelligence to have murdered Master Sir James Zwinge?"

"Very stupid, m'lud. Wouldn't be at all good Intelligence tactics. Not at all." For a moment, Captain Smollett blinked solemnly, digesting this new thought.

"Not even if Master Sir James had discovered that Master Ewen was working for the Poles?" Lord Darcy asked.

"Hm-m-m. Probably not. Much better to pull Master Ewen out, move him to another post, give him a new identity."

"Thank you, Captain Smollett.

"Now. As you have seen," his words took in the entire company, "there is some question about whether Master Ewen could have committed this crime by Black Magic, and so skillfully hidden the evidence thereof that his complicity in the crime was undetectable. I put it to you, my lords, Your Grace, gentlemen, that he could not.

"Father Patrique." He looked at the Benedictine. The priest bowed his head. "Yes, my lord?"

"You have examined Master Ewen since his arrest, Reverend Father?"

"I have, my lord."

"Is Master Ewen's Talent as strong, as powerful, as effective as that of Master Sean O Lochlainn?"

"My lord Advocate . . ." The good father then turned his attention to my lord of London. ". . . And may it please the Court . . ."

"Proceed, Reverend Sir," said my lord the Marquis.

". . . I feel that, while my own testimony is adequate, it is not the best. In answer to your direct question, my lord, I must say that Master Ewen's Talent is weaker, far poorer, than that of Master Sean O Lochlainn.

"But I put it to you, my lords, that this is not the best evidence. Observe, if you will, the relative ease with which Master Sean conquered Master Ewen in the battle of wills at the *Manzana de Oro*. Observe how very simple it was to break the spells on Master Ewen's room lock and upon the carpetbag in which he carried his tools. I beg your pardon, my lord Advocate, if I am out of order."

"Not at all, Reverend Sir," said Lord Darcy. "But I will ask you once more. Will you testify that Master Sean's Talent is much more powerful than Master Ewen's?"

"It is, my lord."

Lord Darcy looked at Grand Master Sir Lyon Gandolphus Grey.

"Have you anything to add to this, Grand Master?"

Sir Lyon nodded. "If it please the Court, I should like to put a question to Commander Lord Ashley."

"Permission granted," rumbled de London. "Ask your question."

"My lord Commander," said Sir Lyon. "You have described to the investigators the use by Master Ewen of the Tarnhelm Effect upon his smallsword. Would you—"

"One moment," said Lord Darcy. "I should like my lord Commander to testify directly. If you would, Lord Ashley?"

"Of course, my lord."

Lord Darcy looked at Sir Lyon. "You want a description of the battle on Somerset Bridge, Sir Lyon?"

"Yes, if you please, my lord."

Lord Darcy looked at Lord Ashley. "If you will, my lord Commander."

Lord Ashley described exactly the sword fight on the bridge.

Then Sir Lyon said, "With the Court's permission I should like to ask the witness a question or two."

"Granted," said my lord de London.

"My lord Commander," said Sir Lyon, "what kind of sword was Master Ewen using?"

"A smallsword, Grand Master. A sword with a triangular cross section—no edge—about two and a half feet in length—very sharp point."

Sir Lyon nodded. "You saw it. Then, when he began to use it, it disappeared?"

"Not exactly disappeared, Sir Lyon," Lord Ashley said. "It . . . it *flickered*. I . . . I find it difficult to explain. It is simply that I couldn't keep my eyes on it. But I knew it was there."

"Thank you, Commander," said Sir Lyon. "Now, if the Court will permit, I will give my testimony. A really powerful sorcerer, such as Master Sir James or Master Sean O Lochlainn—"

"Or yourself?" Lord Darcy asked suddenly.

Sir Lyon smiled. ". . . Or myself, if you insist, my lord Advocate. Any powerful sorcerer could have made his sword so completely invisible as to be totally undetectable."

"Thank you," said Lord Darcy. "The question I wish to put before the Court is this: Is it possible that a man of Master Ewen's limited Talent—even though it was of Master grade—could have acted out a rite of Black Magic and then covered it up to such an extent that neither Master Sean O Lochlainn nor the combined Talents of the other Masters of the Guild at the Convention could have failed to discover what he had done?"

"Absolutely impossible, my lord," said Sir Lyon firmly.

Lord Darcy glanced back at the Benedictine priest. "What say you, Reverend Father?"

"I agree completely with Grand Master Sir Lyon," Father Patrique said quietly.

Lord Darcy turned to look at the Marquis of London. "Is there any need at this point, my lord, to call to the Court's attention the testimony of Master Sean O Lochlainn, Master Sorcerer, that he could detect no Black Magic involved in the murder of Master Sir James Zwinge?"

"You may proceed, my lord. If such evidence becomes necessary, Master Sean's testimony will be called for if and when it is needed."

"Thank you, my lord. We have"—Lord Darcy paused and looked the group over again—"then the evidence before us that Sir James Zwinge was killed by ordinary physical means. There was no Black Magic involved in the murder of Sir James Zwinge, and yet the evidence shows that he was alone in his room when he was stabbed at approximately nine o'clock and when he died half an hour later. Now, how could that be?

"I put it to you that we are far too prone to accept a magical explanation, when a simply material explanation will do."

He leaned back in his chair, but before he could say anything, Sir Thomas Leseaux raised his hand. "If I may, my lord, I should like to say that any theory of this murder which includes thaumaturgical processes would be mathematically impossible—but I do not see how a man could have been killed in the middle of a locked room by ordinary material means."

"That is why I must explain the Crown's case," said Lord Darcy. "Although, I repeat, the evidence is all before you.

"The point we have all tended to overlook is that a man need not be in the same room with another in order to kill him. There was no one else in Goodman Georges Barbour's room when he was stabbed, true —and yet he fell so near the door that it is not quite possible but very probable that someone standing in the hall stabbed him."

"Come now," said Commander Lord Ashley, "that may be possible with Goodman Georges, but it certainly does not apply to Master Sir James."

"Oh, but it does, my lord Commander," Lord Darcy said. "Given the proper implement, Master Sir James might easily have been stabbed from the hallway outside his room."

"But—through a locked door?" asked Lord John Quetzal.

"Why not?" asked Lord Darcy. "Locked doors are not impermeable. The doors to the rooms in the Royal Steward are very old—couple of centuries or more. Look at the size of the key required to open them. And then look at the size of the keyhole required to admit such a large, heavy key. Although the door to Sir James's room was locked, its keyhole was easily large enough to admit a one-inch wide blade."

Lord Darcy looked at Master Sean O Lochlainn. "You have a question, Master Sean?"

"That I do, my lord. I agree with you that the blade that stabbed Master Sir James came in through the keyhole. At your suggestion, I took scrapings from the keyhole and found traces of Sir James's blood. But"—he smiled a little—"if your lordship will pardon me, I suggest a demonstration of how a man could be given a high downward stab through a keyhole."

"I agree," said Lord Darcy. "First, I must direct the Court's attention to the peculiar bloodstain near the door. A full description of that bloodstain appears in the written record."

My lord the Marquis nodded. "It does. Proceed, my lord Advocate."

Lord Darcy turned and looked to his right at Lord Bontriomphe. "Would you ask Sir Frederique to bring in the door?"

Lord Bontriomphe reached behind him and pulled

a cord. The rear door opened and Sir Frederique Bruleur, followed by an assistant, brought in a heavy oaken door. They placed it in the center of the room between the area of yellow chairs and the Marquis' desk, and held it upright.

"This demonstration is necessary," said Lord Darcy. "This door is exactly similar to the one on Sir James's room. It is taken from another room of the Royal Steward Hotel. Can all of you see both sides of it? Good."

"Master Sean, would you do me the favor of playing the part of your late colleague?"

"Of course, my lord."

"Excellent. Now, you will stand on"—he gestured —"*that* side of the door, so that the door handle and keyhole are on your *left*. For the purposes of this demonstration, I shall play the part of the murderer." He picked up a sheet of paper from Lord Bontriomphe's desk. "Now, let's see. Lord Ashley, might I borrow your sword?"

Without a word, Commander Ashley drew his narrow-bladed Naval sword from its sheath and presented it to Lord Darcy.

"Thank you, Commander. You have been most helpful throughout this entire investigation.

"Now, Master Sean, if you will take your place, we shall enact this small play. You must all assume that what you are about to see actually occurred, but you must not assume that the words I use were those that were actually used. There may have been slight variations."

Master Sean stood on one side of the door. Lord Darcy walked up to the other and rapped.

"Who is there?" said Master Sean.

"Special courier from the Admiralty," said Lord Darcy in a high-pitched voice that did not sound like his own.

"You were supposed to pick up the envelope at the desk," said Master Sean.

"I know, Sir James," said Lord Darcy in the same high-pitched voice, "but this is a special message from Captain Smollett."

"Oh, very well," said Master Sean, "just push it under the door."

"I am to deliver it only into your hands," said Lord Darcy, and with that he inserted the tip of the sword blade into the keyhole.

"Just push it under," said Master Sean, "and I'll take it. It will have been delivered into my hand."

"Very well, Sir James," said Lord Darcy. He knelt and, still keeping the tip of the sword blade in the keyhole, he pushed the paper underneath the door.

Master Sean, on the other side, bent over to pick it up.

And, at that point, Lord Darcy thrust forward with the sword.

There was a metallic scrape as the sword point touched Master Sean's chest.

Immediately Lord Darcy pulled the sword back. Master Sean gasped realistically, staggered back several feet, then fell to the floor. Lord Darcy pulled the paper from beneath the door and stood up.

"Master Sean," he said, "happens to be wearing an excellent shirt of chain mail—which, unfortunately, Master Sir James was not.

"You see, then, what happened. Master Sir James, bending over to pick up the proffered envelope, presented his left breast to the keyhole.

"The sword came through and stabbed him. A single drop of his blood fell—half of it falling upon the carpet, the other half upon the presumed message. The blade itself would stop the flow of blood until it was withdrawn and Master Sir James staggered back away from the door.

"He collapsed in a state of shock. His wound, though deep, was not immediately dangerous, since the blade had not severed any of the larger blood vessels, nor pierced the lung. There was some bleeding, but not a great deal. He lay there for approximately half an hour.

"The weapon had, however, cut the wall of the great pulmonic aorta to such an extent that there was only a layer of tissue keeping it intact.

"At half past nine, Master Sean, who had an appointment with him at that time, rapped on the door.

"The noise of the knocking roused Master Sir James from his stupor. He must have known that time had passed; he must have been aware that it was Master Sean at the door. Lifting himself from the floor, he grabbed at his desk, upon which were lying the key to his room and his silver-bladed contact cutter. He cried out to Master Sean for help.

"But this increased strain was too much for the thin layer of tissue which had thus far held the walls of the pulmonic aorta together. The increased pressure burst the walls of the blood vessel, spurting forth Sir James's life blood. Sir James collapsed again to the floor, dropping the knife and his key. He died within seconds."

Master Sean arose from the floor, carefully brushing off his magician's robe. Sir Frederique and his assistant removed the door.

"If it please the Court," the Irish sorcerer said, "the angle at which my lord Darcy's thrust struck my chest would account exactly for the wound in Sir James's body."

Lord Darcy carefully put the sword he was holding on Lord Bontriomphe's desk. "You see, then," he said, "how Master James was killed, and how he died.

"Now, as to what happened:

"We must go back to the mysterious Goodman FitzJean. That Tuesday morning, he had discovered that Goodman Georges was a double agent. It became necessary to kill him. He walked up to Goodman Georges' room and knocked on the door. When Goodman Georges opened the door, FitzJean thrust forward with a knife and killed him. Naturally, there was no evidence that anyone was in the room with Georges Barbour, simply because there wasn't. Fitz-Jean was standing in the hallway.

"Barbour had already discovered FitzJean's identity and, earlier that morning, had sent a letter to Zed—Sir James Zwinge. FitzJean, in order to keep his identity from being discovered, came here to London. Then he managed to get hold of a communication, which—so he believed—reported his identity to the Admiralty. It was, he thought, a letter to the Admiralty reporting the information from Barbour which disclosed FitzJean's identity. He immediately went up to Sir James's room, and, using that same envelope, which, of course, would identify it as an Admiralty message, tricked Sir James into bending over near the keyhole"—Lord Darcy gestured with one hand—"with the results which Master Sean and I have just displayed to you."

His eyes moved over the silent group before him.
"By this time, of course, you all realize who the killer
is. But, fortunately, we have further proof. You see,
he failed to see the possibility of an error in his as-
sumptions. He assumed that a letter sent by Barbour
on the morning of Tuesday, October 25th, would arrive very early in the morning of Wednesday, the
26th, the following day. He further assumed that
Barbour would have sent the letter to the Royal
Steward Hotel, and that Barbour's letter, plus his
own communication, was what was contained in the
envelope addressed to the Admiralty by Sir James
Zwinge.

"But, he failed to realize that Barbour might not
have known that Sir James was at the Royal Steward, that indeed it was far more probable, from that
point of view, for Barbour to address the letter to Sir
James here at the Palace du Marquis."

He rose from his chair and walked to the desk of
the Marquis. "May I have the envelope, my lord Justice?" he asked.

Without a word, the Marquis de London handed
Lord Darcy a pale blue envelope.

Lord Darcy looked at it. "This is postmarked
Cherbourg. Tuesday October 25, is marked as the
posting date, and is marked as having been received
on Wednesday morning, the 26th. It is addressed to
Sir James Zwinge."

He turned back toward the group, and noted with
approval that Chief Master-at-Arms Hennely
Grayme had moved up directly behind one man.

"There was one peculiarity about these communications," he continued blandly. "Master Sir
James had given to his agents special paper and ink,

a special blue sealing wax, and a special seal. These had been magically treated so that unless the envelope was opened by either Master Sir James himself or by Captain Smollett, the paper within would be blank. Am I correct, Captain Smollett?"

"Yes, m'lud."

Lord Darcy looked at the envelope in his hand. "That is why this envelope has not been opened. Only *you* can open it, Captain, and we have reason to believe that it will disclose to you the identity of the so-called Goodman FitzJean—Sir James's murderer. Would you be so good as to open it?"

The Naval officer took the envelope, broke the blue seal, lifted the flap, and took out a sheet of paper. "Addressed to Sir James," he said. "Barbour's handwriting; I recognize it."

He did not read the entire letter. When he was halfway through, his head turned to his left. "You!" he said, in a low, angry, shocked voice.

Commander Lord Ashley rose to his feet and his right hand reached toward his sword scabbard.

And then he suddenly realized it was empty, that the sword was halfway across the room, on Lord Bontriomphe's desk. At the moment of that realization, he recognized one other thing—that there was something pressed against his back.

Chief Master-at-Arms Hennely Grayme, holding his pistol steady, said, "Don't try anything, my lord. You've killed enough as it is."

"Have you anything to say, Commander?" Lord Darcy asked.

Ashley opened his mouth, closed it, swallowed, then opened it again to speak. His eyes seemed to be focused upon something in the far distance.

"You have me, my lords," he said hoarsely. "I'm sorry I had to kill anybody, but . . . but, you would have thought me a traitor, you see. I needed the money, but I would never have betrayed the Empire. I didn't know the secret." He stopped again and put his left hand over his eyes. "I knew that Barbour was a Polish agent. I didn't know he was a double agent. I thought I could get some money from him. But I . . . I wouldn't have betrayed my King. I was just afraid someone would think I had, after that."

He stopped, took his hand down. "My lords," his voice quivered as he tried to keep it even, "I should like to make my confession to Father Patrique. After that, I should like to make my confession to the Court."

The Marquis de London nodded at Lord Darcy. He nodded back at the Marquis. "You have the Crown's permission, my lord," said Lord Darcy, "but I must ask you to leave behind your scabbard and your jacket."

Without a word, Commander Lord Ashley dropped his sword belt on the chair behind him, removed his jacket and put it on top of it.

"Chief Hennely," the Marquis de London said, "I charge you to take this man prisoner upon his own admission. Take him to the outer room, where the Reverend Father may hear his sacramental confession. You will observe the laws pertaining thereto."

"Yes, my lord," said Chief Hennely, and the three of them left the room.

"And now, my lord Advocate," said the Marquis. "Would you kindly report the full story to the Court and the witnesses present."

Lord Darcy bowed. "I shall, my lord.

"I first began to suspect Ashley when I saw that, according to the register, he had come into the hotel at 8:48 on Wednesday, giving as his business there the delivery of a message for Master Sean—and yet *he had not even attempted to locate Master Sean until 9:25,* when he spoke to Lord Bontriomphe. But that is neither here nor there, my lord. Here is what happened.

"As he told us, Ashley needed money. I will explain why in a few moments. He attempted to sell a secret he did not have and could not prove he had. Finally he was reduced to accepting a payment of one hundred golden sovereigns from Georges Barbour merely to identify himself.

"On Monday night when he arrived in Cherbourg, he went to Barbour to identify himself and was told that he would be paid the following morning. Then, Tuesday morning, Commander Ashley was told to take the hundred sovereigns to Goodman Georges.

"At that point, he panicked—not as you or I might think of panic, but cold, frightened panic, for that is the way Ashley's mind works.

"He knew that once he took the money to Barbour in his own *persona*, Barbour would recognize him. Besides, he knew that his scheme had fallen through, since Barbour was a double agent. So he went up to Barbour's room, and, when Barbour opened the door, Ashley stabbed him, using a cheap knife he had bought for the purpose.

"Then he reported the murder, assisted by the fact that the concierge of Barbour's rooming house had, fortunately for him, been out for a few minutes before Lord Ashley arrived. But he also found that, in the meantime, the information as to his identity had already been sent to Zed. Therefore, he had to cut off that information; he had to prevent it from reaching the Admiralty."

Lord Darcy took a deep breath. "In a way," he said, "you might say that I assisted him. Naturally, I did not know at that time that Ashley was a killer. Therefore, I made a request that he transmit a message to Master Sean. That enabled him to get into the Royal Steward Hotel.

"At 6:30 Wednesday morning, the mail from Cherbourg was delivered to the Royal Steward. Master Sir James picked up his at 7:00. Then, having decoded the messages he received, he went down to the desk and asked a man whom he trusted, Goodman Paul Nichols, to hold an envelope for an Admiralty courier, and at the same time he sent one of the hotel boys to the Admiralty with a message for Smollett to pick up the packet.

"Sir James returned to his room, followed by the Damoselle Tia. There followed the discussion and argument which all of you have heard of. When Tia left, Master Sir James locked his door for the last time. At 8:48 Lord Ashley arrived, ostensibly looking for Master Sean. He walked up to the registration desk and started to ask for Master Sean. But Paul Nichols immediately assumed that he was the courier from the Admiralty."

Lord Darcy gestured with an open hand. "This can't be proved, of course, but it fits in precisely. Nichols must have said something like this: 'Ah, Commander, you are the courier from the Admiralty to pick up Sir James's packet? And what could Lord Ashley do? He said, 'Yes.' He took the packet. Sir

James's room number was on the outside of that envelope, and Lord Ashley went directly to that room.

"Then he and Sir James played out some version of the little act that Master Sean and I enacted."

He made a slight gesture with one hand. "And there I should like to point out a peculiar thing. Murderers are quite often—more often than we like to think—very lucky. It is quite possible that sheer luck could have allowed an ordinary person to kill Sir James in the precise manner in which he *was* killed. An ordinary person, if luck were with him, could have made that thrust through the door after having decoyed Sir James into just the right position, and the results would have been the same as they actually were.

"But that was not the way that Commander Ashley operated. The Commander has one advantage: Occasionally, in times of emotional stress, he is able to see a short time into the future.

"I call your attention again to that keyhole. The door is thick. The keyhole, though large enough to admit the blade of a Naval sword, allows very little play for it. There is no way to aim that blade except in the direction the keyhole guides it.

"Even when Sir James was maneuvered into position by the Commander's use of the letter under the door, the odds against Sir James's being in precisely the right position were formidable.

"Just think of the positions it is possible to take to pull a piece of paper from under a door.

"The attitude which Sir James actually assumed is the most likely one, but would any reasonably intelligent murderer depend upon it? I think not.

"This, then, was another of the many clues which

led me to identify Commander Lord Ashley as the murderer. Because of the emotional tension he was undergoing, his prophetic ability allowed him to *know*—know beyond any shadow of a doubt—precisely where Sir James would be and when he would be there. And he knew exactly what he would have to do to get Sir James into that position.

"Sir James would not allow Commander Ashley in the room; he would not unlock the door for him. Therefore, Ashley had to kill him by the only means available. And because of his touch of the Talent, he was able to do so.

"The sword went through the keyhole in a straight line. A single drop of blood fell—half of it on the carpet, the other half on the envelope.

"I think that is perfectly clear. Lord Ashley then returned the envelope to his pocket and his sword to his sheath. That is why I asked him to leave both jacket and scabbard."

He gestured toward the chair where the Commander had left his sword belt and jacket. Master Sean had already looked the jacket over.

"You were right, my lord," he said, "there's a smear on the inside of his jacket pocket, and I have no doubt that there'll be another inside the scabbard."

"Nor do I," agreed Lord Darcy. "Let me continue. At that point, Lord Ashley realized something else. He realized that one man—and *one* man only—knew that he had picked up that packet.

"I don't know exactly how Paul Nichols died, but I respectfully suggest to the Court that it was something like this:

"Commander Lord Ashley arrived back in the lobby just at 9:00 and saw Nichols leaving. The hallway toward the back door is easily visible from the lobby; he must have seen Nichols leaving his own office.

"He went back and told Nichols some kind of story, and lured him into the furniture room. A quick blow to the head and a rope around the neck"—Lord Darcy snapped his fingers—"and Goodman Paul Nichols was eliminated as a witness.

"Then, I think, panic must have struck Lord Ashley again. Standing there in that closet, over the body of a man he had just strangled, he wanted to see what was in that packet. He tore it open, scattering pieces of blue sealing wax over the body of the man he had just killed.

"And, of course, he saw nothing, for the papers came out a total blank. I presume he burnt those papers later. It would have been the intelligent thing to do.

"But he still had one more thing to do. He had to relay my message to Master Sean.

"He found Lord Bontriomphe in the lobby and—well, you all know what happened after that.

"However, I'd like to point out in passing that Lord Ashley actually *returned* to the lobby around 9:10, although he did not speak to Bontriomphe until 9:25. The obvious assumption is that he was afraid to speak to any sorcerer for fear that his emotional state would give him away, and that not until he saw Lord Bontriomphe could he find the courage to speak to anyone."

Captain Smollett raised his right hand and the golden stripes of rank at his cuff gleamed in the gaslight. "A question, m'lud, if I may." His normal hearty complexion now seemed somewhat grayed. It is not easy for the head of an Intelligence operation to discover that one of his most trusted men has betrayed him.

"Of course, Captain. What is it?"

"I think I understand what the Commander did and how he did it. What I don't understand is *why*. D'you have any idea, my lord?"

"Until just a few hours ago, Captain, that was the main thing that bothered me. His motive was a desire for money. As a matter of fact, a conversation I had with him yesterday at the Admiralty showed that he could only think of betrayal in terms of money. Every motive that he attributed to other possible suspects had a monetary basis.

"But, until the raid at the *Manzana de Oro* I did not understand the motive behind the motive. I did not know why he needed money so badly.

"Master Ewen MacAlister has made a full confession, and since this is merely a Court of Inquiry I can tell you what it contained without bringing him here as a witness." He paused and smiled. "At the moment, I am afraid that Master Ewen is in no condition to appear as a witness."

He placed the tips of his fingers together and looked down at the toes of his boots. "Master Sorcerer Ewen MacAlister, in the pay of the Polish Government, was working with the Sidi al-Nasir of the *Manzana de Oro* to obtain Commander Lord Ashley's services as a Polish agent by blackmailing him.

"When the wheel spins—when the card turns— when the dice tumble—a gambler feels a momentary surge of psychic tension. That is why the gambler gambles—because of the thrill. Lord Ashley's advantage was that when these surges of tension came, he was occasionally able to see what the winning play would be.

"Not often, mind you; the tension was not that great. But it gave the Commander what gamblers call an 'edge.' The odds in his favor were increased. The Commander won when he played—not always, and not spectacularly, but regularly.

"The Commander's rare ability, of course, is not detectable by the sorcerers who work in any gambling club. It cannot even be detected by a Master Sorcerer." He looked at Sir Thomas Leseaux. "Am I correct, Sir Thomas?"

The theoretical thaumaturgist nodded. "You are correct, my lord. That particular form of the Talent, since it deals with time, and since it is passive rather than active—that is, observational in nature—is undetectable. Unlike the clairvoyant, whose Talent allows him to see through space, and, occasionally, into the past, the precognitive sense which operates into the future, is almost impossible to predict, train, or control."

Sir Thomas Leseaux shrugged slightly. "Perhaps one day a greater mathematician than I will solve the problem of the asymmetry of time. Until then . . ." He shrugged again, and left his sentence hanging.

"Thank you, Sir Thomas," said Lord Darcy. "However, it is possible for a sorcerer to thwart, under certain circumstances, the precognitive sense. Master Ewen MacAlister proceeded to act upon the gambling devices at the *Manzana de Oro* when, and only when, Commander Lord Ashley was playing.

"The Commander began to lose. Before he knew it, he was deeply in debt—and because of that he did what he did."

Lord Darcy smiled. "By the way—and this is

something that Master Ewen made a great point of in his confession—I should like all of you to think for a moment of Master Ewen's position on Somerset Bridge last night, when he suddenly realized he was faced by a man who was predicting his every action. However, that is by the bye.

"Actually, My Lord Commander was able to penetrate his crimes because of fantastic good luck. He did not plot his actions; he merely acted on impulse and managed to commit one of the most baffling crimes it has ever been my good fortune to investigate.

"And then by an equally fantastic stroke of *bad* luck, he was betrayed. He is an adroit and cool man when faced with danger; he can act or he can lie with equal facility. Excellent attributes in an Intelligence agent, I must admit. But the lie he told in Sidi al-Nasir's office simply did not hold water. Yesterday afternoon, when we were looking for Paul Nichols, I asked you, Captain, if you had any notion of where he might be hiding, of where the headquarters of this Polish espionage ring might be. And you said you had no notion, none whatever.

"But, in Sidi al-Nasir's office this evening, Lord Ashley calmly admitted that he owed the Sidi some one hundred and fifty golden sovereigns, a rather large amount of money even for a Commander in his Majesty's Navy.

"His explanation to me was that Naval Intelligence had long suspected the Sidi and that he, the Commander, had contrived to get himself into debt so that Sidi al-Nasir would propose that the Commander pay the debt off by acting as an agent for His Slavonic Majesty.

"That is why I say that his luck, at that point, had turned from fantastically good to fantastically bad. In actual fact, Commander Lord Ashley had no notion that Sidi al-Nasir was in the pay of the Poles. He had got himself into debt at the *Manzana de Oro,* and the Sidi had threatened to inform you of that fact. What would you have done, Captain Smollett, if you had been so informed? Would you have cashiered the Commander?"

"Doubt it," said Smollett. "Would have had him transferred, of course. Can't have a man who gambles that way in Intelligence work. I don't object to gambling in itself, my lord; but a man should only gamble what he has—not upon his expectations."

"Exactly," said Lord Darcy. "I quite understand. There would, however, have been a black mark upon his record? He would have had little chance to rise above his present rank?"

"Little chance, my lord? I should say none whatever. Couldn't give a man Captain's stripes with a mark like that against him."

Lord Darcy nodded. "Of course not. And Ashley knew that. He had to do something to pay off Sidi al-Nasir. So he concocted this fantastic scheme to pry money out of a man whom he knew to be a Polish agent. As His Grace the Archbishop of York remarked to me yesterday, there is no evil in this man. There is, as you can see, only desperation. I think we can believe his statement that he would not willingly betray King and Country.

"Had Sidi al-Nasir made his proposition to My Lord Commander two weeks ago, or even only a week ago, none of this would have happened. It is my personal opinion that if al-Nasir had asked Lord

Ashley to pay off his debt by betraying his country before tonight, his lordship's facile mind would have come up with the same lie that he told me this evening, except, Captain Smollett, that he would have told it to you.

"What would you have said if—say, a week ago—the Commander had come to you and told you that, by deliberately going into debt, he had trapped the head of the local Polish spy ring into betraying himself? That he, Commander Ashley, had been asked to become a double agent and could now become—if the term is proper—a triple agent? Be honest, Captain, what would you have said?"

Captain Smollett looked at his knees for what seemed a long time. The others in the room seemed to be holding their breaths, waiting. When Captain Smollett raised his eyes it was to look at the Marquis de London rather than at Lord Darcy. "If it please the Court, my lord," he said slowly. There was pain in his eyes. "I am forced to admit that had things come about the way Lord Darcy has just outlined them, I should have believed Commander Lord Ashley's story. I should very likely have recommended him for promotion."

At that moment, the door opened, and Father Patrique came in. He was followed by Commander Lord Ashley, whose face was pale and whose wrists were encased in padded shackles. In the rear came the watchful-eyed Chief Master-at-Arms Hennely Grayme, his pistol holstered, but his hand ready.

"My Lord Justice," the priest said gravely, "it is my duty to request the attention of the Court."

"The Court recognizes the Reverend Father Patrique as *amicus curia,*" the Marquis rumbled.

"My Lord Justice," the good father said, "My Lord Ashley, a Commander of the Imperial Navy of Our Most Dread Sovereign the King, wishes, of his own free will, to make a statement and deposition before this Court."

The Marquis de London glanced once at Lord Bontriomphe, who was taking down everything in his notebook, then back at Lord Ashley.

"You may proceed," he said.

# 23

FORTY MINUTES LATER, Lord Bontriomphe looked over his shorthand notes and nodded thoughtfully. "That winds it up," he said. "That covers everything."

Commander Lord Ashley was gone, to be escorted to the Tower by Chief Hennely and a squad of Armsmen. The Court of Inquiry had been officially adjourned.

My Lord the Marquis surveyed the room and then looked at Lord Darcy. "Except for a few minor details in what was said, you gave us the story of Ashley's activities quite accurately. Satisfactory. I might say, *most* satisfactory." He looked around at the others, "Does anyone have any questions?"

"I have a question," said Sir Lyon Gandolphus Grey. He looked at Lord Darcy. "If I may, my lord, I should like to know why you were sure that there was no direct link between Master Ewen MacAlister and Commander Lord Ashley."

Lord Darcy smiled. "I couldn't be absolutely certain, of course, Sir Lyon. But it seemed most probable. Master Ewen was doing his best to get the Damoselle Tia to worm the secret out of Sir Thomas Leseaux. Would he have tried so hard if he had known that Lord Ashley was willing to sell it? Or, rather, claimed he had it to sell? That would have been much simpler than trying to get a stubborn child to betray everything she loved."

"But how did you know she wasn't a willing spy?" Sir Thomas asked.

"There were several reasons," said Lord Darcy. "Of course, ecclesiastical commissions had twice given her a clean bill, but there were other indications. She had gone to Sir James and argued with him, and that was hardly the behavior of a spy. A spy would have acted immediately, not argued and walked out. And a well-trained spy does not—as Tia did—throw a note from one of her fellow agents into a wastebasket and forget about it. Also—while there was the possibility that the conversation in the *Hound and Hare* might have been an act put on for my benefit— the subsequent attempt to do away with her was a strong indication that it was not. Therefore, she had, as she said then, actually intended to tell everything to the King's Officers."

The Dowager Duchess of Cumberland said: "Ironic, isn't it, that while all the Armsmen of London and half the Imperial Navy have been struggling to discover one man's identity, that letter was actually here all the time, in that envelope."

Lord Darcy reached out for the blue envelope on Lord Bontriomphe's desk, where Captain Smollett had placed it. He held it up. "You mean this?" he

asked rather apologetically. "I am afraid it wouldn't
have done us much good to look for that information
here."

"Why not?" the Dowager Duchess frowned. "Because of the spells?"

"Oh, no," said Lord Darcy. "Because of the fact
that this envelope and its contents did not exist until
an hour or so ago.

"The handwriting, while a passable imitation of
Georges Barbour's, is actually my own. I had a
chance to study Barbour's hand thoroughly yesterday afternoon at the Admiralty Office.

"You see, I wanted Ashley's confession. We actually had very little evidence. I knew *what* he had
done, and *how* he had done it, by reasoned deduction.
There is, of course, the evidence of the blood in his
jacket pocket and in his sword sheath, but we
couldn't count on its being there. We needed more
than that.

"So—this letter came into being. After all, you see,
Ashley couldn't have been *certain* that the information from Barbour had been sent to the hotel. Since
I knew that he had opened the envelope from the hotel at his first opportunity, I also knew that what he
found were blank sheets of paper. He had no way of
being sure that those sheets had contained the information that was so dangerous to him.

"The letter was a necessary deception, I think—
and if you will cast your mind back, Captain
Smollett, you will recall that I did not once tell you
that the letter had actually come from Barbour."

"So you didn't," said Captain Smollett. "So you
didn't."

"Well, my lords, Your Grace, gentlemen," the
Marquis de London said, "this has been a rather

strenuous night. I suggest we can make the best use of what is left of it by getting some sleep."

\* \* \*

The eight guests left the Palace du Marquis in a body. With the exception of Captain Smollett, they were all headed for Carlyle House.

There had been still another guest present, Lord Darcy knew, a guest who would remain behind until the others had left.

Behind the Vandenbosch reproduction in my lord Marquis' office was a sliding panel, and beyond that a small alcove. When the panel was open, anyone sitting in that darkened alcove could see through the cloth of the painting and observe and hear everything that took place.

Only the Marquis, Lord Bontriomphe, and Lord Darcy had known that someone had been in that alcove during the official inquiry which had resulted in the arrest of a killer, but it was not until some two months later, in Rouen, that Lord Darcy heard anything further from that hidden observer.

A package was delivered to Lord Darcy's residence by a King's Messenger. It was not a large package, but it was fairly heavy. There was a note with it which read:

My Lord Darcy:

Again we are indebted to you for your brilliant work in the protection of Our Realm. We understand that you were so unfortunate as to lose the valuable .40 caliber MacGregor which you so obligingly used for the demonstration at Westminster.

Since we deem it fitting that any weapon of this kind worn in Our presence should be Our gift, We are sending you this package.

   We would have you understand however, that it is *not* a purely ceremonial weapon, but is to be used in the course of your duties. If We hear that it is hanging on the wall of your trophy room in a golden frame, or other such foolishness, We will personally come over there and take it away from you.

JIVR

Inside the box lay what was probably MacGregor's finest creation: a handcrafted, man-stopping, .40 caliber handgun. The gold and enamel work on it made it as beautiful as it was deadly. On both sides of the butt, in hard enamel, were Lord Darcy's personal arms: *Ermine, on a fess gules, a lion passant gardant or.* In the golden tracery work surrounding the shield were the lions of England and the lilies of France.

# FRED SABERHAGEN

| | | |
|---|---|---|
| ☐ 49548 | **LOVE CONQUERS ALL** | $1.95 |
| ☐ 52077 | **THE MASK OF THE SUN** | $1.95 |
| ☐ 86064 | **THE VEILS OF AZLAROC** | $2.25 |
| ☐ 20563 | **EMPIRE OF THE EAST** | $2.95 |
| ☐ 77766 | **A SPADEFUL OF SPACETIME** | $2.50 |

## BERSERKER SERIES

**Humanity struggles against inhuman death machines whose mission is to destroy life wherever they find it:**

| | | |
|---|---|---|
| ☐ 05462 | **BERSERKER** | $2.25 |
| ☐ 05407 | **BERSERKER MAN** | $1.95 |
| ☐ 05408 | **BERSERKER'S PLANET** | $2.25 |
| ☐ 08215 | **BROTHER ASSASSIN** | $1.95 |
| ☐ 84315 | **THE ULTIMATE ENEMY** | $1.95 |

## THE NEW DRACULA

The *real* story—as told by the dread Count himself!

| | | |
|---|---|---|
| ☐ 34245 | **THE HOLMES DRACULA FILE** | $1.95 |
| ☐ 16600 | **THE DRACULA TAPE** | $1.95 |
| ☐ 62160 | **AN OLD FRIEND OF THE FAMILY** | $1.95 |
| ☐ 80744 | **THORN** | $2.75 |

**ACE SCIENCE FICTION**
P.O. Box 400, Kirkwood, N.Y. 13795

S-12

Please send me the titles checked above. I enclose _____.
Include 75¢ for postage and handling if one book is ordered; 50¢ per
book for two to five. If six or more are ordered, postage is free. California, Illinois, New York and Tennessee residents please add sales tax.

NAME_____

ADDRESS_____

CITY_____STATE_____ZIP_____

# H. BEAM PIPER

| | | |
|---|---|---|
| ☐ 24890 | **FOUR DAY PLANET/LONE STAR PLANET** | $2.25 |
| ☐ 26192 | **FUZZY SAPIENS** | $1.95 |
| ☐ 48492 | **LITTLE FUZZY** | $1.95 |
| ☐ 26193 | **FUZZY PAPERS** | $2.75 |
| ☐ 49053 | **LORD KALVAN OF OTHERWHEN** | $2.25 |
| ☐ 77779 | **SPACE VIKING** | $2.25 |
| ☐ 23188 | **FEDERATION (5¼″ x 8¼″)** | $5.95 |

**ACE SCIENCE FICTION**
P.O. Box 400, Kirkwood, N.Y. 13795

S-10

Please send me the titles checked above. I enclose _____.
Include 75¢ for postage and handling if one book is ordered; 50¢ per book for two to five. If six or more are ordered, postage is free. California, Illinois, New York and Tennessee residents please add sales tax.

NAME_____

ADDRESS_____

CITY_____STATE_____ZIP_____

Classic stories by America's most distinguished and successful author of science fiction and fantasy.

| | | |
|---|---|---|
| ☐ 12314 | **CROSSROADS OF TIME** | $1.95 |
| ☐ 33704 | **HIGH SORCERY** | $1.95 |
| ☐ 37292 | **IRON CAGE** | $2.25 |
| ☐ 45001 | **KNAVE OF DREAMS** | $1.95 |
| ☐ 47441 | **LAVENDER GREEN MAGIC** | $1.95 |
| ☐ 43675 | **KEY OUT OF TIME** | $2.25 |
| ☐ 67556 | **POSTMARKED THE STARS** | $1.25 |
| ☐ 69684 | **QUEST CROSSTIME** | $2.50 |
| ☐ 71100 | **RED HART MAGIC** | $1.95 |
| ☐ 78015 | **STAR BORN** | $1.95 |

▲ **ACE SCIENCE FICTION**
P.O. Box 400, Kirkwood, N.Y. 13795                S-02

Please send me the titles checked above. I enclose _____.
Include 75¢ for postage and handling if one book is ordered; 50¢ per
book for two to five. If six or more are ordered, postage is free. California, Illinois, New York and Tennessee residents please add sales tax.

NAME_____

ADDRESS_____ _____

CITY_____ STATE_____ ZIP_____

# ANDRE NORTON

"Nobody can top Miss Norton when it comes to swashbuckling science fiction adventure stories." —*St. Louis Globe-Democrat*

| | | |
|---|---|---|
| 07897 | **Breed to Come** | $1.95 |
| 14236 | **The Defiant Agents** | $1.95 |
| 22376 | **The Eye of the Monster** | $1.95 |
| 24621 | **Forerunner Foray** | $2.25 |
| 66835 | **Plague Ship** | $1.95 |
| 78194 | **Star Hunter/Voodoo Planet** | $1.95 |
| 81253 | **The Time Traders** | $1.95 |

*Available wherever paperbacks are sold or use this coupon.*

**ACE SCIENCE FICTION**
P.O. Box 400, Kirkwood, N.Y. 13795

Please send me the titles checked above. I enclose _____.
Include 75¢ for postage and handling if one book is ordered; 50¢ per book for two to five. If six or more are ordered, postage is free. California, Illinois, New York and Tennessee residents please add sales tax.

NAME_____

ADDRESS_____

CITY_____STATE_____ZIP_____

S-03

# MORE TRADE SCIENCE FICTION

Ace Books is proud to publish these latest works by major SF authors in deluxe large format collectors' editions. Many are illustrated by top artists such as Alicia Austin, Esteban Maroto and Fernando.

| | | | |
|---|---|---|---|
| Robert A. Heinlein | Expanded Universe | 21883 | $8.95 |
| Frederik Pohl | Science Fiction: Studies in Film (illustrated) | 75437 | $6.95 |
| Frank Herbert | Direct Descent (illustrated) | 14897 | $6.95 |
| Harry G. Stine | The Space Enterprise (illustrated) | 77742 | $6.95 |
| Ursula K. LeGuin and Virginia Kidd | Interfaces | 37092 | $5.95 |
| Marion Zimmer Bradley | Survey Ship (illustrated) | 79110 | $6.95 |
| Hal Clement | The Nitrogen Fix | 58116 | $6.95 |
| Andre Norton | Voorloper | 86609 | $6.95 |
| Orson Scott Card | Dragons of Light (illustrated) | 16660 | $7.95 |

*Available wherever paperbacks are sold or use this coupon.*

**ACE SCIENCE FICTION**
P.O. Box 400, Kirkwood, N.Y. 13795

Please send me the titles checked above. I enclose _____.
Include 75¢ for postage and handling if one book is ordered; 50¢ per book for two to five. If six or more are ordered, postage is free. California, Illinois, New York and Tennessee residents please add sales tax.

NAME_____

ADDRESS_____

CITY_____STATE_____ZIP_____

S-15

# Gordon R. Dickson

| | | | |
|---|---|---|---|
| ☐ | 16015 | Dorsai! | 1.95 |
| ☐ | 34256 | Home From The Shore | 2.25 |
| ☐ | 56010 | Naked To The Stars | 1.95 |
| ☐ | 63160 | On The Run | 1.95 |
| ☐ | 68023 | Pro | 1.95 |
| ☐ | 77417 | Soldier, Ask Not | 1.95 |
| ☐ | 77765 | The Space Swimmers | 1.95 |
| ☐ | 77749 | Spacial Deliver | 1.95 |
| ☐ | 77803 | The Spirit Of Dorsai | 2.50 |

Available wherever paperbacks are sold or use this coupon.

**ACE SCIENCE FICTION**
P.O. Box 400, Kirkwood, N.Y. 13795

Please send me the titles checked above. I enclose _____.
Include 75¢ for postage and handling if one book is ordered; 50¢ per
book for two to five. If six or more are ordered, postage is free. California, Illinois, New York and Tennessee residents please add sales tax.

NAME_____

ADDRESS_____

CITY_____STATE_____ZIP_____